Clare Clark is the author of *The Nature of Monsters*. Born in 1967, she graduated from Cambridge with a double first in History, and now lives in London with her husband and two children.

SAVAGE LANDS

It is 1704 and, in the swamps of Louisiana, France is clinging to its new colony with less than two hundred men. Into this hostile land comes Elisabeth Savaret, one of twenty-three women sent from Paris to marry men they have never met. With little expectation of happiness Elisabeth is stunned to find herself falling passionately in love with her husband, infantryman Jean-Claude Babelon. But Babelon is a dangerous man to love. Witness to Elisabeth's devotion is another of his acolytes, Auguste, a young boy despatched to act as go-between with the 'redskins'. When both Elisabeth and Auguste find their love challenged by Babelon's duplicity, the consequences are devastating.

Books by Clare Clark
Published by The House of Ulverscroft:

THE NATURE OF MONSTERS

CLARE CLARK

SAVAGE LANDS

Complete and Unabridged

CHARNWOOD
Leicester

First published in Great Britain in 2010 by
Harvill Secker
The Random House Group Limited, London

First Charnwood Edition
published 2011
by arrangement with
The Random House Group Limited, London

Detail from Guillaume de Lisle's 'Carte de la
Louisiane et du Cours du Mississipi'
(Covens & Mortier, 1742) reproduced by kind
permission of the David Rumsey Map Collection,
www.davidrumsey.com

British Library CIP Data

Clark, Clare.
  Savage lands.
  1. Louisiana- -History- -To 1803- -Fiction.
  2. Historical fiction.
  3. Large type books.
  I. Title
  823.9'2–dc22

  ISBN 978–1–44480–574–1

Published by
F. A. Thorpe (Publishing)
Anstey, Leicestershire
Set by Words & Graphics Ltd.
Anstey, Leicestershire
Printed and bound in Great Britain by
T. J. International Ltd., Padstow, Cornwall

This book is printed on acid-free paper

For Flora,
my American girl

Every man calls barbarous anything he is not accustomed to; it is indeed the case that we have no other criterion of truth or right-reason than the example and form of the opinions and customs of our own country.

Nothing fixes a thing so intensely in the memory as the wish to forget it.

— MICHEL DE MONTAIGNE

1704

Before

His Majesty sends twenty girls to be married to the Canadians and to the other inhabitants of Fort Louis, in order to consolidate the colony. All these girls are industrious and have received a pious and virtuous education. Beneficial results to the colony are expected from their teaching their useful attainments to the Indian females. In order that none should be sent except those of known virtue and of unspotted reputation, His Majesty did entrust the bishop of Quebec with the mission of taking these girls from such establishments as, from their very nature and character, would put them at once above all suspicions of corruption. You will take care to settle them in life as well as may be in your power, and to marry them to such men as are capable of providing them with a commodious home.

— ANNOUNCEMENT TO THE
CONGREGATION OF FORT LOUIS,
LOUISIANA, MARCH 1704

On the nineteenth day of April in the year of Our Lord 1704, the *Pélican*, a recently captured Dutch vessel of some six hundred tons, weighed anchor and headed for the open sea. Elisabeth stood on the main deck with several of the other girls, her hand raised to shade her eyes as the spires and towers of La Rochelle dwindled against the horizon. It was a fine day, unseasonably warm, the storms of the past weeks washed clean from the sky. Above her the men hauled on ropes or hung like spiders from the rigging, shouting to one another above the sharp slap and crack of the sails, but for once none of the girls spoke, though Marie-Françoise de Boisrenaud reached out and took the hand of little Renée Gilbert, who swayed a little, lettuce pale. Though exorbitantly overloaded, the heavy-hipped ship slid smoothly through the unruffled water, her company of twelve attending gunboats fanned out behind her, the creamy wake unfolding from her stern like a wedding veil.

It should have been over by now, her fate decided. With October barely a week old and a ship readied in Rochefort, the bishop had declared it probable that most of the girls would be settled by the new year. On the day that her godfather was to take her to Paris to meet the coach, she had stood in her attic bedroom, her

5

hand on the iron latch of the window, gazing out through the rain-speckled glass at the crumpled clutter of roofs and chimneys heaped up against the smoke-grimed sky, and she had thought, *When the leaves return I shall be married.* Beyond the barricades of the weaving mills and the dyehouses, the bare trees ran through the sky like cracks in ice. The window frame was old and warped, the paint peeling in scabs. She ran her finger along the cold loop of the latch as the wind rattled the loose panes, and the draught made her shiver.

From the shop her aunt called her name, her voice wilting on the last syllable. Elisabeth turned away from the window, holding her arms tight across her chest for warmth, but she did not answer. It seemed to her that though she was not yet gone, the room had accustomed itself already to her absence. The bed in the corner of the room had been stripped of its sheets and rugs, its drapes knotted up so that the mattress might be aired. The door to the press hung open, its shelves and compartments empty but for a few yellowed sheets of the paper her aunt insisted upon to prevent the stained wood from spoiling the linens. The ewer and basin with their pattern of faded forget-me-nots had been rinsed and wrapped and put away in the kitchen, and there was no fire laid in the small grate. Even the old writing desk was bare, its curved legs buckling as though they might give way without the steadying disorder of books and pamphlets and catalogues and papers that habitually crowded its surface. Elisabeth stroked its scarred

6

top, tracing the grain of the wood with her finger. Though elaborately carved at the feet, the desk was the work of an unskilled woodsmith, its table insufficiently deep for its breadth, its fragile legs ill-suited to so sturdy a piece. Beside them the squat legs of the ladder-backed kitchen chair straddled the floor with the stolidity of a taverner on market day.

Again Elisabeth heard her aunt calling for her and again she did not answer. Instead she pulled out the chair and sat down. The frayed rush seat had always been too high and it comforted her to feel the familiar press of the desk's underside against her thighs. Sometimes, on those too few occasions when she contrived to sit here all day, she had undressed at night to find the shape of it printed in secret lines on her skin. The desk was shabby, ink-stained and scabbed with candle wax, its single splintery drawer split with age and clumsily nailed together, but she was filled with a sudden longing to take it. It was impossible, of course. Even if her aunt had agreed to such a notion, each of the twenty-three girls was permitted only a single trunk.

Elisabeth had packed the books herself, taking out some of the heavier linens her aunt had selected from the shop. She did not tell her aunt. Her aunt thought like most women and considered a tablecloth or a set of handkerchiefs of considerably greater value than the words of La Rochefoucauld or Racine. If it had not been for her godfather, she would never have managed to accumulate even her own modest library. A respected merchant, Plomier Deseluse was no bibliophile, considering books a pitiable proxy for the pleasures of company and of cards, but he was both prosperous and good-hearted. When Elisabeth's uncle had died, he had settled upon her a small allowance from which she might purchase what he referred to as the necessary niceties. It would, he said, serve her until she was of an age to be wed.

'Elisabeth!'

Elisabeth set her palms flat on the desk. There was an ink stain on the longest finger of her right hand, a pattern of freckles on the back of her left like the five on a die. Her hands at least she might take with her. She closed her eyes. Then she lowered her head and set her cheek upon the desk, inhaling its faint smells of old varnish and ink powder. The King would buy her books from henceforth. The arrangements had been brokered by the bishop, whose diocese of Quebec had recently been extended to contain the new settlement in Louisiana. In addition to her trousseau, each girl would receive a small stipend from His Majesty's Ministry of the Marine to support her until she was married, for a period not to exceed one year. Deseluse considered the bargain to be more than reasonable. There were perhaps one hundred unmarried men in Louisiana, many in a position to support a wife. The girls would have their pick of them.

Downstairs a door slammed.

'For the love of peace, Niece, must I shout myself hoarse?'

Without opening her eyes, Elisabeth raised her head a little. Her nose brushed the desk as, very

8

lightly, she pressed her lips against its waxy surface. Then, unsettled by her own foolishness, she rose and walked quickly across the room. She did not turn round as she closed the door behind her and descended the stairs towards her aunt.

★   ★   ★

Deseluse had been late. As her aunt hastened to greet him, her hands smoothing invisible creases from her skirts, Elisabeth watched the dark shape of his carriage beyond the swirled glass of the windows, heard the impatient jangle and slap of a horse shifting in its traces, the raised voice of a man objecting angrily to the obstruction. The afternoon had darkened, though it was hardly three o'clock, and the lamps were already lit, bright as coins in their buttery brass sconces. In their glow the long polished counter gleamed like a thoroughbred. Elisabeth leaned against the brass measure that ran the length of the counter, feeling its sharp edge press against her belly.

She had loved this shop when first she had come to live here. Accustomed to the frugal plainness of her father's home, she had thought herself awoken in a jewel box. She had gazed in wonder as her aunt took down the heavy bolts of silk and velvet and gossamer mousseline, billowing them out so that her customers might appreciate their fineness, the grace of their fall. Along one wall of the shop were tiny drawers containing buttons of every shape and hue, buttons of shell and bone and polished metal and every shade of coloured glass that flashed like firecrackers when you held them in the light. She had not known there were so many colours in the world. Sometimes, when she was supposed to be working on her sewing, she had crept into the shop and hidden beneath the counter, aching to dip her hands into the rattling drawers of buttons and throw them into the air, to pull great spools of colour from the reels of ribbons and trimmings and threads so that she might fill the air with their brilliant patterns. She had not thought then that it was possible to be oppressed by the ceaseless cram of colour and stuff, that sometimes, when the day was ended, she would desire only to slip into the lane behind the shop and tip her head back, restored to herself by the grimy grey pallor of approaching dusk.

'Elisabeth, my dear.'

Plomier Deseluse stepped into the shop, shaking the wet from his shoulders like a dog. His wig, bulky and horned in the old-fashioned style, glinted with rain. Elisabeth bobbed a curtsy, inclining her head.

'Sir.'

'Come out from behind there and let me kiss you. It is not every day that I despatch a ward of mine to be married.'

Elisabeth's smile stiffened as, obediently, she stepped out into the shop and allowed her godfather to embrace her. He smelled of claret and wet wool.

'Officially I suppose you are now a ward of the King or some such, but we should not let such formalities prevent a fond farewell.' He took a large handkerchief from his pocket and blew his nose loudly into it. 'This is your box?' Leaning out into the damp lane, he gestured at the coachman to load the trunk onto the back of the carriage. When the door clicked shut behind him he shivered. 'Wretched miserable weather.'

'Please, come warm yourself by the fire,' Elisabeth's aunt said hastily. 'May I bring you some tea? A little port wine?'

Deseluse shook his head.

'We should leave directly.' He nodded at Elisabeth. 'You are ready?'

'Yes, sir.'

'Then let us be off. The roads are hardly safe in darkness.' He bowed to Elisabeth's aunt. 'Good day, Madame. My wife wished me to tell you that she shall call on you tomorrow. It seems a woman can never have enough dresses.'

Elisabeth's aunt bared her teeth in a smile. Her teeth were yellow, a slightly darker shade than her complexion.

'I hope, sir, that you too shall come back and see us, though Elisabeth is gone. We should be most obliged.'

'Yes, yes, well, I am sure,' Deseluse said and he gave his shoulders another brisk shake. 'Now, Elisabeth, you are ready?'

Elisabeth looked at the smooth gleam of the counter, at the bolts of cloth stacked on their deep shelves, and she thought of the long afternoons when she had thought she might die of the dullness of it. On the wall her shears hung from their blue ribbon, their blades slightly parted. Her fingers twined together, the tips hard

11

against the points of her knuckles.

'Come along, now,' urged her aunt.

Slowly Elisabeth turned. The door was open and outside the rain flurried in petulant squalls. Pulling up the hood of her cape, she touched her lips to her aunt's yellow cheek.

'Godspeed, Niece, and may God bless you.'

'Farewell, Aunt.'

'Write and tell us how you find things. Your cousins shall be curious. Louisiana. Imagine.'

'Imagine,' Elisabeth echoed, and she rolled up her mind like a length of ribbon so that she might not.

★   ★   ★

Of the twenty-three girls, seventeen would be travelling from Paris. Some of the girls had connections to the convents and missions of Paris; others, like Elisabeth, had been proposed to the bishop by patrons of his acquaintance. Twenty-three girls between the ages of fourteen and eighteen, girls of high moral character, not all of them well-born, but all raised in virtue and in piety, fine stock from which to breed a new France in the New World.

Twenty-three girls who might otherwise never be wed.

She knew only that the men of Louisiana were mostly soldiers or civilian officials in the pay of the King. Some were Canadian, the rest French. One of these men would become her husband. She had signed a contract to make it so. For fifteen *sols* a day and a trunk of linen and lace,

12

she had sold herself into exile, property of the King of France until, in a savage land on the other side of the world, a man she had never met might take her in marriage, a man of whom she knew nothing, not even his name.

If such a fate was preferable to the future that had beckoned her in Saint-Denis, married according to the arrangements of her aunt or confined to repeat forever the same dreary day behind the counter of the mercer's shop, there was poor comfort in it. It was miserable to be a grown woman, more miserable still to be a grown woman with neither the funds nor the affections a grown woman must have at her disposal if she was to contrive her own future. As a child Elisabeth had liked to lie on her belly beneath the table in the kitchen, a book on the floor before her. It was warm in the kitchen and friendly. She had lain beneath the table and the words in the book and the hiss of the fire and the grunts and slaps above her as Madeleine kneaded the dough for bread had wrapped themselves around her like a blanket, muffling time. When it was dinner the old servant had been obliged to bend over, her breath coming in short puffs as she threatened to sweep Elisabeth from her hiding place with her sharp-bristled broom. Elisabeth had laughed then and tickled Madeleine behind her fat knees and thought how, when she was a woman, she would make her home under a table where the world was all stories and swollen ankles.

Then her father had died and Madeleine had gone and Elisabeth had been sent to live with her father's sister in Saint-Denis. In her aunt's house there were boys and wooden crates under the kitchen table where her aunt kept the china, wrapped carefully against breakage. Elisabeth was ten then and hardly a girl at all. Her aunt required her to work in the shop during the day, or to help with the house. Elisabeth read at night beneath a candle that guttered in the midnight draught from the window. Sometimes, when she lay down to sleep, the night sky had already begun to curl up at the edges, exposing the grey-pink linings of the day, and she could hear the heavy wheels of the vegetable wagons as they rumbled down the lane. Her aunt complained about the candles and rebuked Elisabeth for yawning in the shop, but the old woman was weary too and her heart was not in it.

A husband was another matter. When she was married, Elisabeth thought, even the nights would not be her own.

* * *

The box was large and flat, tied about with string. At his master's instruction, the coachman set it on the table in the main parlour of the coaching inn. Though the taverner had informed them that several of the other girls were already arrived, the room was empty and ill-lit. The fire in the grate smoked and beneath the choke of it the inn smelled strongly of soup and spilled brandy.

'Well, go on then,' Deseluse said, his spirits somewhat restored by the arrival of a large glass of Madeira wine. 'Open it.'

Elisabeth hesitated.

'What is it?' she asked.

'Proof if any was needed that no one ever learned wisdom from reading books,' the merchant observed drily to the taverner, and he pressed a coin into the man's palm. 'Why don't you open it, my dear, and see for yourself?'

Elisabeth did as she was told, lifting the lid from the wooden box. The silk inside was a milky green, the green of the tiny jade tiger that the bookseller kept on his desk in the shop behind the cathedral. The tiger had been brought from the Orient by the bookseller's brother, against its will Elisabeth supposed, for its curiously human face was contorted into a furious scowl. She would never again enter that shop, she thought suddenly, never again hear the arthritic jangle of the bell over the door as it opened or breathe in the smell of dust and leather and patent medicines that caused her nose to wrinkle and her heart to lift, and she fumbled with the box, striking her wrist painfully against its sharp edge.

'Take it out,' her godfather urged, and he leaned into the box and scooped clouds of green into her arms. The quilt spilled from her embrace to sweep the floor, the cool silk heavy with feathers. The taverner whistled.

'Goose,' Deseluse said. 'From the Périgord. The finest down in all of France.'

Elisabeth stroked the quilt and the heaviness of it was like the heaviness in her chest.

'Thank you,' she said. 'It's beautiful.'

'A wedding present,' he said. 'With a good

15

wife beside him and a good quilt on top of him, a man may sleep like a king.'

'Better still the other way around,' the taverner rejoined with a leer that, at the merchant's frown, he quickly adjusted to deference. 'May I fetch you another glass of that, sir?'

When the taverner was gone, Deseluse took the quilt from Elisabeth and laid it carefully across the back of a wooden settle.

'There is something else in the box too. Something I was given that I thought might amuse you. Here, let me.' He reached into the crate and drew out three heavy volumes bound in tooled leather. 'Handsome bindings. Worth a few *livres* I shouldn't wonder.'

Elisabeth's hands reached out like a beggar's. 'For me?'

'Well, they are not for that impudent taverner, that is certain!' He turned the top volume on its side so that he could read the spine. '*Essais Volume I* by Michel de Montaigne. With two and three to follow, if you have appetite enough for them.'

Elisabeth gasped as, without ceremony, he hefted the three books into her arms. Montaigne's *Attempts*. Her father had spoken to her of Montaigne, had called him one of the great sages of the modern world, and it had immediately intrigued her, that a man of eminence would label his life's work so.

'Attempts!' Deseluse declared, shaking his head. 'It would appear that Sieur de Montaigne had a thing or two to learn about salesmanship.'

But Elisabeth did not laugh.

16

'Thank you,' she whispered and her voice shook a little. 'I — I don't know what to say.'

'Heavens, my dear, they are only books. Thank you will do very well.'

Much later, after supper when at last she was able to escape to her room, Elisabeth opened the first volume. The pages were uncut, the book folded in on itself like a secret. Elisabeth ran a finger over the inked lettering of the frontispiece and the urge to cut the pages was like a stitch in her side. But she did not. She thought of the other girls in the parlour and she twisted, constrained even in recollection by the sticky, stifling bounds of their obedient inconsequentiality, and she told herself — not yet.

All through the months of waiting in Rochefort, when the war with the English necessitated delay upon delay and she thought she might die of the other girls and their prattle, she had not succumbed. The volumes remained in her trunk uncut. Sometimes at night, for comfort, she took them onto her lap, stroking the leather bindings, running her finger over the fine gilded lettering. On the voyage, perhaps, if it was bad and she could not endure it, perhaps then she might permit herself the first chapters. A mouthful or two, just enough to sustain her.

She would keep the rest for Louisiana.

* * *

Now, the wind-fattened sails bulged contentedly as the ship traced a wide arc away from land. The dark stain of the sea widened and spread.

17

Far off on the horizon, the port stretched narrow, no more than a ravelled thread hemming the sky before it pulled tight. Then it was gone.

The girls shifted, murmuring among themselves. Pulling herself up on to the rail, Elisabeth leaned out, stretching her neck into the wind. Beyond the prow the sea spilled over the lip of the horizon, tipping them towards their future. Elisabeth wrapped her arms around the rail, tasting salt and the nostrum sting of tar, and thought of St Augustine, who believed that the earth was as flat as a stove lid and that it floated on water like a slice of orange. Astronomers had proved one thousand times over that the world was a globe, but still she found herself thinking of the place where the oceans ceased, the sigh of the ship as it was borne over the fall into the abyss.

Slowly, in a shuffling line, as though shackled together, the girls trailed back towards their quarters. Elisabeth did not follow them. In the distance a dark smear above the indigo line of the sea looked like land. She knew it was not land. Ahead of them stretched the Atlantic sea, one thousand inscrutable leagues of water and wind and English warships. Beyond that, if they should survive it, lay the islands of the New World.

Elisabeth stared out to sea for a long time. In Rochefort the towns-folk had called Louisiana 'the drowned lands'. They muttered of a barren swamp inhabited only by boy soldiers and wild Canadian hunters, a pestilent wilderness stalked by wild animals and wilder men. Above her, on

18

the orlop deck, animals rattled and stamped in their cramped pens. The hold was too crowded to accommodate them, packed tight with muskets and gunpowder, barrels of flour and wine and bacon, bolts of cloth and miles of rope and twenty-three trunks crammed to bursting with the newly acquired necessities of a stranger's bride. When at last she turned away, squeezing her eyes shut, the brightness of the sun repeated itself on her darkness in patterns of red.

Behind the narrow ladder that led to the foredeck, she drew the book from her pocket. The wood smelled of salt and warm varnish. Elisabeth drew her knees up to her chest, making a kind of lectern of them, and fingered the fraying ribbon that marked her place. Homer's *Odyssey*, translated into French. A cheap cloth-bound copy, printed on cheap paper.

'An epic journey,' the bookseller had said when she paid for it.

'Except that Odysseus comes home,' she had replied, and she had hurried out of the shop before he could answer.

It was near the end of September and still the heat was insufferable. They lay beneath a palmetto shade, but even out of the direct strike of the sun the air was viscous, too thick to breathe. The boy squirmed on the pile of reeds that served as a bench and scratched fiercely at the insect bites on his chest. His eyes ached in the bleached-white afternoon. The screech and hum of the dark forest pressed itself into the cracks between the beating of gourds and shrieking of flutes and the caterwauling that passed for singing. There was not the slightest stirring of a breeze. Inside his too-tight boots, his feet were swollen and raw with heat and blisters. He had grown a full inch in the months since leaving La Rochelle and the sleeves of his shirt barely covered his wrists. The Louisiana sun had burned the backs of his hands red.

In his home town of La Rochelle, down by the wharves where the curses of the sailors spiralled in the sea-salty breezes like stalks of straw, they had called the savages *peaux rouges*, redskins. Kicking at coils of rope as he loitered, the boy had imagined a race of scarlet men, bright and smooth as cherries. But in this, as in so many other things, he had been disappointed. The savages were not red. They were brown. Some had a coppery hue, but most were just brown. Their skin was drawn all over with tattoos, as

20

though they attached their limbs to their bodies with yards of black twine. Even their faces bore patterns, some so frantic that it was difficult to distinguish the ordinary features of eyes and mouth. Their hair fell in heavy braided tails down their backs, adorned with bouquets of feathers. They made no attempt to cover themselves. Their nakedness did not shame them. When they danced and stamped and sang, disporting themselves with their gourds and their drums, their cocks slapped the scrawl of their thighs and the chords in their necks strained against the webbing of their inked skin.

Their women were barely more modest. They covered themselves only with a strap upon which was placed a one-foot-wide sash of fur or bristles, painted red, yellow and white. Their breasts swung and shifted as they walked, the older women's slack and empty, the nipples large as a palm, the younger ones round and high, bouncing a little so that it seemed to the boy that they winked at him. He stared at them, ashamed and angry at the agitation they aroused in him.

Like their menfolk, the female savages were snarled with tattoos. Many had stripes of black the full length of their noses and down their chins, dividing their faces in two like trees marked for felling. Their scribbled-on skin was greased with bear oil, their black hair too. When one of them bent before him to offer him a slab of the rough yellow cake that passed among their kind for bread, the sharp musky reek of her caused him to flush and he was stricken by the sudden and powerful urge to strike her, the

21

blood itching in his clenched fists. It was well known that the savages were as carelessly carnal as animals.

He sank his hands into a platter of pumpkin as she stood and moved noiselessly away. Her bare toes were ringed with circles of dark dots. He thought of the time in La Rochelle when he and his cousin Jean had hidden behind his uncle's house and watched as his uncle raised his new aunt's skirts and pressed her against the wall, his stubby fingers scooping her breasts from her stays. Jean had nudged him so hard then that he had fallen noisily against the wall and his uncle had heard them and come after them with a rod. He could not remember the beating but he remembered his aunt's blue-white breasts and her thick white thighs, the skin puckering as she tightened them around his uncle's waist.

Heaping food onto his plate, the boy ate swiftly, urgently, in the savage manner, without a spoon. The juice from the pumpkin was sweet and thick as syrup. He lifted his plate and drank it, then wiped up the last sticky smears with a wad of cornbread. Only when the meal was over and the savage women were gathering up the empty baskets and clay dishes did he raise his eyes and stare again at the sway of their breasts, the hitch of their polished buttocks as they walked. The carpenter, watching him, whistled and several of the men laughed. The boy shrugged and his neck reddened as he spat his contempt into a curved palm.

Later, when the fire of the sun had burned itself out and night drifted against the split-log

22

palisades that encircled the settlement, the savages danced again. They made a ring of twenty or thirty and, to the sound of a whistle and a drum made from an earthen pot and a strip of deerskin, they danced into a line and then back into a ring. The boy thought of the sailors in La Rochelle, the vigorous jigs scraped out on the fiddle, the gold in their ears and in their teeth. The night was illuminated by torches of bound cane twice the height of the tallest man and as wide around. The savages' faces shone in the orange glow. Shadows jumped against the palisades and the dark mound of the temple where they kept the bones of their ancestors all piled up like an unlit fire. The drums beat louder, rattling like sticks between the boy's ribs. In the huts of the warriors hung the shrivelled scalps of their enemies. The skin was yellow, the hair as brittle as dried seaweed.

When finally the dance was finished, the men were taken to their sleeping quarters, an upended beaker of dried mud with a roof of palmetto leaves. At the entrance to the cabin a young savage woman waited, her hands clasped together. She wore a mantle loosely around her shoulders and, beneath its hem, a small child clung to her leg, its cheek against her thigh. Speaking a few words in her own tongue, she gestured at the group of men, asking them with her hands if they had all that they required. The ferret-faced carpenter from Nantes made a show of shaking his head vigorously, thrusting the finger of one hand through the circle made by his forefinger and thumb on the other. The men laughed and groaned, slapping him on the shoulder as they pushed him ahead of them into the cabin. Inside bearskins had been laid by way of cots upon the packed earth floor.

At the threshold, drawn by some impulse he could not explain, the boy turned towards the savage girl, one hand fluttering out from his side. The girl hesitated, her eyes dark and shuttered, and the shells in her ears gleamed. The boy parted his lips as though to speak but he said nothing. He let his gaze drop. Slowly the girl bent down and lifted the child onto her hip, her heavy black plait falling over one shoulder. The infant twined its arms around her neck, its legs around her waist, pressing its face against her cheek. The girl raised her head once more towards the boy, like a deer scenting the air. Then, drawing the child closer, she walked away into the darkness.

★ ★ ★

The men were restive that night. It was widely known that the chief of the savages had offered to the commandant as many women as there were men in the party and that the commandant had refused him, setting his pale arm against the chief's dark one and gesturing with his hands to indicate that the flesh of one should not touch the other. From the pallet next to his, the carpenter leaned over and jabbed the boy in the ribs. His finger was sharp as an awl.

' 'Course, it's worst for you, ain't it?' he jeered. 'For a man of your appetites and experience, the lack of it must be torture!'

The men laughed as the boy cursed and hunched himself into a ball.

'I think the infant is crying,' one of the others taunted.

'Fetch a woman to suckle him,' said another.

'Fetch one for each of us!' protested a third.

Amid the laughter the blacksmith they called Le Grand noisily passed wind. The men laughed harder. The one with the scar beneath his eye, whose work the boy did not know, slid a flask of *eau-de-vie* from his pocket and passed it around. When it reached the boy, he snatched it up and drank with a practised toss of his wrist, steadying himself against the burn in his breastbone. The carpenter began a lurid tale of a pair of doeskin breeches and two red-haired seamstresses from the Vendée. As the flask emptied, the men's tales grew wilder, the coarse words thickening the darkness like flour. From his place at the centre of the circle, the boy listened and his scalp prickled with scorn and longing.

Later, as the men mumbled and snored and a mosquito sang its high-pitched whine like a secret in his ear, the boy lay awake, his hands still and his throat dry, waiting for the headache that threatened at the base of his skull. He was accustomed to sleeplessness. In La Rochelle, in the screened-off bedchamber the boy had shared with his five brothers and sisters, he had leaned out of the narrow window when the others were asleep and watched the shift and jostle of the masts in the harbour as they scraped the star-barnacled sky.

Now he lay upon his back, staring up into the night, and the tears seeped from him like sweat. On the ship there had been other boys like him, four of them in all. Together they had learned how to mend rope and wash decks, to scale the rigging in all conditions, to read a compass and to endure without a sound the regular beatings of the boatswain. At night they had boasted in whispers about the adventures they meant to have in the New World. They worked to gain their passage, nothing more. Not one of them meant to stay a sailor.

The first to fail had been the band's self-appointed leader, a gap-toothed whelp with a pirate's swagger and hair the colour of apricot preserves, who had reminded Auguste powerfully of his cousin Jean. The boy had grown feverish shortly after the ship had set sail from Havana, where she had stopped to take on supplies; even as he succumbed to delirium, the other two had begun to complain of chills and pains in the back and joints.

By the time the passengers disembarked at Massacre Island, all three of the other boys, and several of the ship's crew, were dead.

* * *

They stayed in the village for three days, during which the savages sang and danced three times a day. Though the afternoons brought violent thunderstorms, the heat did not break. But the commandant showed no sign of haste. He was a slight man with a fair complexion, almost

26

undersized, but though he was hardly twenty years of age there was an authority to him that was not easily disregarded.

While it was his older brother and founder of the colony who was acknowledged as the finer soldier, it was widely agreed that in matters of politics and diplomacy it was the commandant who held the advantage. The heat and caprice of the wild lands did not diminish him, nor did the strange ways of the savages discompose him. His father had departed Dieppe for New France as a young man, and all twelve of his sons had been familiar from birth with the singular language of the Huron savages who were the Canadian settlers' closest allies. The southern tongues were not like Huron, but the commandant's mouth had adjusted itself quickly to their strange shapes. Whether dealing with man or savage he bore himself always with a quiet assurance, as though nothing could occur that he had not already anticipated.

He made no objection to the savages' rituals. On his chest he bore a tattoo in their fashion, a twisted mass of vipers with forked tongues, inked by a Pascagoula during preparations for war. Though he hated tobacco, he always smoked the pipe of peace they called *calumet*, drawing several long puffs in the manner of the chief. It was an outlandish-looking thing, the *calumet*, a hollow length of cane decorated all over with feathers so that it resembled several fancy ladies' fans tied together.

When the commandant permitted the savages to smear white dirt in circles upon his face, the boy was ready to snigger, had his hand cupped in readiness, but, when he sought about him for an accomplice, the men's faces were blank. Le Grand was the only one to catch his eye, his face creased with a warning frown. Awkwardly the boy looked away, his cupped hand thrust stiffly into the sheath of his armpit.

On the third day a savage offered his back to the commandant, who, to the boy's astonishment, bowed his head and climbed upon the red man's shoulders. Another savage held his feet, and in this manner they progressed to a stake sunk in the centre of their village, while the other savages made noisy music with drums and calabashes filled with pebbles. When they reached the stake, the commandant was set down upon a deerskin, his back towards the chief. The chief placed his hands upon the commandant's shoulders and rocked him as though he were a fractious infant that would not sleep. Each warrior of the tribe then approached the stake and struck it hard with a wooden club that the men called a *casse-tête*, calling out in their own tongue.

At last they were finished. The boy rubbed his eyes with his fists and tried not to yawn. It was so very hot. His eyes stung and his head felt dull, heavy and swollen. He had a sudden memory of his mother on a hot day, snoring on a stool outside their house, her head tipped backwards, a dish of thick green beans set between her thighs. Stealing up on her, Jean had placed one of the bean pods in her open mouth and run away. They had watched from behind the tavern

28

wall as she spluttered and woke, spitting the bean from her mouth and upsetting the dish in her lap. He remembered still how foolish she had looked, scrabbling in the dust for the beans, and the anger that had scoured the base of his throat. He had ducked behind the wall so that she would not see him, but Jean had stood there with his hands upon his hips, openly laughing at her. His mother had said nothing. She had not struck him nor had she informed Jean's father of his son's offence. The people of La Rochelle had considered his mother a weak and silly woman.

The boy set his chin on his knees, staring at the ground. A little way off a black insect about the length of his finger rested in the dust. With its long folded legs, the insect resembled in shape the grasshoppers he had caught in France, though it was much larger. The boy wriggled forward on his bottom, trying to get a closer look. The creature's head was long with wide-set eyes and a pronounced jaw like the head of a horse. The boy wondered if it stung, then if it was injured. It seemed so still. On its back four small wings gleamed vivid purple. The insect twitched, shivering on its grass-stem legs. The boy flinched. Then it was gone.

Squatted in a half-circle on their haunches, the savages watched in silence as the commandant had two of his men unload the presents they had brought and set them out upon the skins. The boy watched too. The presents were for the most part commonplace items: knives, axes, small mirrors, copper rings, combs, kettles, glass beads, even hats and stockings. The stockings were red.

Without rising from their haunches, the savages shuffled closer to the array of gifts, reaching out to touch with one finger the teeth of a tortoiseshell comb, the silvered handle of a mirror. The commandant placed a string of beads in the chief's lap. The chief held it up to the sky, blinking as the glass flashed darts of green light. The boy thought of his sister, then. There was a dress that she had had once that she had always said would look fine with a string of green beads. He could not remember the dress or whether it too had been green.

Marguerite had been the kindest of his sisters. She would be married by now and living with the butcher on the rue d'Armagnac. Only the baby Jeanne would be left at home. The boy thought of his mother, nudging the cradle with one foot as she bent over her darning. She had cried sometimes from the bruises, the tears little shards of ice in the rough wool. He blinked, shaking his head clear as the chief laid down the green necklace and stood to inspect the remainder of the presents. Several of them he picked up and examined more closely. The largest kettle had a dent in its belly.

One of the savages, bolder than the rest, suddenly took up a hat and placed it upon his head. Then he stood. Apart from the hat he was quite naked, his coppery skin glossy and almost hairless. The commandant nodded gravely and clapped his hands and, when the savage tipped the hat over his eyes and stamped his feet by way of dancing, some of the men clapped too.

The boy bit his lip. The hat was unexceptional, even plain, its modest brim trimmed only with dull silver braid. There were hundreds of such hats pressed onto bent heads in the crowded streets and wharves of La Rochelle, which, together with black coat and downcast eyes, made up the livery of the careful and the conservative. A hat of that kind was as ordinary as bread, inviting not the faintest attention or curiosity. And yet, set jauntily atop the savage's oiled black hair, as the Indian leaped and spun, jabbering in his frenzied tongue, it made no sense at all.

When the dance was finished, the savages rolled their gifts up in the deerskins and carried them away. The chief waited, still seated, his hands set lightly upon his thighs. The commandant said something to him in his language. The chief inclined his head and his eyes narrowed. Raising his hand to his men, the commandant nodded.

This time four of them were required to bring the two wooden crates that had sat so low in the pirogue as it inched its way upriver. The commandant had the men set the crates before the chief. There were smears of red on the carpenter's breeches; in the damp air the iron fastenings that secured the chests had already rusted. The commandant clicked open the first crate. The chief watched intently, without blinking.

Slowly, the men lifted a large bundle of sailcloth from the crate and set it on the ground.

It was tied all around with twine, like a corpse. The knots were obstinate, and it took a moment or two for the carpenter to fumble them loose. Stripping the twine away, he knelt and unrolled the bundle. Inside were four French muskets, their barrels oiled and glossy. The chief's face twitched, his lips peeling from his brown teeth like a fox scenting a chicken coop. From the second chest the men took another bundle and spread it out, revealing a considerable supply of lead and powder.

The commandant placed his hands together as though in prayer and bowed to the chief. Then he gestured at the guns. The chief nodded. The commandant gestured to one of the men, whose name was Doré. If he had a trade, the boy did not know it, but Doré had come to Louisiana from New France with the commandant and he was well accustomed to the unnatural ways of the savages. Cracking his knuckles, the Canadian pulled an apostle from his belt before hoisting a musket and upending it.

The squatting savages shuffled closer, their eyes round with fascination and fear. Beneath their chins their brown knees gleamed like polished wood. Deftly Doré measured out the black powder and poured it from the apostle into the muzzle of the barrel, before ramming the lead down with an authoritative grimace. When he rotated the cock, the savages' heads tilted to precisely the same angle, and they blinked rapidly as he tap-tapped the fine priming powder into the flash pan and slid the lid closed. Then he turned the cock and raised the musket to his shoulder, closing one eye.

The crack of the gun caused several of the savages to cry out in terror. The white men laughed out loud, urging Doré to reload. Even the commandant smiled and shrugged and held his hands out, palms flat, towards the chief. As for the boy, he was filled with a sudden surge of exhilaration. His heart pounded and he hooted wide-mouthed as he watched the savages blinking uncertainly, peering at the instrument that had emitted so violent an explosion.

Grinning, Doré held out the gun, inviting inspection. Shakily the savages stretched their necks, jabbing their heads like chickens as they darted looks at the gun. None dared to touch it. Doré let the musket drop. The savages watched, motionless, as once again he loaded the weapon, primed it and lifted it to his shoulder. Then he fired. For a moment the echo of the shot hung in the humid air. Then it was gone, drowned out by the violent screams of the birds.

★   ★   ★

That evening, the commandant summoned the boy and quietly informed him that preparations were being made for departure early the next morning. Their business with the Houma was complete. In addition to a good supply of ground maize and vegetables, the chief had given the commandant a number of fowls and four of the savages of the village to serve as guides as far as the next settlement, some twenty leagues north. They would leave at daybreak.

All, that was, except the boy.

It was, the commandant said, a matter of diplomacy. Strong alliances with the savages were essential if the French were to hold their position. The colony boasted fewer than one hundred soldiers, many of whom were weakened by sickness, and, with war in Europe, there was little hope of more, at least for the present. Meanwhile the English, already well established in the lands to the east, were determined to extend their territories. Given the threat of English dominance in Europe as well as the New World, the French had hoped for assistance against them from the Spanish forts at Pensacola and at Veracruz, but the former was weak and the latter at too great a distance, and Spain had proved an erratic ally.

The commandant's voice was low and steady. He did not speak to the boy as the other men did, as though he was slow or a girl. With so acute a shortage of men and no military stations to buttress the wedge of French occupation between the strongholds of St Lawrence in Acadia and the handful of small forts in the south, the commandant explained, the French position was perilously ill-defended. Their only hope of securing the newborn colony against the English threat lay in the forging of strong alliances with the many savage nations situated along the length of the St Louis River. Through the bestowal of gifts and favours, the French might secure the allegiance of these savage tribes and, when required, induce them to war against their enemies. Such a stratagem had served the

34

French well in the north. Now it must be depended upon to secure the vast empire of Louisiana for France until it grew strong enough to support itself.

'All counted, and in a nation that extends perhaps one thousand leagues, we number fewer than two hundred souls. Only half are soldiers. If we are to claim Louisiana for our King, each Frenchman must do the work of one hundred. You included.'

The commandant leaned forward, pressing his hands between his knees. Beneath his unbuttoned shirt the snakes writhed and licked at his chest. The boy tried to hold his gaze, but his face burned hot and he feared that the trembling in his mouth would betray him. He gazed at the ground as, in the same steady voice, the commandant confided that the course of such diplomacy was not without difficulty. The savages were brutish and unreliable, some nations particularly so. Only a year before, three Canadians had been massacred while they slept by Alibamon savages with English muskets and lances.

Now, despite swift retaliation, it was rumoured that the English were once more stirring up dissent among the Alibamons, urging them to raids against the French. More ominously, the Chickasaw, one of the most powerful nations in Louisiana, had declared their allegiance to the English. It was essential that the tribes who had promised to support the French might be depended upon.

Over the years, the commandant explained, he

had made many caresses to the Ouma nation, for their situation close to the confluence of the St Louis and Red rivers gave them a strategic importance. Some years previously the commandant had helped them to resolve a dispute over territory with their neighbours, the Bayagoulas, and in return he had always been favourably received. Now he required certain proof that they might be depended upon. It was for this reason — and at this the commandant cleared his throat and set his hand reassuringly upon the boy's shoulder — that the boy would not accompany the exploratory party as it continued northward. He would remain here in the village with the Ouma. He would live with the savages.

The boy heard the commandant as though still aboard ship, the words gusting and echoing in his ears. He was to master not only the trade language of Mobilian but also the savages' local tongue so that he might act as interpreter for the French who should pass this way. In addition he was to familiarise himself with the habits and associations of the tribe, their affiliations and their enmities, and report to the garrison accordingly. His presence in the village would permit him to keep a close watch on the tribe's plans and engagements, their dealings with neighbouring nations and, in particular, any skirmishes or preparations for war.

'You shall be my eyes and my ears, young man. The next best thing to me remaining here myself. Can you do that?'

The feather cloaks of the Ouma had eyes. When they danced and the cloaks leaped upon their shoulders, the eyes seemed to roll and wink, sometimes in jest but more often in warning. The eyes of the dancers rolled too, showing the whites. The boy's throat burned but he ducked his head all the same.

'Good man. We shall not be assured of Louisiana until we hold the hearts of her savages in our hands. How big are your hands?'

The commandant nodded at the boy, a smile pressed into the corner of his mouth. The boy hesitated and then extended his hands, palms up. The commandant cuffed him lightly on the shoulder and stood up.

'Big enough, surely,' he observed wryly, looking down at the boy. 'After all, how large can the heart of a savage be?'

The boy said nothing. His face was stiff as an old sail. The commandant dismissed him, but before the boy had taken three paces he heard his name. He turned back, his heart fierce in his chest. He kept his gaze upon the commandant's boots.

'You may live among them, *mon fils*,' the commandant said. 'But you must never forget that you are not one of them. It is simpler to make a savage of a Frenchman than a Frenchman of a savage.'

'Yes, sir,' he whispered.

The commandant sighed.

'The women of this nation know nothing of restraint. It is their belief that when the time comes that a woman must depart this life and must traverse the narrow and difficult bridge to the Grand Village of the hereafter, only those

37

who have — who have indulged their lewd natures will cross easily.' He drew in his breath sharply. 'Master the savages' tongue but remember always that you are a Frenchman. Serve your King with honour. When it is time, we shall return for you.'

★ ★ ★

The leave-taking ceremony was concluded, the preparations almost complete. The chief had repaired to the temple to exhort the savage gods to look favourably upon the expedition and grant it safe passage. A procession of savages accompanied the white men down the hill to the river, stamping their feet and beating drums. It was still early, but the day was already oppressively warm. By the bayou the close-set copse of trees offered no respite but, like a huddle of perspiring men, gave out its own sour-smelling heat.

The boy waited by the copse, half hidden by a brake of cane, watching as the men loaded the last of their supplies. Their faces were scarlet and shiny with sweat and they slapped in vain at the veils of biting insects that hung about their necks. In the muddy shallows the pirogues rocked gently. They were heavily laden, the savages' deerskins mounded in the bow; inside the crates the chickens squawked, scratching and banging their wings against the wooden sides. The boxes of lead and powder were set with care upon a folded pad of sailcloth so that they might remain dry.

It was time for the party to depart. The commandant called the boy's name. He did not answer. Instead he watched as an alligator cruised the far side of the river, only its nostrils and its hooded eyes visible above the yellow crust of the water. One of the men had told the boy that to snare human prey, alligators had been known to call out to passers-by in the voice of a child.

The boy did not know whether to believe this or not. On his first day at the garrison at Mobile, he had seen the dog belonging to the commissary bitten by a rattlesnake. The beast did not even live a quarter of an hour, but swelled up so much that it was unable to move and died with a ghastly choking, as if it had swallowed its own tongue. Astounded by the speed of its demise, the boy had regarded its passing less with sympathy than a kind of grisly enthralment, but now, as the men uncoiled the ropes securing the pirogues and with a great deal of shouting and splashing pushed out into the wide stream, he felt a sharp pang of grief for the poor dead creature and his nose prickled. He rubbed it roughly with the back of his hand.

Raising his gun the commandant saluted the village with two volleys of musketry.

★   ★   ★

Upstream against the current, the pirogues made slow progress. It was several minutes before they reached the bend in the creek and passed out to one another in their garbled tongue, the last of

39

the natives turned away from the river and began to climb the path back to the village.

The boy leaned against a thick staff of cane, his fingers seeking out the swollen ridges of its joints. He felt hollow, as though the soft parts of him had been carried away upstream, bundled up with the deerskins and the squawking fowls. On the other side of the creek, the alligator rose again, paused and sank out of sight. The stream smoothed and steadied and continued on its way.

They were gone.

He was all alone, cast adrift among the savages. He spoke not a word of their language. He knew none of their names or whether indeed they possessed any. He knew nothing of where he was, except that the French garrison was eight days' travel away, through forests and swamps swarming with every kind of terror. He had not the faintest notion when he might see one of his countrymen again.

As he stepped out from the cane brake, the boy trod in a hillock of soft earth and a swarm of red ants spread like a rash across his boots and up over his bare ankles, setting his skin on fire. There were ants inside his boots. As he tugged them off, the boy once again felt the prickle of tears behind his eyes. The missioners claimed that there were savages who strangled their babies before they might be baptised and burned their bodies on the fires in their temples to appease their idols.

His skin burned, but the boy thought of the alligator and dared not rinse his feet in the river.

Instead he pulled up a handful of grass and scrubbed at his feet and ankles, pressing down hard to crush the ants that clung on. The sap in the grass stung his inflamed skin and streaked it green. He rubbed earth on the sorest patches. Then wearily, his too-small boots in his hand, he set off barefoot up the path towards the village.

He was twelve years old and a boy no longer.

Gently, Elisabeth cradled her left hand in her right, stroking the ring's smooth curve with her thumb. Again the fire caught, the flames licking her ribs with their hot tongues. The impossible absurdity of it stopped the breath in her chest and she hugged herself, her eyes squeezed shut, holding the dizzy tilt of it tight inside her. Had she not, of all of them, been the most distrustful, the only one indifferent to the insinuating drip of hope? Had she not despaired at the empty-headed idiocy of the lot of them, their wilful forgetfulness, the tenacious vigour with which they clung to their fantasies of prosperity and contentment? During those interminable lurching days, when it seemed that the world would be forever water and the ill-tempered priest La Vente limped the decks in search of sin, it was her contempt for her fellow passengers that had sustained her. Contempt and the certainty that, whatever the miseries of the voyage, the fate that awaited them at the end of it would surely be worse.

And yet, and yet. Raising her left hand she gazed at the ring on her finger and then swiftly touched it to her lips, closing her eyes to inhale the secret salty smell of her palm. It had been the order of the Ministry of the Marine that, excepting mealtimes, the girls be confined to their private quarters for the duration of the voyage, so that their virtue might not be corrupted by the coarseness of the ship's crew and its cargo of young soldiers. When she remembered the darkness and the suffocating smell of them all together, the smell of hair and skin and stale powder and desperate, desiccating monotony, all crated up in damp salted wood, she had to swallow, so unaccustomedly sour was the taste of scorn upon her tongue. There had not been one among them with any book-learning, any scholarly curiosity, nor so much as an ounce of common sense. Closeted together they were as foolish as a coop of clucking chickens.

In the main the chickens had endured the voyage without protest.

They had occupied themselves with sewing and tittle-tattle and to Elisabeth's despair they had chafed against neither. Their tongues moved as deftly and as decoratively as their fingers. As their needles darted and flashed, Levasseur the infantry officer grew broader and braver than any man alive, René Boyer the gunsmith and Alexandre the master joiner more skilful and prosperous. The men's blank faces were endowed with proud noses, firm chins, kindly blue eyes; their houses were furnished with comforts, their larders with meat and wine and exotic fruits.

At dinner, the chickens clustered around the trader La Sueur, who had been in Louisiana the previous winter, begging him for more details of their establishments and their future situations. The brash trader, long married and the father of five children, had amused himself by ranking the men of the colony according to their physical attributes, his sly allusions causing the chickens to flap and cackle. Elisabeth had observed his manipulations and had felt a flush of angry shame at their suggestibility. It had irked her then that La Sueur thought her no different.

Perhaps she was not so different after all. The thought began wryly, but the joy rose quickly in her and she could not keep it in. She had a sudden urge to laugh out loud, to spin wildly around the narrow room until she was dizzy. Instead she wrapped her arms over her chest, hugging herself tight, her fingertips finding the sharp wings of her shoulder blades, her lips together and her eyes closed, feeling herself swell with the bursting giddy miracle of it.

Was she truly the same person who, in exasperation, had thrown her book to the ground and demanded of the girls to know why, if their situation was so fine and the men of Louisiana so handsome and prosperous, was it that the King himself had been required to purchase them a wife? They had looked at her, then, and the bruised bewilderment in their eyes had made her want to scream.

Later that day Elisabeth had found herself accosted by Marie-Françoise de Boisrenaud, a girl a little older than the rest, who had quickly established herself as cock of the roost. The daughter of a squire from Chantilly, Marie-Françoise was a practical, pale-haired girl who had made it her business to become acquainted with the present situations of all of the bachelors of Louisiana. From an initial catalogue of fifty or sixty eligible men, and taking proper account of prosperity, position, age and health as well as congeniality and a pleasant appearance, she had proceeded to compile a list of the twenty-five she regarded as the colony's best prospects. Among the chickens she had become known, not without gratitude, as the Governess.

'We have been sent here to do God's will,' Marie-Françoise rebuked Elisabeth, and she raised her voice so that the other girls might be certain to hear her. 'Do you dare to know better than Our Lord, to tell us what we should hope for?'

'The Lord may tell you all He pleases,' Elisabeth had answered, and she had glanced over at the chickens who dropped their eyes hastily and busied themselves with their sewing. 'I know only that the only proper protection against disappointment is to expect nothing.'

Aside from causing Marie-Françoise's mouth to pull tight as a stitch, Elisabeth's words had not the slightest effect. As the weeks lengthened into months, the chickens traded the men like the cards in a game of bassette, snatching them up or frowning over them and fingering them before letting them drop. They mocked Elisabeth for her books and her gloominess, threatening her with the assistant clerk of the King's storehouse, Grapalière, who was ancient and toothless and, as a result of an accident with a musket, had an iron hook for a right hand.

Elisabeth only shrugged. She did not care if they thought her proud. When at last the interminable voyage reached its end, they would be unloaded like barrels of salt pork and sold, if they were not deemed to have turned, to the highest bidder. If Elisabeth might in time contrive to accept her fate, she for one would not conspire in the preposterous pretence that it would all end happily.

She knew it now, of course, the lunacy of hopefulness, though she dared not submit to it. He possessed more than enough for them both, a sanguinity that was almost carelessness, and the simplicity of it in him took her breath away. It was like a lamp inside him, so that he was always brilliant with it. He dazzled her. That first night, that first perfect night when she was his and he hers, one before God, she had watched him as he slept and she had understood that this would be her part, that she would arch herself about him with her vigilance always, the glass around his flame so that he might burn the brighter. His face had been loose in sleep, like a child's, his limbs sprawled and his hands curled open upon the sheet. Outside the night had hummed, alive with insects, and it had seemed to Elisabeth that she listened to the singing of her own heart.

Twenty-three girls and he had chosen her. He told her that he had never considered another but she knew it was not so. She remembered him. When they had at last arrived at Mobile, there had been a welcoming party of sorts but, though some of the chickens attempted cheer, the mood was subdued. Fever had struck the ship as it sailed from Havana; some twenty of the soldiers and crewmen on board the *Pélican* were dead. As Elisabeth trailed with the chickens onto the dock, all of them gaunt and several feverish, she noticed him, standing a little way off. The heat was overpowering, the windless air clinging to them like damp cobwebs, but he stood easily, as though he were quite comfortable. She watched as his eyes slid over them one after another, skimming across her and past her without snagging. Then she had only held her head a little higher, swaying on legs rendered unsteady by the shiftless solidity of the earth, and turned away to follow the ragged crocodile of girls to the commandant's dwelling. These days she tried not to remember it. When the image came to her unbidden, something opened inside her and the depth of it made her dizzy.

She shook her head, swinging her legs to the bare floor. It was late. She should already be dressed. For the first time since she had come to Louisiana, there was a coolness in the air. She took the blanket from the bed and wrapped its weight around her shoulders, burying her face in its coarse weave. It smelled of leather and tobacco and, faintly, of stale wine. As she breathed it in, tasting its distillation in her mouth, her belly tumbled and she clenched her hands into fists, pulling the blanket tight around her shoulders until it held her close, its beard-rough lips pressed to the line of her jaw. She closed her eyes, one cold hand pressed tight against the throb of her neck, giving herself up to the lack of him.

A sudden brisk banging at the door caused her to startle. Curling herself into a ball, Elisabeth

47

burrowed into the disordered bed, her nose pressed into the pillow. There was another flurry of knocking, causing the wooden latch to jump in its rest.

'Elisabeth? Are you there? Elisabeth?'

It was Perrine Roussel, the wife of the carpenter. Elisabeth hugged her knees, her face hidden in the blanket, and waited for her to go away. Despite everything, the chickens still contrived to call round. They peered around her cabin and urged her to join with them in grumbling about the shameful conditions in which they were expected to live. They complained of the mosquitoes, of the inadequate housing, of their husbands and, most of all, of the dearth of proper white flour for bread.

The savages did not grow wheat. The planter Rivard had twice attempted to grow it at his concession at Bayou Saint-Jean but, though the first signs of growth had appeared promising, both times the grain had succumbed to rust in the final weeks of ripening and rotted on the stalk. Few others had followed Rivard's example. Most of the settlers were soldiers or craftsmen from France's cities. They possessed little knowledge of farming and less inclination to learn. Not one among them had journeyed halfway across the world to labour in the fields. Besides, the colony lacked tools and oxen. Some of the men raised small gardens behind their cabins as they had done in France, but for everything else they were dependent upon the savages, who had no cows or pigs and made their greasy yellow bread from ground corn. There was no bacon, no fresh pork or beef, only the tough, stringy meat of wild creatures hunted in the forest. As for white flour, that staple of every respectable French home, it was an expensive luxury, available only when the ships brought it three thousand miles across the sea.

The chickens deemed the situation intolerable. Just the day before, Anne Negrette and the others had told Elisabeth that they meant to take their objections to the commandant to protest the impossibility of surviving without it. They had urged her to come with them, had declared it imperative that they all stick together. Now they sent the carpenter's wife, to ensure her attendance.

'Elisabeth? Elisabeth Savaret, are you there?'

A grey shadow stained the stuff that covered the far window, the tip of a nose dark against the pale cloth. Then it was gone. That was yet another of the chickens' objections, the lack of glass in the colony. The window frames in all the cabins were instead covered with stretched sheets of *platille*, a thin linen stuff that lent to the streakily limed interiors a kind of muted stillness, as though they were under water.

Elisabeth loved it. Behind their blank white windows, soft in the filtered light, the two of them were perfectly alone, the neighbouring cabins forgotten. And, unlike glass, the *platille* let the breezes in while keeping out the harsh glare of the sun. Sometimes, in the searing heat of the summer, she had stepped inside the cottage and it had been almost cool.

Elisabeth squirmed down the bed, pulling the

quilt over her head, burying herself beneath its comforting weight. Of all the things she had brought with her to Louisiana, he loved the sea-green quilt the best. He liked to tease her that he would have married her for the quilt alone and, when he took it in his arms and danced with it about the cabin, twirling its skirts in sea-green swoops, she laughed, swallowing the prickle of disquiet that caught in her throat.

She had laughed too when he told her she was beautiful, but behind her apron she had crossed her thumbs, pleading with the Fates that he might never see it was not so. For all her efforts, she could not rid herself of the fearfulness. When she signed the marriage contract that would formalise their betrothal, her hand had trembled so uncontrollably that she had pressed down too hard on the pen and split the nib, leaving a dark puddle of ink upon the paper. The curate had sighed and reached for the sand. He had only smiled. Taking her ink-stained hand in his free one, he had dipped the broken pen in the puddle of ink and signed his own name.

Jean-Claude Babelon. She murmured it under her breath, tasting the shape of it. Savaret was a brisk name, its syllables contained tightly within the private recesses of the mouth. Not so Babelon. Babelon was all in the lips. When she spoke his name, she could feel her mouth softening, her lips parting as though they readied for a kiss. Elisabeth had always disdained the English practice of a wife taking her husband's name upon their marriage. Now she found herself envious of it. In England, each time she was introduced to a stranger, each time she signed a letter or wrote her name on the flyleaf of a book, each time someone called to her across the street, she would declare herself his. In England, she would shed her old name like a chrysalis and emerge newly made into the world. Elisabeth Babelon. But that was not the French way. In Louisiana, as in Paris, she would always be Elisabeth Savaret.

The quilt smelled of him. She inhaled and again her body stirred. The longing in her was pure and brilliant, like light in glass, and she wondered suddenly if this was the secret they shared, those empty-headed chickens, if somewhere deep in their down-stuffed hearts, they had understood what she had never even guessed at, for all her book-learning: the certainty that a man and a woman might share of themselves completely, their souls and spirits as indivisible as two wines poured together in a single bottle. These days she had to struggle to recall the girl she was before him, when her self was all in her head and her body was only trunk and arms and legs, its passing appetites satisfied by a warm cloak or an apricot tart.

She had not opened her books since she had arrived here. There was a shelf above the table, a plank set on makeshift brackets, bare but for a couple of dusty dishes and a knife with a broken handle, but she had not troubled to unpack them. As she reached into her trunk, she touched the worn covers lightly as an archaeologist might touch the relics of a bygone time, with a kind of respectful bafflement. On the tooled leather of

Montaigne she paused, tracing the scrolled pattern very slowly with one finger, remembering the ache she had felt for it during the endless months in Rochefort. Then she had closed the trunk and pushed it under the bed.

She did not talk to him of poetry or philosophy, of science or astronomy. When they talked, they spoke of themselves. Sometimes, late in the liquid darkness, he told her of his dreams. For now he was merely an ensign, the lowest rank of commissioned infantry officers, but he meant to be rich. Sometimes she joined with him in imagining the pleasures of their future life. More often she lay with her head upon his chest and her hand flat upon his belly so that she might listen to him: the pulse of his blood, the quiver of his nerve-strings, the whisper of his lips against her skin.

As for the words, they still occupied her skull, their insect thrum never perfectly silent, but she cared nothing for them. With him, in this strange land, where the swamp whispered and the vast fruits swelled and rotted, she was flesh, all flesh. The weight of her, once densely crammed into her head, now tangled itself luxuriously about her ribs and tingled in her limbs. Her skin eased and opened. Her muscles melted. Even her bones softened, so that she moved with the indolence of a sun-drunk cat. He had breathed his warm life into her. And, when he touched her, his lips and fingers exquisitely unhurried, every freckle, every tiny hair was his, each one charged and spangled with the light of him. To look at him was like looking at the sun. When she forced herself to close her eyes, his face remained before her, branded scarlet on the underside of her lids.

Three days after their arrival, the commandant of the colony, a Canadian by the name of Jean-Baptiste Le Moyne de Bienville, had given a party. By then most of the chickens had regained something of their strength and spirits. There had been food and a great deal of rather sour wine. Elisabeth had stood a little apart, observing the swallowed disappointment on both sides. Insofar as they were accustomed to gentlemen, the girls knew only the citizens of Paris or of Rouen, soft-palmed men with powdered hair and scented handkerchiefs. The men of Louisiana, whether French or Acadian, were rough and awkward, their manners poor and their clothes worn and patched. They in their turn sought useful wives, the broad-hipped, spade-handed type of wives who might build houses and bear children in the same afternoon and still have supper on the table when they got home. Most of the girls gathered in Bienville's parlour looked frail enough to be blown away by a sneeze. Only Marie-Françoise tipped up her chin and bared her teeth as she worked her path around the men, her smooth brow concealing a frenzy of calculation.

Sometime after the others he had come. From her corner she watched him pause on the threshold. He stood there for a long time, one hand flat against the jamb, observing the gathering, his uniform coat unbuttoned and his sword low on his hip. Once again Elisabeth found herself drawn by his indifference, the amused detachment that seemed to set him apart from the rest, and she named them vanity and pride. It hardly surprised her that when at last he entered the room, he crossed directly to Jeanne Deshays who, even diminished by sickness, remained the most beautiful among them.

The evening was almost over when the commandant brought him to her. He was taller than she had guessed and slighter, his hands narrow with long tapering fingers. His face was sunburned and, when he ceased to smile, the creases around his eyes drew pale streaks in the brown skin. The two men conversed together for a moment, something light-hearted about the Spanish garrison at Pensacola, before Bienville excused himself and turned away. He had regarded her thoughtfully, suppressing a smile, and in her confusion she had muttered something foolish about the weather. When he raised an eyebrow, she stared at the floor, insinuating herself into the gaps between the planks.

'Elisabeth Savaret,' he said as though the words amused him.

She nodded, almost a shrug, and did not look up.

Gently he placed his fingers beneath her chin and brought her face up to his. To think of it still caused her skin around her jawbone to thrill.

'Elisabeth Savaret,' he said again, and the smile tugged at his lips. 'I have a question for you. Will you answer it?'

'Perhaps.' Her voice was hoarse.

'Perhaps?'

'It depends upon the question.'

'A reasonable condition.' His face was so close that she could see the flecks of gold in his grey-green eyes. 'Very well then, this is my question. What in the world is it that vexes you so?'

★ ★ ★

The next day, the day that Louise-Françoise Léfevre died, he called for her. Afterwards he said laughingly that it was her ill temper that drew him to her, that alone among the straining, sickly girls for sale, she had flint and fire. He was a Québecois, he said, born to snow and ice. He was powerless to resist fire. She kissed him then and did not tell him that the fire was all his, that, before him, the rage in her was all ash and the thin sour smoke of disenchantment. In the brightness of his own flames he forged her, dissolving her chill metal to a stream of liquid red.

He had gone on an exploratory voyage, something to do with minerals and mines. It was a hazardous journey, for the mines were situated in the territory of the Nassitoches tribe, requiring him to travel through nations who were enemies to the French, but he assured her that he would be in no danger. He knew the country well. The previous winter, when there had been no ships and barely enough food, and the commandant had feared the men of the garrison would starve, he had billeted them among the natives, who had taken them in and fed them. On board the *Pélican* La Sueur had cocked an eyebrow as he described these billets and the willingness of the savages to satisfy every one of the Frenchmen's particular needs.

'Do you see now why the colony needs you so?' he declared. 'A man without French wine must slake his thirst with Indian beer.'

The trader's chivalry was always blade-bright, calculated to cut cleanly. Aboard ship she had thought her own hide too thick for it. Now, as she huddled beneath the quilt, crushing the skirts of her dress, she was glad that La Sueur had taken ill in Havana and was not yet come.

She tried to summon the trader's face, pallid and sweaty with fever, but instead it was the bodies of the savage women that came, their glistening breasts and their supple bellies and the languid roll of their smooth coppery limbs. They gathered in the shade of the canebrake behind the garrison, their deft fingers twisting the dried leaves of the palmetto into baskets. Their bodies were perfectly smooth, like brown fish, for they stripped the hair from their skin with a paste of shell ash and hot water.

They were not like the slack-mouthed whores of Paris. Their faces proffered no invitation. Their unclothed bodies were a fact, their polished skin declaring their sex with neither pride nor shame, like animals. They knew nothing of modesty or restraint. The thought of him in the embrace of one of those women, his skin against hers, his fingers tangled in her black

56

hair, his lips upon her lips —

Elisabeth buried her face in the blanket, forcing the image away before it could bring ill luck. As she inhaled, filling herself with the smell of him, the dread gave way to shame. What kind of wife doubted her husband so, when he had given her no cause to doubt him? He had promised himself to her before God, his voice clear and unfaltering, the secret smile pressed into the side of his mouth. He was hers as entirely as she was his, her lawful wedded husband to have and to hold and to hold and to hold, till death do us part.

Except that she must not think of death, nor of fear, not yet, not while he was gone. Soon he would be home, perhaps even today. Until then, her faith in his safety was all she could give him, a fiery circle of devotion inside of which, if she held steady, she might protect him from harm.

They were nearly all of them married now. The fever had forced a number of postponements but still, throughout August, there was a steady stream of marriages at the small, unadorned chapel inside Fort Louis. Aboard ship, Marie-Françoise had urged her intimates to coyness. By holding themselves aloof, the well-made girls would demonstrate to the cream of the colony's bachelors that they were worthy of their consideration. It was only the least desirable of the girls who had any reason to hurry.

The girls had nodded solemnly then, but none had heeded her advice. Even the beautiful Jeanne Deshays had succumbed to courtship within a matter of weeks. Her husband was judged something of a catch, a high-ranking officer with a meaty face and considerable influence. Elisabeth, herself three days wed, had attended her marriage. Jeanne, still weak from her illness, had recited her vows like a shopping list.

Once the formalities were complete, there had been celebrations at the house of Jean Alexandre, the master joiner. Most of the men of the garrison attended, and he had promised he would come. For more than two hours she watched the door, light-headed with the lack of him and the boom and crack of the evening storm. When at last he entered the cabin, wet with rain and already engaged in conversation with several of his fellow officers, her heart flew from her chest.

'Do you mean the short one with the squint? I hear her pots last the longest,' Anne Negrette asked her then, but she did not answer. Her breath came quickly and her spit tasted strange in her mouth. He did not cross the room towards her. With the others he paid his respects to the newly-weds, clapping the groom on the shoulder and saying something that made him laugh. The savagery of her jealousy then caused her ears to sing. For a shameful moment she hated them all, the bride and groom, the men with their faces foolish with drink, the shirt that lay against his chest, the finger and thumb that cupped his jaw, the sheen of rain upon his forehead. She looked away, then, and her apprehension caught like a bone in her throat. He was so substantial in his separateness, so complete. He looked exactly as he had before they were married.

It was late when at last she persuaded him to leave. The storm had passed and the white moon was bandaged in gauzy cloud. She had held his hand with both of hers and he had kissed her, covering her mouth with his and pressing her up against the splintery boards of the cabin. The freshly washed darkness was soft and fleshy, alive with the shriek of cicadas and the throaty calls of frogs. She had not resisted him. The recollection of it caused her skin to flush. They might so easily have been discovered. There might have been snakes or alligators or poisonous scorpions in the long grass. Her feet had been bare, her shoes kicked off in the darkness. When they were spent, they had leaned against the cabin, their heads together and their fingers entwined, and listened to the men's laughter and the sawed-out fiddle strains of the gavotte until the fever came upon them again and they ran home together, the taste of each other sharp upon their tongues. Early the next morning, when dawn came, she had returned for her shoes. When she found them, they were soaking wet and frosted all over with the glistening trails of slugs.

Occasionally she wondered if any of the chickens felt as she did. Perhaps little Renée Gilbert, whose husband was a cannoneer almost twice her height. There was something in the set of her mouth when she gazed up at him that Elisabeth recognised. She thought sometimes that she would like to say something to her, but she never did. It was better to hug it close, where she could keep it safe.

Besides, she never saw Renée alone. Though they lived with their husbands and were burdened with the duties and responsibilities of marriage, the chickens were as much in each other's company as they ever had been. And still they strained to assimilate Elisabeth into their sorority. It baffled her and stirred her also, their refusal to be rebuffed. She thought now that perhaps it was her anger that drew them to her, the hope that its sharp edges might be pressed into the service of their dissatisfactions, of which there were many. Perrine had made it clear that they thought Elisabeth's indifference to their poor circumstances a betrayal of their guild. By consenting to survive on bread made from savage corn or, worse still, sagamity, a kind of savage porridge made from the same coarse grain, Elisabeth made it easier for the commandant to order the rest of them to follow suit.

'But what is it you object to so?' Elisabeth protested. 'The savage bread is not what we are accustomed to, but then what here is?'

Her answer had provoked Perrine, but Elisabeth knew that it was not really about the bread. It was the pleasure she took in her husband that truly offended them and her refusal to conceal it. They considered the extravagance of her delight not only ill-suited to the harshness of their situation but an affront to the rest of them. They frowned when they saw her with him, and whispered among themselves. It was some time before Elisabeth understood that they were frightened of her. She unbalanced things. The narrow slice of swamp that lay between

60

them and the precipice of the world was already treacherous enough.

Of course they grew accustomed to it in time. There was little else they could do. As for marriage, there were only two girls that remained to be accounted for. Just yesterday Elisabeth had seen Marie-Françoise by the garrison, pale as paper after her illness, the lines around her mouth scratched on in black ink. The dark hair of which she had been vain had clung to her scalp, coarse and provisional, and she had walked tentatively, as though afraid of the ground.

Still, she lived. The man to whom she had, to her great satisfaction, contrived to become engaged had not proved so fortunate. Late in September, with their marriage less than seven days away, he had succumbed to delirium. His decline was rapid. Two days later Marie-Françoise had stood pale and bewildered as his household effects were sold at auction, the proceeds shared between his mother in Quebec and his brother at Versailles. The other girls had made sure to visit her, taking with them trifles to lift her spirits, but Elisabeth had declined to accompany them. She knew they thought her heartless and she was sorry for it, but still she would not go. Her bliss was new and fragile and she was afraid. Misfortune was contagious. These days when she saw Marie-Françoise in the settlement, she had to fight the impulse to cover her eyes. Misery swarmed about the Governess's shoulders like a cloud of flies.

Elisabeth sighed and, stretching, pushed

61

herself up to sit. The morning was almost gone. His good boots stood by the door, their heels worn down at the backs, and his laced hat hung on a peg, its brim ghost-marked with dried sweat. *We are all waiting*, she thought, *for you to come back and occupy us*. Perhaps even at this very moment he was climbing out of the tilting pirogue, his boots sliding on the rush-slippy mud of the dock. The pirogues would be laden with food for the colony, and he would have to stay a while with the other officers to oversee the unloading of the provisions into the warehouse. Left alone, the men were careless and inclined to steal. She could see the two notches between his eyebrows that deepened when he was conducting business. It was the only time he was solemn. She wanted to reach out and smooth the furrows away with her finger, to place her lips lightly upon that place so that she might feel his breath hot against her chin, and then, slowly, very slowly, to draw her lips down the bridge of his nose and across the unshaved bristle of his upper lip to his mouth. He would pull her to him then and she would feel him firm and solid in her arms, and the parts of her that without him were rough and broken off and shameful would once again become smooth and whole and true.

Hurry home, she whispered, and beyond the blind window the birds screamed, their throats raw with longing.

Many weeks were to pass before the boy was able to approach the bayou without straining for a glimpse of the expedition. Then winter came. There would be few travellers in winter, the savages told him. In winter the big river froze in the north and the white men waited by their firesides. He was not hungry. The harvests had been good and much food stored for the lean months. Besides, the savage hunters were skilful. There was always meat.

The boy grew taller. The bones of his face sharpened and his red hands hung from the poles of his arms like flags. To put on his boots became an agony. Though he endured the torture of them for as long as he was able, he was at last obliged to abandon them for shoes of the savage style that they called moccasins, fashioned from deerskin and ornamented with a pattern of tiny coloured beads. The moccasins were warm and well-fitting, but he hacked off the beads with the tip of his knife. As for his coat, he refused to give it up, though the pinch of it pulled at his shoulders and chafed the skin beneath his arms. The cuffs kinked, pale stripes marking the old seams. Even then they hardly grazed his wrists.

He lodged with a warrior and his wife, a quiet round-faced creature who treated him with the same glancing affection that she accorded her own half-grown litter of infants. A quick study, it was not long before he had picked up the rudiments of their tongue but, favouring the isolation accorded to the uncomprehending, he spoke little. In La Rochelle as a boy, he had lain for hours upon his stomach when it rained, watching the insects with whom he shared his quarters. He had observed that the spider held her silk upon a reel inside her own body and that she lived not upon her web but in a silken tunnel that she spun alongside it and in which she ate her prey; that in the winter, when the ice came, the flies by his pallet grew feeble and could barely crawl, but those close to the fire remained vigorous, rubbing their hands together like conspirators. The cold ones were easy to catch. The boy had peered at them through the cracks in his fingers, noting the great red eyes, the transparent wings, the four black stripes on their backs, and then he had crushed them, pressing the tips of his fingers hard into his palm.

Now the boy watched the savages, and he saw that many things that the men had told him were true. He saw that the Ouma men wore bracelets and necklaces of bone and feathers in their hair as if they were women and that some even carried fans. He saw that they ate untidily and seldom used spoons, that they worshipped fire and water and trees, that they feared owls above all creatures, for their cries foretold the death of a child. He saw how they made magic with the straw-filled corpse of a dead otter and listened to their dreams, for they believed that their guardian spirits came to them in visions to advise and warn them of danger. He saw that not one among them, not even the chief, thought it possible that a man might capture words in his hands and fix them to a page. Not for the first time the boy wished he knew how writing was done.

He saw all these things, and his scorn tasted pleasantly sharp upon his tongue. But the boy's eyes were sharp and he saw other things too, things that no one had troubled to tell him. He saw that the greatest possible care was bestowed upon the children of the savages by their mothers. He saw how those with surplus wealth were expected to distribute it generously. He saw that far from being raised as warlike, boys were taught never to fight among themselves and those that breached this commandment were banished as punishment to a hut some distance from the village, as persons unworthy to live among their kinsfolk. Most startling of all, he saw that it was a boy's mother, not his father, who owned the hut in which they lived and all the utensils and chattels contained within it. It was his mother to whom he looked for instruction and guidance, the mother's brothers who disciplined him when he transgressed.

For a long time the boy puzzled over this. He studied Issiokhena, with whom he lodged, and Baiyilah, her husband, and the kinsfolk who came in and out of their hut as though it were their own. His ears squinted with the effort of listening, of understanding. And so he learned that when a savage boy spoke of his brothers and sisters, he spoke of his cousins. His mother's brothers he called not uncle but father. It was to be several months before he grasped that the savages had arranged matters the wrong way round so that a savage child reckoned his descent through not his father's but his mother's line. The father was regarded fondly enough but was granted little respect and no authority. At night the boy lay in his bed of skins, turning this over and over in his mind. It was an uncommon mistake. In France, and in all civilised nations, a boy's father was, for better or worse, the key to him.

The boy's father's name had been Auguste Guichard. It was the boy's name also but no one in the village used it. Though he repeated it many times, the French sounds were slippery in the savages' mouths and they could not keep hold of them. Instead, in the first months, his fellows called him *Nani*, which in their language meant fish. They said it was for the paleness of his skin, but the boy knew that they made fun of him. From the first he had shown himself a poor swimmer.

When they called him *Nani*, Auguste's mouth tightened and he refused to answer. The name endured a little while before it withered and died. No new one grew in its place. When it was necessary to refer to the boy by some kind of name, they called him only *Ullailah*, or boy by himself.

The savage boys stopped gesturing at the boy to join in their games before he had readied himself to accept. He watched from the shadow of the palisades as they tossed wooden dice or threw spears at rolling stones to see who could come closest to the place where the stone would finally stop. He thought of Jean. It was not difficult to imagine Jean squatting among them, his sharp knees poking holes in his breeches as he coached them in the rudiments of *mia* and hazard. Ever since Auguste could remember, his cousin had always been in the middle of everything. There was something about Jean that drew boys to him like lice. When he ran, he never troubled to glance over his shoulder. He knew they would follow.

Auguste had watched him and watched him but, though he had tried to copy his cousin, he had never caught the trick of it. He could only observe that in La Rochelle there was a shape to the air that fitted around Jean exactly. It was not the same for Auguste. The air inside him did not match the air outside. When he breathed out the other boys could smell it.

Once he had found a wasps' nest beneath the eaves of his mother's cottage. He had watched it for almost an entire afternoon and he had seen that though most of the wasps came and went unmolested, one wasp seeking entrance to the nest was set upon by the others and stung to death. When they were gone, Auguste picked the dead wasp up by its wings and studied it closely. He could see nothing about it that was different from all the other wasps.

In La Rochelle the grey seas of France had hurled themselves against the land like capricious giant-children, one moment cradling a ship in the palm of one hand, the next snapping it carelessly in two. They demanded unceasing attention and applause, and their tempers set the tempers of those who lived alongside them just as the sun set the hour of the day.

The river of the savages, which they called *misi sipi*, or big stream, was a different kind of monster altogether. It eased through the throttle of swamp and forest like a great yellow snake, languid and muscular, exhaling the thick reeks of fertility and decay. In La Rochelle the frontier between water and land was sharply drawn, marked out by the perpendiculars of cliff and castle wall. The savages' river knew no such boundaries. It sprawled tideless in the sleeping waters of creeks and bayous and seeped into the swamps and forests, where its dark quiescence gave the illusion of solid earth. Everywhere a frenzy of vegetation erupted from its skin, propelled by a fierce and vulgar prodigiousness. Even in winter the curves and planes of the landscape disappeared beneath a dissipation of trees, bushes, vines, canes, mosses, ferns and flabby fungi. Roots and branches twisted over one another, coiling and clasping in a thousand sinuous embraces. Cypress knees pushed through mats of decaying leaves like thrusting cocks, while hanks of matted Spanish wig hung from the clefts of every tree limb, clothed only in the filmy veils of spiders' webs. On warm days the wet air throbbed with the shameless fecundity of it.

Auguste watched it all, as he had been instructed. He noted the visits of the neighbouring tribes, keeping count of them by a system of different coloured pebbles. He heard no whisper of enmity towards the French and no rumours of war. No Englishmen visited the village. In the early summer there was a brief skirmish with the Tunicas, who were the Oumas' neighbour, when a warrior of that tribe seized two women of the Ouma as slaves, which brought a swift and violent reprisal from the Ouma warriors. Otherwise all was quiet.

Auguste watched and he waited. Sometimes he even forgot to wait. Along with the other boys, he assisted in the fields, clearing and preparing them for the spring planting. Along with the other boys, he received instruction in the arts of running and of hunting, in the dressing of skins and the fashioning of weapons. The savage children were given their first bows and arrows and their first toy spears as soon as they could walk, and many were already skilled in their use. To test them one of the old men of the savages secured a clump of dried grass, twice the size of a fist, to a pole the height of a small tree. The first boy to bring down the hay would receive a prize. Auguste watched as the tallest of the boys, whose name was Tohto, drew and fired eight arrows into the air, setting them off so rapidly that the first one reached the ground only after the eighth was despatched. His friends whooped and cheered. The elder did not smile.

'Hunting is not simply a matter of dexterity, my son,' he said gravely. 'To be a great hunter you must learn the virtues of endurance, of patience, of humility. And accuracy too,' he added, his eyes bright in his lined face. 'Look.

You have lost eight arrows but the grass has lost not one hair from its head.'

The guns brought to the village by the commandant remained in the chief's hut, wrapped tightly in their skins. Auguste was clumsy with a bow and arrow, but his foot was noiseless and his eye was quick. Afraid of the forest, he swiftly learned the shape of it. In the forest silence was not an absence, a hole requiring the darn of chatter. It was hardly silence at all, alive as it was with the creak of frogs, the chatter of the birds, the shiftless slop and suck of the water, but beneath the clamour there was a breathlessness, a sense of suspense, of secrets hidden in the treacherous ground.

Auguste grew skilful in the imitation of the calls of the forest birds so that they might be lured into the snares that the savages hung in the trees. He collected the insects of the forest and studied them, examining the tilt of their wings, the hinged fragility of their legs. Sometimes, if the creature was unfamiliar, he sketched the shape of it into the dust with a sharpened stick so that he might fix its particulars in his head. He observed the pitcher plants like cones of rolled paper, the achechy with its roots rich with red juice like chicken's blood. It was the job of the women to gather the plants for dyes and medicines, and it caused them great merriment to observe Auguste upon his knees, digging with his fingers in the wet black soil.

One day one of the women approached him and quietly suggested that he cultivate a garden alongside the village vegetable plots. Her words

70

caused the sharp wings of his shoulder blades to jut fiercely from his back. After that he ventured further into the forest where the women could not see him.

As for fishing, the savage boys whittled rods and painted plugs and spinners in much the same way that the boys had done in France, but Auguste preferred the method of the elders, sliding one hand into the stream and waiting for a fish to nudge it. He learned to set all of his attentiveness into his fingers while his eyes followed the dragonflies above the water, cutting the air into slices like slivers of coloured glass.

He had grown accustomed to his solitude by the time the dog took him as its companion. It was a yellow pup with a foxy face and a slouching gait, and when it sniffed about him its brow wrinkled suspiciously. Its ribs protruded from beneath its rough coat. Wild dogs were common in the village, some of them so accustomed to human proximity that they were almost tame, and Auguste paid the creature little heed, expecting it to tire of him and wander away. It did not. It made three neat turns and settled beside him, its nose tucked beneath its hind leg. When at last Auguste rose from the riverbank, the dog rose too, its tail pressed down between its haunches. When Auguste turned to look at it, it looked away, as though pretending its presence was an accident, but when he took a few steps towards the village, the dog followed several paces behind.

It reminded Auguste of a game his sisters had liked to play. Several times he swung round without warning, and each time he turned the dog was quite still, its white-whiskered muzzle lifted in a posture of alert disinterest. When they reached the village Auguste begged Issiokhena for a little deer meat and held it out to the dog. The dog frowned and did not come closer. Auguste was obliged to throw the meat into the dust at the dog's feet. The dog snatched it up and fled into the shadows. Auguste waited as the shadows lengthened and thickened, but it did not come back.

That night Auguste dreamed of Jean and of his sisters. He woke with a heaviness in his chest, listening to the light breathing of the savage children on their skins beside him, and when dawn broke he rose and went out.

He was almost at the palisades when he sensed that someone was following him. He turned. The dog looked away. Auguste hesitated. Then he thrust his hands in his pockets and walked towards the forest, his tuneless whistle snagging in the rising chorus of songs and shrieks that heralded the day.

She dreamed about it when he was gone, the images in bright fragments like shards of broken glass catching the light. His gold-flecked eyes in a plump infant face. His long fingers in dimpled fists. A lean, sunburned face and a creamy new one, cheek to cheek, like a slippage in time. His secret smile tucked into the corner of a puckered baby mouth. Plump arms twisted round their necks, making of them a three-headed whole. Alone, night after night, she picked over the pieces, cutting her fingers on their sharp edges, and the wonder of it was as sharp in her as remembered desire. But when at last he came back to her and they lay tangled together beneath the sea-green quilt, his fingers tracing the undulations of breast and belly, she said nothing. She wrapped her arms around him and her legs too, sealing his skin against hers and forcing out the spaces between them. Sometimes, when he slept, she gazed at him, seeking in his man's face the child that he had once been, and it grieved her, the years that she had lost.

As the months passed and the other women grew peevish and then fretful, sharing confidences and herbal infusions that might be relied upon to stimulate the womb, she received the first ghostly spasms of her monthlies with a slackening in her belly that she knew for

73

gratitude. To the bewilderment of the other women, she had refused the acquisition of a native slave, declaring it an unnecessary expenditure while there were no children. Now she prayed nightly that she might be spared the trial of conception. For all that they had been married a full year, the prospect of sharing her husband with another remained unendurable.

She knew better than to speak of this with him. He declared her tough, fearless, stubborn to the point of pigheadedness, and he relished the perversity of her. Her refusal of a slave delighted him as much as he claimed it infuriating, not least because the King had not paid the army in two years. He called her his tigress, his little alligator, and laughed gleefully when she complained of the foolishness of the other men's wives.

'It's little wonder they distrust you,' he crowed, his hands circling her waist. 'Those doxies cling to one another like drowning rats on a raft. It is a reproach to them all when you manage quite well all by yourself.'

And so she did, almost. She was thankful to be free of the trifling gossip of the women, their sour faces and constant complaints. They took comfort in each other's miseries, bemoaning always the dearth of things, their dissatisfaction sucking the vigour from the air around them until Elisabeth could hardly breathe. They traded boils and blisters, raw hands and aching backs, poor slaves and poorer husbands. When occasionally one among them contrived a kind of jest, their laughter was disagreeable, grudging, wrung from them like water from laundry.

In her own cabin Elisabeth could close her eyes and smile and know herself quite happy. All the same it was lonely turning always from the chickens' companionship, and it grew lonelier still when in time they ceased to offer it. Jean-Claude was absent from the settlement a great deal. Despite the small gardens that the wives had begun resentfully to cultivate, the settlement continued to produce almost nothing for itself, and it was his job to ensure that there would be sufficient food to see the colonists through the winter months. To this end he travelled not only to the neighbouring tribes but sometimes even to the Spanish fort at Pensacola.

At first Elisabeth did nothing during his long absences. She walked dreamily around the town, along the river, or she simply lay in bed, her limbs sprawled, luxuriant with recollection. Once she took from her trunk a book of poetry and tried to read it, but her eyes raced ahead of the words, her belly warm with poetry of its own, and she closed the covers and knew that Jean-Claude was right, that books were the solace of those who did not live.

But the days were long and idleness loosely woven. She grew restless, the longing for him fidgeting in her fingers. One afternoon as she slept, the fear crept upon her and in the helpless space between waking and sleeping she saw him sicken, his pale face glazed with sweat; she saw him set upon by savages, his red blood pooling in the dark shadows of the canebrake, leaking into the thick yellow water of the river.

75

She rose then and, though it was the hottest part of the day, she built a fire and lit it and set the iron on it to heat while she gathered all his shirts and his neckcloths that were piled together in a basket. They smelled of air and the leaves of the bush where they had been spread to dry and, very faintly, of him. Quickly she set the pressing board on the table and, wrapping a cloth around it, laid the first shirt out on its surface. Then, seizing the hot iron, she leaned down upon it with all her strength, forcing the nose of it into the rough seams. Her hair clung to her brow and dark circles spread beneath her arms as she moved between the pressing board and the fire, hardly able to wait for the iron to grow hot again. That evening, when dusk came and with it a little coolness, she placed her hand upon the pile of his clothes, and for the first time in days she felt him close to her. She knew then that he would come home.

After that it became her habit to prepare daily for his return. She swept the hut fastidiously and scoured the table with sand. She turned the dried-moss mattress and spread the sea-green quilt. She gathered branches of the flowering plants that flourished on the perimeters of the settlement and arranged them in a savage jar decorated all over with loops and whorls. She begged, bought and bartered for cuttings and seeds and cultivated their garden, her knees dark with dirt as she plucked out the weeds and tucked the dampened soil carefully around the growing plants. She went early to the market, when it was hardly light, and in a clumsy pantomime of gestures she had the savage women show her how their beans might be crocked, their tough meat stewed until it was tender enough to be cut with a spoon. She traded a lace collar for baskets of peaches and plums and wild apples and the whortleberries that he loved, and she busied herself with canning and preserving, sealing the jars with wax from the candleberry tree.

She made lamps with the wax too, boiling the berries with hot water in the kettle until the pale green wax rose to the surface and filled the cabin with its sweet smell. It was a kind of drudgery, but more than that it was a hex. Each bottle that she filled for him, each lamp that she set upon the shelf, was a link in the chain that joined her to him, and with each link the chain grew stronger, pulling him home.

That expedition took Jean-Claude away for many weeks together. When at last he returned, thundering upon the door with both fists and calling out to her to show herself to him, she almost wept with relief and the shock of him. She had forgotten his face a little.

Later she curled herself against him, her hands spread wide upon his chest, and closed her eyes, inhaling deeply to draw the smell of him into the depleted parts of her as he talked of the places he had visited, the strange savage customs he had witnessed. He told her of the Pasagoulas's love of brandy and of the Tunicas, whose chief wore always a silver medal on a blue ribbon and carried a gold-topped cane that had been sent to him by the King of France. The Tunicas, he said, raised fowls aplenty but would not eat them, so that when he had proposed their purchase, he had been obliged to pretend to their chief that he wanted them as pets.

'Perhaps, I should keep my word,' he suggested, his lips so close to hers that she could hardly keep from licking them. 'Bring them to live here. After all, I know how you love to be surrounded by chickens.'

Elisabeth laughed, twining her arms about him.

'Oh, I have missed you so,' she murmured.

'You sweet-tongued deceiver.' He kissed her on the forehead, his beard tickling her nose. 'I would wager you do not think of me once from the moment I leave until I am back here in your bed.'

'True,' Elisabeth conceded. 'Thank heaven the wood store is not full. Where else could I have hidden old Grapalière and his discarded breeches when you came back so unexpectedly?'

Jean-Claude laughed, and he pressed his face against her neck, shifting his weight so that she could feel him hardening against her. It amused and aroused him to be teased in such a way. Elisabeth was glad he did not tease her back. Somehow the fear was always with her, clinging to the soles of her feet like a shadow. She could not shake it. Sometimes she longed for him to be afraid too.

Raising his head, he parted her lips with his tongue and kissed her. She closed her eyes, melting against the warmth of him. When the kiss was over, he raised himself on his elbow to look at her, one hand upon her belly. She smiled up at him dazedly, memorising all over again the flecks of gold in his grey-green eyes. He touched his mouth lightly to her forehead. Then, abruptly, he sat and swung his legs round to the side of the bed. The air was chill against her bare skin as he reached for his breeches, the first smoky breath of winter visible as he sighed and stood.

'I have to go,' he said.

'Now? But you are only just come home.'

He shrugged, his back to her as he pulled his shirt over his head.

'I have business at the tavern.'

'Tonight?' She tried to laugh. 'They shall surely not expect you tonight?'

'On the contrary, I was supposed to have gone there directly. Now where are my boots?' Still fumbling with the buttons of his breeches, he leaned over to kiss her briefly on the mouth. 'Do not wait supper for me. I shall eat there.'

'But I have meat for you. And whortleberries.'

'They'll keep.'

'Don't go,' she pleaded, no longer troubling to conceal her dismay, and she reached up to caress his neck. She felt the twitch of his muscles beneath her fingers as he leaned past her to retrieve his discarded neckcloth. 'Please. Not tonight.'

'Come now,' he said, with a wry smile, pulling away from her embrace as he straightened up to arrange the cloth around his neck. 'For weeks you have been spared the affliction of a stinking husband clogging up the place. You expect me to believe you are not a little bit glum that I am come home?'

Her eyes flew open.

'How can you be so cruel? I have done nothing but long for your return. Without you I am — I am nothing.'

His fingers stilled. He looked at her and his smile contracted to a twist that caused her skin to shrivel.

'I am going to the tavern, Elisabeth,' he said coldly. 'Not New France.'

'I — forgive me.' She attempted a smile. 'I have spent too much time with the other wives. I have learned to be a scold.'

Jean-Claude shook his head at her, rolling his eyes. Her heart unclenched.

'Then unlearn it forthwith or, God help me, I shall go back up the St Louis this very night and take refuge with the savages.' He laughed softly through his nose, touching his lips to her forehead. 'Believe me, a man can suffer no greater misery than a shrewish wife.'

The first days of November blew in on a flurry of wind and spitting rain. Elisabeth was entirely happy. In the winter the upper reaches of the river froze and the men no longer made their long expeditions north. The winter months were devoted instead to repairs around the settlement, to planning and preparing, to waiting for spring. The cabin was full of him, the scatter of his discarded coat and boots, the greasy smears of breakfast on an abandoned wooden plate, the dent of his head in the moss pillow on their disordered bed. It astounded her, the delight she took in caring for him.

It was not just Elisabeth who was grateful for winter. The brisker air lifted spirits dulled by months of stifling heat and humidity and brought an end at last to the cursed mosquitoes. The warehouses were adequately stocked and the forest a fine source of firewood. It was generally agreed among the settlers that a little French weather was by no means unwelcome.

Their sanguinity was short-lived. That winter, the winter that heralded the year of 1709, was the bleakest anyone could remember. Elisabeth's crowded shelves grew empty. The supplies in the warehouses dwindled. By February they had run out. The commandant despatched an emergency expedition to nearby savage villages but the savages had little to spare and the men returned

81

with less than a quarter of the anticipated rations.

There was hardly any meat. Rabbits were scarce, deer scarcer. The men shot scrawny squirrels and scoured the shreds of flesh from the bones with their teeth, while the women foraged in the swamps and forests around the town for acorns and edible roots. The garrison was sealed and the unmarried soldiers once more billeted upon the natives. Only the taverner Burelle scraped up an income of sorts. The maize beer brewed by the savages was neither as strong nor as flavoursome as French wine, but it served at least to blunt the rodent gnaw of hunger. In Burelle's modest dwelling, the oak chest by the fireplace was crammed with darned stockings and lengths of faded silk ribbon.

In so small a settlement it was hard to keep secrets. Hunger soured the breath and sharpened eyes and tongues. Marie-Françoise de Bois-renaud accused Renée Gilbert of entering her storehouse on the pretence of returning a dish and stealing a handful of chestnuts. Perrine Roussel came close to blows with the wife of the ferret-faced carpenter over the just apportionment of a small crop of the tasteless mushrooms that grew among the roots of the walnut tree at the edge of the forest. Jean-Claude had Elisabeth salt the meat he brought to her when it was dark and store it in a barrel he had concealed behind the woodpiles in the outhouse.

'How on earth did you manage it?' she asked him the first time, her eyes round as he unwrapped the bloody haunch of venison from his pack. 'I thought there were no deer.'

'There are always deer for the hunter who knows in which direction to point his musket.'

'But so much of it! What about the others?'

'If the others lack meat, then they must devise their own ways of getting it. The wise man makes sure to hunt alone. Tonight it is just you and me and a feast fit for a king. What else could possibly matter?'

She touched her fingers to the meat, thinking of the wives and their hungry eyes, their snatching fingers. Let *their* husbands bring them meat, she told herself, if they care enough to do so, and she took his face in her hands and kissed him. He tasted of tobacco and the medicinal sting of *eau-de-vie*.

'Meat,' she murmured. 'You work miracles.'

She was frugal with the meat and it lasted a good while. The sacks of Indian corn they pushed beneath the bed, wrapping them in deer-skins to protect them from the mice. She did not ask where they had come from but measured out the grains carefully, half-cup by half-cup, and afterwards going on her hands and knees to pick up any that might have spilled. Once she heard footsteps in the lane outside and she froze, her fists closing over the gold kernels like contraband.

They ate in darkness, stealthily, an old blanket over the *platille* window and the lamps blown out, spooning up thick gravy in the dying light of the fire. The river was frozen above the red-painted post that marked the border between the Ouma and their northern neighbours, the

Bayagoulas. There could be no venturing north. There were rumours that the Chickasaw, stirred up by the English and in league with several of the smaller savage nations, planned an attack on the depleted garrison. The attack did not come. Shrivelled with cold and famine, the town closed in upon itself, hunched against the blasts of the north wind as the desolate seabirds shrieked in the ice-grey sky.

The sacks of corn grew lean. In the bitter early mornings, when fingers fumbled buttons and the damp chill cut through bone, Elisabeth watched the pinched grey faces of her neighbours as they toiled with wood and with water. Two or three of them were big with child. She covered her head with her patched scarf and did not meet their eyes, muttering the required pleasantries with lips that were clumsy with shame and a choked-up sort of anger at the weight of their wretchedness.

Sometimes she went with them to the forest in search of food. They spoke little, their eyes blunt with hunger and fatigue. When she discovered a fistful of sour late mulberries or a straggly half-dead patch of wild onions, she took only a few and thrust the rest at the others, refusing their gratitude. Afterwards, alone in the cottage, she pulled the sack from its hiding place beneath the bed and ran what was left of the corn through her fingers, inhaling its old-barn smell before putting it back, pulling the deerskin tight over it as though she was tucking an infant into bed.

One night in March, Jean-Claude brought

wine. They drank it in bed directly from the bottle, wiping their mouths on the backs of their hands. The wine was Spanish, thick with sunshine and the turned-earth sweetness of blackberries. The embers of the fire caught in the bottle and spilled jewels of dark red light on the sea-green silk of the feather quilt as he protested bitterly against the stifling confines of the settlement, the dull and narrow preoccupations of his fellows. He declared himself bored beyond the limits of reason by the political manoeuvrings of the garrison officers, their petty jostlings, their fixation with favour and with hierarchy.

'They rot here with their seals and their promises, scouring the horizon for boats that might bring them a word of praise from the minister-in-waiting for this or the third undersecretary to the commissary of that. They are truly a pitiable lot, these Frenchmen of yours. The colony of Louisiana covers almost two thousand miles of bountiful St Louis River and they cluster here like timid children clutching at their mother's skirts, waiting to lick the leftover smears from her baking bowl? No wonder their wives starve and their mewling infants too.'

'The river is frozen solid,' Elisabeth protested gently. 'Even the hardiest of you hairy Québecois cannot travel when the river is impassable.'

'Do you know what they do, these countrymen of yours?' Jean-Claude frowned and took another gulp of wine. 'They write angry letters to the Minister of the Marine accusing Sieur de Bienville of selling fifty barrels of the colony's best gunpowder to the Spanish in exchange for gold. Perhaps he did so. Perhaps he did not. But the colony endures, though the same minister in his elegant house in Paris would not risk a fingernail to save it. The whole army of Louisiana numbers hardly more than one hundred, of which one quarter are not fit to fight, but somehow the commandant sees that we hold our position here against all the odds. In the Mediterranean we are at war with the Spanish, but the commandant maintains his own private peace with Pensacola. He has made us safe. Why should it concern me that the esteemed Bienville may or may not grow rich on the proceeds of gunpowder he has contrived, through a miracle, not to require?'

Elisabeth smiled. 'You cannot expect the commissary to think as you do. I am as much an admirer of the commandant as you are but, whatever his abilities, the gunpowder is not his to sell.'

'There, you see, you are as French as the rest of them. You all believe that you can bring the rules of Paris here. But this is not Paris. Look at your Frenchmen stamping their feet and dashing off their furious letters on the King's paper. How will those letters reach France when there are no ships to take them?'

'They are idiots, it is true.'

'They would be better to sell the paper and the ink and be done with it. At least there would be profit in it.'

'Your cynical posturing does not convince me. You are not half so much a Diogenes as you pretend.'

Elisabeth uncurled herself lazily, stretching her arms high above her head. Reaching out, Jean-Claude caught her wrists in one hand and pulled her towards him, his other hand seeking the hidden warmth beneath her skirts. Elisabeth sighed and leaned in to him.

'You Parisians are all the same,' he murmured. 'I might defend myself against your accusations if I had the first idea what it was you were talking about.'

Elisabeth laughed and took his head between her hands, tipping his face up towards hers. He smiled at her and the miracle of him squeezed her heart like a fist.

'My love,' she whispered. 'You shall never have to defend yourself to me. Not if you live to be a hundred.'

It was several months before spring came and men of his kind returned to the village. From their place in the canebrake, Auguste and the dog watched them as they mounted the bluff, two of them, tall and short, accompanied by a native servant. He did not know them. They were not soldiers. The tall one was a gaunt man in the white collar of a religious. His right arm was in a rough sling and he walked jerkily, shrugging off the solicitudes of his stocky sandy-haired companion. Behind them walked the servant, all slung about with bags and pouches and carrying a small wooden box upon his head.

Before the men reached the village palisades, they were greeted by several of the elders bearing the *calumet*. Auguste watched as the sandy-haired man spoke to them urgently, chopping at the air with his hands. Then he slipped away, the dog silent at his heels. At the edge of the forest, where the savages cut the trees for daily use, he unbelted the hatchet at his waist, testing the sharpness of the blade against his thumb. He paid no heed to the *rat-a-tat-tat* of the red-capped woodpecker nor to the paint-bright hummingbird that darted between the white bells of the convolvulus. He chopped wood until the buttery sun melted in the sky and the nerve-strings in his neck and shoulders sang in protest.

It was dark when he returned to the village. As he gathered with the others to eat, he learned that the visitor was a pastor with a mission upriver, many days' travel away. He had come to the village once before and talked to the villagers of the white man's Great Nanboulou, who had no body and in whose fire the wicked must burn for many, many moons. He had claimed himself the Nanboulou's chosen instrument on earth. Now it seemed that he was powerless to call down that god's powers to expel the evil spirits that plagued him. Weak with sickness, he travelled to Mobile in search of the pale-faced medicine man whose powers might prove stronger than his own.

As was customary, the chief of the village made accommodation for the priest and his companion in his own hut. When the pastor learned that there was a French boy living among the savages at the village, he asked that the boy be sent to him there so that he might report upon his progress to the commandant at Mobile.

At the threshold of the chief's dwelling, Auguste hesitated. Only the elders of the village were permitted to enter without the chief's express summons. Cautiously he peeped in. In the centre of the hut a cane torch burned, as thick around as a child, exhaling its black breath towards the roof. The silver-haired priest sat stiffly upon a pallet, propped against his wooden box, a book upon his lap. Across from him, his companion sprawled upon his stomach, picking at his teeth with a sharpened stick. A callused heel poked through the hole in his stocking.

The pastor looked up from his book.

'Ah,' he said, nodding. 'Come. Come in.'

After months of hearing only the savage language, the French words came as a surprise. Auguste did as he was bid. He saw that the missioner's left ear was torn, his cheek scored with half-healed gashes, and that the cloth that wrapped his arm was rusty with dried blood.

'Do you have a message for the garrison, boy?' The priest moved his arm and the pain showed on his face. 'Anything that the commandant should know?'

Auguste hesitated.

'At first harvest, Tunica warriors seized two squaws and took them as slaves,' he said slowly, fumbling for the words in French. 'The Ouma raided their village and broke the men's heads.'

'The usual savage caper, then. And the English? You have seen a white man?'

'No, sir. You are the first.'

'Is that so?' The priest considered Auguste thoughtfully. 'Then let us talk together a while. I am Père Jouvet. Perhaps you know of me, of my mission at the Nassitoches?'

Again Auguste shook his head. The priest pressed his lips together in a line.

'You do well here, boy? You make headway with the savages?' Auguste shrugged.

'A man of few words. But you have mastered their language, have you not?'

Though the priest's tone remained courteous, Auguste noted the pale flare of his nostrils, the tightening of his fingers in his lap. It would serve

90

no purpose to anger him.

'I listen carefully,' Auguste said slowly. 'And I watch.'

'Good, good. A man cannot hope to civilise the savage unless he knows what he is up against, knows their language, shares their food.'

'I don't mind the food. The food is good.'

The priest frowned. His hand now lay open on his lap, palm upward, the forefinger lightly circling the pad of the thumb.

'Do you know how I came to be injured? A young warrior of my mission desired his uncle buried in our church, though the dead man had never once set foot across its threshold. When I refused him, the warrior set upon me with arrows. One struck me here upon the ear, another in the arm. I tried to pull it out, but the head was stuck fast in the sinew and the stem broke off in my hand. It is there still.'

Auguste thought of the deer he had butchered the previous week. Where the arrow had struck the beast's shoulder, its bloody flesh had been stuck with tiny shards of bone, like fishes' teeth.

'Do you pray to God?' the priest asked.

The boy hesitated, then shook his head.

'No, Father,' he answered. 'There is no church here.'

'Not yet perhaps,' the pastor replied. 'But there shall be. There shall be churches all across this God-starved land. Until then you must worship God in the church of your heart. In the wilds of the forest it is easy to stray from the path of virtue, but remember this. The white man who turns his back upon the light of the Lord is no better than the idolatrous savage. Learn from God and not from your fellow man.'

The priest broke off, his shoulders racked by a fit of coughing. He gestured at Auguste as he struggled to regain his composure.

'Some water, if you please,' he croaked. 'On the floor. A bottle.'

The stubble upon his chin gleamed white against the grey of his skin. Auguste crouched, squatting in the savage way. By the missionary's pallet, there was indeed a leather water bottle, its belly worn shiny with use. Beside it a leather pouch lay open, its dark throat glinting with treasures. The flame from the cane torch caught the dull burnish of tooled gold upon the spine of a battered-looking book and, a little deeper in, the precise glint of glass. The tips of Auguste's fingers burned. With his two thumbs he eased the cork from the neck of the bottle and held it out to the priest who drank deeply, closing his eyes.

'I have learned things from the Ouma,' Auguste said quietly as he moved his arm as he had been taught to raise the bow, in a single smooth arc. 'About animals and birds. About plants.'

The priest lowered the bottle, belched quietly and, wiping his mouth with the back of his hand, gestured to Auguste to return it to its place. Unhurriedly Auguste drew his hands from his pockets. The bottle was warm. Pushing the cork hard into the neck with his thumbs, Auguste thrust it into the open pouch and closed the flap.

'The men of the Nassitoches worship symbols

of the male phallus,' the priest said. 'But it is not the savage who grieves the Lord most deeply. The savage is rude and heathen, but there remains in him the grace of God's creation, when man was naked and knew it not. Not so the white man, who knows the Lord's commandments and breaks them daily with his drinking and his gambling and his abominable lechery. Why do you squat like that? Stand up like a man so that I can see you.'

Auguste scrambled to his feet, his fists deep in his pockets.

'Your counsel is wise, Father,' he murmured.

'And your coat is too small. You have become a man since you came here.'

Auguste shrugged. The priest let his hand drop back into his lap.

'The warrior who wounded me did so because he could not countenance his uncle's exclusion from the blessed kingdom of Heaven,' the priest said quietly. 'There is not one among the Canadian *coureurs* who would think of it. Now do you wish me to hear your confession?'

Auguste cast a wistful glance towards the door where the dog waited for him, its whiskered muzzle pale in the gloom. Then, withdrawing his hands very carefully from his pockets, he bowed his head and mumbled something about speaking ill of another and drinking brandy. When he had given the boy his penance, the priest lifted his hand, marking out a cross in the air with two raised fingers.

'Lord, bless this Your humble servant. Make a sword of his will, that it might cut the sin like a canker from his heart, and set the shield of virtue in his hand, so that he might serve all his days as a valiant foot soldier in the service of Thy great name. Amen.'

★ ★ ★

Many moons were to pass before news reached the Ouma that the priest with the arrowhead in his arm had perished at Mobile. Auguste received the news with fleeting pity and not a little relief. The Ouma made fire with a dry stick spun briskly between the palms inside a hollowed branch of wood, as though they whipped milk for chocolate. He had feared that it would not be long before talk reached the mission at Nassitoches of the French boy who could call down fire from the sun at his pleasure.

For weeks after the priest's departure, he worried that the missioner would find the burning glass missing and return for it. In preparation Auguste rehearsed a story about finding it in the mud by the bayou and keeping it safe. But, though he waited, the priest did not come back. The moon had begun to fatten again when he called the savages to witness a miracle.

It was unusual for the boy to call attention to himself. Curious, several of the Ouma drew closer, making a ragged circle around him and his yellow dog. Placing some dry agaric upon a chip of wood, Auguste drew the stolen glass from one pocket and a small jar from the other. He raised his hand for silence. With a flourish he reached into the jar and sprinkled some of the contents over the glass. Then, drawing the focus of the glass upon the tinder, he bid the fire come. There was a pause and then the agaric began to smoke. Putting his mouth to it, Auguste blew. The flame burst forth, a brilliant orange flower.

The savages could not contain their awe and astonishment. Like children they clamoured for him to make fire again. Auguste performed the same trick four times and each time the savages gaped and blinked, gazing from the glass to Auguste's face and back again. When he held out the glass for their inspection they looked at it sideways, as if it might harm them.

Later that same day, the chief of the Ouma called Auguste to him. He wished to obtain the glass. He offered generous terms, but Auguste refused him. The chief protested and then pleaded. If Auguste would only show him how the magic was performed, he might set whatever value he chose upon the instrument. The chief would see to it that the price was paid by all the families of the village.

Auguste was silent for a long time. Then gravely he told the chief that what he asked was impossible. The glass had been his uncle's, the only brother of his mother, who was long dead. For years Auguste had tried to bring fire from it but he had never succeeded. He had thought the contraption useless. Then, only a few nights ago, his uncle had come to him in a dream. In that dream, he had told Auguste of the secret of the glass. Then he had taken his nephew's hands in his and bid him swear that he would never part with it. Auguste would not dishonour his uncle.

He would keep the glass, but for as long as he remained in the village, he would use it to summon fire for the Ouma whenever they desired it. In return he wished for nothing but their continued kindness and their kinship.

The burning glass altered forever Auguste's standing among the savages. Possessed of mysterious powers and yet remote, reserved, frugal in his appetites, he was unlike any white man the savages had ever encountered. As a second winter passed and then a third, he came to be esteemed as a man of learning and of wisdom. He grew tall, though his body remained knobby and narrow, and his child's voice cracked and split like the shell of a nut. His tendency to silence strengthened his reputation. And still the commandant did not return. Instead, when the thaw came and the trade on the river began once again to move, it was a Canadian ensign who came to the village, in search of a young Frenchman with a yellow dog of whom the Ouma were more than a little afraid.

The child came in May. It was rainy season, the sky sagging above Mobile like a mouldy mattress, and behind the bluff, where the ground was low, all the houses were flooded. The damp jammed its fat fingers between the timbers of the cabins and paddled the mortar of clay and oyster shells that filled them. Nothing dried. In Elisabeth's garden the pumpkins swelled, their leaves greasy with mud. The cabin smelled of rot. Jean-Claude had been gone from Mobile for nearly two months.

She had only just begun to show. The sickness that had tormented her lingered for days afterwards, the bleeding much longer. There was a fever, some manner of poison in the blood brought on by the ceaseless rain, the unwholesome thickness of the air. She dreamed vivid, fevered dreams. In her dreams, over and over, she unwrapped the meat and opened the sacks of corn beneath the bed and stirred the stew in its pot over the fire and, pressing the food into her mouth with both hands, she ate and ate and ate, until her belly swelled, splitting the skin in two. When she woke, she saw them, the faces of the wives, pressed against the *platille*. The wives brought her crocks of peas and sagamity. When she refused them, they went away with pursed lips, muttering about the sin of false pride. Elisabeth only lay on her back and stared up at

97

the rough palmetto stripes of the roof until they repeated themselves on her closed eyes.

The midwife came frequently, impatient to justify the yearly stipend that the commandant had recently threatened to cut. A brisk woman with red knuckles and a sharp chin, Guillemette le Bras had assigned herself to the post when the colony's first *sage-femme* had succumbed to a summer epidemic, but in two years she had been required to attend only five births. Nobody could be certain why so many of the women of the colony appeared barren. As with the corrupted flour and the sour wine that came from France, some said that it was the unwholesome climate of Louisiana that had spoiled them, others that the gallant minister responsible for their despatch had known them already rotten in Rochefort and had sent them all the same.

The new priest came too, entering without ceremony and taking a stool at the foot of her bed. Rochon was a Canadian, arrived from the Jesuit seminary in Quebec, a man of rather greater girth than stature and an easy manner as yet undampened by the rains or the pinch-faced, limp-legged sternness of La Vente. He did not appear discomfited by Elisabeth's silence. He clasped his hands beneath his round belly and regarded her thoughtfully.

'So you are the scholar,' he said and Elisabeth raised her head, stone-heavy with weariness, and looked at him because there was no mockery in his voice.

'I am the unruly seminarian,' he said, and she blinked and pressed her elbows into the emptiness in her belly because there was no mockery in that either and because his flat, inflected French was just like her husband's.

'No longer, surely,' she murmured.

'The categorisations of others have a way of sticking.'

They were both silent then, caught in their own thoughts.

'I think you are not much like the other women here,' he said finally.

'They do not like me.' She swallowed. 'I cannot blame them.'

The Jesuit shrugged cheerfully.

'The soldiers at the garrison dislike me also. Perhaps they shall come around to us in time.' He smiled, looking around him at the cabin. 'No books?'

Elisabeth hesitated, then shook her head.

'One day, I suppose, we may see books at Mobile. A hospital. A church. A decent pâtisserie, God help us. It is not easy to imagine.'

His kindness was unbearable. She stared up at the palmetto roof as the Jesuit studied her, his stubby fingers steepled against his lips.

'It would make no difference, you know,' he said gently. 'Well, a pâtisserie perhaps. But not a church. The mysteries of God's purpose on earth are no plainer in carved pews. As for books, even the scholars among us see only darkly. Churches and books cannot substitute for faith. We must accept His will.'

'And if we cannot?'

'Then there is nothing for it but a glass of good wine.'

Then it was June. Elisabeth grew stronger. As the flood waters receded so too did the blackness in her. There was food in the settlement again. No one wanted to remember winter. She scrubbed the cabin clean, replacing the planks that had rotted in the floods. From a trader in the settlement, she acquired a rough lime ground from seashells to whitewash the walls and fresh nettle-bark linen for the windows. She washed the dried slime from the inside of the jar covered with whorls and filled it with flowering grasses. In the garden she knelt in the drying mud, clearing the choke from the roots of the vegetables. When the first peas came she bottled them. Their grassy scent was very sweet.

Rochon visited often and she was glad to see him. In the hot blue days of summer, loosed from the tyranny of fever, she slept easily once more. Many women in Louisiana lost children. The midwife had told her it was the unhealthy air that did it, the stench of the corrupted swamp, and Elisabeth knew it to be true. Only a savage god would kill a child for punishment.

She worked hard in the garden. When she parted the leaves of the Apalachean bean plant and saw the ripening beans hanging in shadowed clusters, or bent down to inspect the spreading stalk of the melon, the leaves as broad as her hand and, among them, the tight pale green fruits, something quickened within her, and she longed for Jean-Claude to come home so that she could show him what she had done. She did not show the Jesuit. But when he came she rose from her knees, wiping her hands on her apron, and sat with him as he ate the food she brought him. There was no one else in Mobile she did that for.

Rochon was unlike any priest she had ever known. He did not speak in sermons. When seeking to propound the wisdom of others, he was more likely to quote the words of poets than the letters of St Paul. His religion was generous, forbearing towards the faults of others, while scrupulously confessing of its own, and his laughter, which began as a rumble within the barrel of his belly and foamed upward to spill from his mouth, was infectious.

Mobile oppressed him. He pushed to be granted a mission among the savages, but so far Bienville had refused him, insisting that he could not be spared. Confined to the settlement, he chafed in his traces, restrained on one side by the petty impieties of the town's inhabitants, on the other by the thunderous religiosity of his superior. His only satisfaction was a small school for the children of savage slaves, where for one hour a day when their duties were complete, he taught the children to speak French, which he had convinced the commandant would increase their utility and enhance their value.

'At least you are safe here,' Elisabeth said.

'A ship in harbour is safe, but that is not what ships are for.'

'You are fortunate. To know your purpose.'

'I only know that I must leave Mobile if I am not to rot from the bottom up.'

Elisabeth was silent.

'Do you know Rabelais' book, *The Abbey of Thélème?*' Rochon asked softly. 'His order of Thelemites had only one rule: do what thou wilt. A joke, of course, but at the same time, absolutely serious. Rabelais was convinced that the free man possessed a natural instinct for virtue and aversion to vice. It was when he was subjected to the unnatural enslavement of statutes and laws that he was turned aside from that noble disposition, for it is in man's nature to desire those things that are denied him.'

'Is that why you seek a mission? Because you are denied one?'

'Not precisely my point. But yes, that is possible.'

'And when you have one, what then?'

Rochon smiled.

'Then I suppose I shall be free most virtuously to regret it.'

'And the savage children?'

'They will not be abandoned. I have found my successor.'

'La Vente? Poor children.'

'You.'

'Me? But — '

'Waiting is not enough occupation for any of us.'

★　★　★

After that, in the late afternoon three days each week, Elisabeth taught the children of the savages the rudiments of the French language.

She conducted the lessons in the cabin on the rue d'Iberville, the infants squatting in two obedient rows on either side of the room, girls to the left and boys to the right. She did not ask their names, but she learned their faces, the way one boy rubbed his ear against his shoulder when he was thinking, the resolve of the smallest of the girls to speak a little sooner and louder than the rest. She brought household items from the kitchen hut and borrowed others from her neighbours, pointing at each one and saying the word for it in French. They were eager pupils, several of them quick. They learned to say yes, no, thank you, forgive me. They learned to count. At night sometimes she dreamed of them, their faces turned upward like two rows of cabbages. When they chorused the words after her, their voices were high and clear.

Sometimes, after the lesson, she gave them apple cider to drink and pieces of cornbread. It pleased her to see the eagerness of their appetites, the glances and whispers that darted between them when they thought she was not looking, but she was glad when they were gone. Then she went out onto the stoop, watching the evening shadows settle in the high trees, so that in the house the silence might unfurl undisturbed, stretching its limbs like a lover across the hard dirt floor, ready for his return.

★   ★   ★

He came back when the ground was dry and Elisabeth as good as healed. He was in high spirits, lifting her off her feet and spinning her giddily around as sunlight spilled through the open front door and warmed the hard dirt floor. She laughed with him and wrapped her arms tightly around his neck, the exquisite ache of his embrace like unshed tears at the base of her throat. When the savage children came for their lesson, she sent them away. It was only much later, as they lay pressed together beneath the sea-green quilt, that she told him about the baby.

'But you are not to concern yourself about me,' she murmured, her lips against his. 'There is time. And I am quite well again, as you can see.'

'As I can feel.' His tongue flickered against hers, his hand sliding down over the curve of her belly. 'Then let us hope you do not succumb again too quickly. There is a great deal more to be said for the manufacture of children than there is for the raising of them.'

The next time she went longer. The sickness persisted and the exhaustion. Her breasts hardened and swelled, and her back ached. At night the child moved like a fish inside her, slipping between her nerve-strings as though through weed and setting the waters inside her to vibrating. She placed her hands upon her belly and it rippled, soft ridges moving in waves across the tautening flesh. A darkening line ran from her belly button into the hair between her thighs, dividing her in two.

It was winter again and he was once more at the settlement. She pushed herself wearily through the work of each day, cutting short her lessons with the savage children so that she might have time to prepare his evening meal. Mild weather meant that food was not so scarce as it had been in previous years but, though she ached for sleep, still she blew out the lamp and put the blanket across the window so that they might eat in the old way, secretly, before the fire. But it was not the same. However hard she tried, she could not make it the same. Her fatigue sapped the vigour from the room. The hours passed sluggishly. When they sat together he grew restless. She thought to suggest she read aloud but she feared his mockery or, worse, his disdain. When supper was finished, he took his hat and went out. He said that walking aided his digestion.

There was a new uneasiness between them. Often they started to speak at the same time, apologising and gesturing at the other to continue before lapsing once more into silence. She watched him as he moved around the cabin, and he shrugged his shoulders at her and frowned, as though the weight of her gaze oppressed him. He did not look up to observe her unclothed as she stepped out of her ragged petticoats as he once had. Instead he busied himself with his boots. Though they lay together still, from time to time, his efforts were straining and brief, his eyes closed and his face furrowed and folded in on itself as though she was not there.

She did not want him. She could hardly bear to acknowledge it to herself but she did not want him. The smell of him, the musk of his sweat and skin and breath, overpowered her. When he touched her, her flesh was reluctant, stupid, determined upon its own boundaries. He set his tongue in her mouth, his fingers between her thighs, he entered her, and yet she remained apart from him, the core of her untouched. Desire, the melting hunger for him that had coursed in her like blood, eluded her. She closed her eyes so that he might not see the truth in her, and waited for him to be spent.

'Promise me it will be as it was,' she wanted to beg him. 'Promise me that, when the baby comes, it will be as it was.'

But she did not dare. It was too frightening,

too unalterable, to speak of such things out loud. Besides, her anxiety provoked him. He was short-tempered, bored from too much time in the settlement and impatient for spring, but he was not cruel nor was he cold. When she put her arms around him and held him against her, swallowing the tears that rose too easily in her throat, he patted her back and brushed his lips across the top of her head. He was a good husband.

But sometimes, when she stood apart from him, watching him when he did not know it, she saw that his eyes slid over her without catching, the way they had at the dock that very first day. They snagged instead on other women's necks, other women's breasts. She saw it and something at the centre of her fell away. At night, when the moon was bright and round and threw sharp shadows on the cottage floor, she lay awake, the infant curling sinuously inside her, and watched him sleep. He looked exactly as he always had, contented and contained, complete within his skin. She could no longer sleep wrapped in his arms as she had always done. The swell of her belly did not permit it.

★   ★   ★

It came in March. Longer than the first but still too soon. The midwife rubbed it with bear oil and dribbled brandy between its lips but the breath was too weak in it and it did not last the night. As dawn streaked the sky, the midwife sprinkled water over the baby and baptised it with the name Joseph, for her own father. Later she called for the Jesuit to perform the proper burial rites.

Neither of Joseph's parents were present at the brief ceremony. Elisabeth was too weak to leave her bed. The afterbirth had crumbled during its expulsion, and the midwife was required to bring it out, piece by piece, by means of an instrument shaped like a crochet hook. The pain was severe and there was a great deal of blood. Afterwards, Elisabeth lay with her knees pressed up against her chest and her eyes fixed on the wall and the grief cramped inside her like the contractions of labour.

As for Jean-Claude, matters of business required his urgent departure. The infant had been dead less than twelve hours when he bid his wife farewell. She did not weep. The emptiness in her yawned black, vaster by far than the husk of bones that contained it. He stood by the side of the bed, his arms hanging limp at his sides, and it seemed to her that he was slighter than usual, less substantial.

'I am so sorry, dearest,' she whispered. 'The child. I should never — it was my fault.'

He shook his head, then, and he pinched the bridge of his nose between his thumb and forefinger.

'Don't say that.' His voice was sharp with anger. 'Don't — you are strong. Damn the child, do you hear me? Damn the child.'

His voice thickened as he knelt beside her, bringing his fist down upon the lumpy mattress. When she held him against her torn, tender body

108

he did not resist her. Through her numbness she felt his dependence upon her and there was comfort in it.

*   *   *

She was not left alone. Rochon came. The women, mollified a little by Elisabeth's continued misfortune, came too, but unlike the Jesuit, they were not content to sit with her in silence. It was among the most certain of their certain principles that company was meat to the convalescent and scandal her strongest physic. They came in pairs, bringing vittles and juicy morsels of town gossip, and set about sweeping and scrubbing and straightening around her, thickening the air with dust and chatter.

They discussed the price of a head of bear oil and the prettiness of Jeanne Deshays' daughter and the sudden and unexpected demise from the fever of Gabrielle Borret's seven-year-old Mobilian slave, because naturally it was never the troublesome ones that were taken. They talked of Angélique Brouyn's milk cow that was grown dry and of rumours that natives in the pay of the English attacked the Spanish fort at Pensacola and of the best way to cook buffalo meat. The subject of greatest interest, however, was the scandal of Pierre Charly, the merchant, whose savage housekeeper had just borne him a son.

Though such infants were hardly unknown, this particular case had caused something of a stir, and the previous Sunday La Vente had taken to the pulpit to argue for the legitimisation of marriage between white man and savage, claiming that otherwise there would be no end to debauchery and the disgrace of illegitimate offspring. His remarks had infuriated the commandant and, though the wives had not yet forgiven Sieur de Bienville for the lack of white flour, in this regard they were all firmly on his side. La Vente was not well liked. His manner was abrasive and his purple-faced piety tyrannical. Worse than either, he ran the most expensive shop in all of Mobile, selling his allowance of flour at ten times the usual rate and a barrel of wine for the shocking sum of two hundred and fifty French *livres*. It was Perrine Roussel who observed that for all his denouncements from the pulpit, the good priest was less a Catholic than he was a Jew.

As the chickens cackled, Elisabeth fixed her gaze upon the peeling lime and said nothing. There was a weight upon her chest like two hands pushing down that made it hard to breathe. Her eyes and her throat ached. She ate when someone set a dish in front of her, but she was hardly aware of the food in her mouth. Sometimes she blinked, startled by a noise or the abrupt awareness that the room had grown dark without her noticing, to find that the food was cold and the spoon lost among the bed rugs.

Inside her belly her womb cramped, wringing itself out like a wet cloth. The emptiness cramped too, shrinking and hardening into something frozen that pressed its sharp edges into the soft parts of her. When she thought of the lost infant, it was with a kind of heavy detachment. Her grief was all for her husband.

One day, when Guillemette, the midwife, came to see Elisabeth, she was accompanied by Marie-Françoise de Boisrenaud. A spinster still, the Governess occupied her days with schooling the colony's children and superintending the conduct of their mothers.

'Do you still bleed?' Guillemette asked Elisabeth.

When Elisabeth nodded, Guillemette clicked her fingers and reluctantly Elisabeth parted her knees. The midwife unwrapped the rag she had knotted about her hips, placing it in a bucket at her feet.

'I had not expected it to continue so,' Guillemette said. 'Of course the afterbirth did not come out cleanly. It is possible that fragments of it remain. Still, you are otherwise well healed.'

'Did you hear that, Elisabeth?' Marie-Françoise admonished. 'Otherwise well healed. You should be satisfied.'

'I am going to give you a tisane of ground pine,' the midwife said as she set a fresh rag between Elisabeth's thighs. 'The treatment is unpleasant. You will bleed very heavily and there will be considerable pain. But it must be endured. The flow will cleanse your womb and you will mend. Take heart. There will be more children.'

The spasm that cramped Elisabeth's abdomen then caused her to whimper. Guillemette regarded her coolly, her knobby hands set upon her hips.

111

'Belladonna is a poison, of course,' she said calmly. 'An excess of it will kill. Taken as instructed, however, it effects only enough harm to the body to provoke it to heal itself.'

'Moderate harm?' muttered Marie-Françoise, rolling her eyes. 'Then I wish you all good fortune. Elisabeth Savaret is not well known for her love of moderation.'

'Nor is she a fool,' Guillemette countered briskly. 'She will do as she is told. With physic of this kind, the perils of intemperance are grave.'

'Intemperance is a sin of pride, Guillemette,' Marie-Françoise replied. 'Its perils are always considerable. Elisabeth would do well to remember that. Our miseries on earth, like our joys, are a matter of divine Providence. Like the farmer in the parable, we reap what we sow.'

A surge of fury split the crust of Elisabeth's exhaustion.

'Since when did a shrivelled-up spinster governess know anything about how to live?' she hissed.

Marie-Françoise's face twisted into a knot.

'You are not the first in the colony to have suffered loss, Elisabeth Savaret,' she spat. 'Nor shall you be the last. You may consider yourself better than the rest of us but, believe me, you are quite mistaken. It would become you to show a little humility.'

The next day Elisabeth swallowed a draught of the midwife's tincture, measuring it out carefully as she had been told. Then she lay upon her bed. Within minutes her stomach began to scream and her mouth to desiccate. Her tongue cracked

112

and, as the tincture took hold of her, every part of her body shook and sweated, convulsed with fever. When the blood came, it was dark and clotted, soaking through the rags to spread in a black bruise on the palliasse beneath her.

On the third day, when she managed to rise from her bed, Guillemette le Bras declared herself satisfied. It was, the midwife admitted, the first time she had attempted such a cure, which she had learned from a book that one of the sea captains had brought from France. The remedy called for mercury but, unable to secure it, she had instead used belladonna, which grew in abundance in the forests close to the settlement. The substitution of one poison for another had proved a matter of good sense. If it was true, the midwife said briskly, that the effects of physic could never be relied upon, the practice of it was not half the mystery that physicians liked to make of it.

When Jean-Claude returned, they did not speak of the infant. He did not ask after his wife's health, only observing approvingly that she had regained her figure. Somehow he had acquired for her a new petticoat and a dress of dove-grey silk, trimmed with velvet ribbon. The dress became her. She did not think to ask how he had obtained it. He had always been clever at such things. At night, in the darkness, he set his hands upon her, folding back time. Afterwards she lay beside him as he slept, pulling his arms around her shoulders like a cape.

★ ★ ★

On a dull, airless day in April, Marie-Françoise de Boisrenaud came to the cottage with a parcel that she dropped without ceremony upon Elisabeth's table.

'It would seem that even our old enemies the Spanish take pity upon us. The commandant returned from his visit there with a chest of items sent to them by the charitable ladies of Havana. The commissary has charged me with the fair disposal of its contents.'

Elisabeth took the parcel, turning it over in her hands.

'Have you heard? The Jesuit Rochon is to take a mission among the savages on the Red River. Doubtless their godless ways shall suit him very well.' Marie-Françoise wrinkled her brow. 'La Vente shall not regret his departure, of course, but perhaps you shall? I understand that he was quite the companion to you while your husband was away. Well, go on then, open it.'

Her jaw hard, Elisabeth set the parcel down on the table and picked at the knots. She had known about the mission, of course. Rochon had told her the news himself. He had laughed at her apprehension, unable to contain his excitement.

'I shall come to no harm,' he had assured her.

'And if you do?'

'Then the last will of Rabelais shall serve as well for me: 'I have nothing, I owe a great deal, and the rest I leave to the poor.' '

The knots were tight and her fingers were clumsy. When at last they came loose, she coiled the string carefully around her hand, pulling it tight. The tips of her fingers whitened.

'We saw it and thought immediately of you,' Marie-Françoise said, her voice sticky with virtue. 'We pray that you shall soon have the need of it.'

Elisabeth pulled open the paper. Inside was a baby's dress of lawn and lace, white, a little worn. Beneath one sleeve there was a neat darn where the seam had torn. Elisabeth stared at it and her jaw clamped tight.

'For me?' she said. 'How very considerate you are. You are quite certain, I suppose, that you shall have no want of it yourself?'

When Marie-Françoise was gone, she dragged the chest out from beneath the bed. The corners of the trunk left pale lines in the hard dirt floor. Lifting the lid a slit, she bundled the dress into it and pushed it once more out of sight. She went to the garrison then, to ask after the Jesuit. The dress remained there for five years, quite forgotten, the lawn browning at the edges and the fine lace working into holes. It was only long afterwards, in the dark days when there was no sense or shape to any of it, that she took it out and wept for each one of them and all that they had lost.

From the first moment that he saw him, Auguste knew that the Canadian was not like the others.

Most of the white men who came from time to time to the village were *coureurs-de-bois*, coarse hunter-traders from the north desirous of satisfying their simple appetites for trade and women. They reminded Auguste of the boys of La Rochelle before they were sent to sea. Hairy-chinned and coarse-mannered, the *coureurs* prided themselves upon their bluntness, their lawlessness and their lack of restraint. They derided the petty curbs set upon their liberty by the officials and priests of the towns, by the chiefs and missionaries in the villages. They drank heavily and gambled whatever they had. The savages were wary of them, for they had guns and they were known to raid the villages for slave concubines, but they did not fear them as they feared their enemies among the savages. The *coureurs* possessed neither the subtlety of the native nor his stark brutality. Their deceptions were as clumsy as their sentiments.

The Canadian ensign was another matter. Like the *coureurs* he travelled alone, with only three Mobilian warriors as guides. Like them he greeted the savages with bonhomie, distributing presents with a reckless generosity, but beneath the affability there was a refinement about him, a

watchfulness that Auguste recognised as calculation. His hands were elegant, with tapered
fingers. His nails were almost clean. The men of
the Ouma were tall but he was taller, more than
six feet, with long legs and the languorous
manner of someone accustomed to admiration.
The crown of Auguste's head barely grazed his
chin. When the ensign clapped him on the
shoulder, Auguste stiffened at the condescen-
sion. He would not be made to feel like a child.

More than any of this, though, it was the
consideration that the ensign gave him that made
Auguste uneasy. The *coureurs* had never
bothered with him much. They noticed him of
course, for a boy sent to live among savages was
an object of curiosity. Sometimes after supper
they liked him to sit with them so that they
might lecture him in words smudgy with brandy
upon the idleness of savage men and the
licentiousness of savage women and the weakness of both for strong liquor.

Occasionally one might nudge him for titbits
of information about the tribe, pretending a
white man's fellow feeling in the hope of
learning something that might advantage their
negotiations, but that was rare. Certainly none
had ever sought him out, as the tall Canadian
sought him out, to converse with him. The first
time, he sat with his long legs folded up on each
side of him like a cricket as Auguste whittled at a
piece of wood with his knife. Curls of pale wood
drifted about his knees and settled on the fur of
the yellow dog that slept beside him.

'What are you making?' the ensign asked idly,

117

twisting one of the curls of wood around his finger.

Auguste shrugged.

'Nothing much.'

There was a silence. The ensign smoked a pipe. Auguste bent over his work, gouging the flesh of the wood with the point of his knife. Then the ensign rose and walked over to the cabin, pulling several strands of palmetto from its fringed roof and swiftly twisting them together.

'There,' he said.

On the palm of his hand was a small dog, its ears and tail cocked, a tiny palmetto tongue protruding from its muzzle.

'Here, take it. It's for you.'

Auguste shook his head, hunching over his knife.

'It's all right,' he said.

'Come on. It's the only trick I know. I have no choice but to oblige you to appreciate it. The savage who taught me despaired of me. I was so poor a pupil it took me a six-week expedition to master the one animal.'

Auguste hesitated. Then he reached out and took the palmetto dog, touching it gently on the head with one finger.

'Does he have a name, your dog?' the ensign asked.

'No.'

'Not even in your head? I mean, you must call him something, mustn't you, when you think of him, even if it is just Dog or Him?'

Auguste eyed him suspiciously, but he did not

118

smirk. He looked at Auguste, his brow creased, as if the question itself was a puzzle to him. Auguste was silent, gazing at the palmetto dog in his hand.

'No,' he said at last. 'Not a word. A picture.'

'A picture.'

'Yes.'

'A particular picture?'

Auguste thought of the yellow dog and in his head it sat, its bottom barely grazing the earth, its muzzle stuck carelessly into the air as if it were about to whistle.

'Yes.'

'But no name?'

'No name.'

The ensign laughed softly and shook his head.

'French, Mobilian, Choctaw, and still you think in pictures? You are a most unusual man, Monsieur whatever-your-name-is. A most unusually interesting man.'

* * *

The ensign's name was Babelon. He remained at the settlement for several days. Auguste grew almost accustomed to the strange questions and the way the ensign cocked his head to listen to his answers, as though the words were a liquid that must be poured into his ear without spilling a drop. To his astonishment he found himself telling the ensign of his life in La Rochelle, of things and people he told himself he no longer remembered, the stone house by the harbour, his sisters with their wide grins and wider-legged

119

gaits, the siren suck and spit of the stone-grey sea. He scratched them into the dust with a stick as he spoke, drawing them out of his head, but still the images jostled forward, noisier than market day, and first among them, as he always had been, was Jean.

'Your cousin sounds like my brother,' Babelon said with a rueful grin. 'My brother was big, taller by far than me and broad as a wall, and he could get the rest of us to do whatever he wanted. It did not matter how vilely he behaved towards us, we followed him like sheep wherever he went. My mother used to say she hoped we were fastened to his boots with invisible threads for she could think of no other explanation that might excuse our pitiful devotion. My mother was not an admirer of devotion.'

Auguste thought of his own mother, the drag of her shoulders, the droop of her mouth, the way she had of slumping at the table at dawn as though the day had already defeated her. The prickle of it discomfited him and he made to scramble to his feet, clicking his fingers at the dog.

'It's late,' he mumbled.

'Ah, not so late. Take pity on me, I beg you. Agreeable company is a rare and precious pleasure in Louisiana.'

He smiled. Auguste smiled too, awkwardly, then swallowed and stared down at the ground. The dog sighed and thrust its nose once more beneath its haunch. There was something about the ensign's gaze, the warmth and the intensity of it, that seemed to shrink the world to the space between the two of them. Auguste was not accustomed to being looked at in such a way.

'You want a woman?' he blurted. 'I can, you know. Arrange it for you. If you want.'

'That I can manage for myself. If I have learned anything in this life, it is that it is a great deal easier to find consolation for the body than for the spirit.'

There were men of the Ouma who lay with men. Of course there had been men like that on the ship to Louisiana too, but it had been different then, furtive and dirty, something for the boys to snigger at. Among the savages such men were accommodated and permitted to practise their perversions openly. They wore the woman's apron to mark them out. Auguste glanced up at the ensign. Babelon smiled, a dry smile tucked into the corner of his mouth, and Auguste's neck flushed. He was sure that the older man knew exactly what it was he was thinking. He reached out and set his hand on the dog's neck, feeling the comforting coarseness of its coat beneath his hand. The dog shifted a little but did not wake.

'I have a wife in Mobile,' the soldier said, his mouth twitching. 'To whom, for all of my mother's admonitions, I am devoted.'

Auguste's blush deepened.

'You have children?' he muttered.

'Probably. But none that I know of.'

Auguste ducked his head, a snort of laughter escaping his nose.

'Your Ouma girls are fine-looking,' the Canadian observed.

121

'Yes, sir.'

'I think we can dispense with the *sir* this far from the garrison. You have a girl?'

Auguste shook his head and immediately regretted it. Usually he lied.

'Keeping your options open?'

'Something like that.'

'Wise man. You know, I never thought I'd marry. Seen too many men stifled that way, the demands, the complaints. The ceaseless scolding. Elisabeth is not like that, thank God. She is strong, self-reliant. Bloody-minded, some might say.' Babelon smiled. 'My mother would approve of that. Fierce as a tigress she was and twice as fearless. I think she would have killed anyone who tried to lay a finger on us.'

'She is in Quebec still, your mother?'

'She died. When I was eight years old. You?'

'My mother is alive. I think. But she is not fierce. Not fierce at all.'

'Then you shall have to do as I have and find yourself a fierce wife instead.' He grinned. 'Don't fool yourself, Auguste. We may have stronger sinews, but it is men who are the weaker sex. Every man needs a fearless woman to fight his battles for him.'

★ ★ ★

It was years since Auguste had dreamed of Jean, but that night his cousin returned to him. He stood on the harbour wall at La Rochelle, his hands upon his hips. Auguste had to tip his head right back to see him. The glare of the sun burned his eyes.

'Come up!' Jean called. 'Come up here!'

'I'm coming,' Auguste called back, though he was afraid. But when he began to climb the wall was smooth and slippery. He could gain no purchase on it. Time and again he tried to climb, but each time he fell backwards the wall grew higher and its surface more slippery. Auguste could no longer see the sun.

'Come up here!' Jean called impatiently, and his voice was muffled, as though it came from a long way off. 'Come up!'

In his dream Auguste felt the slide of hot tears on his cheeks, the sick chill of humiliation in his belly.

'I can't do it,' he whimpered. 'I can't do it!'

But Jean was gone.

The next day Babelon left, headed north. Auguste did not say goodbye. He watched him leave from his hiding place in the canebrake. All that afternoon, as he skinned deer and scraped the hair from the hides for soaking, he thought of Jean. When he closed his eyes, he could still bring to mind his cousin's voice, with its distinctive ragged edges and its sailor's disregard for nicety but, though he screwed up his face with the effort of it, he could not summon Jean's face.

★　★　★

Ensign Babelon returned to the Ouma three more times before winter came, each time remaining in the village for some days after his business was complete. The chief always extended him a warm welcome. Auguste watched carefully and knew why. In addition to the corn he purchased for the settlement and the presents he brought to reinforce their friendship, Babelon brought with him a selection of French goods for private sale, including muskets and powder and frequently brandy. The arrangement was conducted discreetly, to both men's advantage.

'The wise man does not dominate the red man, nor does he seek to civilise him,' Babelon said to Auguste. It was the last expedition of the year before the ice came, and he was in no hurry to return south. 'He observes their customs and directs them to his own ends. If a white man snatches a native woman from her own village, the savages will come after him and break his head, as many a doltish hunter has discovered. But if he comes to the savage chief in friendship, then the chief shall offer him women as he offers him meat, for his greater comfort.'

Auguste was silent.

'It is habit that makes a man stupid. We purchase our slaves from the local traders in the marketplace and yet still we reward the Choctaw with a rifle for every Alabama scalp they bring us, because that is how it has always been. It is the purest kind of idiocy. What possible profit can be gained from a scalp without the savage still attached?'

Auguste wanted to ask him then why it was that Babelon told him these things, but he did not. The soldier was, like him, a servant of the commandant. They were on the same side. All the same, he watched him closely, careful to mistrust his companionship, and held himself tightly, so that the soldier might find nothing in him to profit by. He could not conquer his suspicion that any man who sought his friendship must surely mean to swindle him.

But late at night, as Babelon talked and the fire sighed and sank, something inside him unknotted a little and he did not resist it. He had never before heard anyone talk as he did. Jean had never had much time for words. For Jean talk was for planning, not for pleasure: at sundown, under the dock, faster, higher, that dog with this stone. But with Babelon the conversation was the game. From him, Auguste learned the art of spinning stories into bright patterns; he came to see the adventure of words, the thrill of another's attention, the sharp delight of provoking laughter. He stopped drawing in the dirt as he spoke, so that he might have all his attention for it. When Babelon clapped his hands together in delight at the story of the missionary's burning glass, Auguste thought he would burst from the triumph of it.

Babelon did not mean to stay a soldier. Wise men wanted to be rich, he told Auguste, for the rich could make the world bend to their will. Auguste shook his head, surprising himself with the strength of his opinions. The white man's world of risk and profit was like iron, he protested. Hard and cold, it required a fire of great intensity to bend it. He favoured the savage way, where those with surplus wealth distributed it generously among the others. There was no need to be rich when the shape of the world was softer and might be altered more easily.

Babelon frowned thoughtfully, nudging a smouldering log with his boot so that a spray of bright red sparks twisted upward in a veil of smoke. Auguste watched them as they burst and flattened into grey ash. He was in no hurry for Babelon's answer. It was in these silences that the threads of understanding seemed to tighten and quiver between them.

'You are wrong,' Babelon said at last. 'The savages want nothing because they have nothing. It cannot remain so. We tame them with presents they cannot hunt or grow or make from clay. And so it goes. They teach us a hundred dishes with Indian corn and we teach them to covet the possessions of their neighbour.'

Babelon never talked to Auguste about the savage women. It was something else that marked him out, that made him different from the other men. But on the fourth or fifth night, when Babelon bid him goodnight and went without ceremony to a hut that was not his, Auguste did the same. It was a brief and awkward encounter. When it was over, she did not speak and he could think of nothing to say. Instead he rose quickly, turning his face from the eyes that gleamed in the darkness, and went outside.

The moon was high, flooding the village with silver light. Beside him his shadow on the hard ground was precise, ink-black. Outside the hut to which Babelon had gone he saw a girl. She squatted with her legs apart and the stream of urine was bright in the moonlight. Her braid fell over her shoulder and on her neck there was a cluster of dark bruises, like sores.

Later, restless on his palliasse, he stared down at his unclothed body, the sparse growth of hair around his genitals, his awkward boyish limbs, and he longed suddenly for Jean, who might teach him how to be a man. But, as he fell at last into sleep, his last thoughts were not of his cousin nor of the girl whose smell he wore upon his skin, but of Babelon, who saw into the heart of him and liked him all the same.

The women stood around the table, chopping and stirring encouragingly as Perrine Roussel lamented their misfortunes. Elisabeth, standing to one side, tilted her head at an angle that suggested attention, watching the spiral of peel that curled away from her knife. It was an unexpectedly warm day for December and the white flesh of the apple was already brown. The apples were her christening gift, the first crop of her own tree. When she had piled them into the basket to bring them, their sweet smell had filled her with a quiet pride.

'Bacon, wine, barrels of flour — all taken direct from the *Aigle* to his own private store,' Perrine protested, holding out hands lumpy with dough. 'From what I hear, the commissary tears his hair out but the commandant has paid off the ship's officers and he is powerless to stop it.'

By the thrown-open door to the yard, Jean-Claude conversed with the widow Freval. The widow did not seem to notice the other women who, as was customary, had gathered in the kitchen to assist in the preparation of the christening meal.

'Two years we have waited for that ship. Two years, *mesdames*, to have the food stolen from under our very noses!'

When news of the *Aigle*'s arrival had reached Mobile several of the wives had wept with joy.

128

Though small, the ship had proved heavily laden, bringing not only food but luxuries so long denied that they had almost forgotten to hanker for them: bolts of fabric and ribbons, cooking utensils, paper and ink, even candles, though these were all broken or melted. There had been building materials too: ropes and knives and nails, and a handful of settlers, among them the widow Freval. With her two young daughters, the widow had taken lodgings with the schoolteacher and had quickly established herself as a dressmaker. The women all agreed she had exceptionally skilful hands.

Elisabeth threw the peeled apple on to the pile on the table and took up another, sliding her knife beneath the skin. Mme Freval was a pretty little thing with soft white arms and a heart-shaped face, which she tipped up towards Jean-Claude, her lips parted in a smile. Though her gown was modest in its cut, it displayed her plump figure to advantage, its dark trim drawing attention to the creaminess of her skin. Her brown hair was caught in a loose knot at the nape of her neck and, as he spoke, she twisted a curl of it between her fingers.

'How then, I ask you, may we share in this rare largesse, we who starve here for the want of decent flour?' Perrine demanded, kneading furiously. 'When we are prepared to pay our esteemed commandant three times the proper price for it, that's when! And who here can afford to do that? Not any of us, that's for certain, not when that very same esteemed commandant has paid no one but himself for three straight years!'

Elisabeth watched as Jean-Claude inclined his head towards the widow, murmuring something that made her laugh. It was a happy occasion. The previous night, some hours before dawn and after a long labour, Marie-Cathérine Christophe had brought forth a healthy son. That morning, at a baptism attended by family and a handful of neighbours, the boy had been named François-Xavier for his god-father, the powder-maker François-Xavier Lemay.

Elisabeth herself had been present at the birth. She had held the labouring woman's hand as she braced herself against the force of her contractions and sponged the sweat from her brow. When the time came for the child to be born, she had pressed down on Marie-Cathérine's knees as Guillemette worked with her hands to draw the infant out. When at last it came, the sound of flesh tearing had been sharp, like ripped silk. As Guillemette cut the cord and spooned watery gruel into the wailing infant's mouth, she had motioned for Elisabeth to assist with the delivery of the afterbirth. She had warned Elisabeth before that the mother might require the belladonna, for she was sore and much fatigued, but Marie-Cathérine had only moaned, jerking with the pain, and expelled the bloody mass in a single fleshy slither. Then she had taken the squalling child into her arms and wept. Elisabeth had wept too but quietly, blinking her tears into her bloodstained sleeve.

It had been her first birth. Afterwards Guillemette had nodded at her.

'You did well,' she had said, and Elisabeth had shaken her head. Her duties had been simple, little more than the boiling of water and tearing of rags and, in the darkest hour of the night, the preparation of a caudle of wine with sugar and spices to boost the labouring woman's spirits. And yet, as she had walked home in the strengthening dawn, the sky pink-tinted and the air sweet with birdsong, she had been overwhelmed by the sudden sense that the world had been created afresh and that she, Elisabeth Savaret, was a part of it.

'I do not know how he dares,' Perrine sniffed. 'Accusing us of shiftlessness when we refuse to till the fields like peasants, while all the while he eats like a king from our very plates!'

She was still raw with it, raw and light-headed with lack of sleep. When she had arrived back at the cabin that morning, Jean-Claude was just waking and she had built a fire and made porridge and coffee and brought them to him. She was dropping with fatigue and yet she was possessed of a fierce energy that made the thought of sleep impossible. Instead she had washed her face and changed her clothes, putting her bloody apron and sleeves to soak in a bucket of lye before taking up a broom and setting about the cabin floor. As the dust rose around her, she thought of the blood-slimed child who had opened his white-blue eyes to gaze up at her in furious astonishment and of the look that had passed then between her and Guillemette, and the dust had caught in her throat and caused her eyes to water.

The widow's two daughters ran through the kitchen, ducking beneath the floury arms of Anne Conaud, the blacksmith's wife, who, red-faced, lifted an iron kettle from the fire. She tutted at them irritably as they slipped through the doorway to wind themselves in their mother's skirts, clamping to her legs like irons and clamouring for her attention. The widow placed a hand lightly on their tousled heads but she did not look at them. Her face was still tipped up towards Jean-Claude's. Elisabeth did not know how the widow had contrived to be invited to the party. Her lodgings were on the other side of the settlement, beyond the place d'Armes. As for blood ties, she was kin to no one.

'For the love of peace, Elisabeth Savaret!' Perrine scolded. 'See how much apple you take off with that peel!'

The widow stooped, taking the girls into her arms and pressing her lips against their foreheads. Jean-Claude watched them in silence, his hands thrust deep into the pockets of his breeches. Elisabeth willed him to look up, to seek her out, but he did not. The widow opened her arms and, seizing each other's hands, the girls ran together through the open door. The widow and Jean-Claude smiled. He placed a hand beneath her elbow. Then they followed them.

Slowly an unpeeled apple rolled from the pile and fell with a thud to the floor.

'Elisabeth Savaret? Where do you think you are going?'

But she was already gone.

Above the screams of the birds, Elisabeth could hear the flimsier cries of the girls as they called out to their mother. The afternoon was bright, the sun a harsh white glare behind its shade of cloud, and she squinted as she hurried down the steps and into the yard. When she reached the mulberry tree, she stopped, aware suddenly of the apple-sticky knife in her hand. They were standing together at the southern edge of the yard, their backs to her, a clear slice of the canebrake that edged the property visible between them. As she watched the widow called out to one of the girls, warning her to take care. Beside her Jean-Claude hoisted the smaller one up into his arms. The child leaned back away from him, her face crumpled with concentration as he pointed upward. There was nothing and then a vividly coloured bird flashed green and scarlet across the white sky.

'Yes,' she cried delightedly. 'Yes, I see it. I see it!'

Jean-Claude turned. Elisabeth hastened backwards, snatching at her skirts, until, bent over a little, she was concealed by the fans of the palmetto. She could hear feet creaking on the planks of the stoop behind her, muffled voices, the distinctive bark of René Boyer's laughter. In the sudden dread of discovery, her feet slipped on the muddy ground and she fell, dropping the knife and bruising her hand against a rock.

Perrine looked up as she returned to the kitchen and took up her knife.

'Whatever happened to you?' she asked peevishly. 'You're white as milk.'

Elisabeth bent her head, pressing the blade of her knife into the waxy apple. It left a smear of mud on the rosy skin.

'Well? Are you ill?'

'No. Perhaps. I don't know.'

Perrine shook her head, expelling a spiteful snort of laughter.

'Why, Elisabeth Savaret, one birth and you could almost be a physician.'

* * *

After the baptism dinner, Jean-Claude was summoned to the garrison and Elisabeth returned home alone. The hectic energy that had sustained her through the day had soured into an exhausted jitteriness. Fatigue fogged her head, making her clumsy. When she heated the stew over the fire, she burned her hand on the iron pot. She sucked the scorched flesh, feeling the blister rise beneath her tongue. She thought then of the tiny infant, not yet a day old, suckling at his mother's breast, and of the indissoluble threads that bound her to Marie-Cathérine and to the child, whether he knew it or not. When Guillemette le Bras had first asked if she might consider assisting her in her midwifery, Elisabeth had hesitated.

'I don't know,' she had said. 'I would not be a popular choice.'

But Guillemette had only frowned, studying Elisabeth with her red knuckles pressed against her hips.

'You are capable and circumspect, qualities of

134

considerably greater worth to a labouring woman than a fondness for tittle-tattle. Surely you wish to be useful?'

The spoon slack in her hand, Elisabeth let her head hang forward. Her eyes closed and she thought of Rochon, who had gone to live among the savages so that he might not rot in a safe harbour. She thought of the widow and her daughters, of a heart-shaped face tipped upward and a smile tucked into the corner of a mouth, and of the rags she soaked each month, the trails of brown blood drifting in the water like smoke.

It was late when he returned, his supper still on the table. Rubbing her eyes, Elisabeth lifted the top plate. The gravy had grown a waxy skin.

'I'm afraid it has spoiled rather.'

Jean-Claude shrugged, reaching for his fork. He was in good humour.

'How was the commandant?' she asked.

'The commandant was uncommonly well.'

Elisabeth brought the pitcher of water. The water splashed a little as she poured, making a puddle on the table.

'You are not usually so glad to see him,' she said as she fumbled a rag from her apron.

'He is not usually so sympathetic.'

'You are sure it was the commandant you saw?'

Jean-Claude gave a muffled laugh, his mouth full of food.

'We talked business,' he said. 'He was most interested in what I had to say.'

'That's good.'

'You should be. With a little managing it

should prove extremely profitable.'

'For the commandant?'

'For all of us. I mean us to be rich, Elisabeth.'

'Rich? Here?'

'There are riches for those with the appetite, even in a place like this.' Jean-Claude took a final mouthful and pushed his plate away, stretching his arms above his head. 'I promise you, we shall not rot in this stink hole forever.'

Elisabeth took the plate and placed it at the far end of the table. She swallowed.

'Should you like apple pie? We baked too much for the baptism dinner.'

When he nodded she placed a large slice before him. There was a scorch on the wooden tabletop where some months before she had distractedly set a scalding kettle. Elisabeth traced the half-circle of it with a finger.

'It went off well today, don't you think?'

'Did it? The infant certainly displayed strong lungs.'

'I thought it went off well. The joiner seemed pleased.'

'When isn't he? That man is pleased by a plank of wood.'

She smiled, biting her lip. Then she took up the pitcher again.

'Here, give me that. I should like to remain dry.'

Elisabeth let him take the pitcher from her.

'I was surprised to see the seamstress there,' she said, watching the flow of water into the cup. 'She is not a neighbour.'

He shrugged.

'It's hardly a big town.'

'You — I thought I saw you speak with her. Was she pleasant?'

'She was amiable enough.'

'Her daughters looked pretty creatures. I wonder at their ages.'

Jean-Claude glanced up at her, his spoon aloft. There was a speck of pastry on his chin.

'Why are you so interested in the seamstress all of a sudden?' Elisabeth coloured.

'I — she's new here. I was just curious. You have a crumb — '

'I do?'

'There. You have it.'

Pushing back her chair, Elisabeth rose, taking up her husband's empty plate. Gathering the other dirty dishes, she pushed the door open and set them with the others for washing on the stoop. When she came back into the cottage, the door slammed behind her, causing the lamp to gutter. Jean-Claude turned round, one eyebrow raised, stretching his arms above his head.

'It's the hinge,' she said. 'The leather's rotted.'

'I'll get more.'

'Thank you.'

He leaned forward on his elbows, regarding her over his steepled fingers. His eyes crinkled.

'Jealousy becomes you, you know,' he said.

'Jealousy? What in heaven makes you think I — '

'Young widows. It hardly matters if they are not comely, or if they drag a bevy of brats behind them like bad weather. They always put colour in a wife's cheeks.'

Elisabeth frowned. He laughed.

'Don't mistake me. I rather like it.'

'Don't.'

'See how fetching your eyes are when they flash. You she-wolf, you.'

'Stop it.'

He laughed again.

'Come, Elisabeth. I only tease you a little. The seamstress is a plain Jane with a litter of squalling pups and the figure to prove it. I may be a dullard on occasion but I am not blind. Come here.'

She hesitated.

'Come here,' he said again, a fraction more sharply. 'And be glad there are no pups here to spoil our pleasure.'

Slowly Elisabeth came round the table until she stood before him.

'You think me foolish,' she murmured.

'Foolish and delightful.'

Taking her head between his hands, he kissed her. The tips of his fingers were hot and urgent in her hair, his elbows tight against her ribs. He had not kissed her like that in many months. She closed her eyes and her head filled with the widow's soft arms and creamy skin and her heart-shaped face tipped up in invitation, cramming her skull until she was seized with anger, anger at the widow and anger too at the miserable doggedness of her imagination. It quickened in her, hot and sharp as desire, and she lifted her skirts where she stood, forcing her mouth against his as though she meant to devour him.

That month she did not bleed. For ten days she waited for the cramps, twisting a rag between her legs, but they did not come. She rinsed the unstained rags and folded them and placed them back in the chest beneath the bed. When the tingling came in her breasts she pulled the strings of her bodice tight, fastening them at her waist with a fierce knot. She said nothing to Jean-Claude. Then one evening, as she prepared supper, the sickness came upon her so strongly that she barely had time to make it to the porch. When he came after her she was leaning on the splintered rail, doubled up with the force of it.

'Are you all right?'

'I — I am better now,' she murmured. 'Go back in. I shall be there directly.'

He turned away. Then he turned back.

'So you are with child again.'

She was cold, her legs unsteady. She pressed a hand to her clammy forehead, pushing away the tendrils of hair, and looked up at him, her neck trembling slightly beneath the sudden weight of her head. He looked back at her, his arms crossed over his chest. He did not smile.

'I don't know,' she said. 'Maybe.'

'You are late?'

She hesitated. Then she nodded.

'How late?'

'Three weeks. A month perhaps.'

One hand clamped to his jaw, Jean-Claude stared out over the yard. She could hear the rasp of his fingers against his ill-shaved chin.

'And so it begins again.'

Elisabeth leaned into the rough rail of the porch, waiting for the dizziness to pass.

'What?' he demanded. 'You expect me to dance for joy?'

'I — perhaps this time — '

'Why should this time be any different?'

Elisabeth was silent. Beneath her, the weeds glinted with silver threads of bile.

'We have been through enough,' he said. 'I cannot believe you want this any more than I do.'

She felt the clatter of his boots on the porch in the palms of her hands, his warm hand on her shoulder. She did not look up.

'Go to bed,' he said more gently. 'I can get supper in town.'

She let him take her arm, lead her into the house. When he was gone she lay on the bed, her bodice still laced. The sickness was not yet passed. She could feel the oily swirl of it at the base of her throat, the dull ache in her belly. She closed her eyes, feeling the room tip queasily around her, but she could not banish the image of him, the frown between his brows, his eyes sharp with a fear that caused her heart to turn over.

When dusk came the *platille* was streaked with pink like the inside of a shell before it faded to dusty grey and then to black. The room was very dark, though it thrummed with the night chorus of the frogs. Like being swallowed, Elisabeth thought, and unseen in the darkness she wept, the tears sliding into her ears.

Some time later she rose and made her way

unsteadily into the other room. The sickness threatened her but she stretched her neck away from it, breathing carefully and swallowing the curdle in her throat. The supper fire was all but burned out. Elisabeth pushed away the blackened wood, sending up pale spirals of ash, and blew on the dying embers, coaxing a tiny reluctant flame for the tallow lamp.

The wick caught, sending shadows leaping against the wall. In the corner, by the table, was the basket containing the few necessities Guillemette considered indispensable for any midwife. Clean rags, bear grease as lubricant and emollient, flasks of syrup to purge and nourish the newborn infant. And tucked in beside them, in an earthenware jar, the tincture of belladonna to cleanse the womb and bring down a stubborn afterbirth.

Setting the lamp on the table, Elisabeth took a cup from the shelf. Then she squatted down before the basket. The sickness and the shadows ducked and slipped about her and she put one hand to the floor to steady herself. On the table the lamp hissed. Slowly she reached in and took the jar from the basket, cradling it in both hands. The jar was savage-made, its mouth stopped with a bung of soft wood. When she held it to the light, she could see the shallow indentations in the earthenware made by the tips of the savage's fingers and she slid her own fingers into them, feeling the fit of it. She thought of the story Jean-Claude had told her of the savage nation of the Taensas, whose temple had been struck by lightning during a great storm and had immediately burned with great force, reducing their idols to ashes. Making horrible cries and all the while invoking their Great Spirit to descend and extinguish the flames, the savages had seized their children and, strangling them, had cast them one after another into the fire. Ten infants were dead before Jean-Claude and the rest of the expedition were able to restrain them. Afterwards the chief had turned furiously upon the white men.

'What if ten is not enough?' he had demanded. 'Shall you protect us then against the wrath of the Great Spirit?'

The tincture was black with a dark vegetable odour. Elisabeth's hand shook as she poured a measure into the cup and carefully placed the sealed jar back in the basket. Somewhere in the darkness beyond the cabin a dog barked. It was late. Soon Jean-Claude would be home. He would slip into bed beside her, bringing with him the tavern smells of meat and tobacco and cheap brandy, and he would fall asleep and the room would be silent but for their exhalations, as quietly he breathed in her air and she his. Her hands were tight around the cup, her fingers stiff. She swallowed, forcing down the knot in her throat, not troubling to wipe away the tears that spilled from her eyes.

Then, very quickly, she raised the cup to her lips and drank.

That winter, when the birds were silent and the mist-veiled air hung in chill swathes over the canebrakes, the dog died. It died in the night, unexpectedly. In the morning Auguste discovered it curled in its habitual pose, nose under its haunch, but when he tried to rouse it, its body was cold and stiff. He buried it in the forest by a weed-choked bayou where the soil was soft and the worms curled like bruised fingers in its black crumb. He did not mark the place. When Issiokhena gave him deer meat, he shook his head and told her the dog had run away. She said nothing, but the pity in her face made him want to hit her.

When winter was over and the thaw come, Babelon came once more to the Ouma village. When Auguste returned from the fields, he saw the ensign leaning on the palisades, a pipe clamped between his teeth. He smiled, and Auguste smiled too and the tightness in his chest shifted a little. Babelon jerked his head towards the boy's ankles.

'No dog?'

Auguste shook his head.

'I'm sorry,' Babelon said gently, and he put one hand on Auguste's shoulder.

'Yes,' Auguste replied, and he stood very still as the shape of the ensign's hand burned through his shirt and into his skin.

143

That night Babelon showed him a letter he had brought from the commandant. It requested that Auguste accompany him upriver to the villages of other savage tribes north of the Ouma in order to assist in matters of translation.

'Pitiful, I know, but for all that I have lived alongside savages since childhood, I have never mastered their languages.'

'You speak some Mobilian.'

'What I have mastered might be covered quite as well with hand signals. It is strange. I had grown accustomed to that dog.'

Auguste shrugged, scouring his prickling nose with the back of his arm. He was not surprised by Babelon's failure to master other languages. Accustomed to shuffling words like playing cards, the ensign would abhor the tongue-tied awkwardness of ignorance. More than that, he was too much himself, his lines too decisively drawn. He lacked the unformed elasticity of self that expands to accommodate the patterns and peculiarities of another's tongue. More than once he had declared Auguste's fluency manifestly unnatural. If Auguste was damp clay, Babelon was a pot, glazed, fired and finished. He could no more bend himself to a new language than a pot could fold itself in two.

The primary purposes of the expedition were to negotiate with the savages for corn and other foodstuffs and, where possible, to acquire slaves who might profitably be traded with the settlers in Mobile. In addition Auguste assisted in the commerce of those goods that the ensign brought from Mobile on the commandant's

144

private account. These were dealt with separately and the skins taken in their payment stored in a separate pirogue.

Auguste asked no questions. It was his job to translate the words, not to make them. The matter was none of his business. But when Babelon had returned south and he was once more alone among the Ouma, he could not shake the persistent mosquito-whine of suspicion that sang in his ear. It was not the commandant's ethics that troubled him. Auguste was no magistrate and cared little for the law. The Sieur might do what pleased him. It was Babelon's duplicity he feared, the gnawing fear that his unquestioning collaboration was exactly what the ensign had counted upon. It tormented him that Babelon might have seen the weakness in him and seized upon it. He had begun to trust in the possibility that the ensign was his friend.

When the next *coureurs-de-bois* passed through the village, Auguste made sure to ask about the commandant and his trade with the savages. Though their accounts differed in some details, the thrust of the story was always the same. Since the founding of the colony there had been allegations of corruption, rumours that the commandant sold Crown supplies for his own profit. But some years ago there had been an investigation, a most rigorous investigation. Many of the settlers had been required to give evidence. The commandant had been tried before a new commissary despatched for the purpose from France and exonerated in every particular.

Generally it was agreed that this brought to a just conclusion what had been a sorry affair. Even among those who suspected that he still contrived to skim for himself a little of the colony's sparse cream, there was a grudging acceptance that Bienville was at least as good a commandant as any other and likely better. With a force of fewer than one hundred men, he had held the territory firm against the twin perils of savage and Englishman. He might feather his own nest a little, as men were inclined to when the opportunity arose, but his devotion to the colony of Louisiana was beyond reproach.

As for Babelon, he was thought to be a decent fellow. He could hold his liquor and he was not a bore or a killjoy like some of his senior officers. Beyond that nobody knew much about him. He was a man who kept himself to himself, they said. Then, tired of the subject, they ran on with their usual tales as Auguste drank from their proffered flasks of brandy and tried not to hope.

★　★　★

The leaves were black underfoot when Babelon returned to the Ouma village, the end of the season's trading. Babelon stood beside the pirogue, regarding Auguste with a smile twisted up into the corners of his mouth into which he pressed his forefinger and thumb, as though he meant to trap it there.

'I understand you have been conducting something of an investigation.'

'I don't know what you mean.'

146

'Really?'

Auguste kicked at the ground with his toe.

'I needed to be sure,' he muttered.

'And are you?'

'Yes.'

'Yes, sir.'

'Yes, sir.'

The smile escaped Babelon's fingers and carved deep grooves of amusement in his cheeks.

'*Vierge*, Auguste, who would have known you were such a suspicious little bastard? It is good to see you again, my friend.'

Auguste nodded. His ears burned.

'Here, help me with these. And careful with that one. There is something for you in it.'

Auguste frowned.

'I am not a savage to be bribed with favours,' he said sharply. 'I have said yes, have I not?'

Babelon glanced up at him, one eyebrow raised.

'For the love of peace, Auguste, I do not seek to buy your favour,' he said. 'As my friend I trust you give it freely. Go on then. Open it.'

The basket had a lid secured with a leather strap. The boy hesitated. Then he knelt down and unknotted the strap. Inside was a curled ball of grey-white fur.

'You can touch it. It's quite tame.'

Carefully Auguste reached out with one finger. The creature raised its pointed slender face, its pink nose twitching, and stretched. Two little pink hands reached up to take hold of the edge of the basket.

'For me?'

'For you.'

'You brought me an opossum.'

'I thought you Frenchmen called them woodrats.'

'I like the Ouma word better.'

'Well, I know you are interested in animals. You can study it or make a pet of it or eat it if you wish to. It is all the same to me.'

Auguste swallowed but still his throat felt very full.

'I cannot accept it,' he said at last.

'But of course you can. What use do I have for a woodrat? I was tricked into taking it, frankly. It didn't cost me a *sou*.'

Babelon stayed for four days. On the last night they sat in their usual places before the fire, the opossum a warm, dense weight in Auguste's lap. It was a frolicsome creature and much favoured by the savage children. They would be disappointed when he gave it back.

'Shall it be difficult for you to leave here?' Babelon asked when the fire was almost gone.

'Leave?'

'You cannot stay here forever. You are too useful to the commandant.'

Auguste thought of the forest at dawn, when the early sun caught in the spiders' webs, and butterflies hung in the air like coloured thoughts, and he wrapped his arms around his chest, pressing tight against the squeeze of his ribs. *I was born by these waters*, the chief of the Ouma had said to him once, when he was first come. *The trees of the forest are my bones, and the creeks and gullies that run between them bear my blood, which is the blood of my nation*. It seemed a long time ago now, when he was still a child.

'Not difficult,' he said at last. 'I do not belong here.'

'It would be fine to have you in Mobile,' Babelon said. 'The winters are long there and decent companionship rarer than wax candles.'

'You have your wife.'

'Yes. I have my wife.'

They were both silent, staring into the fire.

'I should like to meet your wife. If you do not object.'

'Why on earth should I object? You shall like one another.'

There was another silence. Then Babelon began to laugh.

'What is so funny?'

Babelon shook his head, convulsed with merriment.

'Your face. How could I not have seen it before? The two people in the world of whom I am fondest and both of you have that exact same way of looking at me, the way you look at me at this very moment, Auguste, if you could only see yourself.'

'What way?'

'As if you do not trust me further than you could throw me.' He laughed harder, his arms pressed against his belly. 'Oh, yes. You and Elisabeth shall like one another exceedingly.'

Elisabeth crouched before the fire, blowing on the damp tinder. Even when the wood caught, and the flames licked up towards the blackened kettle, she remained where she was, her arms around her shins. The pains in her belly eased a little when she squatted.

Jean-Claude leaned against the jamb of the door, his head tipped back and his arms crossed over his chest. He might have passed for a man ten years younger, Elisabeth thought, watching him out of the corner of her eye. Most of his fellows in the garrison had begun to sag, their bellies pouching over their breeches, their turkey jowls slack above the knots of their neckcloths. Their faces, besieged for years by a strong sun and stronger liquor, were blotchy and scribbled with red. It shocked Elisabeth to see the indefatigable Jean Alexandre limp down the rue d'Iberville with his stiff-legged old man's gait, or Jeanne Deshays' husband, who always smiled at her as though the effort might undo him, his yellowy eyes like battered coins in their little purses of flesh. It shocked her more to see Jeanne's daughter, a poised and pretty child of almost six. When she looked at Jean-Claude, it was possible to pretend that no time had passed at all.

It was fortunate, perhaps, that they possessed no looking glass. Elisabeth knew that she was hardly the smooth-faced young girl who had first come to Louisiana. Though she had not spread and slackened like the other wives, grey streaked her hair and the skin around her eyes was worn and creased. The old strength was lacking in her. The second infusion of belladonna had taxed her gravely and months later she continued to be crippled by violent cramps. It had been another long winter, not cold so much as relentlessly wet, the low sky bulging and dripping in wet pillows, and several times she had succumbed to fever and to chills upon the stomach. The boy Auguste had brought savage remedies, offering them to her uncomfortably, without looking at her, and she had thanked him, and when he was gone she had poured them away. She had had quite enough of medicine.

She no longer assisted Guillemette le Bras. She had told the midwife that her husband objected to the work and Guillemette had only nodded, jutting her sharp chin. She had not attempted to change Elisabeth's mind. Some time later Elisabeth learned that the midwife had asked Marie Nevette to take her place. The news had come as little surprise and yet it had pained her. The wife of the gunsmith was well liked among the women of the settlement. Besides, she had a child of her own.

Elisabeth stirred the sagamity so that it would not stick to the bottom of the kettle and burn. Beneath the table she could see her trunk, its lock rusted, and the mark on the floor where Guillemette's basket had once been. When she had returned the basket to the midwife, it had contained everything that might be required for a lying-in. Everything, that was, but the tincture of belladonna. Months before, when at last she had been able to rise from her bed unassisted, she had wrapped it in a cloth and taken it outside. The very thought of it in the basket had become unbearable to her.

She had thought she would hurl the jar into the trees. She had imagined it, the dark impact of it in the shadows, the furious cawing and crashing as the birds took flight. But as she stood on the porch, she thought of the jar smashing, the fugitive liquid leaping up to splatter her hands. She thought of its vile fumes rising like wood-smoke, twisting in the air to insinuate them-selves into her mouth, her nose, through the jelly of her eyes and the cracks in her coarsened hands, and the agitation had caused her stomach to turn over so sharply she had thought she might vomit. Half bent with the effort of it, she staggered across the yard to the wood store and, reaching behind the woodpile, she thrust the jar deep into the barrel where once they had hid-den meat. Clattering back the lid, she had tumbled logs over the barrel until it was quite sealed up.

Elisabeth turned back to the pot, forcing the spoon through the thickening mixture. Usually it was her favourite time of day, before breakfast, when the light in the cabin was grey and soft as though filtered through dust and the ease of sleep still hung about them. When the porridge was ready, she lifted it from the fire and carried it to the table. She gripped the handle of the kettle tightly, so that she might not think of the cramps. All those months ago, when at last she had ceased to bleed, she had thought herself drained of it, like a calf hung upside down. She had imagined the tubes of her veins round and empty, like little mouths. Now when her monthlies came, the violence of them shocked and distressed her.

Her husband held his plate out.

'I still cannot judge which catches the truth of him better, a pale-faced redskin or a red-skinned paleface,' Jean-Claude mused, resuming their conversation as she spooned out a steaming helping. 'It seems that he possesses too much of both to be easy with either.'

'He is easy with you.'

'No. He is devoted to me. That is something different.'

'Must he really come tonight? You shall suffer no lack of him after tomorrow.'

'I have already asked him. You shall not mind it when he is here.'

Elisabeth sighed and set down her spoon. The cramps were growing more severe. She longed for her husband to leave so that she might huddle alone beneath the sea-green quilt.

'Admit it,' he said. 'You are fond of the boy.'

'Of course I am.'

'And he is perfectly smitten with you. A love-struck swain.'

'Goodness, what nonsense you do talk!'

Standing up, Elisabeth touched her dry lips with the tip of her tongue and drew in a cautious breath. She took her husband's empty bowl and set her full one inside it.

'But of course he is,' Jean-Claude insisted. 'Do you not see the way he looks at you?'

He fluttered his eyelashes at his wife and she smiled in spite of herself, shaking her head.

'He is only a boy.'

She turned away from him, but he caught her by the waist, pressing his lips to the nape of her neck. She leaned back against him, the bowls held tight against the pain. They had been married many years and it was no longer his habit to kiss her at breakfast. Even in her distress, there was solace in it.

'Of course he is frightened of you too,' Jean-Claude murmured into her hair. 'He is not stupid. But he worships you. He dreams of doing this to you. And this too.'

'No — '

'But of course. He is — what? Fifteen years old? Sixteen? It is likely all he thinks of. As for this,' he murmured, his hands more insistent, 'oh, he would surely die for the chance — '

Elisabeth's stomach cramped and she hunched over, almost dropping the bowls to the floor. Soon the bleeding would start. She forced a smile, twisting out of his embrace, and set the bowls down with a clatter upon the table.

'You should go.' The words stuck to the roof of her mouth. 'It would not do to keep the commandant waiting.'

As if he had not heard her, Jean-Claude lifted Elisabeth into his arms, his mouth hard against hers. The sweat was cold on her brow and at the nape of her neck and little silverfishes darted through the darkness of her closed lids. She thought she might faint. Setting her down on the tumbled quilt, he pushed up her skirts with one hand, fumbling with the other at the buttons of his breeches.

When he lay upon her, his weight on her distended belly caused her to whimper.

'As for this,' he murmured, his breath hot against her neck, 'if I ever catch him dreaming of this, I'm going to break his bloody head.'

★　★　★

By nightfall Elisabeth had begun to bleed. She moved slowly, uncertain of her limbs, and when she stirred the stew the smell of it caught in her throat and made her gag. Her forehead was hot but she shivered. She was starting a fever. She poured water into three cups and set three wooden plates upon the table.

Over the winter Jean-Claude had fallen into the habit of bringing Auguste back for supper four or five nights each week. In the early days, Elisabeth had endeavoured to plead against such regularity, but she had had little success. Auguste was lodged with the locksmith, Le Caën, whose wife had died of yellow fever two years previously. The housekeeping was left to his daughter, a girl of perhaps nine years old, who stared at Auguste as he ate his solitary meal, her mouth blooming buds of blood as she picked the skin from her chapped lips. It was, Jean-Claude insisted, uncongenial and, desirous to please him, Elisabeth had relented. To her considerable surprise, she had grown not only accustomed to the boy but fond of him.

It was not just Auguste's manifest devotion to her husband that softened her towards him, nor was it the comical little woodrat he called

Ponola, the savage word for cotton fluff, that he sometimes brought with him to amuse her. It was the quiet intensity of him. He put her in mind of the savage women who came to trade with the French women on market day. He had the savage's way of listening with his body as well as his ears, the savage's habits of stillness and moderation. He did not swallow all the air in the room or set himself between them as the other men did, demanding the wholesale transfer of Elisabeth's consideration to their own petty complaints and preoccupations. It was not that he was silent, though he spoke as he ate, frugally and with care, but that, unlike the rest of them, he did not wish to silence them. They were not required to act out an approved style of marriage before Auguste.

Elisabeth wondered if he had had a mother among the Ouma. He did not say so, though he told her that his own father had died when Auguste was no more than an infant. His mother had married again, a porter at the shipyard. He had been a rough man and quick to anger. His mother had been frightened of him. She had not been a fierce woman like Elisabeth, he had said once, and Elisabeth had laughed, startled by the remark. He wished she had been, he added awkwardly. Perhaps if she had been fierce they might have been happy. As Elisabeth and Jean-Claude were happy.

Elisabeth had thanked him then and turned away, covering her face with her hands. For, if it was true that they were happy, it was true too that they were at their happiest when Auguste was with them. He was the looking glass in which they could admire themselves. When Auguste was there, Jean-Claude was at his most charming and affectionate, alternately teasing her and declaring her perfections, and she in her turn was blithe and wry as he liked her, rolling her eyes at Auguste in rueful disbelief. After supper they would sit before the fire, Elisabeth with her mending on her lap, and sometimes the men would talk and sometimes they would sit in easy silence, Auguste watching them covertly, from his place by the door, as Jean-Claude reached out and quietly covered her hand with his.

It was not so always when they were alone. Then the spitting fire and the silence had a way of drying out the air between them, until it cracked and split and Jean-Claude uncrossed his restless legs to pace around the cabin. She had to force her attention then to her work so that she might not be tempted to beg of him what it was that vexed him so. The question only ever served to vex him further.

★ ★ ★

It still stirred her, the click of the door latch lifting, the murmur of his voice beyond the wooden door. There was desire in it, even after all this time there was desire, mixed in with anxiety and a straining kind of hope that all would be well. On evenings like this one, when she was sick and brittle and her need for him was stronger than her resolve, it took considerable

157

effort to remain where she was and greet him with the dry amusement he loved in her.

'So, what news today?' Elisabeth asked with a smile as the two men came into the cabin. 'Who accuses whom of what?'

The effort of speaking made her giddy. She bent over the stew kettle, gripping the spoon so tightly that her knuckles showed white. Dropping his boots, Jean-Claude padded across the room in his darned stockings, sliding his hands around her waist. Auguste looked away.

'That looks good,' Jean-Claude murmured.

He was in a good temper. Dizzily she closed her eyes and leaned against him.

'The stew or the wife?'

'Sweet flesh both.'

'If you were fool enough to attempt a stew with meat as old as mine you would be chewing it till morning.'

'That seems hardly a matter for complaint.'

Elisabeth laughed shakily and pushed him away.

'Auguste, please forgive my husband's nonsense. I am glad you could come.'

'I fear I come too often, Madame.'

Elisabeth had given up protesting that he address her by her name. Her insistence discomfited him and did nothing to change his habits.

'Your last decent meal for some weeks,' she said instead, spooning out stew and sagamity. The smell of it sickened her. 'Come. You should make the most of it.'

Auguste took the plate she held out to him.

158

His fingers grazed hers and he took an abrupt step backwards, spilling a little gravy on the floor.

'I — I am sorry. How clumsy I am.'

'We are all clumsy around Elisabeth,' Jean-Claude said.

Rolling her eyes at Auguste, Elisabeth handed a heaped plate to her husband and smeared some gravy over another for herself.

'Don't listen to him,' she said. 'Let us eat.'

They sat at the table, Jean-Claude at the head with Elisabeth and Auguste on either side of him, as was their habit. Elisabeth watched her husband as he spooned up the food, his legs braced and his eyes on his plate. Tomorrow he would be gone again.

'You are not hungry?' Auguste asked Elisabeth. 'You look pale.'

'I tasted the stew too much while I was cooking,' Elisabeth lied. 'It has spoiled my appetite.'

She sipped a little water to steady her stomach, cradling the cup in both hands. She could feel the heat of Auguste's gaze on her hot face.

'So,' she said. 'What news from town?'

'I thought that was a wife's duty,' Jean-Claude replied, his mouth full. 'To expose the confidential business of others.'

'You forget that nobody tells me anything.'

'True. And you forget that you have never been the least interested in anything that they had to say.'

Auguste smiled. He waited as Jean-Claude

lifted his spoon again and began once more to eat.

'I have news,' he said then. 'I have acquired a cabin.'

'But that is wonderful, Auguste,' Elisabeth replied, touching her tongue to her lips. She had the drifting sense that she might faint. 'Where?'

'Rue Condé Dugné is the second cabin in New Mobile, at the corner of rue de Pontchartrain. It is not large but it has a fine garden. You would like it, Madame.'

'I'm sure I would.'

'Until it's infested with all your various grotesqueries,' Jean-Claude observed, his mouth full. 'Fortunately for me, Elisabeth prefers her vegetables edible. Perhaps your wife will too. A man with a house must find himself a wife.'

Auguste smiled.

'Thank you, but I shall settle for a housekeeper.'

'Ah, so like our friend the merchant you favour *le marriage naturel*? How long I wonder before she is keeping house for a litter of little *mestifs*?'

Mestif was the settler word for children of mixed blood. Elisabeth shook her head at her husband.

'Leave the boy be,' she said gently. 'You embarrass him.'

'Nonsense. Auguste is a man of the world. He knows better than to hold out for a wife when the French girls that fetch up here are unfailingly both plain and disagreeable. Do not make that face at me. You know it as well as I.'

160

Elisabeth closed her eyes, pressing her hands down on the table as a wave of nausea rolled through her.

'Madame?' Auguste's voice seemed to come from a long way away.

'She sulks because she knows I am right. If you are finished, Auguste, we should be going. They will be expecting us.'

'Perhaps you should stay here with your wife,' Auguste murmured. 'See how white she is.'

'You spend too much time with savages. French women are all this colour.'

Auguste did not laugh. He waited, his hands upon the back of his chair. Under the table Elisabeth could see one of his big toes poking through a hole in his stocking. The suck of her sickness was powerful inside her. She raised her head a little, setting her stomach to pitching.

'Go,' she urged. 'Please. I am a little tired, that is all.'

Auguste hesitated. Then he walked away. She heard the creak of leather as he slid his feet into his boots, felt the flare of sharp night air against her neck as they opened the door and slammed it shut behind them. Dragging herself to standing, she pressed her nose against the *platille* that covered the window, steadied a little by the chill on her hot face.

It must have been the breeze that made the men's voices sound so close.

'It's true. But I see Alexandre with his boy, who is the very spit of him and so strong and vital, and of course I envy him. Who would not? Without sons to bear him forward, a man's life is so fragile somehow. So fleeting.'

'It is not too late. Perhaps this time — ?'

'No. If indeed she is with child, she will lose it. She always does.'

Auguste murmured something in reply but the words vanished, swallowed into the swamp of the starless night. Elisabeth's skin was prickly with gooseflesh. She clutched her arms about herself, tasting in her mouth the curdled-milk tang of dread. Her legs shook as a sudden spike of sickness pushed up into her throat. Turning, she vomited violently into the crock of sagamity.

Afterwards, she covered the pot and washed her face with water. Then she sat before the fire, her hands folded in her lap. She was still sitting there when he returned. The tallow had burned out and the fire too, though the dying embers glowed red through the crust of ash. He was drunk and, from the force with which he shouldered open the door, in ill humour. He swore as he struggled with his boots, dropping them noisily before turning towards bed. He was almost upon her when he saw her, her face *platille*-pale in the darkness, and the shock of it caused him to stumble.

'*Sacrement!*' he cried out angrily. 'Lurking like a thief in the pitch darkness, what is wrong with you?'

She did not flinch. She looked up at him and the grief and the shock in her caught, exploding in a great blaze of fury.

'With me? What is wrong with me?'

'What the devil — ?'

'You told me you did not want children. You

162

said so. You said we — that I was all you wanted.'

She was on her feet now, her fists clenched before her, her eyes coal-bright. Jean-Claude's hands fell to his sides. He blinked, steadying himself on the back of a chair.

'It has happened again, hasn't it?'

'It always happens.'

'Oh, I know.'

'It happens because it is what you wanted,' she shouted. 'What you have decided for us.'

'What I have decided? For God's sake, Elisabeth, what the devil has it to do with me?'

'It has everything to do with you. It was what you wanted. I didn't want — I never wanted — I —'

She sagged suddenly, the fire all burned out.

'It was for you,' she whispered, and the ash drifted in her, ice-cold. 'I did it for you.'

Jean-Claude stared at her, his eyes hard. Then he passed his hands over his face.

'Go to bed, Elisabeth.'

'It was for you.'

'*Vierge*, Elisabeth — '

'When I told you I was with child you said — you said you did not want it. You said that we could neither of us endure it.'

He stared at her then and a muscle jumped in his cheek. In the gloom Elisabeth's lips were grey-blue.

'You think this is my fault? My fault that you cannot keep a child in your belly?'

Elisabeth swallowed. She was empty, numb. She felt nothing. She clenched her fists tighter, trying to hold onto the numbness, the nothing.

She could feel herself falling.

'It was what you wanted,' she said again, her voice cracking, and the crack split her in two, like a split log, all the way through.

'Enough, for God's sake! You are gone mad.'

She had never seen him so angry. When he slammed the door she did not move. She knew that if she moved she would awaken. She would feel. She did not think to weep and yet the tears fell, running unchecked down her face. She stood quite still as the hollowness inside her stretched wider than the bones that contained it.

He came to bed much later, bringing with him the smell of brandy and stale sweat. At some time in the night he reached for her. His hands and his breath were hot against her skin, his need urgent and quickly sated.

'That's better,' he murmured afterwards and she squeezed her eyes tight shut, so that she might not weep again.

Soon afterwards he began to snore. She lay awake until the *platille* at the window greyed and the clatter of the birds stirred the sun to rising. Then she must have fallen asleep. When she woke, the window was bright with low-slanting sun and he was gone.

For Auguste Mobile was to prove a kind of heaven. He had not grieved to leave the nation of the Ouma, just as he had not grieved to leave his mother in La Rochelle. He belonged in neither place. In the savage village as in the port of his birth, he had chafed against the structured hierarchies into which he had been required to fit, never finding the ease or the fearlessness required for friendship. He had become accustomed to the sense of wrongness that rested like a stone on his chest. He still did not know quite how it was that it flavoured his voice or his breath or some other vital part of him with the unmistakable stink of otherness, but he knew that it did and he had long since ceased to fight against it. It was as much a part of himself as his eyes or the scar on his arm.

With Babelon and Elisabeth it was different. There was a space for him alongside them and its shape was his shape. There was no trick to it. He breathed out and his breath matched the air around him. It was so ordinary that at first he hardly trusted it. He was hesitant, discomfited by the proximity of them and shy of their easy intimacy. He was dismayed by the blatancy of his presence in their house, like a clumsy spinster aunt. When he ate with them, he excused himself early so that they might resume the proper business of being two.

He did not know exactly how it had changed, only that it did, so that by the time the spring came he was a part of them and they of him. It did not go unnoticed. A few of the townspeople remarked upon it. Even the locksmith Le Caën, a man of few words, was heard to jest about the woman with two husbands, the words sloshing about in his mouth in a swill of Burelle's home-brewed liquor. Beside him his daughter bent her head silently over the opossum, her chapped lips moving, her pressed-together brows low over her fierce black eyes.

Then it was spring. On their last evening together, as they prepared to depart for the first expedition of the year, Auguste watched Elisabeth's white face and he was filled with a sudden and terrible dread that their winter bonds, once unknotted, might never again be rebound. Unable to imagine how the two of them would reach each other across the lack of her, he embarked upon the journey with a heavy heart, unleavened by the play of light upon the water, the bursting green newness of the freshly awakened forest. To his surprise, he missed the opossum, which he had left in the care of the locksmith's daughter. At night the blanket over his feet was cold and insubstantial.

Babelon too began the expedition in foul humour. Though he said little, it was clear that he and Bienville had quarrelled. At the village of the Little Tomeh, which was the first of their destinations, he bid the savage guide to watch over the pirogue containing the commandant's private goods but not, as was usual, to unload it.

166

'We shall return it to him just as it is,' he said with a grim smile. 'Let us see how he likes that.'

And later, when Auguste made imprudent mention of the commandant, his face darkened.

'That miserly bastard would have all of Louisiana for his own estate. Well, let me tell you, I for one am no dumb slave.'

But Babelon was not possessed of the stolidity of character that allows a man to fix obstinately upon ill temper. As the Mobile River rolled the leagues away from beneath them, he could not subdue his delight in being free of the constraints of the settlement. It seemed to Auguste that as they made their way towards the nation of the Talimali, Babelon grew taller, his rising spirits thickening his muscles and pressing the beard from his chin.

The Talimali were refugees of the Apalache nation, Catholics who had fled their villages in the Spanish east to escape attack by bands of Alabama and Apalachicola raiders in the pay of the English. They spoke a strange tongue that was part savage, part Spanish, and so different from their neighbours that Auguste was required to spend much time among the women and children of the village, inducing them with small gifts to talk with him and assist him in his learning. They did so willingly. It was Bienville who had granted them land on the Mobile River on which to settle, and they were grateful.

When some days later they came to the village of the Mouvill, whose language resembled that of the Chickasaw, Auguste did the same. After that, in each new nation, it was his habit to squat

167

in a place where he might draw in the earth as he talked. In each place a circle of children would quickly gather around him, pointing at his pictures and shrieking with mirth at his mistakes. The entertainment was always short-lived. Auguste's stiff tongue would soften, his shoulders would drop, and, as their language spread and stretched within him, the children would return to their games and their chores, only occasionally remembering to take notice of the stranger in their midst.

'How do you remember it all?' Babelon asked him late one night. The fire was almost burned out and he kicked at it to summon a flame. Auguste shrugged. 'No, really. How do you hold all that nonsense in your head?'

Auguste was silent, considering the question.

'I suppose it's like places,' he said at last. 'My mother's room in La Rochelle, say, or the hut at the Ouma. Or your own cottage. When you are away from it, you have to remember, to think, yes, the oak chest is there, the table there. You wonder, is it the right window where the *platille* is coming away in the corner or the left? But when you are there you do not have to remember. You know it without thinking. Of course it is the right-hand window where the nail is missing. There it is, right in front of you.'

'Nails missing?' Babelon said drily. 'In my house? I think perhaps you are not acquainted with my wife.'

Auguste smiled and said nothing. Except that it is your house I am thinking of, he thought. The nail is missing and the flap of loose *platille* is

168

marked with a small smudge of orange rust. The oak chest has a chip in its lid the shape of a pumpkin seed and the faded blue cloth on the table, embroidered at the hem with paler blue silk, is the same colour as her eyes. There is a basket of woven palmetto on the table that she sometimes fills with fruit. She likes plums best, particularly the dark purple ones with the golden flesh. The top of the table is marked with knife cuts and, on the corner closest to the fireplace, there is a black half-circle where a hot kettle has scorched it. She places her hand over the mark sometimes, palm flat, when she is thinking, and spreads her fingers. She has a pattern of freckles on the back of her right hand like the five on a die.

The fire sighed, sinking into soft ash.

'It must be hard to leave her,' Auguste murmured.

'I have grown accustomed to it.'

'But when she is in poor health — ?'

Babelon raised an eyebrow.

'I have grown accustomed to that too.'

'Of course the climate is not wholesome.'

'The climate suited her well enough once.'

The two men were silent, staring into the dying fire.

'Time is not kind to women,' Babelon observed at last. 'As their skin slackens it seems that their nerve-strings do too. When I first met Elisabeth nothing daunted her. She was so strong, so — brave.'

'Fierce.'

'Fierce, yes.' Babelon smiled. 'You should have

169

seen her, so indignant over this or that.' The smile faded. 'She is not fierce any more.'

'She has been ill.'

'Unceasingly.'

Auguste thought of Elisabeth's ashen face, the purple shadows smudging her brown eyes, the tightening around the corners of her generous mouth and across her knuckles as she bit down on the pain. She always fought fiercely against the pain.

'It must fatigue her,' he murmured.

Babelon sighed, kicking out at the fire with his heel so that sparks rose in a red arc against the dark night.

'Believe me,' he said. 'It fatigues us both.'

★ ★ ★

They remained in each village for several days before continuing north to the great nation of the Choctaws. Much of the land remained uninhabited, uncleared. As the river rolled out behind them, the sharp corners of Elisabeth's absence softened and Auguste found himself adapting to the shape of the traveller's life, the slap of the paddles, the tumble of the water, the shriek and stretch of the forest, the sharp, strong smell of men one behind the other in the hollowed-out intimacy of a small pirogue or beneath makeshift tents of bent reed canes covered in cloth, which the French called *baires*. As they made their way from the low delta through the plains and almost as far as the mountains of upper Louisiana, Auguste found his curiosity inflamed by the innumerable species of plants and insects that flourished there. Many were unfamiliar to him. He gathered those specimens that caught his eye, took cuttings and seeds for his garden at rue Condé. In the evenings, after camp was struck, he bent over them, studying their singularities and sketching them in the dust to set them more firmly in his memory.

'For the love of God,' Babelon protested one evening. 'Anyone would think you had never seen a leaf before.'

'This is no ordinary leaf,' Auguste replied, holding up the flower in his hand. 'Look here. See how it grows upward, curling around to make a kind of hollow belly? When insects enter them this flap here lowers like a lid so that it cannot escape.'

'Why does it wish to trap insects?'

'It eats them.'

'A carnivorous plant?'

'Yes. The Ouma consider it a powerful remedy against fever. A love potion too.'

Babelon peered more closely at the plant.

'Intriguing.'

Later the ensign rummaged in his pack and brought out a small book tied around with a strip of leather into which was tucked a stub of pencil.

'Here,' he said, proffering them to Auguste. 'You should keep a proper record.'

Auguste shook his head awkwardly. Paper was scarce and he had never learned to use a pencil.

'I should only spoil it.'

171

'Better you than I,' Babelon answered and he jammed the book in the younger man's pocket. Auguste kept it there for days, feeling the nudge of it against his thigh as he squatted over his dust pictures. But when at last he opened it and summoned the pencil in his fingers, he found it surprisingly obliging and accurate.

'These are good,' Babelon observed some days later, flicking through the pages.

'I have used too many pages. Here, please. Take it back.'

But Babelon would not.

★　★　★

When at last they gained the first village of the Choctaw nation, they received troubling news. Some weeks previously, two Englishmen, envoys of the governor in Carolina, had visited a Chickasaw village only a few leagues from their far border with the Choctaw. They had brought eight packhorses loaded with merchandise and stayed in the village for eight days. During that time they had repeatedly impressed upon the Chickasaw chiefs that a friendship with the English was essential to that nation's prosperity. To secure that friendship they offered not only gifts but also advantageous trading terms.

Auguste let the silence settle. Then very quietly he asked the chief how it was that he knew such things.

'The Chickasaw have long been our adversaries,' the chief replied. 'The prudent warrior knows the business of his enemies at least as well as his own.'

'And what answer did the Chickasaw chiefs give the Englishmen?' Auguste asked.

The chief shook his head. He did not know. He knew only that the envoys had brought guns and gunpowder to the Chickasaw and that the Chickasaw chiefs had not refused them. In addition, the English had asked permission to return, and this too the Chickasaw chiefs had not refused.

Auguste nodded. Then he turned to Babelon and translated what the chief had said.

'Those bastards.' Babelon frowned, his fingers drumming on his thighs. 'Those slippery savage bastards.'

'Our people have made many promises to the Chickasaw that we have not honoured,' Auguste murmured. 'More presents, trade advantages, a fort in their province. So far they have received none of them.'

'But they smoked the *calumet* with us, did they not, accepted the gifts we gave them? So they declared their allegiance to us, to the French Crown.'

'And when we smoke the *calumet* with the Choctaw, we bind ourselves in allegiance to their neighbour, who is also their oldest and most powerful enemy. It is to be expected that the Chickasaw keep an open door to Carolina. Their eastern boundary is very susceptible to English attack.'

'So they betray us.'

'Not yet. But it is by no means improbable.'

The Choctaw chief, who had remained silent, spoke then to Auguste in his tongue. His face was grave.

'What does he say?' Babelon demanded impatiently.

'He suggests we go directly to the Chickasaw and declare our friendship to them. He believes that they are still anxious to keep faith with us, but we must offer them caresses and assure them of our steadfastness.'

Babelon shook his head.

'That is impossible. We are expected back in Mobile. There is business there that cannot wait.'

'Surely the commandant — '

'What the devil has the commandant to do with this?'

Auguste hesitated.

'I have translated poorly,' he said at last. 'The chief is adamant. If we do not go there presently, we risk our friendship with his nation as well as with the Chickasaw.'

'Well, then we must take that risk,' Babelon retorted. 'The Chickasaw are not our only allies in this godforsaken place.'

He glared at Auguste, who flinched and looked down at the ground. The chief of the Choctaw observed them and said nothing. Babelon sighed.

'Does it not strike you as questionable, how much the honoured chief knows of his enemy's business?' he said more gently. 'If the English have made approaches to the Chickasaw, then it is likely they have come here also. Who is to say that this is not a trap, an ambush?'

174

'The chief is a man of honour.'

'Honour? Auguste, he is a savage. Like all the other savages we have purchased his allegiance with gifts, with guns. Perhaps the English offer better terms. No. Tell the chief that we shall go to the Chickasaw but that first we must warn the commandant. Bienville knows this game of old. If there is something rotten here then he will smell it.'

Auguste hesitated. Then he did as he was bid. He chose his words carefully. The chief frowned. Then he nodded.

'You are quite certain?' Auguste asked when darkness had fallen and the dancing was begun. 'That we are to return to Mobile?'

'And from there to the Mississippi. The Natchez expect me.'

'But — '

'Auguste, do not be naive. Can you not see that this is exactly what the English want? To distract us from the business of trading, of securing supplies for the settlement, until we are too weak to withstand their assault?'

Babelon's face was shiny and in his eyes Auguste saw only the flames of the cane torches, leaping yellow in their curved glass shades.

'The Choctaw would not betray us,' Auguste said quietly. 'They have pledged their allegiance most solemnly.'

'Their solemnity is hardly at issue. Whether the Choctaw are in the pay of English masters or whether they are only their dupes, the end is the same. They send us to the Chickasaw and, in all likelihood, to a trap. We lose nothing by caution.'

175

Auguste was silent.

'With the river in flow, it should take us no more than a matter of days to reach Mobile. Then, well, it is a question for the commandant. Let him decide.'

The current was swift and, as Babelon had predicted, they were returned to Mobile within the week. From the river they went directly to meet with the commandant. Auguste told Bienville what he knew, then, as instructed, he waited outside as the commandant conferred with Babelon. When the two men emerged, they informed Auguste that he was to return to the Choctaw village with a guide and require of the Choctaw chief that he attend the commandant in Mobile at his earliest convenience. As for Babelon, he would travel directly to the Mississippi so that the business interests of the settlement might not be compromised.

Auguste accepted the commandant's orders. When they had been dismissed, the two men walked slowly back towards the dock. It was raining, a fine drizzle that clung to their coats.

'A drink at Burelle's?' Babelon asked.

Auguste shook his head.

'You must be impatient to see your wife.'

'She will look even better after another drink. So will the woodrat, come to that.'

The thought of the opossum gave Auguste a tiny squeeze of pleasure. At the corner of rue Condé, he stopped and bid his friend farewell.

'Godspeed,' he said. 'Go safely.'

'And you, sir. And you.'

Auguste turned away.

'Just one thing more,' Babelon called after him. 'Any chance of having that quire I loaned you? I may be required to keep a log of things. You know.'

Auguste fingered the familiar square of the book in his pocket. In the time that he had had it, the stuff of his coat had grown corners to accommodate it.

'Of course,' he said, and handed it reluctantly to Babelon, who slid it into his own pocket. 'The drawings . . . I am sorry if I have used too many pages.'

'On the contrary,' Babelon protested. 'With your pretty illustrations to enliven them, perhaps even business accounts may prove tolerable.'

When Babelon had gone Auguste lingered in the street, biting at his thumbnail. Then he turned and walked slowly towards the rue de Tonti. He tried to fix his thoughts upon anticipation, of the opossum who would scramble onto his shoulder and nip gently at his ear, of the tulip tree in his garden that would be just coming into flower, but they slid away from him and he thought instead of the commandant, who, before dismissing Auguste, had poured wine for the three of them and raised his glass.

'To effective espionage,' he had said, tossing back a gulp. He wore no neckcloth and his shirt was open, revealing the twined mass of serpents inked upon his chest. The wine had been sour. Later, when the bottle was empty, Bienville had shaken his head.

'Surely the chief of the Chickasaw is not such a fool as the Choctaw would have us believe.

Does he not know how the perfidious English whistle down his kind like turkeys from a tree? And for what? For a few muskets? More favourable terms of trading? Do not mistake me, I am only too familiar with the imperatives of commerce. But the English? The English worship profit as the savage worships the sun, not for the warmth of it on his back, but because without it day would never come. Treachery runs in their veins. There is nothing, I swear it, not kinsman nor country nor the kingdom of God Himself, that an Englishman would not sell at the right price.'

Every month of that dreary winter began with the faint fresh breath of hope and ended in cramps and clotted blood. Then it was spring again. Jean-Claude went north.

When the rains came, the river burst its banks anew and the houses in the lower part of town were once more flooded. The residents were obliged to rely on their pirogues to get about town and Elisabeth made room for the family of Renée Gilbert, whose home was several feet under water. Confined to the cabin the two women waited, the children peevish and fidgety about them. Elisabeth bitterly begrudged the violation of her solitude. She was irritated by Renée and exasperated by the children, whom she found both tedious and exhausting. When the smallest one overturned a pitcher of milk, she struck him. Renée's affronted silence lasted for days.

The rains fell without ceasing. In its mud hole the fort rotted from the foundations up, its wooden bastions crumbling beneath the weight of its cannon. Bienville had brokered an uneasy alliance between the Choctaw and the Chickasaw in which both nations pledged their friendship to the French, and the chiefs of the two nations had both spent some part of the winter in Mobile. It did not prevent the English from stirring up trouble. If they succeeded in provoking the Chickasaw to attack, the town would have precious little hope of holding out against them.

Then, in a violent storm that lasted three days, the half-built church was flooded, the altar and makeshift pews smashed to sticks, and the single field of Indian corn that the commandant had prevailed upon the settlers to plant was destroyed. Worst of all, the warehouse was ravaged. There had been no ships from France since the *Aigle*, and even before the rains goods of every kind had been in perilously short supply. By the time the tempest blew itself out, there was almost nothing left.

Miserable, impoverished and fearful, the townspeople complained bitterly. The locksmith Le Caën, with several other tradesmen, led a delegation to the commandant to persuade him to move the town to the mouth of the river. There was, they declared angrily, no worse possible place for a settlement than this sodden swamp in the middle of the woods.

Bienville listened to their exhortations and sent them away.

The rains were still falling when Jean-Claude's expedition returned with food and with slaves. There was not enough of either. The expedition remained in the town for three days while their cargo was recorded and stored in makeshift huts erected in the garrison high on the bluff, and the slaves were quickly sold to those settlers of the town who could afford them. Then, once again, Jean-Claude and his guides ventured north.

And still the rains did not cease. As the floods

rose, tongues soured and rumours bobbed like logs on the surface of the scummy water. Renée declared bitterly that the commandant was a pig, too proud and too stubborn to admit the mistake made by his brother in situating the town in a swamp. Others went further. Some said that Bienville kept the settlement in Mobile solely because it was a good distance from the harbour at Massacre Island and the convoluted business of transporting cargo between the two made it easier for his agents to abscond with stolen goods; others claimed that he invented the threat of an English ambush simply to divert attention from his own incompetence. But though there were threats of reports to the Minister of the Marine and even of formal complaints to the King, nothing was done. No ships came and there was no paper for letters. For all the notice paid to them by the mother country, the drowned lands of Louisiana might have been sluiced from the surface of the earth.

It was almost June when the skies cleared and the waters slunk back to their summer positions on the margins of the settlement. Renée and her family returned to their home and made what repairs they could manage. During the sweltering months of summer, a crew of twenty slick-skinned Apalache natives toiled against the white-hot sky, cutting and dressing timbers for a large stockade and rebuilding the bastions that supported the cannon. That summer six soldiers died from the fever.

The garrison for all of Louisiana now numbered fewer than sixty men.

For most of that summer, Jean-Claude was away from Mobile. In their two lines in the cabin on rue d'Iberville the savage children chanted French words, making music from everyday phrases. One day, when they were gone, Elisabeth pulled her trunk from its place under the bed. The leather was mildewed, the lock rusted shut. She ran her fingers over its rough mouth. Then she pushed it back out of sight. The commandant did not approve of teaching savages to read or write. He thought book learning among slaves not only unnecessary but hazardous. But when the children came for their lesson two days later, she waited as they chorused their greetings and then she held up her hand.

'Today,' she said, 'I have a different lesson for you.'

The children waited. Elisabeth took a breath. Then she sat before them, her hands in her lap, and she began to tell them the tale of the *Odyssey*. She spoke of Telemachus, whose father was missing, and of his mother Penelope, surrounded by young men who endeavoured to persuade her to accept her husband's disappearance and to marry one of them. The story came awkwardly at first, its details half forgotten, but as she continued Elisabeth found that Homer's verses returned to settle on her tongue, their song familiar in her mouth. The children gazed at her, their eyes wide. She knew they did not understand her. When she was finished they were silent. Then, shyly, they filed away, leaving Elisabeth sitting alone in the cabin. She sat there for a long time as the darkness settled about her and the words hummed inside her like bees.

The next time she taught them words that would be useful in the fields: hoe, till, machete.

It was almost August when Jean-Claude returned. He was burned dark by the sun, the beard mossy on his chin. It was only when she hastened to embrace him that she saw the slave. Bare-headed, with long black hair that fell almost to her knees, she waited in the lane, her eyes set demurely upon the ground. She wore a long white linen dress of mulberry bark that skimmed her hips and her high, round breasts, and the skin on her face and arms was smooth and coppery-brown. She was very young.

Elisabeth's stomach fell away.

'You're back,' she said.

'So many weeks gone and that is all the welcome I get?'

Elisabeth raised herself on tiptoes and, putting her arms around her husband's neck, kissed him on the mouth. As he held her in a close embrace, she opened her eyes and looked over his shoulder. The savage girl stared at her without blinking. Her eyes were almost black, her brow high and strong. She was very still.

'Welcome home,' Elisabeth murmured and, tugging his hand, she pulled him into the house. Perhaps, she thought, if she slammed the door hard enough, when she opened it again the savage girl would have gone. 'It was a profitable expedition?'

'For Sieur de Bienville certainly.' He flung himself into a hard chair, tipping backwards. 'Again. Thirty able-bodied slaves and every *sou* they raise goes into his coffers.'

'Not exactly his, surely?'

'Then you do not know Sieur de Bienville.'

The door stood open. In the frame of it the girl stood like a wraith, her white dress bright as a candle-shade against the afternoon sun, the shape of her body dark and clear.

'Jean-Claude?' Elisabeth swallowed. He frowned, then turned to look.

'Ah.'

He clicked his fingers at the girl, motioning at her to enter. As she walked, her body rippled inside the linen dress, slippery shadows that defied the demureness of her attitude. She stopped before Elisabeth. She smelled of bear oil and warm skin, a musky, carnal odour. Quickly Elisabeth covered her face with her hands, inhaling the familiar scent of her own fingers.

'Did I say thirty slaves?' he said blandly. 'Better make that thirty-one.'

'You bought a slave? But I thought — '

'Who said anything about buying? She was — a gift.'

'A gift?'

'A little something for my trouble.'

'But we agreed — '

'No. You agreed. It is become absurd, Elisabeth, this caprice of yours. Every other household in the town, if they are not paupers, has some manner of slave.'

'So? Since when did we give a fig for anyone else?'

'I give a fig for affectation. And it is become an affectation, this nonsensical obstinacy of yours. She will do the heavy work, water, wood, cleaning. You will be free to teach your savage pupils whatever nonsense it is you teach them, and for whatever else you choose besides.' He frowned at her impatiently. 'What possible reason can you have for refusing her?'

★   ★   ★

The girl's name was Okatomih. Though she was dressed in the costume of the Natchez, she was not a Natchez herself but of the Yasoux nation, whom the Natchez had raided some months before. Elisabeth knew nothing more of her than that. Okatomih knew no French and Elisabeth nothing of the savage tongues of the north. The few words she knew were either Pascagoula, picked up from the savage women who traded their wares at the market, or Alibamon, which was the commonest tongue among the slaves, but the girl only shrugged at her, her face blank. Elisabeth was obliged to instruct her in mime, pointing and performing the required actions. The slave observed Elisabeth's efforts with her unblinking black eyes and said nothing. It filled Elisabeth with a fury at the same time murderous and hopelessly impotent. She longed for the girl to demonstrate her impudence, to fail in her duties, so that she might punish her.

185

In this, as in everything else, the slave confounded her. She wore her hair as Elisabeth instructed, in a tight braid, and her face in an expression that was not so much defiant as defiantly blank. She kept herself and the kitchen hut reasonably clean. She was always early to rise, folding her deerskin and placing it on a shelf beside the salt crock. She pounded the corn and washed the pots and household linens. She swept the floors. There was always flour in the flour barrel and wood in the wood store. Unlike Elisabeth, she was also an accomplished cook and even brewed a delicately flavoured savage liquor that resembled French beer. Elisabeth had only to serve the meal and afterwards set the dirty dishes outside the door. When the master was at home, the slave was forbidden from entering the cabin. On this last point Elisabeth was perfectly clear.

As for Jean-Claude, he appeared well satisfied with the arrangement. He showed not the slightest interest in the girl herself except on occasion to remark upon the flavour of a particular dish. It was the women of the settlement who concerned themselves with her diligence. In the weeks after Okatomih's arrival, several of them called upon Elisabeth to inspect her and to advise upon the principles of slave management. Most of the settlement's slaves were from the nation of the Chetimacha, with whom the French had long been enemies, and their shortcomings were only too well understood. The women studied the girl with narrowed eyes, unwilling to concede that

Elisabeth might have made the better bargain.

'Well, I suppose she looks strong,' Renée Gilbert remarked. 'The poor sort have an infuriating habit of wasting away.'

'And the lively ones of making a run for it,' Perrine Roussel warned, waggling a finger. 'You will need to be vigilant. Whip her seldom but watch her like a hawk.'

In this, at least, Elisabeth was obedient. However resolutely she determined to disregard the slave, her gaze was drawn again and again to the high smooth brow, the slanting eyes, the pulled-back hair like a cap of black silk with its swinging tassel braid, the mesmerising pass of the broom back and forth across the floor, the press of her fresh, ripe flesh against the linen of her dress.

In all the years of their marriage, Jean-Claude had never been so present in the cabin as he was at those times. When the slave's hands encircled a pot, her brown fingers splayed, when the tip of her tongue dampened the corners of her mouth, when the perspiration gleamed on her brow, he was there. He was the pot, the mouth, the brow, the broom that moved in her hands with breathless languor. The girl moved and he moved with her, darkening her shadow, thickening her hair, seasoning her breath with his favoured tobacco. When she bent and her heavy braid fell forward over her shoulder, it was his shadow hands that brushed it aside, his shadow lips that pressed themselves greedily against the stretch of her exposed neck. When she raised the spoon to her mouth, testing the flavour of the stew, it was

187

his flesh she tasted, his juice she wiped from her chin. The lucidity of the images, and their unreasonableness, tormented Elisabeth.

She was short-tempered with the savage children, rebuking them sharply for slips of gender or of pronunciation. They grew wary of her. Then, one day, on the boys' side of the cabin, there was a space in the line like a missing tooth. One of the older boys had not come. When she demanded of the others why he was not there, they did not answer. The smallest girl opened her mouth but the girl beside her elbowed her hard and she blinked and pressed her lips into a line. The lesson passed slowly. When it was over the children did not linger. They hurried from the cabin in silence. It was only when they reached the end of the lane that Elisabeth heard their voices, high and clear, singing the strange music of their own tongue.

Elisabeth sat on the stoop, watching the mosquitoes spread like mildew across the darkening sky. In the past when she had wished to hide from the excesses of her imagination, she had found solace in labour. She had toiled until she was exhausted, finding a kind of refuge in fatigue, in the immediacy of blisters and aching muscles. Now that was the slave's work. Elisabeth was instead required to busy herself with the finer tasks, the making of soap, the sewing of clothes, the preserving of food. None of them required the skull-stunned grind to which she had cleaved so gratefully. None of them caused the sinews in her shoulders to shriek and the sweat to run into her eyes, so that

188

she could no longer hear the voices or see the pictures that flapped like coloured bookplates in her head.

Books, the comfort for those who do not live.

Early the next morning, when it was hardly light, Elisabeth knelt by the bed and once more tugged the trunk from underneath it. The key would not turn in the lock. In the end she was required to break it open with the axe they kept in the wood store. When she lifted the lid, the smell of damp leather and paper stirred so powerful a nostalgia in her that for a moment she closed her eyes, besieged by the remembrances of a self she had thought long shed. The window with the curled iron latch that rattled when the wind blew. The slag of roofs and chimneys heaped up against the sky, crusted with lichen and streaked with bird droppings that gleamed white in the pink Parisian dusk. The battered writing desk with its too-frail legs piled with disordered towers of books and pamphlets and catalogues and papers. Yellow candlelight on the print-black page. The sentences cleaving themselves to the hidden parts of her, drawing her deeper and deeper into their private embrace until the whole world was a pool of light in which she swam, words swarming about her like fish.

She reached in, spreading the books out before her. Homer's *Odyssey*. Racine. *The Thousand and One Nights. Essais Volume II* by Michel de Montaigne. She ran her fingers over the tooled cover. The leather was cool and slightly sticky, like the palm of a hand. Then, very carefully, she

189

opened it. On the frontispiece, mould spread in flowers, their grey petals speckled with black. She ran a fingertip over the inked lettering. She had never written to Paris of her safe arrival in Louisiana nor had she received any letters from Paris. It had not been expected. In all those years, she had hardly given a thought to the shop in Saint-Denis, the silk of the polished wooden counter and the sharp edge of the brass measure, the heavy bolts of silk and cambric and fine wool, the rattling drawers of buttons and the reels of ribbons and trimmings and threads, Mme Deseluse in her brightly coloured gown sucking her teeth as she tutted over the mousseline held out for her inspection by her anxious and ingratiating aunt, and in her memory everything was precisely as it had been when she left it. Now, for the first time, she wondered if the shop were still there.

Later, when the girl came in from the kitchen hut, Elisabeth slammed the trunk shut and pushed it back into its place beneath the bed. The slave regarded her silently, the broom slack in her hand as Elisabeth took up the axe, clamping the book beneath her arm. Grains of rust sprinkled the floor like sugar.

'To work,' Elisabeth snapped, jabbing with her elbow towards the broom. Snatching down the knife from the shelf above the table, she marched across the sunlit yard towards the wood store.

The door stood open, as she had left it. She set the axe in its usual place, standing it on its handle so that the metal blade would not be dulled by damp. The stack of logs was high,

190

readied for winter, and the air was sweet with resin. For a moment Elisabeth stood quite still, watching the sun-spangled dust turning idly in the doorway. She thought of the barrel behind the log pile, its lid pressed down by the weight of wood, and of the jar inside it, interned in its wrapping of rags. As the years passed, the tincture would thicken and dry up, the jar falling into pieces in its rags, a corpse in its winding sheet, she thought, and there was comfort in the ghoulishness, an easing of something at the back of her throat that had been knotted a long time.

The log pile had been stacked in steps so that they formed a kind of bench or settle. Elisabeth hesitated, the Montaigne heavy in her hands. She looked out into the yard. It was silent, low clouds muffling the sky, and the slave was nowhere to be seen. Though there was surely no need for stealth, she closed the door furtively, lifting it to ease the gritty drag of it against the dirt floor and leaving an opening just wide enough to cast a washed-out ribbon of daylight across her lap. When she stroked the worn green leather of the cover, something turned in her belly, a longing not so much for the book itself but for the unexpected stirrings within her of her childish self, whom she had thought long dead.

She sat there for some time, the book upon her lap. Then, very carefully, she inserted her knife between the sealed pages and cut.

★ ★ ★

191

She roused herself only when the light began to drain from the page and her eyes ached from squinting at the smudgy print. It was late and rain drummed on the roof of the wood store. It occurred to her that it had been raining some time. Her back and her neck ached, and her shoulders were clenched tight as fists, but there was a lightness inside her that caused her to catch her breath. She closed her eyes so that she might hold it tight inside her, but already it had begun to fade, the press of her own anxieties dark against the weaknesses in it.

Sighing, she stretched upward, turning her head to ease the stiffness in her shoulders. In the watered-down light the black words danced above her fingers: *I have never seen a greater monster or miracle in the world than myself.* She thought of the Jesuit Rochon, whose ease and humour had so little of the Catholic Church about it. She thought of Renée, of the children who had come to her for lessons, of her husband who loved her for a fierceness that was all his and who feared nothing in the world but the throttle of her frailty. She thought of the books she had smuggled from France rotting in the trunk beneath the bed. She thought of Okatomih, who had been a prisoner and was now a slave.

A sudden white flash drew sharp black lines around the log pile. The rumble of thunder that followed it was long and violent. She could feel the force of it rattling in her throat. Rain hammered at the roof. She stood, the book hugged tight to her chest. There was another knife blade of lightning, the crack of thunder. The storm was close. For a moment she hesitated. Then, taking off her apron, she wrapped it several times around the book and placed it high on the log pile where it might not be seen. Then she opened the door.

Immediately the wind snatched at it, slamming it wide on its flimsy hinges so that she had to battle to secure it. The rain lashed her face and, at the boundary of the yard, the line of oaks bucked like ships. Wrapping her arms over her head, Elisabeth ran towards the cabin. Her hem dragged through the mud, setting curls of wood shavings floating in the puddles like pale feathers, and the wind tore at her hair and ripped roughly at the ragged cypress tiles of the roof, but the wildness of the storm filled Elisabeth with a kind of exhilaration and she tipped her head back, crying out to the tumultuous sky and kicking her heels out behind her as she ran. When the lightning came, the white force of it illuminated her like a lamp.

At the porch she hesitated, watching the rain dance in frenzied patterns across the yard, and abruptly all the wildness in her was gone. It was late and she was cold and the day's duties were undone. She shivered, squeezing the rain from her skirts and from her hair. Then she turned and went in to the cabin. It was only as she knelt before the grate in her sodden dress, coaxing the reluctant fire to unfold a second flame, that she felt once more the force of the lightning in her and the brilliance, a faint electricity that prickled in her hair and in the soles of her feet so that the next morning, when she awoke to a drizzly grey dawn, she did not think to inspect the damage done by the tempest. Instead she pulled a blanket from the bed and crossed the yard to the wood store, sidestepping the chaos of broken branches that littered her path. The rain tapped lightly on the roof above her as, curling up as comfortably as she was able, she unwrapped the Montaigne and once more began to read.

It had been, Babelon told Auguste, an act of Providence. Had it not been for the hurricane, which damaged the merchant's pirogues and dragged his own downstream against his will, he would not have encountered the merchant as he did, on a turn of the river far from any native settlement, and shared with him a fire and some food. He would never have known that there were merchants who dealt not in furs and hides but in curiosities, marvels of the New World, both natural and man-made.

This merchant had once sold to a Prussian nobleman three dragon's eggs and the feathers of a phoenix. In recent years, however, he had favoured the collection of more natural phenomena. There was, he had told Babelon, a growing fashion in Europe for grand gardens, which was no longer satisfied by the ordinary flowers and trees of such temperate regions. Discerning noblemen wished their gardens to inspire awe and incredulity, and they were willing to pay handsomely for unusual specimens. The merchant was not himself a horticulturist, but he understood vanity and he understood profit. In the company of two guides, he travelled between the savage nations, trading trinkets for persimmon and pitcher plants. The practice was protracted and often perilous but, after several months of such commerce, his two pirogues were laden with hundreds of carefully wrapped and boxed specimens.

It was no difficult matter, then, to show the merchant the notebook of Auguste's sketches. The merchant had turned the pages eagerly. Several of the drawings showed plants for which there was considerable demand, several more species with which he was unfamiliar. When Babelon informed him that Auguste had a garden in which he cultivated many of Louisiana's native plants for his own study, and that, moreover, Babelon himself could ensure their safe delivery to the merchant's ships, the merchant closed the notebook and set his hands one on top of the other on its cover. The negotiations extended over the days that followed, but it was price they haggled over, not principle. By the time both men prepared to leave the village, an agreement had been reached.

Auguste's uncertainty infuriated Babelon. He declared it absurd, unreasonable, childish. There was, after all, nothing in the least unlawful in the arrangement. The plants were entirely Auguste's to do with as he wished. Private matters of business were permitted, even encouraged, in Louisiana so long as a man's personal business in no way compromised his loyalty to the colony. France was at war and could spare no ships. Wages were three years in arrears. In such times, the commandant himself commended resourcefulness. A man could not live on an unpaid salary alone. There was nothing in the arrangement that Auguste could possibly object to.

Auguste admitted as much. And still he continued uneasy. He distrusted Babelon's impatience, his airiness, the enthusiasm that was almost anger. He disliked the scorn with which Babelon teased him for his timidity and his youth as much as he disliked his own failure to divest himself of either. He detested the way that his friend, who had never before shown the slightest interest in his garden, now crouched close to the ground, running his hands over the leaves as though they were coins. Most of all he hated that his fate was to be sealed by an act of Providence. Auguste had always mistrusted Providence. She liked to watch you squirm.

★   ★   ★

He had grown accustomed to it, of course. And he had loved the work. It had never ceased to delight him: the clustered seeds in their boxes, the cuttings in their bracelets of damp earth, the flowers laid between paper leaves and pressed to gauzy translucence. The merchant had urged Babelon to consider no plant too ordinary, for virtually every native of Louisiana differed in some particular or other from its European cousin, and so everywhere he went, Auguste gathered flora of every manner and description. And so that he might know them more closely, for each plant that he collected he brought back another to his garden and set it to growing there, so that he might observe its seasons and its habits.

He observed too the habits of Le Caën's

daughter and the opossum, for the child brought the creature often to the cabin. On the first occasion she pushed the animal into his hands, ducking her head and walking away from him very fast. Auguste put his face against the creature's soft fur and inhaled its musty smell.

The next time he shook his head.

'See,' he said as the creature squirmed in his arms. 'She would rather have you.'

The girl bit her lip.

'No,' she said, but she reached out a hand all the same and touched the creature on its head.

'She is more yours than mine now. I should like it if you would keep her.'

The child said nothing then but the gladness lit her face like a lamp.

The next time she came, she brought a plant.

'For you,' she said shyly and, though it was but a common iris that might be found anywhere thereabouts, he thanked her gravely and planted it where she might see it when she came. The girl herself grew as fast as a weed, her long limbs bent up around her as she squatted to inspect the plants. She seldom spoke, but when he told her their names she nodded, her brow creased and her dark eyes fierce with attention.

Babelon came to the cabin also. He brought money, Spanish *piastres*. One day, he joked, there would be something in Mobile to spend it on. It was years since Auguste had seen money of any kind, and he hid it in a bag in the rafters of his cabin. The beds of his garden grew crowded. The one Alibamon boy who tended the place when he was away became three. Before long, Auguste was obliged to dig out some of the more commonplace among his collection to make room for new arrivals. He took to adding careful sketches to the boxes of plants he sent with Babelon and, as he grew more courageous, suggested notes to Babelon, who scrawled them in the margins.

The merchant was well satisfied. Before long he was sending with Babelon crumpled lists of plants that he wished Auguste to seek out for him. When Babelon spread them out to read them, Auguste recognised the particulars of his friend's spiky hand and he was glad. It made him feel closer to the unknown trader to know that he too was not a man of learning.

The merchant's lists were vague and frequently incomprehensible — he asked for 'the plant with the knife-shaped leaves that bears a crimson flower' or 'the low small tree whose white flower resembles a hedge honeysuckle' — but Auguste was a paleface with a savage's knowledge of the forest, and he made a fine detective. He had an instinct for the kinds of plants that might delight a Frenchman, however common they might be to Louisiana. As summer melted into autumn, he collected the seeds of the mulberry, the blueberry, the sassafras, of the walnut and the hickory, of the many diverse kinds of Louisiana rose and the lush sweet-shaded flower that the settlers called lion's mouth, which in summer turned the plains of the Natchez pink. He gathered specimens of the flat-root, the rattlesnake-herb, the poison-arrow creeper, the maidenhair fern, the toothache tree and all the other favourite remedies of the savage medicine man, and had Babelon write out instructions for their manufacture.

His fascination was stronger than his uneasiness, and more persuasive. It entranced him to imagine the seeds of this land breaking open in the French earth, the cuttings he had taken so carefully stretching out their wild green arms towards the French sun. The King of France had a room in his palace made entirely of looking glasses and a garden filled with the plants of the New World. And one day a tulip tree would grow in the marketplace in La Rochelle, and the boys of the town who were now men would marvel at the heavy pink-lipped cups of its blooms and stare out to sea, the limits of their small lives pressed tight around their ribs.

★   ★   ★

Then winter came. The expeditions stopped and the plants blackened and shrivelled in his garden. Auguste went to Marie-Françoise, the schoolteacher, and asked awkwardly if she might teach him his letters. By spring he could write his name and simple words. By spring he was older and the resolute green in the muddy soil filled him with hope.

The rains were gentler that year. As the months passed and the bag of *piastres* in the roof grew heavier, Auguste was able to laugh a little at his callower, more mistrustful self. When he supped at the Babelon house he took fruits for Elisabeth from his garden, which she set in the palmetto basket in the centre of the table. The rim of the old basket had begun to unravel, slivers of sharp grass sharpening its edges. Elisabeth too was not as she had once been. Time and hardship had sapped her old poise. Instead there was a kind of tightly sprung agitation about her that put Auguste in mind of a humming-bird. Her eyes were never still but darted after her husband, shadowing his slightest shift. She was very thin.

In the winter, when Babelon had travelled to the nearby village of the Bayagoulas to buy corn, she had come to his house. It was late, the darkness chill against the windows. He had opened the door and she had been standing there, her head bowed, and at the sight of her his blood had leaped in his veins and he had taken a step backwards with the force of it, and she had come in.

He had not known what to say. That is, he had wanted to say a thousand things, all of them wrong, but she had spoken first and, rushing out the words as though she had rehearsed them, she had asked him to take her to a savage village so that she might consult with a medicine man. She had heard that there were things that the savages could do for women like her. To help them. Then she had hung her head.

'Help me,' she had whispered. 'I do not know what else to do.'

They had never before been alone together. When he nodded his agreement, she reached out her hand and she touched him very lightly with the tips of her fingers on the back of his hand.

Her fingers were icy. Thank you, she said, and she opened the door and, glancing quickly about her to make sure that she was not observed, she left.

The next day, he took money from his pouch in the roof and went to Burelle, who was known to keep a little gunpowder for customers who did not ask for credit. Two days later he walked to the village of the Pasagoulas a small distance from the settlement, where he spoke with the medicine man. When the tincture was ready he took it to Elisabeth, concealed beneath a basket of vegetables.

When he knocked at the door of the house on rue d'Iberville there was no answer. Auguste hesitated and turned away. On the other side of the street, the old wife of Burelle the taverner hailed him from a chair set out in the sun. She had a rug around her shoulders, another over her knees. He nodded at her, the basket held tight against his chest.

'Leave them with me,' the old woman rasped. 'I'll make sure they get 'em.'

Auguste shook his head, his arms cradling the basket.

'Thank you but — '

'You think I can't be trusted with a few mouldy vegetables?'

Behind Auguste the door scraped open.

'Madame,' he said, turning with relief towards Elisabeth. But instead of Elisabeth, it was the slave who stared back at him. Auguste was surprised. He had never before seen her in the house, had only ever observed her as a shadowy presence as she worked in the garden or brought platters of food to the cabin door, the whisper of her feet on the rough planks causing Elisabeth's back to stiffen.

She was young and very beautiful. When she held out her hands for the basket, he held it tightly against his chest. Across the street old Burelle's wife strained forward, her wrinkled neck extending from the shell of her blankets.

'Where is your mistress?' he asked.

The slave did not answer. Above the tilt of her cheekbones her dark eyes were fixed upon his but he could see no coldness in them, no anger or hidden grief. He could see nothing at all. Then abruptly she turned and, leaving the door open behind her, she walked back into the cottage. He followed her, setting the basket of vegetables on the table. She did not turn. As she walked the roll of her haunches pulled the linen of her dress tight over her buttocks and the braid of her hair swung, revealing two dark bruises on the back of her neck.

On the other side of the room she pushed open the yard door, jerking her head towards the wood store. The flare of pale sun caught in the linen of her dress, sketching the shape of her darkness against its bright whiteness as she walked slowly across the yard towards the cooking hut.

Auguste stared at the wood store. The rickety door stood a little ajar. He hesitated. Then, the old woman craning after him, he hurried away.

★ ★ ★

203

It was some days later that Babelon returned from the Bayagoulas. Almost immediately they were summoned by the commandant. There were alarming reports from the Spanish fort at Pensacola. Savages in the area surrounding the fort had been armed by the English, who were determined to force the Spanish to cede the stronghold. For almost a month these savages had posted themselves at the gates of the garrison, holding the soldiers there as virtual prisoners. Those men who had ventured too far from safety were brutally attacked. None had yet been killed, but several were badly wounded. The fort was not sure how long it could survive the siege.

Bienville had thought the fort at Mobile better protected, surrounded as it was by small nations friendly to the French, but he was no longer so sure. It was not only the proximity of Pensacola to Louisiana that concerned him. Today he had received word that the Alabama, with whom he had thought to have made peace, had ambushed the nearby nation of the Mobilians, the French's closest allies. The Alabama had attacked unexpectedly and at night, slaughtering fourteen and making off with women and children.

'The same story,' the commandant said grimly. 'English guns. English gunpowder. If we are to safeguard our savage alliances, we must retaliate immediately.'

By nightfall a force of French and Mobilian soldiers had been mustered. They would depart for the Alabama the next day. In the meantime

Bienville summoned an emergency meeting of the chiefs of the neighbouring nations, so that they might once more pledge kinship and join together in the protection of the French lands against enemy attack. When that was done, he himself would travel north to the great nations of the Choctaw and the Chickasaw. If the English were intent upon trouble, then the French could afford to lose the friendship of neither.

That night Auguste did not take supper at the rue d'Iberville. Instead he sat upon his own stoop, chewing on a piece of cornbread and slapping away the mosquitoes as the liquid darkness thickened, submerging the familiar contours of the garden. He would be gone for many weeks. When he returned it would be summer. He would not see the tulip tree flower. The thought of it filled him with a melancholy that was almost grief.

It was late when Babelon came. Auguste half rose.

'What news? Is something happened?' he demanded.

Babelon shook his head.

'I was restless. I needed a walk.' Reaching into his pocket he pulled out his flask. 'A walk and a drink.'

He sat down beside Auguste and uncorked the flask with his teeth, upending it into his mouth before handing it to Auguste. The brandy was fine, strong but mellow, without the customary firewater burn.

'Good, huh?' Babelon said. 'You can keep a

man in a sewer but you can't make him drink piss.'

Babelon was drunk. As he set clumsily about filling his pipe, Auguste thought of Elisabeth alone in the Babelon house. He pictured her sitting at the table in the light of a single tallow lamp, one hand pressed over the burned black mark on the tabletop, the other tracing with one finger the zigzag weave of a palmetto basket filled with fruit, as her ashy shadow flickered restlessly behind her on the wall.

'Your slave,' he said abruptly, startling himself.

Babelon stretched out a hand, plucking the flask from Auguste's fingers. Tipping his head back, he took a long gulp of brandy.

'God, that's good.' He sighed happily, wiping his mouth with the back of his hand. 'My slave? She's clean, quiet. She works hard. In the main I'm satisfied.'

'So I see.'

' 'So I see'?' mocked Babelon. 'Ah. I see you attempt the *double entendre*. Very clever.'

Auguste did not reply.

'Satisfied, I get it. You imply — but what is it exactly that you imply, Auguste?'

Still Auguste was silent.

'Can it be that you consider my private affairs your concern? Perhaps you seek to instruct me in how to manage my finances? Or how to fuck my wife? You'd like that, wouldn't you? To fuck my wife?'

Auguste stared at his knees as the shriek of the cicadas scraped like a slate down his spine. He had never felt so young or so foolish.

'No?' Babelon stretched his face in a parody of astonishment. 'The woman you follow about like a dog with his tongue out? Don't tell me you are a man of principle? But of course you are. You were raised by savages.'

'Go home, Babelon,' Auguste said softly.

'Oh, don't worry, I'm going. But let me tell you something before I go, since those bastard savages don't seem to have taught you the first thing about civilised behaviour. Here, among white men, there are rules, and the first rule? Keep your fucking nose out of other men's business.'

Auguste did not know how long he remained there on the porch once Babelon was gone. He knew only that he missed the soft, warm weight of the opossum in his lap and that against the black of the sky, two owls swooped and cried, faint gleams of warning in the moonless dark.

Is not man a wretched creature? Because of his natural attributes he is hardly able to taste one single pleasure pure and entire: he is not wretched enough until he has increased his wretchedness by art and assiduity.

She did not know what exactly it was in Montaigne that stirred her. He wrote of war and religion, of marriage and friendship, of fear and the power of the imagination, of drunkenness and lying, of the sweet gratification of scratching an itch and the pleasure of playing with his cat. His book had no form and reached no conclusion. Frequently its reasoning wandered from the point, drifting off into reverie before circling back to its origin and then stopping abruptly, without apology.

It was not so much a book as a discourse, interrupting itself, scolding itself and frequently laughing at its own jokes, but she devoured it as a b oy consumes sweetmeats, peeling apart the paragraphs so that she might know precisely the taste of every part of it. Some days, when his words pierced her with the precision of his understanding, she stood before him as though naked, and his compassion was a balm that soothed the raw and ragged scars of her. Other days, provoked to protest by his rueful assertions, she argued out loud, gesturing at the page as though he might see her and declaring herself determined to prove him wrong. Always he awoke something in her, something that she had forgotten in herself or something she had never known. Whether they touched her or provoked her or caused her to hoot with amusement, his words splashed in her like sunlight, setting long-buried seeds once more to germination.

It entranced and troubled her, that it was possible to know another person in the world so absolutely as she knew this man. She knew her husband's flesh better than her own, the landscape of its dips and knots, but he had never shared himself with her as Montaigne shared himself, without limits, his erudition always tempered by his unflinching honesty and his generous heart. Would Jean-Claude have admitted to her that his memory was rotten, that he struggled with basic mathematics and had never mastered chess, that, until recently, he had not known that yeast was used to make bread? Would he have confessed to her that sometimes, to his delight, the smell of a kiss lingered a whole day upon his moustache? Once, perhaps, in the beginning. Would he examine himself as Montaigne examined himself, clearly and without sentiment, never flinching from the truth?

Montaigne thought friendship a more precious gift than the sexual ardour between a man and a woman. Though he acknowledged that the fires of passion burned more brightly, he declared them rash and fickle, subject to attacks and relapses. Since passion was a matter of the body, he declared, and not of the mind, it was subject to satiety. It comforted Elisabeth to pity him. On the matter of love, she told him, tapping the woodcut on the frontispiece, he was simply wrong.

Once, only once, Jean-Claude surprised her with her head bent over the book.

'What's that?' he had asked without curiosity, and she was startled to find herself flushing.

'Nothing,' she muttered, and she tried to push it down into the chair out of sight but something in her awkwardness aroused his curiosity and he bent down and took the volume from her, letting it fall open in his hands.

'*Desires are either natural and necessary, like eating and drinking; natural and not necessary, such as mating with a female; or else neither natural nor necessary, like virtually all human ones, which are entirely superfluous and artificial.* What the devil kind of nonsense is this?'

'It's just a book. My godfather gave it to me when I left Paris.'

'Why?'

'He thought I should like it.'

'He could not think of something more useful?'

'He gave me the quilt also.'

She smiled up at him hopefully, but Jean-Claude appeared not to hear her.

'Listen to this,' he said. '*Baboons falling madly in love with women are an everyday occurrence.*' He turned the book over. 'Who is this lunatic?'

'He's not a lunatic. He's a Frenchman. From Bordeaux. Do not be misled by the baboons. He writes of every subject under the sun.'

'Baboons included? Although I think of our garrison and I am obliged to concede that the man may have a point.'

Snapping the book shut, he handed it back to her. Elisabeth felt the weight of it in her lap. Then she held it out to him.

'Why don't you take it?' she said. 'For the expedition. You will like it, I know you will.' She hesitated. 'Perhaps when you return we might talk about it.'

'You are attempting to educate me, is that it?'

'It is a book for real people, not scholars. What I mean is, it is written not to make one feel stupid, as so many books are, but to make one understand things. The important things.'

'And what are they, pray?'

'To know ourselves. Entirely and truthfully, without evasion.'

Jean-Claude snorted derisively, snatching the book from her hands.

'Elisabeth, I swear to God — this town may soon be besieged by the English and yet you sit here with your head in a book when the other women are laying in food? Since when did this important business of knowing ourselves keep anyone from starvation?'

'Things are not yet so bad,' Elisabeth murmured.

But he was already halfway to the cabin. She found the book when at last she followed him in, abandoned face down on the table, its pages crushed awkwardly within its covers. She wrapped it carefully and hid it behind a muddle of corn-brush heads and broken dishes on the high shelf over the table. She no longer kept it in the wood store. Several times since his return, Jean-Claude had brought bundles to the house and hidden them behind the woodpile. He did not tell her what was in them and she knew better than to ask.

'Keep the place locked,' he told her. 'In this town you can't trust anyone.'

★　★　★

It was Montaigne who urged her not to be afraid, to untangle need from desire, conviction from zeal, learning from good sense. He counselled her to look about her, to accept not the judgements of others, however highly she held them in esteem, but to judge for herself. And always he gazed into the depths of his imperfect self and set down what he saw there, obfuscating nothing.

Rare is the life which remains ordinate even in privacy. Anyone can take part in a farce and act the honest man on the trestles: but to be right-ruled within, in your bosom, where anything is licit, where everything is hidden — that's what matters.

She went to Guillemette le Bras and begged her pardon.

'I should like to assist you again,' Elisabeth said. 'If you ever have need of me.'

The midwife regarded her coolly, her red knuckles clamped beneath her sharp chin.

'Marie Nevette is my assistant now,' she said.

212

'The commandant will pay for only one.'

'I — it would not matter. I don't care about the money.'

'Oh?' Guillemette raised a thin eyebrow.

Elisabeth hesitated.

'The night that François-Xavier was born,' she said quietly. 'I shall remember it always.'

'It was an easy labour.'

'I know. I know there will be others that are not. But I should like to help you. This place, the rains and the heat and the mosquitoes, the hunger, it is as though it wants only to break us, to make thieves of us and beggars, to drag us down into its own godless mud. I cannot change Louisiana, but I can examine my own conscience. I can try to be good.'

'There is no halo for a midwife's assistant. Only blisters and broken nights.'

'Then I shall make do with those.'

'And no pay?'

'For now. If I am useful to you perhaps the commandant will change his mind.'

'I admire your optimism. Let me think about it.'

Several days later Guillemette came to the cabin. It was afternoon and she waited on the stoop as the savage children filed out. Then she reached down and picked up a basket, covered with a sheet of nettle-linen that she placed in Elisabeth's arms.

'Here. You will take your instructions from Marie Nevette.'

'Of course,' Elisabeth said, and she hugged the basket to her chest.

'Check the basket and make sure all is in order. Anne Negrette is expecting, but not due for several months. We shall hope for more.'

'Yes. And thank you.'

Guillemette inclined her head, a slight smile softening her sharp features.

'I do not know who or what changed your mind. But I am glad of it.'

★   ★   ★

Spring came and Jean-Claude went north. Each day, when the work was done, Elisabeth curled up with Montaigne. As the weeks passed, she got into the habit of opening the book at random so that she might enter his thoughts as if she entered a room and disturbed him there. Sometimes she did not read but only looked at the woodcut of the author pasted into the frontispiece, holding his wise and weary gaze and touching her fingertips to the creases that lined his face. She came to know his opinions on sleep, on names, on prayer and on the affection of fathers for their children, and all the time his words worked upon her like fingers gently loosening her bonds. He examined her, as he had examined himself, with tender exasperation, and he knew her too.

When her monthlies ceased, then, and her breasts began once more to tingle and swell, it was perhaps not so surprising that to Elisabeth the child in her belly was a part of this awakening, a creature brought to life not only through the simple bodily act of a man lying with a woman but also by the bringing to life of those hidden parts of her that for so long had been but insensible flesh. She was not sick as she had been with the others. Indeed she glowed with new vigour. She had been unwell for so long she had forgotten the sheer pleasure of strength, of eagerness. Every day she told herself that she was mistaken, that the pain and the bleeding would come, but the strength in her grew daily and she did not believe it. Not this time. She was filled with a new certainty that rendered everything about her sharp and clear, as though it were outlined in black ink. Though she was afraid, the elation was stronger. It rose in her throat in reckless bubbles.

This one was different from the others. From the very start, Elisabeth felt the fierce vehemence of his attachment, as though he dared her to fight him, and her gladness was touched with sorrow for the others who had gone before. So distinct were the sensations of him that had she not known him tethered tight in her womb, she might have thought that he moved through her, flashing fishlike in her blood, spinning along the cables of her nerve-strings. There was no part of her that was not stirred by him.

His son. He was a boy, she was sure of that too. A son, flesh of her flesh, with Jean-Claude's tapered fingers, Jean-Claude's tucked-away smile. The thought of it stirred her, so that the soft parts of her prickled with a luxuriance that was almost desire. Alone in the cabin, she held her husband close, her hands flat on her belly and her eyes tight shut. She thought she had never loved him so well as she loved him now.

It was the tonic that had done it, the medicine of the savages. Somehow it had unpicked the snarled-up knots and twists of her cat's-cradle womb and spread it out anew, flat and smooth and ready. She imagined Auguste's face when she told him, the pleasure that would light his face, the duck of his head as he tried to contain it. The tips of his ears would turn pink. He had learned much from the savages, but it surprised her that Jean-Claude said he was a fine negotiator. It seemed to her that he had not yet mastered the savage art of concealing his feelings. They would have him stand as godfather, if the baby held. If the baby held. She added the provision quickly, appalled by her own recklessness, and held her thumbs tight. Nothing provoked Providence to vengeance more quickly than conviction. It was for that reason that she told no one of the baby. The longer the words remained unspoken, the stronger the hex that kept them true.

★   ★   ★

The trees grew heavy with fruit and in the savage fields the pumpkins fattened. It was harvest time. The settlement waited, but the English attack did not come. Like the other wives Elisabeth hoarded food. She bought earthenware pots from the savage market and had Okatomih help her with the bottling. The sun was hot as the slave bent over the fire, her hair damp with the steam as she boiled the crocks to prevent spoiling. When the pots were full, Elisabeth took them to the wood store.

The hut was warm. The stale air smelled of sweet cypress and metal. It tasted like blood. The bundles were half concealed behind the log pile, heaped on top of one another and wrapped in dirty sailcloth. When Elisabeth had finished stacking the crocks against the wall, she hesitated. Then she touched one of the bundles, feeling the coarse grain of it between her fingers. It was greasy, thick, without the fibrous weft of savage cloth. Whoever had secured the bundles had been careful. The corners of each one had been folded into sharp triangles and secured with canvas straps. Elisabeth ran her hands over the uppermost bundle, expecting the grind and slip of grain, but instead the shape of it was hard with distinct edges. She pinched with her fingers, feeling a curved hollow, like a water pipe. She frowned, puzzled. Then she covered her mouth with her hands. The taste of metal was sour in her throat.

She took the pots back into the house and stored them under the table. When she sat down to eat she set her bare feet against their cool bellies and thought of the plump fruit sealed tight inside, its flesh fattening with sweet syrup.

⋆ ⋆ ⋆

An uneasy calm settled over Mobile. Elisabeth passed her days in the broken-down cane rocker beneath the shade of the front porch that faced out towards the street, lulled by the heat and the

217

chair's monotonous pendulum creak. The linen grew grimy and weeds sprouted between the planks of the cabin. The other women frowned as they passed her sprawled in the rocker and whispered among themselves. Once the wife of Burelle the taverner, who lived across the lane, limped over and stood before her for a long time, her little red eyes bright in her slab of a face, before she shrugged and, turning, limped away.

Elisabeth liked it best in the evening as the sun slanted low and the mosquitoes danced in the lavender sky. It was easier to dream in the twilight, when the air was soft and warm as flesh and the edges of things slackened and blurred. She could imagine him then, her son, fat-legged and curious in the dust, or at the corner of the road, calling out to her and all grown up. He would be a tall boy, naturally, with tapered fingers and a wide brow, the image of his father. But when she looked up at him and took his hands, it was not Jean-Claude's handsome face she saw upon his shoulders but Montaigne's, his neat round head and unkempt beard and hooded eyes, his wise and steady gaze, and the calm words that curled from his fingers onto the indifferent page.

There you see what it means to choose treasures which no harm can corrupt and to hide them in a place which no one can enter, no one betray, save we ourselves. We should have wives, children, property and good health, if we can; but we should not become so attached to them that our happiness depends upon them.

She hugged her belly then, feeling the corners

of the book press into her flesh, and though she understood the wisdom in Montaigne, the fine-grained gloss of learning and reason, she grieved for him. He never truly loved, she thought, and with all the fierceness of grief, she strained for her child's safe arrival and her husband's safe return.

When the commandant was at last assured that the English soldiers were not coming, he despatched a detachment of five men to the village of the Alabama who had offered corn for the French storehouses. Only one of the pirogues returned. One day's journey from the first village of the Alabama, a band of savage warriors had ambushed the French expedition, killing three of them and leaving the others for dead. The savages had been armed not with the weapons of the natives but with English muskets and lances.

The injured men were taken to Bienville's house, where their wounds were bound and a mission mustered for reprisal, twenty soldiers from the garrison and almost one hundred savage warriors raised from neighbouring nations. It returned with a string of prisoners whom they paraded through the town roped together like cattle. The prisoners moved noiselessly in the dust, their heads held high, their blank faces impossible to read. Among them was the warrior who had boasted of killing two of the white men. In full view of his fellows, he was bludgeoned to death, scalped and his body thrown in the river. Such was the justice of the savages, that blood must be avenged by blood.

The rest of the prisoners were sold to the settlers as slaves.

Bienville's swift and violent reprisal against the

Alabama restored an uneasy almost-peace to the region, but it was not long before emissaries from the Choctaw brought worrying news. Yet again the English had attempted to secure the allegiance of their close neighbour and foe the Chickasaw, showering them with guns and promises of favour. Though much desolated by disease, the Chickasaw remained a proud and fierce people, their martial instincts little dimmed by misfortune. The Choctaw were afraid. They beseeched the French for bullets and gunpowder so that they might defend themselves.

The commandant was in no doubt as to the gravity of the situation. He arranged immediately to return with the emissaries to the nation of the Choctaw so that he might present to the chief of the largest settlement two barrels of gunpowder and a renewed pledge of allegiance. While Babelon and Auguste took the *calumet* to the chiefs of the lesser villages, Bienville himself would continue to the village of the *minko*, or high chief, of the Chickasaw.

'Better times lie ahead,' he told Auguste as he bid him farewell, his pirogues heavy with goods he could not spare. 'We shall have peace.'

★   ★   ★

It was some weeks later, when Babelon and Auguste were lodged at the Choctaw village of Grey Rock, that the commandant's orders reached them. They were to travel to the Chickasaw directly. Once there Babelon would remain only for as long as was demanded by savage custom before returning to Mobile. As for Auguste, he was to remain there for as long as was necessary, learning their language and reporting back to Bienville any significant political or commercial activity.

'So, once again you are become a spy,' Babelon murmured.

'No,' Auguste answered grimly. 'I am become a hostage.'

The journey took several days. When they reached the place where the Choctaw and the Chickasaw nations met, their Choctaw guides refused to travel any further, and Auguste and Jean-Claude were forced to continue on alone. They did not talk about the English or about the savage threat. Auguste would have been happy not to talk at all. Instead he was obliged to listen as Babelon talked in ever wilder terms about trade and commerce. They would cultivate great gardens of plants for the nobility of Europe, great nurseries of slaves for the cultivation of the New World. When Auguste remarked sharply that he thought Babelon a soldier, Babelon replied only that he meant to resign his commission. Did the commandant not have him already working as a merchant, trading with the savages for food? His dealings in slaves had meanwhile gained him something of a reputation among the *coureurs*.

'The difficulty with slaves, of course, is the unreliability of the merchandise,' he said. 'The savage slave has a habit either of escaping or of dying in captivity. Neither is good for profit.'

'I shouldn't think that their first concern.'

'But it is mine. Which is why as soon as I am able I shall set up a business for their exchange. I mean to trade them for slaves from Guinea. It is perfect, don't you see? How can a savage slave run away to his village when his village is hundreds of leagues away across the sea? If he insists upon dying instead, then let him die on the voyage there at the trader's trouble and expense.'

'And your Negro?' Auguste asked. 'What if he dies on you?'

'He shall not. The Negro makes an altogether better slave. That is why I propose to offer three savages for every two of them. That way everyone is happy.'

'Shall you not need the commandant's consent?'

'Perhaps, but then the commandant and I have had business dealings before to our mutual satisfaction. I have always found him a reasonable man.'

Business. The murmur of it rose from Babelon like flies from dung. It flavoured everything he touched, everything he said. It seemed to Auguste that he could not put bread on his plate without Babelon evaluating its potential for resale.

'It is fortunate that your banishment is only for the winter,' Babelon remarked more than once. 'We shall not miss much of the plant season.'

Later, when they were almost at the Chickasaw, he turned to Auguste almost casually.

'I thought I might talk to your boys about the garden. See what we can salvage before the season ends.'

Auguste thought of Babelon in his garden, his greedy fingers crushing leaves, tearing up roots.

'No,' he said.

'Why on earth not? We have time for another shipment before the river freezes.'

'No. I — it's over. The business. I have had enough of it.'

Babelon frowned. Then he laughed.

'Come now. You don't mean that.'

'Yes,' Auguste said. 'Yes, I do.'

'But why?'

Because of you, Auguste wanted to say. Because I do not like what you are becoming, what you have become. Because I cannot bear the way you look at me, the way you talk to me, as though I am for sale too. Because I no longer trust you.

Instead he shrugged.

'I am tired of it.'

'Tired of it? Tired of success? Of making money?'

'Is that so extraordinary?'

'Extraordinary? It is complete bloody madness.'

When Auguste protested, Babelon held up the flat of his hand.

'Please,' he said. 'I am in no temper for another of your sermons. Do as you wish. You are hardly the only man in Louisiana capable of picking flowers.'

They did not speak of it again. For the

remainder of the journey, they sustained an imitation of their old familiarity. It was not always uneasy.

But something between them had changed. It was not a dwindling of affection, for in the new distance that divided them Auguste felt the sharpness of love more acutely than ever. The ties that bound them had not loosened. Instead, in a manner Auguste hardly understood, they had twisted and tightened so that Auguste could no longer move easily within them. At night when he remembered their evenings together at rue d'Iberville, there was a barb in his throat that made it hard to swallow.

He was to blame, he understood that. It was he who had changed. Babelon was exactly as he had always been. After supper he settled beside the fire with Auguste as he always had, threading his words together like strings of brightly coloured beads, and when it grew late, as he always had, he went to a hut that was not his. And though it was true that Babelon's interest in commerce had intensified, that his passion for trade and profit played like a bow over the very nerve-strings of him, it was as much true that he was no less Babelon because of it. If anything, his zeal served only to emphasise the contours of his nature, so that he was made more himself than ever.

It was Auguste who had lost the knack of being himself. He grew impatient, quick to anger. He picked fights with Babelon over matters upon which he had never before held strong opinions. He drank too much. He did not understand it, except to perceive, dimly, that somehow whatever it was that served to link his thinking mind and his physical self had been severed. There were times when his hands moved and their movement startled him. It was as though he occupied himself only fitfully and even then frequently without conviction. It was a discomfiting feeling, to be at the same time inside himself and quite separate from his own sensations and responses. He observed the vehemence of his moods, the physical ferocity of his antagonism, and it unnerved him. In his head he considered himself perfectly disinterested.

After seventeen days of travelling, they reached the Chickasaw nation. Though the chief greeted them with the customary displays of friendship and the white men responded as tradition demanded, Auguste had the good sense to be afraid.

When it was time for Babelon to return to Mobile, the men embraced. Auguste closed his eyes as he pressed his friend's back and his heart tightened with something that was almost homesickness.

'Keep a garden,' Babelon called as he stepped into the pirogue and motioned to the guide to push off. 'If you must be imprisoned here, you might at least turn it to your advantage.'

Auguste did not trust himself to answer. As the pirogue pulled out into the fast water at the centre of the stream, he turned and strode briskly away up the bank. Babelon called out after him, something about being wary. Auguste did not turn round nor did he slow his pace. It was only when he reached the village that he opened his fists and let the last of his dismay run like sand from his uncurled fingers.

⋆ ⋆ ⋆

At first Auguste's presence among the Chickasaw aroused suspicion and hostility. As he passed through the village, he cast behind him a shadow of suppressed whispers and silences. Discourses were bundled up and away from him as he approached, just as the more genteel women of La Rochelle had bundled up their skirts in winter to avoid dirtying them in a muddy puddle. The *minko* had lodged him with an elder by the name of Chulahuma. Sometimes, when he woke in the night, he could see the eyes of the elder gleaming in the darkness.

But Auguste was a good hostage and a good spy. Cautious by temperament, he had a gift for indistinctness. Desirous neither of savage companionship nor of the deference customarily demanded by his kind, he obscured himself in the ebb and flow of a life to which he had long been accustomed. The rhythms of it soothed him. He did not hunt with the men, for they did not wish it, but he fished and made tools and sketched, eking out the rough paper he had brought with him from Mobile. There was solace in the unfamiliar freedom from responsibility, from the care of any living thing.

There was solace too in isolation. The Chickasaw were not like the Ouma. They did not pretend to find a place for him among them. To them he was a paleface, unfathomed and unfathomable, separated by the uncrossable chasms of colour and civilisation and the Catholic Church, and Auguste was content to keep it so, though his religion amounted to little more than a vague feeling of dread and a powerful fear of death. He had gone to Mass in Mobile once when he returned from the Ouma, just to see. The church in La Rochelle had coloured glass and incense and men in tall hats who chased away boys like him and Jean when they crept in for the warmth of it, but the chapel in the fort had proved to be not much of anything, just a hut with a rough cross on the wall. Auguste had not known whether to be consoled or disappointed.

As the last weeks of summer thickened and set, Auguste grew fluent in the Chickasaw tongue. Otherwise there was little to do. The English did not come, only the occasional Canadian trader in search of deerskins. Time hung heavy on him. It was almost by accident that he began once more to gather the insects and plants that caught his attention. He sketched the beetles that the Chickasaw ground for dye and the thorn apple that was used in Chickasaw medicine, inducing as it did a condition of waking sleep close to idiocy. He sketched the traders too, surreptitiously. He grew deft at capturing a face in a few lines. The likenesses were accurate and unkind. When Chulahuma saw them, he laughed and took the charcoal from his hand so that he might make marks on the paper of his own.

★　★　★

And so it was that Auguste lived among the savages quietly, without ceremony or stealth. He seldom spoke unless first spoken to and never asked a question nor proffered an opinion. Such directness was unnecessary. The Chickasaw village, like most villages, resembled a water pouch; though by and large it retained its contents, there was always enough leakage to identify what was inside.

Auguste learned much. He learned that the Chickasaw were skilled in the art of diplomacy, keeping as their friends both English and French and ensuring that each always thought themselves at a slight advantage, so that they might find themselves in a profitless alliance with neither. He learned too that they found the lure of trade enticing and liquor of any kind irresistible, for liquor induced in them the dream state in which they conversed with the spirits of their ancestors. Several of the Chickasaw warriors were drunk a good deal. Sometimes Auguste drank with them, though not to encourage the voices in his head. On the contrary, he drank to shut them up.

Meanwhile he sent word with those traders that passed through that all was steady. At night he lay on his cot of stretched deerskin and rehearsed Chickasaw words in his head. He thought that if he dreamed in Chickasaw he might find peace. Night after night she came to him when he slept. In his dreams she was always big with child, implausibly big, so big that her arms could not reach around her, and always beside her was the slave, so close that they might have been joined together like freaks at the fair, her splayed slave hands dark against her mistress's swollen belly.

Then one day a band of elders from a village far off in the western-most part of the Chickasaw nation came to the village. Auguste was at the river. When he returned to the settlement at dusk, he met a group of hunters also returning to the village. They carried a pair of deer suspended on poles. The beasts' heads lolled back, their throats and bellies pale in the dwindling light, and, as the men walked, the swinging carcasses scattered petals of blood on the foot-pressed earth. They were almost at the village when they saw a band of their own men walking swiftly to meet them. Their faces were grim. One of them muttered something to the leader of the hunting party that Auguste did not catch. The hunter nodded. Rapidly they walked over to Auguste. One took his fishing pole and basket. The other two seized him by the arms and hustled him forward.

'What are you doing?' he protested. 'Where are you taking me?'

They did not answer. When he resisted them, they twisted his flesh, half lifting him from the ground. He called out to the other hunters, pleading with them to help him, but they did not move. The warriors dragged him to a windowless hut of mud and palmetto, sunk low into the earth. In the dim light he could make out a worn deerskin thrown on the dirt floor and, in one corner, a pot of water and some cold corn porridge, cut into rough squares. Otherwise the hut was empty. There was a slash of white, turning the men into statues.

'Why?' he cried out. 'What is my crime?'

There was the slap and pull of leather as the door was fastened against him and then, for a moment, silence before the thunder exploded into the sky like a cannon.

He remained in the hut for two days. It rained incessantly, battering against the mud roof of the hut. No one came. Soon there was no more water. Time kinked and stretched. Sometimes he was very afraid. His imagination betrayed him and his bowel also. The damp seeped into his bones. He was very cold.

It was late on the third day when they came for him. When they hauled him out he stumbled, overcome with dizziness and the clean chill of the air. It had stopped raining and he had not heard it. He gulped the air like water and caught his own powerful animal stink. The men dragged him towards the *minko*'s hut. Smoke rose like flour in the darkness. He knew both men from the hunt. He thought of the deer swinging from the pole by its hooves, eyes rolled back in its sagging head, tongue slack. A skilled hunter could skin and gut a deer in four incisions. Again his bowel turned to water, and he whimpered in fear and disgust.

There were perhaps twelve of them gathered there, ranged in a half-circle around a pyramid of wood thatched with palmetto brush. The wood was wet and the fire hissed and spat. In the reluctant flames the men's faces were polished copper. Pressing on his shoulders, Auguste's guards forced him down into a squat. He blinked, gazing up into the circle.

From his place at its centre, the high *minko* regarded him expressionlessly. Then he nodded. Auguste felt his arms jerk from their sockets as his wrists were twisted behind his back and tied tightly with a strip of leather. When they released him he fell forward, striking his nose upon the ground. There was a rock embedded in the mud and the pain was flat and dull. He felt the gush of blood, tasted its metalled warmth and the cold mud upon his lips. Blearily he raised his head.

'Raise him up,' ordered the high *minko's* speaker, for it was the custom that the chief himself remain silent when among his council. Auguste lurched forward as an arm hooked beneath his forearms and hauled him roughly to standing. Fingers twisted in his hair close to his scalp, forcing his head backwards. He imagined the slice of the knife around the base of his skull, flesh peeled expertly from bone. A warm rush of urine bloomed upon his thighs.

'Witness the faithless deceiver. May vengeance be ours.'

The high *minko* raised his right hand. A warrior stepped in front of Auguste, a leather flog held aloft. There was a silence taut as a violin string and then a wild burning pain as the lash caught him, marking the crook of neck and shoulder in sudden scarlet.

'The oath of kinship is a sacred pledge binding our nations together in the sight of our

232

ancestors,' intoned the speaker. 'There is no greater offence beneath the sun than treachery.'

The lash came again. Auguste cried out.

'The warrior who would harm those to whom he is contracted in friendship must be burned to ash and his spirits banished to drift alone and in great agony. What say you?'

Slowly the warrior raised the flog.

'If your nation is betrayed,' Auguste whispered, 'then I am also. I know nothing of any treachery. I swear it.'

The lash bit. Scraps of thought rose from Auguste's head like moths. Only the pain made sense.

'You collect the thorn apple to dull our senses. You steal the likeness of every pale-faced stranger who passes through our village. But still you know nothing. Do you think our great nation eyeless, witless?'

Auguste swallowed, his tongue clumsy in his shrivelled mouth.

'Honoured *minko*, the plants, the drawings — they are but amusements. They signify nothing.'

The lash came again, deeper this time. The ring of faces smeared and slid.

'See the fire that burns for you, betrayer. Do you not think the time nigh for confession?'

Auguste's eyes closed. A hand jerked back his head, so that his shoulder screamed.

'What would you have me confess?' he pleaded. 'I know nothing.'

'Then the burden of your heart's treachery shall weigh your spirit to the earth forever to relive in ceaseless anguish the agony of your death. Men, prepare the fire.'

Auguste trembled as he raised his head.

'Kill me,' he whispered, 'and you shall bring down upon your nation all the righteous rage and vengeance of my people, whose blood you foully and baselessly shed.'

When the lash cracked the air, his legs buckled.

'It is our vengeance you should fear, the vengeance of a blameless nation lured by treachery and false promises into certain slaughter at the hands of its old enemies,' the *minko's* speaker cried. 'Did you truly think us so easily duped, that at your bidding we would walk obediently into the bloody ambush of the Choctaw and never smell the trickery of it?'

Auguste blinked in disbelief at the speaker, his drifting senses sharpened by shock.

'See how the white man's silence speaks more strongly than his denials.'

'You are wrong. Your charges are baseless. We wish you for our allies.'

This time the lash came twice. The wound curled back its red lips to reveal a white gleam of bone.

'Do you call our kinsmen liars, paleface?'

'Not liars, sir,' Auguste said with an effort. 'But mistaken.'

'Mistaken? Mistaken about the English trader who is not English but a brother of yours, bound in the pay of your own chief? Mistaken about the English musket he promises us for every Choctaw prisoner we bring him? Or mistaken about the false brother who eats of our meat only to despatch us to slaughter?'

A dreadful cold took hold of Auguste. He knew then that he would die. Summoning all that remained of his strength, he raised his head.

'On all counts mistaken,' he said again.

A man in a cloak of feathers moved in front of Auguste. It was Chulahuma. Above his head he held a stick the thickness of a man's wrist. It gleamed wet in the firelight.

'Why must you persist in your deceptions?' the *minko's* speaker shouted. 'Your calumnies can but dishonour you further.'

Somewhere far off there were raised voices, the crack of a musket. A youth entered the circle at a run, a burning torch held aloft. Auguste saw how the sinews stood out on Chulahuma's neck as he brought the stick down with all his strength. Something in Auguste's shoulder exploded. There was a rushing slackness in Auguste's limbs and he knew he would faint.

'Can't you see?' he whispered as he began to fall. 'My honour is all that is left of me.'

When it was winter Jean-Claude came back to Mobile. By then there was no disguising her condition. She turned as he pushed open the door and he looked at her and she smiled, willing him to smile too.

'Look at you,' he said, and he opened his eyes wide and shook his head and twisted up his mouth. She took his face in her hands. He was almost smiling.

'You're home,' she said softly, and though she blinked the tears spilled from her eyes and ran down her cheeks.

'Surely it is not so bad as all that,' he replied.

And she laughed a choked-up laugh, feeling his beard coarse and unfamiliar against her palms.

'You have been gone so long. I — thank God you are safe.'

He nodded, pulling away a little.

'And you?' he asked without looking at her.

'As you see.'

'How far along?'

'Five months, maybe six.' She smiled despite herself. 'See how well it goes?'

'You do look well.'

'It is a boy, I'm sure of it. He kicks like a cavalryman.'

'Does he now?'

'A son,' she breathed. 'Oh, my love, imagine it. Our own son.'

Jean-Claude sighed. Then he turned away.

'Just remember how it has always gone before,' he said. 'And spare us that.'

* * *

Some nights later she woke. He was not there. Throwing back the rugs, she rose from her bed. In her belly the infant shifted sleepily. She put her hands on the swell of him, feeling the insistence of his knees beneath her skin.

'Go back to sleep,' she whispered.

The yard was quite still. Above the dark lace of the trees the moon was nearly full, its white gleam smeared with grey like dirty fingerprints. It cast sharp shadows on the hard earth and frosted the shingled roof of the kitchen hut. Elisabeth leaned against the splintery jamb of the doorway, rubbing the chill from her arms. Somewhere an owl hooted.

He had been restive ever since his return. She had expected it. Every winter he chafed against the fetters of convention and routine, of boredom and idleness. The petty hierarchies and trifling pre-occupations of the town's inhabitants provoked him to exasperation. Even the companionship of Auguste had proved small consolation for the miseries of the winter months. Without him, Jean-Claude's imprisonment would weigh upon him unbearably.

All the same it startled her, the turbulence of his repressed vigour, the intensity of his distraction. It crackled in the air around him until he burned like a lamp. No part of him was still. He paced figures of eight in the cabin until she thought she would go mad with it. Even when she begged him to sit, his feet tapped and his fingers drummed the table so forcefully she felt the rattle of it in her teeth. And yet he was not ill-tempered. Sometimes, as she worked, he would steal up behind her and seize her by the waist, laughing as he spun her in a giddy gavotte. When, laughing too, she pulled away from him, he pressed his mouth on hers, his appetite for her as abrupt and immediate as it had been when they first were married.

Elisabeth was grateful. She remembered how he had been before, how he had recoiled from the swell of her, and she was glad of it. But she feared for the child. When he thrust himself inside her she was sure that he would damage the infant, dislodge him. She begged Jean-Claude to be gentle, but the fever was on him and he did not hear her. Afterwards she reached out for him so that she might soothe them both, but he twisted from her embrace, one leg already in his breeches.

He could not be still. And yet he sought no society. He did not go to the tavern. He drank brandy on the yard steps, staring out into the over-grown garden, his boots tapping out a ceaseless rhythm against the rickety boards. The liquor eased the frenzy in him. It helped him sleep.

A breeze stirred the trees, lifting the strings of Elisabeth's undress. She shivered. Then she turned and went back into the house. The next morning, as she lit the fire for breakfast, he pushed open the door. His face was tight with triumph.

'Is breakfast ready?' he asked. 'I am ravenous.'

Elisabeth set the pot of sagamity on the fire.

'Soon,' she said, and she did not look at him.

When he put his arms around her, he smelled of brandy and the brackish salt of the sea. She could feel the energy coming off him like heat. He wrenched at the strings that fastened her bodice, forcing his hand inside to close around her breast. She murmured protestingly, pulled away. When he caught her again, his arms were tighter, his fingers more insistent as he pressed his lips against the nape of her neck, his teeth, crushing her to him. She could feel the hardness of him against her buttocks.

Inside her belly the baby kicked.

'Not now,' she muttered, twisting from his embrace.

He held her tighter, his tongue insistent against her ear.

'Please,' she said. 'The porridge will burn.'

His fingers closing like a vice around her jaw, he twisted her face to meet his, his mouth closing over hers, biting at her lips, her tongue. She could hardly breathe. The child turned inside her.

'Please,' she whimpered.

He let go of her jaw, moving fractionally away from her. She tried to put her hands to her face but his arm still held her, clamping her arms to her sides. With his free hand he ripped open his breeches, bundled up the loose skirt of her undress. Then, with his arms clasped tight around her ribcage, he drove himself hard inside her, twice, three times, a final juddering thrust. Then he let her go. She staggered forward, clutching at her skirts, at the swell of her belly.

'There,' he said. 'The porridge is hardly yet hot.'

★ ★ ★

That night and the next she went early to bed, her knees drawn up, the curve of her belly safe inside them. The second night she woke and he was not there. As she had before, she rose and went again to the door. She did not know what drew her, only that she needed to see it, the unruffled still of the night, the silent kitchen hut.

She could not have sworn it was him, not with complete certainty. It was dark, the new moon a lightless bubble rimed with silver. There were other men of his build, his height. It might have been anyone.

She told herself to go back to bed. But she could not move, could not look away. Beside the kitchen hut the figures moved. Then they were still. The night was warm. It vibrated with the songs of the frogs and cicadas, histrionic as a Greek chorus. The figures divided, resolving themselves into two. Then they were gone.

Elisabeth remained there for a long time, staring out into the dark yard. When she breathed in and out, her breathing was almost steady, but there was a hole inside her that she could not fill with breath. She felt as though a part of her had been cut off. Her mind was gone, her heart too. There was no pain, only nothingness. The pain would come, she knew that. Till then, she could only stare into the darkness. She had no notion of what came next.

Time passed. He did not return. The moon was a blur of tarnished silver behind the clouds, the wood store a dark shape like a threat. Something in her chest stretched, tender as an old bruise. Elisabeth straightened up, setting her spine stiff as a broom handle. When she took down a rush light and lit it, her hands were steady. She cupped the flame with her hand, so that the draught would not extinguish it. Then she walked across the yard to the kitchen hut.

The door stuck. Elisabeth had to kick it hard to open it. As greasy yellow light splashed around the hut, Okatomih scrambled groggily to her feet, the deerskin clutched about her. Her face was smudged with sleep. Elisabeth bent down so that the light flared in the hidden area beneath the cooking ledge. The pots were stacked as they always were, covered with a weighted cloth against snakes and venomous spiders. The space was not large enough to serve as a hiding place.

She turned round. The girl watched her. She said nothing. Elisabeth stepped close to her, holding the light up to the girl's face so that she blinked against the smoke of it. She did not step back. For one wild moment Elisabeth imagined what it might be like to dash the dish of burning oil into that imperious face, the hair shrivelling back from the high brow, filling the air with its acrid stink, the flesh sliding from the blades of her cheekbones. She held the lamp higher. The girl blinked again but did not move. Elisabeth stared into the flame. A plume of black smoke twisted from its frayed yellow tip. She breathed in the meaty smell of the molten fat, the heat of it sharp upon her skin. Then she blew out the light.

Hardly knowing what she was doing, she reached out and closed one hand around the girl's throat. The slave did not struggle, though her pulse beat like a bird against Elisabeth's palm. Elisabeth squeezed her fingers, watching the twist in the girl's face, the bulge of her eyes. A far-off part of her mind wondered if she might be going mad.

'If you ever so much as look at my husband again, I'll kill you,' she said. 'Do you understand me?'

The girl did not reply. Elisabeth pushed her backwards. The itch in her fingers was overwhelmingly strong. She bit down on her lip, her fingertips pressing down into the pliant muscle, and the stirring in her belly was a kind of lust. A stripe of moonlight lit the slave's face, her wide-open eyes. There was no fear in them, only a dull resignation. They were the eyes of someone already dead.

'What am I doing?' Elisabeth said, and the burst of laughter that broke from her was shrill and sharp. 'You don't understand, do you, whore? Not a single fucking word!'

With a disgusted thrust she pushed the girl away. The slave stumbled backwards, striking her head hard against the wall of the hut. Elisabeth snatched up a pot, holding it like a weapon before her, but the slave did not rouse herself in attack. Half crumpled against the wall, she closed her eyes and waited, her only defence one brown hand held up against her bruised neck and one brown forearm like a strap over the curve of her belly.

*   *   *

When at last he came to bed, Elisabeth pretended she was sleeping. He was clumsy from drink, dropping his boots and stumbling over them on his way to bed. When he climbed in beside her, he smelled of liquor and tobacco, of men. He slept heavily, sprawled on his back with his mouth open, one arm thrown wide.

Elisabeth did not sleep.

Later, in that dislocated stretched-out hour when night unhitches itself from time and day is unimaginable, she reached out with her left hand and set it upon his neck. The skin was looser on the muscle than the girl's, and harsh with stubble. She closed her hand, pressing her fingers into each side of his neck. He did not stir. Her fingers tightened. She could feel the tendons as they shifted and slipped. Then she let go.

It grew light eventually, the first fingers of dawn powdering the darkness a dusty grey. Murmuring in his sleep, he turned towards her. His cheek was crumpled, marked with creases by the tumbled rugs. He looked both very old and very young, like a turtle turned out of its shell.

Tears pricked her throat.

Setting her head beside his, she matched the tip of her nose to his, the backs of her fingers light upon his lined cheek. She could hardly bear for him to wake. She might have done it. A little more pressure, just a little more, and she could have held things steady. She could have rewound time. She could have forced back the hands. She might have arranged it right, so that the clock showed always a day in November a little before dawn, when she was his and he was hers, for all eternity.

No one thought Auguste would survive the journey. He was feverish, his wounds corrupted and the bone badly broken. He cried out when they lifted him and laid him in the bottom of a pirogue upon a bed of skins and Spanish beard. As they made their way south towards Mobile, the Jesuit, who had learned something of native medicine during his time among the Nassi-toches, applied a poultice of the root of the cotton tree to his damaged shoulder and had his boy dribble a hot decoction of china root between his lips to promote sweating.

It had taken all Rochon's guile and persuasive-ness to convince the high *minko* to release the injured man into his care. He had been obliged to remind him several times of the brutal reprisals that had followed the murder of the French missionary Saint-Cosmé by the Chitim-acha ten years before, and the perpetual state of war that had since blighted that once-great savage nation. As for the ambush, he pledged an oath in God that the French commandant would not rest until the agitators were uncovered and turned over to the Chickasaw for punishment. Thus would the two nations be reconciled, drawing their alliance afresh in the blood of a common foe.

The priests at the seminary in Quebec, who some fifteen years before had struggled vainly to contain their pupil's merriness, would surely have been startled to observe him possessed of such sombre authority as he displayed before the elders of the Chickasaw, but then a man may find himself possessed of considerable gravity when he holds the life of another in his hands. The high *minko*, mistrustful of the Jesuit but more fearful of plunging the Chickasaw once more into a bloody war with France and all her savage allies, reluctantly concurred. He promised a pitiless revenge if the white man failed him.

Their course to the settlement was a straightforward one, for the upper reaches of the Mobile River would bear them directly to the coast. Still, it was a perilous journey. The winter had been wet and the river was unruly, roaring into unexpected rapids and rolling with rotted trees. They could not be certain that the Chickasaw did not double-cross them. They dared not hunt, or light a fire, or make camp in the open spaces by the river. Nor did they consider it prudent to take refuge with the Choctaw. Instead they travelled at night, risking the treacheries of the stream so that they might evade discovery, and when daylight came they set their *baires* in the tangled confusion of deep forest, always posting one of their number as a sentry to keep watch.

As the days passed, Auguste grew hectic with delirium. His dreams pitched and plunged on the black water and in the heat of fever they were thick with the bodies of the dead and dying, their skulls striking dully against the hull of the pirogue, their nails scoring its bark. He saw pale fingers that reached up from the depths to pluck at him and woke screaming to the ministrations of the boy, who closed his hand over Auguste's mouth and hissed at him to hold his tongue.

It took thirteen nights to gain the boundary of the settlement. By then Auguste's fever was broken and he was quiet, his breathing weak but steady. As soon he was able, Rochon sent word to the commandant only to discover that the Sieur had been summoned to the Spanish fort at Pensacola on a matter of urgency and was not expected back for some days. The Jesuit had been away from the settlement for some years, but he had not forgotten the town's aptitude for intrigue and alarmism. Informing the commissary only that he had arrived as instructed, he returned his patient under cover of darkness to his own house on the rue Condé, taking care to promise Auguste's slave recompense if she kept her master's presence there a secret.

*   *   *

Quiet at last and still, Auguste slowly regained his senses, though his shattered shoulder continued to trouble him greatly. The slave treated his wounds with sassafras and brought him infusions of white willow bark to muffle the pain, but the skin of it was no thicker than the skin on hot milk and the pain was always there when he moved, sickening and exultant. During the first long nights, when exhaustion unshackled his spine and stretched the skin on his face tight over his skull, he tried to steal around the edges of it, in search of the places where sleep was, but his dreams were wild and bright with fear, and when he startled awake the anguish of movement caused him to cry out. He drifted through the dark hours in a haze of fatigue and pain, time crumpling and stretching so that minutes lasted hours, and then suddenly at midnight it was dawn and the slanting sun caught the *platille* at the window and set it alight.

When he saw the gleam of white in the darkness, he thought it was the moon grown suddenly full, or perhaps the sun come up without him, and he glanced at the window, but there was no light in it, and the *platille* was dark as a drawn curtain against the night. He closed his eyes so that he might not see what was not there. It distressed him, how fearful he had grown of himself, and he thought to call for the slave, so that she might bring him willow tea and tallow lights and the ordinary reassurance of her presence in the room. And then there was the scrabble of feet on his legs, claws sharp through the blankets, the press of soft fur against his forearm.

'Ponola?' he whispered and, though his shoulder screamed, he lifted the opossum onto his lap and held its slight body tightly to him. It squirmed, stretching up its muzzle towards his face, its cold, damp nose nudging his chin. It was then that he saw the girl. She stood at the foot of the bed, her dark hair tangled like shadows across her face, and her eyes were bright in the darkness.

'I've taken good care of her,' she murmured. 'Just like I promised.'

'Yes. Thank you.'

She said nothing more but only nodded, fixing him with her fierce eyes. When dawn came the slave found her curled into a question mark on the dirt floor, her frown pressed smooth by sleep and her arms folded into a pillow beneath her head. The opossum raised its head from its nest among the bed rugs, sniffing the air as the savage carried in the dishes of tea and watery gruel and set them on the stool beside the bed. When Auguste opened his eyes, she helped him to sit.

'She come every day,' she murmured quietly as she spooned the hot liquid into his mouth. 'When you gone. Watch the house. Watch the garden boys. Every day the same.'

Auguste swallowed, waiting for the sedative to congeal over the pain in his shoulder. The girl did not stir. But she opened her eyes a crack, like a child playing hide-and-seek, and watched as the slave fed Auguste and changed the dressings on his shoulder.

'I could do that,' she said when the slave had gathered up the dishes and the dirty bandages and taken them outside. 'I am good at taking care of things.'

'You should go home,' he said gently. 'Your father will be expecting you.'

But the girl only shook her head and picked at a splinter on the bedpost, and Auguste closed his eyes as the pain blurred and the sleep inside him grew stronger.

'You should go,' he said again later. 'You are

not supposed to know I am here.'

'Going away won't stop me from knowing.'

And she dipped the dipper into the pitcher of water on the stool beside him and held it to his mouth and, though she spilled it down his chin, Auguste drank and said nothing, because her stubbornness was a solid thing that turned like dust in the room. The day lengthened and he drifted in and out of himself, and when the scream in his shoulder roused him she was still there and the opossum was a warm almost-weight on his legs and he slept a little more and his dreams were ragged and strange but there was no blood in them.

When he woke again it was dusk. The slave moved silently about the room, lighting a tallow lamp that she set beside his bed and fetching the gruel that she had set upon the table. Auguste roused himself groggily, fumbling among the rugs for the opossum, but it was gone.

'The girl?' he asked as the slave knelt beside him, raising the spoon to his lips, and the slave said nothing but only jerked her head at the door, and Auguste let his head fall back upon the pillows so that the spoon rattled against his teeth, spilling hot gruel down his chin.

The door banged open. Auguste looked up as the girl staggered in, clutching the slopping pitcher before her. The front of her dress was soaked through.

'We must have a new pitcher,' she declared breathlessly. 'This one spills.'

★ ★ ★

It was on the eighth day, which was the Sabbath, when the knock came at the yard door, two sharp raps. It was late, the lights of the settlement extinguished. Auguste heard the girl and then the murmur of a man's voice on the back stoop. His stomach closed like a fist. When the girl came back into the cabin she was alone. She shut the door, her thin arms clamped across her chest.

'It's the commandant,' she said.

Auguste breathed out.

'Then we should let him in.'

The girl scowled.

'It has been bad for you today.'

'I am well enough for the commandant. Go. Bring him in.'

The girl made to say something. Then, still scowling, she turned and walked slowly towards the door. Using his good arm, Auguste pressed his fist into the mattress, knuckles white, and struggled to sit up.

★ ★ ★

Bienville stayed with Auguste for almost one hour. From where she squatted on the stoop, the girl could hear his voice, a low rumble that rose from time to time to an angry clatter like a thunderstorm. She could not hear Auguste. When at last the commandant took his leave, he left as he had come, slipping out through the backyard, taking the narrow alley that led out onto rue de Pontchartrain. It was a dark night, the new moon brittle as a bitten wafer. The girl watched him from the shadowed porch, her arms tight around the opossum. When she was certain he had gone, she stood and very quietly pushed open the door to the cabin.

Auguste was sitting on the side of the bed, his feet on the floor, his good arm wedged against the bedpost as he struggled to push himself upward. His face was chalk white and glazed with sweat.

'Quickly,' he said, and she ran to him, untangling the twisted bed rugs to release his legs. Then she bent down and took the chamber pot from its place beneath the bed.

'No,' he muttered, and the word caught stickily in his mouth. 'Not that.'

'Then what?'

'Go to the tavern on rue Saint-François. Tell Ensign Babelon your father wishes to see him. A matter of business. Tell him there is profit in it.'

'But — '

'Tell him to meet him at the old Daraque cabin at the back of town. One hour.'

The girl kicked at the chamber pot. Then she shook her head.

'I cannot.'

'Do not refuse me. I must see the ensign tonight.'

'I cannot,' she said again, and she stared at the floor.

'For the love of God, child, are you become my gaoler?'

'No.'

'Then what?'

She raised her head and stared at him with her

252

black eyes, chewing at her lips, her fingers twisting before her in knots.

'My father is dead.'

There was a silence. Then Auguste cleared his throat.

'When?'

'A few months maybe. Summertime.'

'The scourge?'

She nodded.

'I — I am sorry. I had not heard.'

The girl shrugged and scuffed at the floor with her bare foot. Auguste sagged against the pillow, suddenly overcome with pain and weariness. He thought of the locksmith, his red eyes sloppy in their sockets as he drained another mug of savage liquor, and of the dilapidated cabin that flooded every spring, the mud slippery as seaweed on the walls, and the prospect of rising from the bed defeated him.

'Moquin,' she said. 'I take messages sometimes for him.'

'Moquin.'

'The powder-maker. He is my neighbour. Might I tell the ensign I brought word from him?'

'The powder-maker.'

'Yes. I could go now.'

Her unexpected eagerness was unbearable. Auguste shook his head, jarring his shoulder, and closed his eyes. The pounding in his shoulder jostled with an overwhelming lethargy, blotting out words, stopping his tongue.

'Tomorrow, then?' When he did not reply she nodded to herself. 'Tomorrow is better. You shall be stronger tomorrow.'

She stood by his bed. The fierceness came off her like heat. He tried to reach for it but the pull of sleep was stronger, drawing him down, closing over him like water.

Immediately the commandant stood before him once again, his face tight with anger.

'A trap. A trap of our making. That was what the Englishman told the Chickasaw elders. How else to explain a French trader in their village offering guns in exchange for Choctaw prisoners only weeks after the Choctaw had reaffirmed their allegiance to France? Of course it stank of treachery. It would have been a simple matter then to convince the Chickasaw that they had been duped, that if they did as the Frenchman urged and raided the Choctaw village for prisoners, they would be walking straight into a Choctaw ambush. That is why they came for you.'

Auguste shifted, sending a shriek of pain down his side. But, though he pressed the fingers of his good hand hard against his eyes, he could not extinguish the expression on the commandant's face.

'Those duplicitous English bastards. It's so obvious I can't believe I didn't see it coming. They knew that we had approached the Chickasaw, feared any alliance we had brokered might hold. So they set about destroying it. They chose a village far from the *minko*, a village where the warriors are restless and ill-disciplined, easily persuaded to bloodshed for profit. A village seldom visited by white men.

They knew that the warriors would not ask questions, that if their man spoke Mobilian in the French manner the Chickasaw would think him one of ours. Once the deal was struck all it took was an English accomplice to alert the *minko* to the treachery of their allies. The *minko* told the Jesuit that this so-called Frenchman paid the Chickasaw in English muskets, for pity's sake, English gunpowder. If he had raised the English standard there he could not have made it plainer.'

It seemed to Auguste that the bones in his shoulder were hot coals, branding his damaged flesh. He cried out for the slave and the girl came, her eyes heavy with sleep, and in a whisper he begged her for willow tea. She stayed with him as the slave prepared it, and when it was ready he gulped greedily at the hot liquid, burning his tongue. And still there was no relief. He lay in the darkness, his eyes wide open, as the commandant's words marched around his head, pounding to the throb of his broken shoulder.

'We shall get the bastard who did this to you, I give you my word. Blood for blood, Auguste, blood for blood. Savage law must prevail. Whether it is us who find him first or the Chickasaw, that bastard son of an English whore is going to wish that he had never been born.'

In the event there was no need for Auguste to send the girl for Babelon. He came himself, the very next day. It was early, the waking sun stretching its arms above the trees, and outside the slave lit the fire for breakfast. He did not knock. As he flung the door of the cabin open, the girl lifted her head.

'Here a week, at death's door, and not one word? For the love of God, man!'

Auguste stared at his friend as though he hardly recognised him, his eyes raw from lack of sleep. Though his shoulder ached, there was a numb emptiness at the pit of his stomach.

'Why the hell did you not send word to me? I did not even know you were back.' Babelon strode across the room. He had grown thin since Auguste had last seen him. His handsome face was drawn, his eyes pouched and restive, the whites yellowed and shot with red. When he frowned, it caused a muscle in his cheek to jump. '*Vierge*, Auguste, what the devil did those bastards do to you? You look like hell.'

Auguste bit his lip.

'Look at you. I mean, how could they? Those — those goddamned barbarians. How could they?'

'They thought I wished them dead.'

Babelon shook his head, his face jumpy with disbelief. He almost spoke, then seemed to think better of it. Instead he paced the cabin, picking things up and putting them down. When the slave came in with tea, he stood so that she might pass him, but he was not still. His legs jumped, his feet tapping the floor and his flexed fingers beating out a rhythm, his body restive as a wasps' nest, Auguste thought suddenly, every part of him constantly shifting and remaking itself.

'It was an Englishman, Bienville says, who betrayed us,' Babelon said when the slave was gone out. 'It is proved apparently, there is not the least doubt of it. So I am to go there, to the Chickasaw. I am to see what I can find out about him.'

'You.'

'Yes. Don't look at me like that. The commandant brought the order to me himself. At dawn, which tells you something. Sieur Bienville has long considered the early hours the preserve of songbirds and slaves. My Chickasaw is lamentable, I know, but he has promised me a translator. I asked for you, of course.'

The ensign twisted his lips into an almost-smile. Then his mouth jumped and it was gone. Auguste said nothing. Beside him a feather of steam rose from the untouched dish of willow tea.

'I — God, Auguste. What the devil did they do to you?'

'Nothing that they would not have done to any traitor.'

Babelon rubbed his face briskly. Then he began, once more, to pace the cabin.

257

'Bienville said it was the Jesuit Rochon who found you, persuaded the Chickasaw to let you go. What a blessed piece of luck. The guy's an insufferable arse-pot, of course, but, sweet Jesus, if he had not happened to be passing through — '

'I find it best not to think on it.'

Babelon snorted.

'I don't suppose we could arrange for him to be roughed up a little in his turn, could we? Missioner or not, I could swear that smug bastard has eyes for my wife.'

The anger came quite unexpectedly, rising like vomit in Auguste's throat.

'Why are you come here?' he demanded. 'What is it you want from me?'

Babelon blinked at him.

'You think you can come here and make your little jokes and it will all be as it always was? Please. Do you think I don't know? That I wouldn't work it out?'

'Auguste, I have no idea what you are talking about.'

'Don't lie to me, you bastard. Not now. Not after all this.'

Babelon's lips moved. His face twitched. His hands danced in front of him.

'Auguste, such feverish imaginings, you surely cannot — '

'Damn you, Babelon. Do you think me a fool? An Englishman pretending to be a French Canadian? A delightful notion but hardly necessary when you have a real French Canadian right there, ready to sell his country for a slice of the profit. A French Canadian with English muskets to trade.'

'I really do not know — '

'You do not know what? How it happened? How you managed to be tricked by an Englishman into betraying your country? Or how you got so greedy for profit you no longer cared?'

'Auguste — '

'Spare me.' Auguste leaned back against the pillows, closed his eyes. Then he called for the girl. 'Fetch the commandant here. Quickly. Tell him it cannot wait.'

'For God's sake, Auguste!'

Babelon's shoulders dropped, the words fading into the silence like smoke. He pressed his knuckles to his lips, his face into a knot.

'Please.'

Auguste hesitated. Then he held his hand up, staying the girl.

'Don't you see?' Babelon hissed. 'It wasn't — I never meant for this to happen. That bastard betrayed me. He said it would be a simple matter. He would take the slaves with the plants. To trade in the Indies. He said no one would ever know. He — '

'And you?'

'I never meant — it was a business arrangement, nothing more. I never thought they would come after you.'

'A business arrangement? Urging our enemies to a violent attack upon our allies?'

Babelon's head jerked up. His face was ugly with fear and disdain, his eyes feverish bright.

'Our allies? Damn it, Auguste, if you think

those bloodthirsty barbarians understand the meaning of allegiance, you are as stupid as Bienville. Look at what they have done to you, for God's sake. They have no concept of loyalty, no allegiance that cannot be simply bought. They defend their own interests, without consideration, as wild beasts do.'

'As you do.'

'Because I see that it is the only way to get anywhere in this godforsaken swamp. It is their rules that apply here, not ours. Our government, our petty alliances, our army of boys and halfwits, they are no more than a pitiful joke. Our countrymen have clung to this land for more than a decade and for what? Every spring our houses flood. Every summer we succumb to fever. Every winter we starve. That is what living as Frenchmen has done for us.'

'So instead you sell us all for your own profit?'

'I told you, the Englishman betrayed me. He set me up. I never meant — that bastard has traded plants with me for three years. I thought I could trust him. He told me he could get those slaves away and no one would be any the wiser. I did not know what would happen to you. Jesus, Auguste, if I had known — '

'Then what?'

'Then of course I would never have agreed to it. You know that.'

Auguste turned his face away.

'Listen,' Babelon urged. 'Listen to me. The guns — I gave the Chickasaw only the first payment. A guarantee. I have more. We could go north, much further north, where they do not know us. We can trade up there. And we shall split the profits. Sixty-forty. What do you say?'

Auguste gaped at him.

'Very well then, I am not about to quibble. Fifty-fifty, straight down the line. There is a fortune to be made out there if you only take it. I shall make you rich, Auguste, I swear it.'

Auguste did not reply.

'Come on, Auguste, what do you say?'

'You mean to pay me off?'

'Handsomely. Call it making amends.'

'And if I refuse?'

'I do not think that would be wise.'

'And why is that?'

'Because you would leave me no choice but to inform the commandant that you were a part of the arrangements.'

'He would not believe it.'

'Oh, I think he would,' Babelon shook his head sadly. 'Is it not you who has traded for years with the Englishman, plants for *piastres*? You may hide away the money but I have the sketches you made, his notes. Perhaps it would have continued for many more years, but you wanted more. We both did. And when in due time the Englishman betrayed us to the Chickasaw, well, they took revenge.'

'You would do that?'

'Only most unwillingly. You know I love you like a brother.'

When Auguste did not reply, Babelon knelt at the side of the bed, taking Auguste's good hand and pressing it in his.

261

'Listen to me, Auguste. There has been enough treachery already, enough pain. Must we betray each other too, spill each other's blood? You are my brother, as I am yours. Let us save each other.'

Auguste said nothing for a long time. When he spoke again it was to accept his friend's terms. He winced as Babelon embraced him, jarring his shoulder.

Their plan was a simple one. Auguste was too weak to travel. He needed time to heal his broken bones, to regain his strength. Babelon would therefore take his order from the commandant and, two days hence, he would travel north as instructed, towards the Chickasaw. Once as far as the Choctaw nation, however, he would pretend illness and take refuge there, for the Choctaw had no reason to suspect him. After a suitable time, he would take his leave of the Choctaw and return to Mobile. He would bring with him the greetings of his Chickasaw hosts and a full description of the English agent who had traded with their warriors and of the English plant trader too. He would furnish the commandant with all manner of information, including a number of contradictory reports as to their whereabouts and their allies among the savages. Bienville would suspect nothing. With Auguste recovered, he would once again despatch them to the savages in search of food.

This time they would not come back.

* * *

It was much later, when night had fallen and the settlement slept, that Auguste sent the girl to the house of the commandant. He came secretly, as he had before, and as before he stayed with Auguste for perhaps an hour. They did not light a lamp. When at last he left, Auguste lay sleepless and exhausted among his tangled bed rugs. Though he longed for rest, his mind ground out old memories like a street organ. He thought of the long evenings at the rue d'Iberville, of Babelon dancing with Elisabeth, spinning her around until they arrived breathless and laughing before him, offering themselves to him like a present. Babelon had grinned and bowed but Elisabeth had turned her face away, half hiding it in her husband's sleeve, and Auguste had known why because, even as he laughed in his turn, he put his hands up to his face too, his splayed fingers making a cage to cover his eyes. It was not Babelon they sought to hide from but each other, the blatancy of the other's happiness, the terrible defencelessness of it.

He thought of Babelon rising from the fireside in the native villages and walking silently away towards a hut that was not his. They had neither of them ever spoken of it. It was not the way, between men. But Auguste had watched him go and, though he had tried not to, he had always thought of Elisabeth then, her rapturous face turned into her husband's sleeve where he could not see it, and his heart had tightened and he had told himself that he pitied her, because the flames of love between a man and a woman burn with a wild fever that, seeking satiety in the body, must in time be satiated and fall to ash, while the love between men grows stronger, the years binding them in a fellowship of minds, of spirits undulled by the drear of the quotidian life, the fickle appetites of the flesh.

'You know, of course, that his wife is with child?'

The words had struck Auguste like a blow.

'No,' he said, and he shook his head, shook it over and over, and though the movement pained him he did not stop. 'No. No. She — she cannot. She — it shall not hold.'

'On the contrary, they tell me she is well advanced.' Bienville sighed. 'Some kind of accommodation shall have to be made.'

Shaking his own head, Bienville did not observe Auguste's sudden stillness, the squeezed-up expression congealing on his face, or perhaps he did, because when the silence had stretched long enough the commandant exhaled a dismal laugh, snuffing it out in his nostrils.

'Unless you seek a wife for yourself, Guichard,' he said, and in the darkness his eyes held pinpoints of light as though the inside of his skull was illuminated. 'By way of reparation.'

Auguste did not answer. He thought of Elisabeth holding a child. Holding her husband's child. She had lost so many. The familiar pattern had repeated itself until it had become the shape of them, the two of them and him and the not-yet-infants, the slithers of slick flesh that bled out of her, screwing her body into twists. He had sat quietly in the creases of space they left when they were gone, laying his silence against her like a dressing, a shield against her husband's disappointment, his impatience. He had thought it would go on the way it always had because that was the way it had always been, because those were the foundations that held them steady. The lingering choke of a husband's passion grown cold. The true and enduring love between men. The attachment to another man's wife that snarled like fishing line around his heart.

He had secured her the savage medicine, had smuggled it to her not because he thought it would work, but because she had come to him and he could not refuse her.

Now she bore Babelon's child and Babelon had said nothing. In all of their planning, he had not once mentioned Elisabeth and Auguste had been glad of it. Now he thought of her dear pale face, the way her gaze followed Babelon about the room, matching the arcs and swoops of him as though he were a kite and she the paper tail, and the pain of it overwhelmed him, that she carried the child of the man she loved, whom he loved also, and the grief sprang from the centre of his bones and massed in swollen wens against the underside of his cheekbones until his face ached and the longing to weep was a wild scream inside him and still his eyes were raw and dry, as though they had been scoured with sand.

★ ★ ★

When he called out in the night, the girl came to him and stood beside him, the opossum in her arms. He had her light a lamp, set it by his bedside. She set the opossum on his lap, rubbing the sleep from her eyes with the back of her wrists as she tugged at the wrinkles in his rugs, settling them more comfortably around him. He watched as the smoke pulled itself from the bright flame, smearing a sooty stripe against the wall. There were damp patches on the lime plaster. In several places it had dropped away. The walls of the cabin had grown fat and weak on the wet ground. Soon the house would fall down. All the houses in this quarter would fall. The bayou was too close, its banks too easily breached. It was how it had always been.

The girl arranged his arm gently, her tangled hair draping it like weed. Then she lifted the dripping dipper of water to his lips and he closed his eyes and drank and, as the water slid down his neck, he knew that Babelon was right, that in Louisiana it was not just houses and ships that rotted, but men.

It was dawn when Auguste bid the girl bring him pencil and his notebook.

'Tear me out a page.'

'This one?'

The page she held out was blank but for a small sketch in the top right-hand corner, a quick likeness of the pungently sweet herb that they called spiked head, much used in cooking by the Chickasaw. Auguste had a sudden vivid sense of himself squatting in a slice of evening light, the triangular pull between eyes, plant and pencil as he drew, and the smell of stewing meat drawing the saliva into his mouth. The simple symmetry of exactness and appetite.

He nodded. Then he asked that she fetch him a handful of whiskery sweet potatoes from the store hut and put them into basket. He told her to select the most bruised among them, those with the first white sprinklings of rot. When the girl was gone out he began to write. *It is decided. The trap is set.* He pressed the rough pencil hard into paper, his fingers white-tipped, his gaze shrivelled to the black point of the lead. *If you love him.* When he was finished, he folded the paper once, and then again, and once more, sealing the words inside. When the girl returned, he set it beneath the potatoes in the basket.

'Take these to the ensign's wife,' he told her. 'Make sure to tell her they must be cooked today or they shall rot.'

The girl said nothing but scraped the floor with her toe, her black brows pressed low over her dark eyes.

'It must be tonight, you hear me? And tell her — '

The girl waited, the frown easing a little as she turned her face up to look at him, and Auguste turned his own face away so that she might not see the tears that filled his eyes.

'There is salt,' he said. 'In the basket. Tell her to look for the salt.'

She could not have said exactly when she knew that the slave was with child. She knew only that, when at last she saw it clearly, she saw too that she had known it from the start.

It was a mild day, warm enough to sit outside in the weak sunshine. Weary, for she no longer slept well, she took a rug to the chair on the front stoop and tried to read there, but the words made trails of ants across the bright page and she could not hold the sense of them. So she put the book down and closed her eyes and rocked the chair, quieting herself and the infant with the rhythmic creak of it. It was only when the shadow fell across her face that she opened them and saw the Jesuit, his hands knitted across the comfort of his belly, and his face split open like a melon.

'Look at you,' he said, and she stood and embraced him because the delight in his face was all hers. They laughed then, because her belly and his made too great a circumference to reach around, and he had bid her sit and she had waved away his solicitousness and she had called for Okatomih to bring out some of the beer that the slave brewed herself in the lean-to behind the kitchen hut.

It was then that she saw it, because he saw it too and his understanding was not slippery like hers but solid and alive, and it kicked out in the space between them, as blunt-boned and insistent as the infant in her belly. As the slave walked towards them, balancing the pitcher of beer, Elisabeth saw as the Jesuit saw, without evasion, the unmistakable indentations pressed into the air by the swell of the pitcher's belly and beneath it the swell of the slave's, round and neat and irrefutable as though it too had been fashioned from clay.

They did not speak as the slave bent down, setting the pitcher and the cups upon the floor. When she motioned to Elisabeth, offering to pour, it was the Jesuit who shook his head, who gestured at her to leave them. He sloshed the frothy liquid into two cups and, pushing one into her hand, raised his own to Elisabeth and, without speaking, tipped back his head and took a long, slow pull.

'Damn, that stuff is good,' he said, and he wiped his mouth with the back of his hand.

When Elisabeth did not reply, he bent down, picking up the book beside her chair and examining the spine.

'Montaigne, eh?' he said. 'The great scourge of mendacity and humbug. This is yours?'

Elisabeth blinked. Then slowly she dragged her gaze up to the book in Rochon's hand.

'Mine? Yes. Yes, it is.'

'Of course the name Michel comes from the Hebrew *Micha-el* meaning 'he who is like God'. An ironic choice for a man whose maxim was 'What do I know?' ' Rochon turned the book over in his hands. 'An extraordinary man. Did you know that as a child Montaigne spoke

269

neither Gascon nor French but Latin? His father arranged that he should hear nothing else for all his first years so that it might become his native tongue.'

'Is that so?' Elisabeth said faintly.

'He never mastered the same fluency in Greek, though surely it was the School of Athens who influenced him most profoundly. Socrates, of course, but Plato too and Aristotle. It was from Aristotle that he understood that though the human soul may vary in quality, it does not change in nature. Though we may judge others and find them wanting, or ourselves for that matter, there is no human vice or virtue that is beyond the understanding of us all.'

Elisabeth closed her eyes, swaying a little so that the cup in her hand slopped.

'*What a wonderful thing it is,*' she murmured. '*That drop of seed, from which we are produced, bears in itself the impressions, not only of the bodily shape, but of the thoughts and inclinations of our fathers!* A wonderful thing indeed.'

'Sit,' the Jesuit instructed, taking her arm, and she obeyed, her knees buckling beneath her so that she half fell into the rocker. 'Praise God that you are with child and near your time. Another's situation cannot make it less so.'

He remained with her until the low sun slipped behind the trees and the air grew thin and chill. He had been in town some days, but he offered little explanation of his return except to say the commandant had called him back on business to do with the Chickasaw, who desired a mission set up among them. Instead he talked of Montaigne and the great Jansenist Pascal and of his time in the Jesuit seminary that had been both a prison and a vast new land. Elisabeth was grateful. The present tipped dizzyingly beneath her feet and she did not dare look down. Instead she rocked back and forth, her arms tight around her belly, and she held tight to her father who was dead and to the books she had read in Paris and the words piled a wall in her skull, to keep out the choke and hold her steady.

Rochon bid her goodnight regretfully, said he would come again. When he was gone, Elisabeth rocked a little but the chair hurt her back and her legs twitched and there was no stillness in her. She paced the cabin, picking things up and setting them back down. Several times she started towards the yard door only to turn away again after a few steps, her rush of resolve quite drained away.

When Jean-Claude returned for supper, it took all of her strength to stay her hands from shaking. She served him his meal in silence. She kept her eyes on the floor, unable to look into his face for fear that she would see him altered, a stranger, or, worse, that she would not. And still her agitation crackled in the darkening cabin, charging the air. She saw it in him, in the tautness of his back, the restiveness of his hands. Beneath the table his leg jigged up and down.

'I am to go north again,' he said when he was finished. He did not sit but stood and came over to where she was. 'We ready the expedition tomorrow. We leave at dawn the day after.'

271

Elisabeth nodded, her head bent over the dishes.

'Oh, and the slave,' he added offhandedly. 'I mean to sell her. It is an inconvenience, I know, when you have her trained, but you must confess you have never liked her.' Jean-Claude dropped a brisk kiss on his wife's head and took his hat from its peg by the door. 'Do not look so dismayed. I shall trade her for one younger, stronger. You shall not be inconvenienced.'

Elisabeth did not know how long she sat there. Certainly it was quite dark when the banging came on the door. When the boy came in, the lantern caught the dirty dishes so that the dried scabs of gravy gleamed black on their pale sides.

'Quickly,' the boy shouted, and the lantern shook in his hand and made shadows jump wildly against the wall. 'You must come quickly.'

Elisabeth pressed her fingers to her brow. The boy was familiar and yet she could not imagine who he was.

'It is Mme Conaud, she is at her time. You must hurry.'

'Surely Mme le Bras — '

'The midwife is already there. There is difficulty. She asks for you. Please, Madame, I beg you, come with me.'

In the lamplight the boy's face crumpled. Elisabeth looked at him and knew him for Anne Conaud's son, whose father had died the summer past of the black vomit. She stood, reaching down her shawl and putting it about her shoulders.

'Come then,' she said. 'Let us hurry.'

* * *

It was late in the afternoon of the following day when Anne Conaud was finally delivered of a baby daughter. She was weak, for the infant had been required to be pulled from her by force and she had lost a great deal of blood, but she would live and the child also.

'Go home,' Guillemette le Bras urged Elisabeth. 'Look at you. You are white with fatigue.'

Elisabeth thought of the cabin and the dirty dishes stacked on the table and the kitchen hut with its door closed tight, and she shook her head.

'You go,' she said. 'I shall remain here and make sure she does not sleep.'

Guillemette protested, but she was dizzy with fatigue and Elisabeth was adamant.

'At least go home and wash, change your clothes,' Guillemette suggested. 'I shall wait here until you return.'

Elisabeth looked down at her bloodstained apron, her skirts smeared with the effusions of the lying-in bed, and she nodded. When she opened the door to the cabin, its orderliness was startling. The floor was swept, the table scoured, the dirty dishes washed and stacked neatly on the shelf. If it had not been for the basket of potatoes on the table, she might have thought the house unoccupied.

The potatoes were whiskery, their flanks dark and spotted. They would not last long. She picked one up, feeling its cool weight in her

273

hand, the spongy give of a bruise against the ball of her thumb, and the skin split, oozing wet flesh. She set it down, wiping her hand on her apron, and saw beneath the other potatoes in the basket the pale corner of a folded sheet of paper.

When she had read it, she folded it again along the precise folds and set it back in the basket. She set the potatoes on top of it exactly as it had been. Then she washed her face and hands, changed her clothes and walked briskly back to the house of Anne Conaud, where Guillemette le Bras was waiting for her.

The girl returned breathless.

'The basket,' he said. 'You — ?'

The girl nodded.

'You remembered, didn't you, about the salt?'

The girl blinked. She had a manner of blinking that squeezed her whole face tight, as though it had been pulled with a drawstring. Then she nodded again and, squatting down, set to gathering up the mess of dishes beside his bed. Though nothing had been said, it had become the way of things somehow, the slave in the cooking hut and the girl in the house.

The questions rose in him like dough and he longed to seize the girl's arm, to demand precisely the words spoken and the silences, the manner of her voice, the set of her face and tilt of her head, whether her hair escaped its pins. Instead he let his hands fall open on the rugs, palms upward. His fingers curled, holding nothing. It was set. There was nothing else to be done.

Throughout that endless day and the night that followed, Auguste lay among his tangled bedclothes, counting time in the pulses of his broken shoulder. The rotting walls of the cabin pressed in on him, sucking the air from his lungs. As the day faded he asked the girl to prop the door open so that he might see into the yard. The plants were shattered bones, slimed about with mud and dead black leaves, and above them the weatherless sky turned away from him, indifferent to the whispered urgency in a cabin on the rue d'Iberville, the humdrum ruination of small lives. Auguste knew the pettiness of his grief even as it cried out in him, the dreary cycle of betrayal and counter-betrayal that marked the human season, but knowing it was not consolation but another grief. Was it now that she opened the letter? Or now? Or did she at this moment take up her knife, the one with the fluted blade and the savage patterns burned into the handle, and take from the pile the first of the whiskery potatoes? On the back of her hand she had a pattern of freckles like the five on a die.

He called for willow tea. It quietened neither his pain nor his imaginings. When he no longer could endure either, he had the girl bring him his notebook and a pencil and asked that she sit for him while he sketched her. Though he worked with a grim doggedness, it was a poor likeness. There was a folded-up quality about the girl on the page, a sulky flatness to her fierce black eyes so that she looked merely ill-tempered. When she asked if she might have it, he tore it out roughly, impatient to be rid of it.

As the hours inched through the mangle of the night, he kept a light burning so that he might not lose the shape of himself in the darkness. Sometime before dawn it rained, and the rain thrummed on the roof of the cabin and slapped against the mud of the lane outside. He thought of the *baire* then, the leaking linen and the holes left in the wet earth when the tent was gone.

276

Rain was a curse for the expeditioner. It dampened his gunpowder, rotted his meat, extinguished his fire, set mould to growing in his clothing. It stiffened his boots. As he waited for the night to end, he thought of the mornings that he too had risen before dawn in the chill grey smear of half-light, the rain whispering at his collar as the savages worked to stretch skins tight over the cargo of the pirogues to keep them dry.

It shocked him to wake and find the morning already well advanced. The dawn expedition had departed while he slept. It was no longer raining. He could hear birds, a dog barking, the steady knock of the axe as the slave chopped wood. Somewhere someone shouted. It might have been an ordinary day.

He did not know how long he lay there before the girl came in. When she saw he was awake she frowned.

'I was waiting,' she said. 'You should have called me.'

The slave brought willow tea, porridge, dressed his wounds. The girl washed his face and smoothed his rugs. Nobody spoke. It might have been an ordinary day.

★   ★   ★

Several times during that morning, he thought to send the girl to the rue d'Iberville. There was nothing she could say, nothing she might reasonably ask, but the longing for particulars burned in him like desire, engulfing reason, and he called for her. When she did not come, his

277

petulance shaded into anger and he shouted, jarring his shoulder so that for a moment he could not breathe. It was the slave who came then. The girl was not there, she said, and Auguste thanked her and sent her away, and the futility of his longing swelled inside him until it threatened to close his throat.

It was a little before noon that the Jesuit came to the house. Auguste heard his voice on the stoop and the girl's also. He called out, but there was no answer. He heard the Jesuit's low laugh. Then the door opened.

'You have yourself a fine guard dog there,' Rochon said with a grin. 'She tells me you had a poor night.'

'It was not so bad.'

'You certainly look a great deal better than you did. I doubt the Englishman shall do so well if they find him. Might I sit?' Rochon pulled out a stool and set it across from Auguste's bed, settling his bulk awkwardly upon it. 'I was half tempted to go with them, you know. In the last days I have found to my consternation that there is a great deal more of the savage in me than I realised. I have yet to decide whether it is the company of the Nassitoches I should blame for it or the Old Testament.'

'The expedition — '

'Left this morning, apparently, though I suspect too late to be of much use. Bienville is hopeful, but then hopefulness is the principal duty of his position. I don't suppose I might have something to drink?'

Auguste listened numbly as the Jesuit talked

278

idly of town politics and of the grumbling feud between the Catholic priests and the Jesuits over the rights to missionise the lower reaches of Louisiana. The questions itched at him like lice but he dared not ask them.

'If we might only establish a school, we might have the savages missionise themselves. Elisabeth Savaret does what she can in their cabin but I should like to see her in charge of a proper school. I meant to propose it to her when I saw her this morning, but she looked so completely exhausted that I thought I would be better biding my time.'

'She is not unwell, I hope?' Auguste asked, struggling to keep his voice steady.

'No, no, though she shall make herself ill if she continues in this way. The Conaud woman has been labouring since Sunday, though, praise God, she was delivered this morning of a baby girl. When I passed Elisabeth on my way here, she was pale as milk and hardly able to speak for fatigue. The poor creature had not been home in two days.'

Auguste felt the bottom of his stomach drop away.

'Two days.'

'It does not sound much and yet it is always startling to me, how quickly sleeplessness disorders body and mind. King Perseus of Macedonia, of course, was murdered in Rome simply by being prevented from sleeping. Elisabeth was not so unfortunate, I grant you, but still she was almost insensible. I had to insist upon accompanying her home. Four times on the way there, she asked that I tell her husband she was come home and, though I told her as many times he was already departed, moments later she would ask again, as though I had not spoken.' He shook his head. 'Still, we must be glad that sleep restores reason at least as swiftly as its lack would steal it away. She will be recovered presently.'

Auguste said nothing.

'Is he a decent man, her Babelon?' Rochon asked after a while. 'His disregard for men of the cloth might be construed with equal reason as brute ignorance or an unconscionable good sense.'

'He — I — ' Auguste broke off, pressing his fingers into the sockets of his eyes. The questions swarmed across his skin, biting into his flesh. The torment of them was unbearable. 'The potatoes. Did she get the potatoes?'

'Potatoes?' Rochon looked baffled.

'I sent potatoes. Did she get the potatoes?'

'Now that you mention it there was, I think, a basket of potatoes on the table. Or apples perhaps. Something sweet-smelling, certainly, and slightly rotten. You sent them? So you are no longer a secret?'

'I — no. Not any more.' Auguste was silent. Then he closed his eyes. 'I wonder if you might come back another time? I am rather tired myself.'

Rochon smiled.

'I would ill wish the fate of King Perseus of Macedonia upon you, my friend. Sleep soundly. I shall come again tomorrow.'

As soon as the Jesuit was gone, Auguste called the slave and, asking her loudly for tea, bid her in a whisper to help him dress. He did not have the strength for the girl's fierce gaze. When at last he was in his breeches, the sweat stood out from his forehead and his head swam with silver.

'Come with me,' he said to the slave and, with painful slowness, they made their way through the mud-choked yard and out into the rue Pontchartrain. Each step required the summoning of all of his strength, the shock of the earth sending jagged spasms of pain like lightning down the side of his broken body. The lanes stretched away from him, tilting and swinging so that he lurched forward, losing his footing. Only the strong hands of the slave on his good arm stopped him from falling. On the rue d'Iberville, several passers-by stopped and called out to him, astonishment sharpening their greetings, but he hardly heard then. Fixing all his resolve upon the toes of his boots, he stumbled on.

When at last they reached the Babelon house, Auguste was a deathly grey, his breath coming in ragged snatches. Half leaning on the wall, his legs slackening beneath him, he closed his fist and banged on the door. The slave Okatomih opened it.

'She sleeps,' she said in Mobilian.

'The potatoes,' Auguste rasped in her own language. 'Bring me the potatoes.'

Okatomih's expression did not change. Turning, she went back into the house. Auguste closed his eyes, releasing himself into the embrace of the splintery wall. His legs no longer obeyed him. He was very cold and hollow too, so that the air roared through him, filling his skull with noise.

'Monsieur?'

Auguste opened his eyes. The slave held out an earthenware pot. Inside it the peeled potatoes huddled together, like fledglings in a nest. He shook his head violently.

'No!' he cried and he seized the rim of the pot and shook it so that the potatoes rattled. 'The basket, where is the basket — ?'

Silently the slave reached inside the door.

There was nothing in the basket but some crumbs of mud and, on the rim, a hardening smear of rotten potato. 'What about the letter?' he demanded. 'There was a letter here, in the basket. What did you do with the letter?'

The slave shrugged.

'No letter.'

'A fold of paper, here in the basket — '

Again the slave shrugged.

'Maybe the mistress took?' she said.

Auguste closed his eyes. The roaring rose up about him like water until he was cold as clay and the dead weight of him drew him down into the darkness until the roaring closed over his head.

It was some weeks later when the body of a French soldier was found by a Canadian *coureur* by the name of François Maurichon. Tangled in the thick reeds that fringed the wide plain of the Mississippi River, it bobbed gently, face down, outspread fingers stirring small circles in the yellow water. Maurichon was wary of alligators, and he cursed under his breath as he pushed through the waist-high water to retrieve the body.

It was no small matter to wrestle it through the undergrowth. Even before he had managed to pull it to shore, Maurichon could see that the dead man was much mutilated. There were deep cuts to his back and shoulders and above the slimy collar of his coat his fleshless skull gleamed pale. It was the savage way to pass a knife around the heads of their dead enemies, slicing around the ears and peeling back the skin of the scalp by the hair. Maurichon hauled the body onto the bank and turned it over. The dead man's head fell back, his throat gaping like a toothless white mouth.

The *coureur* shuddered. Hacking a few fronds from a nearby palmetto bush, he hastily covered the body and retreated to the bluff to smoke and consider his options. A little later he made a search of the reeds. Tethered to a low tree, he found an abandoned pirogue and the man's pack, sliced open like a belly. Maurichon was not afraid. His musket was oiled and loaded, though the savages would be long gone by now. He thought of the bloated body, the eyes eaten from the eye sockets by fish. It had plainly been in the water many days.

All the same there was no mistaking the dead man. There was not a man in Louisiana who did not know Ensign Jean-Claude Babelon.

1719

After

The Kingdom of Louisiana is larger than the one of France. The climate is very mild and temperate. One inhales good air and can enjoy a perpetual spring, which contributes to the fertility of the soil of this country which abounds in everything.

In the upper part of the Mississippi one can see mountains filled with gold, silver, copper, lead and mercury which facilitate commerce. The savages have been domesticated by the French settlers, and they treat in good faith and without restraint, having nothing to fear from one another. As gold and silver are very common, and as the savages do not know their value, they exchange pieces of gold or silver for the European merchandise such as a knife made of steel, a steel axe to cut wood, often for a small mirror, a little dash of brandy or other things similar to their tastes.

Plans have been made for a new city which will be the capital of Louisiana. They call it New Orleans. There are already more than 600 houses which are practical for those that inhabit them. Its port is magnificent, of such great length and proportion that it will conveniently enclose vessels which come from all parts of the world.

The Catholic religion is making great progress through the tireless zeal of the missionaries. The frequent instruction given to the catechumens, in addition to the good example of the recent converts, attracts the idolatrous Indians (and unbelievers) to the joys of Jesus Christ and they ask in earnest to receive baptism.

Great care is given to the education of children, and good order reigns everywhere due to the attention and care of the principal officers of the Company.

— EXTRACT FROM A PAMPHLET
DISTRIBUTED AMONG INVESTORS
IN PARIS, c.1719

As was customary, the ship docked first at Dauphin Island. As they eased slowly into the small harbour, the sun was low, slanting into their eyes. The sea was a dark green, the island no more than a humped black rock against the fading sky. By the time that the anchor was set and the sails brought down, night had fallen. They did not go ashore. In the previous months, as the trickle of colonists had become a stream, Dauphin Island was become something of a shanty town, a tumble of temporary cabins thrown up for the new arrivals. Some had waited months for boats that might take them to their concessions. In the morning a sloop would take them to Mobile. Until then, they would be safer to remain aboard the *Baleine*.

In her narrow bunk that night, as on so many nights, Vincente le Vannes reached into her bodice and drew out the folded square of paper. She opened it carefully. The paper was worn soft as muslin, the picture on it split in several places along the deep creases, but still the delicate watercolours glowed jewel-bright in the smoky light of the candle.

The sea was a vivid aquamarine and beneath the pale sky the purple mountains were marbled with pink gold. Above the spires and turrets of the elegant city, fresh breezes swelled the sails of a three-masted ship and tumbled the feathered branches of an exotic tree. A curious-looking creature scrambled up its trunk, its elongated cat-body crowned with the face of a wizened old man. In the fore-ground merchants and sailors in bright blue silk coats jostled with sturdy savages, naked but for loincloths and head-dresses of brightly coloured feathers.

Louisiana. Vincente tasted the word as she traced a fingertip over the familiar silk of the painted ocean, the parapets of the fortified city. For months before she had left Paris, the talk had been all of Mr Law's Louisiana where pearls might be fished in abundance and the streams rolled on sands of gold, where the savages worshipped the white men as gods, and silver was so common it was used to pave the public roads. Immense grants of this enchanted land had been sold to the wealthiest men in the kingdom, and every day the rest had scrambled with the stockjobbers in the rue Quincampoix to snatch for themselves a share in the Mississippi Company which would make nobles of them all. Some had grown so rich already that a new word had been minted to describe them: *millionaire*.

The engraving had been thrust into her hand by a man selling the *Nouveau Mercure* from a stall close by the entrance to the convent. He had not asked for payment and she had known it immediately as a sign, though what it signified exactly she could not have said. At the very left of the picture a missionary in clerical garb sat at a table, holding aloft a wooden cross. Before him a savage raised his eyes to Heaven in a transport of ecstasy, his crossed hands pressed against his heart. He stood in the shadows, his pale countenance creased with thick black lines, as though the weight of the small cross caused him excessive strain.

The abbess's face had been soft and powdery, like a floured bun. Several times at the close of the day, when the twilight drifted in the cloisters and the novices were called to vespers, she had placed her hands upon Vincente's head and blessed her.

'Go home now, child,' she had said, and her voice had been gentle and full of kindness. The thought of it caused Vincente's eyes to prickle.

'For many are called,' Vincente murmured, 'but few are chosen,' and she ran her thumb over the missionary's lined visage, stroking at first, then pressing hard into the page until the page crumpled.

The ship rocked gently, setting the light to dipping. Pushing the engraving aside, Vincente reached under her pillow and brought out her Bible, opening it at the Book of Proverbs, but, though she tried to fix herself upon its commands, she found none of her usual consolation in its numbered certainties. Instead she reached out and once again took up the engraving, smoothing it out across the Bible's opened pages. Absently she ran a finger across the purple mountains, around the curve of elegant dwellings along the harbour wall. She wondered who lived there, whether her husband would own a house in the town, and she thought of the attic apartment in Paris, the cramped rooms with their mean windows, the ceilings that sloped low above the too-large furniture. The fireplaces were small, the light poor. In winter it was impossible to keep warm; in summer the sun baked the blue slates until the heat became insufferable. They might have found more comfortable accommodations elsewhere in the city, but her father was adamant. Whatever the treacheries of fortune, he insisted, they must remain in the Place Royale. It was the address that signified, he told them, the company a man kept that distinguished him and set him in his proper place. In the Place Royale a man, sooner or later, would find himself rich.

Then he had sold her. Her father knew people and he understood the value of the few assets he still possessed. When a nobleman who was cousin to someone high up in the Ministry of the Marine sent word from Louisiana that he had need of a wife of virtue and industry, M. le Vannes had professed himself only too willing to oblige, subject to certain terms. It had been Vincente's mother who had informed her of the arrangements. Vincente had stared at her mother's powdered face and remembered her sister Blandine's furtive whispers, the jab of her nudging elbow as she described to the round-eyed Vincente the terrible things a man could demand of his wife when it was dark and the drapes around their bed shut tight.

'What did he get for me?' she had demanded. 'Thirty pieces of silver?'

Mme le Vannes had only smiled.

'Regrettably, child,' she had said lightly, 'you are not worth half that amount.'

Still, he had sold her. A daughter in exchange for shares in the Mississippi Company and a grant of two hundred *livres* for the purchase of a trousseau. By the time Vincente knew of it the papers had been signed, the details confirmed. At supper that night her father had patted her shoulder and declared it a great triumph, for stock in Law's Mississippi was rarer than hen's teeth. Her mother had contemplated her in exasperation.

'If you insist on regarding as a misfortune marriage to a man whose estates yield harvests of gold, you are more suited to a madhouse than that damned nunnery,' she had declared. 'It is I who must find a seamstress skilled enough to make a bride from skin, bones and sackcloth.'

Later she had overheard her mother talking with her father in the parlour.

'I suppose we should be grateful Louisiana is so far away,' her mother had said. 'At least the Comte cannot consider the bargain of his purchase before it is paid for.'

Her father's laugh had seemed to Vincente the bitterest betrayal of them all.

The light spat, belching smoke. It was almost all burned out. Vincente rubbed her eyes and abruptly the hole inside her opened, pushing against the constraints of her bodice. She swallowed, pushing it down, but it pushed back, stretching into the sockets of her arms, the base of her throat. Vincente hesitated. Then from the pocket of her skirts she took the bread and cheese that she had smuggled from the dining room in a napkin. She had promised herself she would keep it till morning.

'Holy Mary, Mother of God,' she whispered as she tore frantically at the clumsy knot that secured it. 'Pray for us sinners now and at the hour of our death.'

Tearing open the bundle, she snatched up handfuls of food and crammed it into her mouth, pressing and swallowing, squeezing up her face as the lumps of ill-chewed bread travelled awkwardly down her throat and pressed themselves against the underside of her breast-bone. When the food was all gone and her hands lay slack in the grease-stained napkin, she lay down, her knees tight against her chest and her pulse hard, and the tears slid quietly from beneath her closed eyelids.

★ ★ ★

It was barely morning when the sloop cast off from the hull of the *Baleine* and made its slow voyage across the dun water towards Mobile. The mists had yet to clear and, in the cobweb dawn, Vincente stood upon the deck, straining for the first smudged sight of land. As the sun rose, rolled tight in the white pastry of the sky, and ropes and sails and shouts snapped around her, she gazed across the harbour, disbelief springing into her mouth like saliva.

The prospect before her bore no more resemblance to the Parisian illustration than it did to the filthy sprawl of Paris herself. Beneath the dough of the sky, the town of Mobile rose like a dismal act of defiance from the chaos of swamps that encircled it. The water was a muddy yellow soup, choked as far as the eye could reach with thick reeds, and the wooden cabins and warehouses circling the harbour were hardly better than cattle byres. There were no palms, no elegant spires. Instead there rose from the water great dark trees with leprotic bark that rotted in hanks from their trunks. Behind them, on higher ground, squatted a hunchbacked fort built of wood, with four bastions and a flagpole from which the faded flag sagged defeated, like a pauper's washing.

When at last the passengers were permitted to disembark, there were no gleaming savages, no men in fine silk coats. The motley crowd was poorly dressed. Several of the soldiers wore no shoes. Behind her several undernourished Negroes loaded luggage into a rough-looking flatboat of the kind peasants used for the transport of vegetables on the Seine. By the time she had departed Paris, she had convinced herself she left it gladly. She had declared herself disgusted with the city's ingrained dirt and covetousness, its clamour for money and courtly favour, the contaminated monotony of its society, the stink of its alleys and the shrieks of the hags selling herb teas and old hats. Throughout the long and comfortless voyage, it had consoled Vincente to consider how enraged Paris must be by the sweet youth of the New World, a land barely older than Vincente, its beauty freshly minted, its warm breezes soft as a kiss upon a lover's cheek. Beside the bloom of Louisiana, old Paris was no more than a toothless harlot, her peeling mask of paint and patches powerless to disguise the sag of her pockmarked flesh, the coarseness of her cynicism.

Vincente descended the gangplank in a daze of heat and stunned dismay. I am here, she thought. I have reached the promised land. When she had left it, Paris had been giddy, convulsed by speculation fever, the talk only of the Mississippi Company and of the magical country they called Louisiana. Every man in Paris had wanted a share in it. At the rue Quincampoix where stocks were traded, bishops and priests had jostled with courtesans, magistrates with prostitutes, aristocrats with their footmen and maids, and her father with anyone he could find. Fights had broken out; a man had been crushed to death in the stampede. For this.

'Mlle le Vannes, my name is Mme de Boisrenaud. I am only sorry that we meet in such circumstances. Why, they brought you the news in Havana, did they not? I do hope that I am not the one to whom the burden falls — you know, do you not, that M. de Chesse, to whom you were betrothed, is dead?'

Dizzy with the airless clamour of the dock, Vincente could only blink loose-jawed at the pinch-faced crone who stood before her. Though her expression was mournful and her skin slack with age, the old woman's eyes were round, almost eager, and she strained forward, nostrils wide, as though she meant to inhale the aroma of Vincente's distress.

'Last September, it was,' she lamented,

shaking her head. 'Every summer it comes, the fever, like a plague on us. Always some lost, though we have none to spare.'

The sourness of the old woman's breath caused Vincente to cover her nose with her fingers. It seemed that though M. de Chesse had been renowned for the robustness of his constitution and had resisted the illness for some weeks, the affliction had at last proved too formidable an opponent, even for him. It had been providential, the old woman said piously, that the gentleman had been resident at the time in the settlement of New Orleans and not at his concession upcountry. It had been possible to summon a priest to him in his final hours. Perhaps it would comfort the Mademoiselle to know that the last rites had been properly given.

Last September. The ship that had brought her here had finally put out from Rochefort two weeks before Christmas. When the old woman patted her sleeve, Vincente could only gape, seized by a bewilderment that was almost outrage. She could not shake the sense that someone, somewhere, was playing a vast and terrible joke upon her.

'Perhaps if your passage had been swifter?' the old woman commiserated, absently testing the silk between finger and thumb. 'We expected you months ago, of course. It really is most unfortunate. You can hardly have the most favourable first impression of our little colony.'

The old woman shook her head, her brow furrowed and a sad smile upon her lips.

'Hardly the welcome you might have hoped for, is it?'

The urge to strike the old crone was sudden and powerful. Vincente pressed her fists against her cheeks, pinching the flesh with her thumbs.

Her intended husband was dead.

The blow could not match the treachery of the place itself, but the shock of it still startled her. In the first blaze of her resistance, and then, later, dulled by seasickness and the heavy drag of inevitability, she had somehow failed to notice how accustomed she had grown to the fact of her marriage. Though a second box containing small household gifts had been stored in the hold, the chest containing her trousseau had, at her mother's insistence, been placed in her cabin, for she had not, her mother had declared, gone to all that trouble to lose the contents to thieves and damp. It had occupied nearly all the available space, and Vincente had been obliged to press its leather lid into use as table and writing desk. The grease stains and ink spots that had begun as a kind of defiance had persisted as symbol of her defeat, their unchanging forms testimony to her surrender. Once or twice she even discovered herself kneeling before the open lid, trailing her fingers in the pale foam of lace and silk. There was something grimly gratifying in the pain, like probing a bad tooth with the tip of one's tongue.

Vincente swayed, the ground shifting beneath her feet as though she were still aboard ship.

'Do you think — I feel rather unwell. Perhaps it would be possible to take a little water?'

The crone peered at her, examining first her

face and then the pearl brooch at her bosom before tilting her head, her mouth busy with sympathy.

'I pity you. I too was betrothed to a man who passed away before we could be married. He was a prominent man, perhaps the most prominent in all the colony, aside from the commandant himself. The influenza, they said. Five days before the wedding ceremony. Five days!'

'May he rest in peace.'

'Indeed. Though there has been precious little rest for those he left behind. Unlike you, I was not protected by the security of a marriage contract.'

Across the dock, half hidden by a heap of barrels and boxes, Sister Marie urged her flock through the jostling crowd. The daughters of beggars and felons, the sixty girls had been plucked from Paris's Salpétrière penitentiary so that they might be brought to America as wives for the rougher sort of settlers. A patched ragbag of a seraglio even in the inns of Lorient, they were worn thin and grey by the voyage. A number of the sorrier specimens had wept without ceasing for the entirety of the passage, prompting one waggish sailor to remark that this was the first seaworthy ship he'd had the pleasure of that carried more salt water inside the hull than out.

During the rough weather, when many feared themselves lost forever, Vincente had discovered one of them crouched on the deck, her arms about her knees, and had bid her there and then

299

to put her hands together and pray for the ship's safe deliverance. The girl, a scrawny creature with a chapped mouth and hair the colour of dust, had gaped at her with slack, pink eyes. Then she had vanished. The Salpétrière girls had a way of disappearing that was almost sinister, slipping through closed doors and the cracks in floorboards like curls of smoke.

Sister Marie looked up, meeting Vincente's eyes. Murmuring something to the girl at the head of the group, she swung round and hustled the girls away.

'It is not for us to question the will of the Lord,' Vincente said tightly. 'Those that trust in Him shall be brought from darkness into His eternal light.'

The crone blinked. Then she inclined her head.

'Your piety becomes you,' she said. 'The orphan girls are to be accommodated with the nuns in the centre of town, but you are to lodge at my house. The commandant considered it the most suitable arrangement, at least for the present. I shall do what I can to ensure your comfort.'

Vincente shrugged.

'I must go where the Lord intends me.'

The old woman's mouth tightened.

'You are fortunate, in that case, that He did not abandon you on Massacre Island,' she rejoined tartly. 'You would be lucky there of a shack fit for a pig.'

★　★　★

300

Vincente watched as a savage woman made her way through the crowd with a basket of food balanced on her head. The smell of fried batter insinuated itself between the salt and rot reeks of the quayside, flooding Vincente's mouth with a rush of saliva. The hole inside her stretched.

'Madame — '

'Now, now, a little jest, that is all. Did the Lord not command us to remain cheerful in the face of adversity, to bear our troubles without complaint? Of course they call it Dauphin Island these days, though most of us consider the old name more appropriate. Thank the Heavens that there are not enough boats to bring over all the human refuse that lands there. The place is full to bursting with felons, convicted felons if you don't mind, murderers and thieves and the good Lord only knows what dregs of humankind, packed off to save your precious Mr Law the trouble of finding decent folk to settle here. And at whose expense, I ask you?'

'Perhaps I might — '

'Everyone here is in a perfect ferment about it, make no mistake. We are grateful only that the commandant keeps them there and not here on the mainland, at least for the present. We have not suffered here this long to be slaughtered in our beds. Of course the savages are a different story. The ones around here are mostly docile. It is the money, you see. They wish to trade with us and know we shall not tolerate their excesses for all their corn and pumpkins. Some can even be prevailed upon to baptise their children, though their practice of the faith would hardly impress

Rome, but upcountry, why, it is said that the tribes are become so wild — '

Steadying her basket with one hand, the savage woman disappeared into the crowd. Vincente whimpered.

'Mme de Boisrenaud, I beseech you, if I might only rest a little, perhaps take some refreshment — '

The old woman's face snapped shut.

'You are in a hurry, I see. Very well then, please, let me waste no more of your time.'

With exaggerated briskness, she set about the arrangements for Vincente's boxes before escorting her charge away from the harbour in silence. They were a little way up the bluff before the impulse to instruct prevailed over her froideur.

'Of course you shall hardly find the advantages of Paris here in Louisiana, but I like to think we are improving. Sieur de Catillon has this last year brought over the colony's first wheeled chair, if you can believe such a thing! Though one cannot help but think he would have found a boat of more use. He must leave it in New Orleans for there is no road cut yet to his concession and none likely, if the Negroes continue so scarce. We scream for slaves, but it is to no avail. As for the savages, well, they either run up and off to their villages soon as captured, or else pine and die. Neither kind is of any use.'

Vincente let the old woman run on. The hole in her was a living thing, dense and muscular. As they made their way along rutted lanes bordered by dilapidated cabins, their windows sealed with rough linen, their roofs askew, it turned inside her, crushing the breath from her lungs. She stumbled, fixing her eyes on the tips of her boots. The thick dust of the path turned them the dull white of old bones.

'This is the Place Royale,' the old woman said as they crossed in front of the fort. Close up the sagging structure had a drunken air, its splintered walls askew. The wood pilings were green and swollen with damp. Vincente thought of the lofty red-brick mansions in Paris rising from the arches of the vaulted arcades, their great windows framed with pale stone quoins, and she was flooded with a despair so fierce that it was almost laughter.

'The Place Royale,' she echoed.

'Across there is the commandant's house and, next to that, the residence where your orphan girls shall be lodged until they are safely wed,' the old woman continued. 'It shall not take long. We suffer from a dearth of every kind of merchandise here. The ladies of Mobile pine for white flour and stockings, the gentlemen for French wine and fresh beef, and the soldiers of the garrison for cheap *eau-de-vie* and vigorous wives. They have set a sentinel at the door, you know, to contain their excesses.'

'The men or the girls?'

The old woman stopped. Then, with her cheeks sucked in, she expelled a snuffling snort of a laugh, her waggling finger aloft.

'Come now, Mam'selle, I am sure that the Sisters will confirm that the girls' conduct thus far has been above reproach.' She leaned in towards Vincente, her eyes beady. 'Or do you know better?'

Vincente thought of the long, starless nights of the tropics, when the thick black ink of the ocean bled ceaselessly into the black drapes of the sky and there was no end to it. Felled by sun-stunned sleep in the hot afternoons, she spent her wakeful nights crouched out of sight at the stern of the ship, watching the white wake unrolling like lace towards Havana. She paid no heed to the muted thumps, the stifled gasps, the sudden bursts of skittering bare feet. They were past White Island by then and she long past caring, adrift in her solitude and the yawning maw of her hunger. In Paris she had eaten little. Her fast was her offering to God, the emptiness in her belly a kind of righteousness. When the Devil came and she could not resist him, she thrust her fingers down her throat to expel the wickedness from her body. Uncorrupted by the grossness of appetite, contained within the strict confines of her fleshless body, she had willed herself pure in His sight, the desires of her heart clear and sweet. Besides, it had infuriated her mother.

She had grown accustomed to hunger. But aboard the *Baleine* it grew into a craving so violent that she was powerless to withstand it. At Havana they had taken on a milk cow, and every day there was milk and cheese and sweet, fresh butter, fat and cool against her ravenous tongue. She swallowed and her fingers stayed in her lap. The weight of the food in her belly kept her steady. As for the orphan girls, what did she care

304

for their reputations? It fell to Sister Marie to keep them from ruin. Their undoing would be the nun's too.

'Come now,' Mme de Boisrenaud coaxed. 'You can tell me.' Vincente looked at the old woman's greedy eyes, her parted lips, and she hated her and the orphan girls and Sister Marie and Louisiana, and most of all she hated the hole that stretched inside her and would not let her go.

'I am no scandalmonger, Madame,' she spat. 'The shepherd who speaks ill of his flock speaks ill of himself. Now, I beg you, I must eat.'

The old woman's face pinched.

'You do me great disservice, Mlle le Vannes. I seek only to ensure that the honourable men of this colony receive wives of equal virtue, but it seems that your Mr Law is satisfied with sending them the very dregs.'

Stiffly Mme de Boisrenaud stalked away. She had no intention of being preached at by a child. She thought of M. de Chesse, whose desperate appeals to physicians both French and native had brought no cure for his disease, and her lips curled sourly. Wherever it was that his godless soul wandered, he was surely congratulating himself upon a fortuitous escape.

On the bluff above the wide yellow river, a handful of plank cabins huddled together, their mud-plastered walls capped with roofs of bedraggled palmetto. Behind them the roughly cleared ground sloped downward towards a cow pen and, further down, another group of shacks, strung about with laundry and built around a circle of smoke-blackened rocks that served as a fireplace. A little downriver, a high fence of logs encircled an encampment of Negroes; upstream a crooked palisade stood sentry against the moss-slung shadows of the forest.

The place was known among the settlers as Burned-canes, for the canebrakes that had been burned to clear the land for occupation. It had exasperated Elisabeth once, the pitiful lack of poetry in the names chosen by the exploratory parties. The colony was pristine, as blank as a fresh sheet of paper, and yet, in drawing up their maps, the men had contrived no more than a list for the butcher: Fish-river, Cat-island, Grass-point, Red-post. When Elisabeth discovered that one curve of the St Louis River had been dubbed Plate-point because the commandant's brother had lost a plate there, she had declared it an outrage and had threatened to take the matter up with the commandant himself. She had not done so then. She would not now.

It was of no consequence. The plantation at

Burned-canes was not theirs. It belonged to a French nobleman whose family name was eminent enough to carry weight among the financiers of Paris. It mattered not at all that the nobleman was a dissolute with a powerful dislike for matters of agriculture. The newly established Mississippi Company, who had pressed the land upon him as a gift, had assured him that he would need to mine only one-tenth of his property to bring up enough gold for several lifetimes. The nobleman, bruised by a series of unhappy speculations, had not hesitated. Mustering sixty sturdy labourers and their wives from the Rhineland, he had set sail from Lorient to claim his spoils.

In Havana the ship had been struck with fever. More than half of the Rhinelanders had died. While he waited to weigh anchor, the nobleman purchased two skinny cows and a handful of Negroes, and closed his ears to the tiresome band of naysayers who shook their heads and declared his schemes fantastical. It took several more weeks to reach Mobile and another month to raise the ships necessary to transport himself and what remained of his men to the plantation. By then he had almost nothing left. Enraged and embittered, he had ordered his foreman to grow something and sought refuge in the newly established settlement of New Orleans, a hardly town of a few shacks, where he consoled himself with brandy and a rash of whores fresh from the prisons of Paris.

It was the foreman's idea to try indigo, which grew wild in those parts. The indigo flourished.

307

His men did not. They were good men for the most part, large in build and uncomplaining in nature, but the climate plagued them, the teeming compost of the air rotting their lungs. Several more fell ill. Even those who resisted the sickness found themselves stupefied by the heat, their skin purpled with fierce rashes. Their feet bloated and decayed in their leather boots and their bowels turned to water. The incessant bites and stings of the insects burst into boils.

A handful of the Rhinelanders had brought wives. The women were broad-faced and large-boned and huddled around the cabins, their flanks pressed together like cattle. There were no children. It was whispered among the cattle-women that the water in Louisiana made you barren. It was whispered too, and very cautiously, that the foreman's wife was a witch.

The foreman, whose name was Fuerst, had acquired his wife at Mobile. It had been Burelle, the taverner, who had brought the widow to his attention. She was not young nor was she lively, Burelle confessed, but she kept a spotless house and she had a slave. Not being one for company, she would not miss the town. Besides, her husband's death had left her in precarious circumstances. Fuerst had sought the widow out that same day. His French was poor, but he knew enough to make himself understood.

Four days later, he and Elisabeth Savaret were married.

★　★　★

Elisabeth sat on a makeshift bench set against the wall of the largest cabin. The palmetto roof cast a little shadow, but still she squinted against the fierce afternoon sun as she bent her head over the torn shirt in her lap. The shirt was made of nettle-bark linen and the rough fabric frayed easily under the coarse needle. Elisabeth folded the seam and stabbed the needle into the thick layer of stuff, pulling the thread tight.

Over by the cooking hut, the savage woman was pounding corn for bread. The steady *thump-thump* of the paddle throbbed in the blood-thick afternoon. Beside her mother the child squatted in the dirt, drawing shapes in the dust with a stick. Her hair fell across her face and her dirty knees were sharp as elbows. It still startled Elisabeth to observe the child's hard, narrow body, her coltish grace, the sprinkle of freckles across the bridge of her nose. None of the other savages had freckles. Elisabeth thought of the day she had first seen her swaddled in her sling of linen, the plump and dimpled infant with her wide dark eyes and her shock of dark hair and her mouth like a bud beginning to open, and she closed her eyes tight, twisting her head as if from a blow, jabbing the needle hard into the shirt's hem.

Wincing, she put her thumb in her mouth. A spot of red blood bloomed in the rough fibres of the shirt's hem. Elisabeth spat on it and rubbed it with her good thumb but it did not come out. She sighed, pressing her fingers into the sockets of her eyes. She knew it was within the means of any woman to be neat in her work, just as it was quite possible for any woman to husband her household's resources, however meagre. It required only precision and vigilance, both of which might easily be learned. Precision and vigilance and a mind wedged shut against the slippages of memory.

She took up her needle once again, but her fingers were clumsy. The stitches came out irregularly, pulled too tight, so that the seam bunched and refused to lie flat. On the bench beside her, a butterfly settled, its wings trembling together like hands. Then, very slowly, it spread them wide. Elisabeth saw that they were a velvety burnt orange, traced all over with a delicate fretwork of black and white, each one as wide as her palm. For a moment it was still, its feelers quivering faintly in the heat, as fragile as a flower pressed between the pages of a book. Then with a flash of orange it was gone.

Some days were just more difficult than others. They required a greater exercise of will. Pressing her lips together, Elisabeth bent her head over her seam, stretching it and pressing down hard with her thumbs. Carefully she pulled the needle through, but the thread caught. It was knotted, looped around itself. She tugged at it to free it. The knot did not give. She pulled harder. The thread snapped.

The cry was out of her before she could stop it. Across the yard the savage woman looked up. Elisabeth frowned, squinting at the needle as she tried to rethread it. The thread was frayed, her hands unsteady. After three attempts she let them drop into her lap and closed her eyes. The afternoon seemed to tip away from her, dizzying in its heat and silence. It was a few moments before she realised that the regular *thump-thump* of the flour paddle had ceased. She breathed in, steadying herself, sliding her precious needle into her collar for safe keeping before folding her husband's shirt and reaching down to place it in the basket at her feet. When she looked up, the slave was kneeling by the cooking hut, the front of her dress unfastened. The savage woman swayed a little, her eyes half closed, her fingers loose in her child's tangled hair as the girl pressed her face against her mother's chest.

'For the love of-!' Elisabeth cried out.

As she strode across the yard, the child ducked her head, wiping her mouth with the back of her small hand, and pressed herself against her mother's side. The nipple of the exposed breast was puckered tight, its brown centre thrusting out like a stalk, pale traces of milk pearling its crumpled folds. There was a dent in the flesh left by the child's nose. The savage woman's hands tightened on her daughter's shoulders. Then she reached up and retied the strings of her dress.

'Have I not made myself clear on this matter?' Elisabeth demanded. 'The child is five years old, not a babe in arms. If she is hungry, there is sagamity enough in the kettle.'

'Yes, Madame.'

The savage woman's voice was gentle. The child looked up at her mother, her lip caught between her teeth. Elisabeth observed the slope of the girl's cheek, the way that the syrupy sunlight caught in the pale down beneath her ear, and she was overcome by an abrupt and unbearable fatigue.

'Now get back to work,' she said wearily. 'There is a great deal to be done.'

Slowly, stiff-legged, Elisabeth walked back to her bench. She sat upright, her back straight, not touching the rough mud plaster of the wall. Once the planks had exhaled the sharp curative tang of cypress and she had not been able to sit outside, for the smell of them had split her open like a chisel. Now the cypress smell was gone. The dried-mud mortar smelled only of stones, of dust. It was a dead smell.

Her hands were quiet now, her pulse heavy and slow. Beside her the gun gleamed dark and sleek in the slanting afternoon silent. Fuerst had shown her how to fire it. She thought of the weight of it, the resistance of the trigger against her finger, the kick in her shoulder as it went off. The birds had startled from the woods in a confusion of wings and cawing.

'I pray you shall never have need of it,' he had said to her. 'But I cannot always be here. You must be able to kill if you have to.'

Once again Jeanne's flour paddle resumed its steady thump. Jeanne. A French name and yet for so long it had tasted foreign in Elisabeth's mouth. She had become accustomed to it though. The slave had grown into the name and the name into her, so that it was no longer possible to see where one ended and the other began. Jeanne was no longer Okatomih and yet she held her old self inside her, like the stone in a plum.

With a concerted effort, Elisabeth leaned down and took a stocking from the basket at her feet. Across the yard the child looked up at her mother. The savage woman nodded. With great deliberation, as though she balanced on a tree branch, the child walked over to Elisabeth.

She eyed the gun.

'Beg pardon, Madame,' she said, her hands curled behind her back. Her accent was already better than her mother's. 'You like me make study?'

Elisabeth slid her hand inside the stocking, stretching out the foot. The girl's eyes were almond-shaped, their heavy lids and thick brows giving her a solemn, sleepy look. Her mother rubbed her with bear oil, in the manner of native children, so that she might be protected from the sun, but she was not yet burned brown. Her skin was tawny, like fruit, and on her nose the skin had peeled a little, leaving a faint trace of freckles smeared with dirt.

Elisabeth wanted to take her in her arms, to crush the child's narrow body against her own. She wanted to bury her face in her neck, to twist her hands in her hair, to kiss her until her lips split with the force of it. Instead she examined the hole in the stocking's heel. It had been darned several times before. Its edges gaped with stitches like broken teeth.

The girl shifted, glancing behind her towards her mother. Jeanne's arms rose and fell as she pounded the corn, the muscles twisting like vines

313

beneath the skin. The child hesitated, coiling her hair around her finger and pulling it into her mouth.

'Madame?' she tried again.

Elisabeth stared at the hole in the stocking. Then she looked up. Behind the child's head, the sun tangled in the trees, its sticky light stretched in strings of burned sugar. There was a dimple in the child's cheek the size of a fingertip. Elisabeth smiled, her lips clumsy, and shook her head. Then she returned her attention to the stocking.

'Not today,' she said, and she spread her fingers inside the stocking until the hole gaped. Still the child did not go. Her toe traced a circle in the dust.

'I like study with you,' the child said.

'Tomorrow perhaps. If there is time.'

Elisabeth could feel it starting, the tightness that closed around her like an iron bodice, the nausea, the fierce urgency for which she could find no object.

'But my mama said — '

'I said no, didn't I?' she snapped, and halfway through its circle the child's toe stopped. Elisabeth hunched her shoulders, her gaze fixed upon the stocking. He was buried in the wretched stretch of swamp that Bienville had chosen for his new capital, though there had been no town then. At her insistence they had taken her to what passed for the grave. Perrine Roussel, who had immediately appointed herself Elisabeth's guardian, protested that it was foolish, dangerous, that she was not yet strong enough to leave Perrine's cabin, but she had to do something. It took three days to reach the place. The ground was sodden, slippery with mud that clung like lead to the hem of her skirt. Parts of the ground had been cleared and pale tangles of roots reached like fingers from the churned earth. She did not remember anything else except that they had half carried her to the pirogue. They told her afterwards that, as she struggled, she had cried out to him by name, beseeching him to help her.

'It would have satisfied him, no?' Perrine had reflected later. 'That it was to him that you turned for protection, even in death.'

'On the contrary, it would have angered him,' Elisabeth had replied, and her eyes had shone hard and bright. 'He always wished me more self-reliant.'

That night, when Perrine was asleep, she had opened her box. It had been Perrine who had insisted upon her sorting those possessions of his that she no longer needed so that they might be sold. Clothes remained in short supply, and even a much-mended pair of stockings might fetch six *livres*. When, after two days in the rue d'Iberville, she had contrived to fill only a small box with belongings of her own she wished to keep, Perrine had grown impatient and taken over the task herself.

Very slowly Elisabeth had lifted her everyday apron from the box. One by one she set the items out on the floor. His laced hat. His linen shirt with the frayed cuffs. His broadcloth coat. His good shoes, scabbed around their wooden heels with mud. All except the lace dress. She covered that with the apron and pushed the box away. Its corners left chalky scratches on the plank floor.

In Perrine's house the clothes looked real. The hat was stained and the leather of the boots worn, their outside edges humped by the bulge of his feet. His feet had been small but broad, his toes tufted with hair. Once a month she had pared his toenails, his feet set between her thighs. Elisabeth touched one boot very lightly with the tip of her finger. She would clean them and oil the leather to preserve it. Perrine might sell whatever else she could, for Heaven knew Elisabeth needed the money, but she could not sell his boots. Good boots were impossible to find in Louisiana.

When he came back he would need his boots.

★ ★ ★

'Madame? Are you well?'

The child's hand was light upon her sleeve. Dazedly, Elisabeth looked up. The girl's face was close to hers. She was frowning, her brows drawn together, her mouth, her impossible mouth —

He had never been hers. The fire in her had burned for him alone, a fierce and private flame lighting a single page, a single face. But the fire in him was like the fire that had consumed Old Mobile. There was no holding it. It leaped from one cabin to the next, hardly troubling to finish with one before starting on its fellow, and hurling itself against the sky as though it would out-blaze the stars themselves. By the time the Mobile fire was finally put out, eleven cabins had been destroyed.

Elisabeth closed her eyes and in the grainy red darkness his empty boots stood set together, side by side.

'Please,' she said. 'Leave me alone.'

The child hesitated. Elisabeth snapped open her eyes.

'Go away!' she cried, and the child's eyes opened round, and she held herself tightly with her thin arms and walked away.

Elisabeth peeled the stocking from her hand. Then, very carefully, she stood and walked into the cabin. Her entire body, her clothes, her hair, were ablaze with despair, her skin so scalded and blistered with it that the slightest touch would have been insufferable.

On the other side of the yard, the girl glared at her mother.

'You should not have sent me,' she said in her own language. 'She was angry.'

Jeanne laid down her paddle.

'Oh, little one,' she said, smoothing her daughter's forehead with her thumb. 'The master shall be home soon. We must have supper ready.'

The child gazed up at her mother.

'Why is the Madame always angry at me?'

'She is angry with us all and with herself too.'

'But why?'

'It helps her forget her sadness.'

'But she has another husband now. Surely she is not sad any more?'

'But of course she is sad, little bear cub. Their

317

tribe is not like ours. Even the most honoured of white men must go alone into the country of their spirits and leave those who would care for him behind. The Madame grieves for his loneliness.'

'Was the Monsieur honoured?'

'No. But he was loved.'

'Then he shall not be lonely for long.'

Jeanne smiled, her mouth twisting a little at the corner, and pressed her lips to her daughter's head.

'You see things clearly, child. It is the Madame who needs our comfort now.'

★ ★ ★

It was almost dusk when Artur Fuerst returned to the settlement. The men were tired and hungry, the mosquitoes already gathering in black clouds against the darkening sky, and they ate the meal that Jeanne had left for them rapidly and in silence, their forks sounding in dull knocks against the rough wooden plates.

In their own enclosure, despite the warmth of the evening, the Negroes squatted beside the fire that with its sour palmetto smoke did something to discourage the insects. They too ate greedily, each dipping into the big tin kettle with his own wooden spoon, scooping up the thick mess of peas and broken biscuits. When they had granted the nobleman his land, the Company had promised him three hundred Negroes to work it. So far Fuerst had received fourteen. The French surgeon who had examined them upon arrival had pronounced them all severely weakened by the privations of their passage. One of them, on account of a sickness he had succumbed to on the ship, was as good as blind. The balls of his eyes had a swirled look, like broken eggs. Fuerst despatched him daily to the bayou, to catch fish. There was little else that could be done with him.

The fire crackled and burst, sending flowers of sparks into the darkening sky. Summoning the Negro he had chosen as leader, Fuerst issued his orders for the following day, taking care to raise his voice so that the whole band might clearly hear him and not lose time in the morning coming to enquire about their duties. In the firelight their faces wore expressions at once assiduous and vacant, and their skin gleamed black-gold, their eyes ringed with yellow. Above the scent of the burning palmetto, he could smell the slaves' animal odour. It made him afraid.

When he had locked the Negro enclosure, Fuerst hurried up the bluff, calling out goodnight to the men as he passed their cabins. He was weary. The raiding parties of the savages were taking their toll. It was not just a matter of the lost livestock, though that was bad enough. Slowed by the heat, the men were further hampered by the need to hold themselves with weapon in hand. They were falling behind.

He did not like it that the men went armed. The Rhinelanders were good workers and not given to complaining, but they were restive. He could not blame them. Back in the Rhineland, when the agents of the newly formed Mississippi

Company had spoken to them so eloquently of the promise of the New World, each man had agreed to be bound to the Company for three years in exchange for a monthly stipend and, when the three years were up, the endowment of thirty *arpents* of his own land. It had seemed a straightforward enough agreement. The previous year the French Crown had granted the Mississippi Company a monopoly on all trade between France and its Eden of a colony for twenty-five years, the sole right to mine and farm the land. All that was wanting was industrious people: men to work the land and to share in its spoils. The Rhinelanders had come eagerly, impatient for this promised land of plenty where savages prostrated themselves before the white man, where deer offered themselves up for meat and settlers paid no taxes and the Company handed out not only rich and fertile land but also the seeds for its cultivation.

Now they knew better. For months the men's stipend had gone unpaid. Trade between settlers had been outlawed and all commerce restricted to the Company's stores, at the Company's exorbitant prices. Nobody could leave the colony without the Company's express permission. Fuerst had heard the men talk. They declared themselves little better than slaves, dragged from Europe as the Negroes were dragged from Africa, to serve a cruel and pitiless master. They meant the Company. But Fuerst was no longer certain that his authority outweighed their discontent.

He pushed open the cabin door, shouldering

its reluctant canvas hinges. Elisabeth sat at the table, a single tallow candle alight before her. She did not look up as he entered. She stared at the wall, away from him, her chin upon her elbows. The smoky flame painted shadows beneath her eyes.

Fuerst said nothing. Instead he sat on the low stool to pull off his boots and set them neatly in their place by the door. Then, pulling off his grimy shirt and hanging it upon its wooden peg, he crossed the room to wash. His body was thickset but not fat, compact bulges of power moving beneath his freckled skin. His face was burned by the sun, his wrists and hands too, red-brown gloves upon his pale bite-spotted arms. He leaned down, plunging his face into the earthenware dish of water left ready for him. Splashes of water gleamed on the dirt floor as he shook his head and rubbed his face and neck briskly with the coarse cloth. When he was finished, he spread it carefully out over the dish to dry. Then he took the clean shirt from the back of his chair and slipped it over his head.

'A man came,' he said. 'From the de Catillon concession upriver. We may use their bull for stud.'

Elisabeth blinked at her husband, as though woken from sleep. She said nothing. Then she rose and, crossing to the plank table that served as a sideboard, she brought back several dishes, each covered with a cloth. She brought plates and spoons and cups, two of each. When she had set them on the table, she took the cloths from the dishes and folded them into neat squares before spooning the food onto her husband's plate.

They ate in silence, Fuerst forking up neat, swift mouthfuls that he chewed with his mouth fastidiously closed. Elisabeth opened her mouth and set her fork inside it. She swallowed. The food caught in her throat. She swallowed again, harder. The nausea rolled through her. Then she dipped her fork once more into her food and raised it to her lips. She looked down at her plate. Food was scarce and others were not so fortunate. She seemed to have been eating for hours. The lumps of food had the air of the French words she practised with the girl, repeated so many times that they ceased to make sense. The thought of placing them in her mouth revolted her.

Fuerst swallowed his last mouthful and set his knife and fork together neatly upon his plate. Yawning, he reached into his coat pocket and pulled out his clay pipe.

'That wasn't half bad,' he observed, as he always did, damping down the tobacco with his thumb.

Defeated, Elisabeth pushed away her plate, dropping her hands into her lap. In the thickening dusk, her upturned palms loomed pale, someone else's hands. The ring on her left hand hung loose on her finger. He had brought it with him from the Rhineland. It had belonged to his mother. He had given Elisabeth her Bible too, with his mother's name in careful ink on the flyleaf.

Fuerst held a lit spill to the bowl of his pipe

and sucked on it until the tobacco pulsed red. Elisabeth breathed in the smoke, tasting it in the back of her throat. It occurred to her that this was something that she liked, the fragrant smell of his pipe smoke. She watched as he took the pipe from his mouth and studied it, his elbows on the table.

After a pause he raised his head and leaned forward a little, his lips parted and the pipe held aloft as though he were about to speak. Elisabeth waited, her back straight. Fuerst regarded the line of her neck, the whorl of her ear, the fine tendril of hair that escaped her simple lace cap, and he closed his mouth, setting his chin on the heel of his free hand. His jaw slackened and his shoulders too, so that he could feel the weight of his head in his forearm. Slowly he lifted the pipe to his lips and inhaled.

'The indigo settles,' he said. 'If we can prevent the weeds from choking the new plants, next year we should have ourselves a very reasonable harvest. The seigneur will be pleased.'

Elisabeth murmured something.

'Of course the seeds should have been set a foot apart, an instruction to which the Negroes showed themselves incapable of adhering, but most look set to prosper for all that. We will not have another year like this one. If we had only been able to secure twice as many slaves — '

'You would have twice the number of mouths to feed.'

Fuerst frowned.

'Well, yes, but with twice, three times the amount of land under cultivation — '

'Are things not hard enough? Even Negroes do not eat indigo.'

The sleeping area was separated from the main room by a plank screen. They undressed in silence, their backs to each other. In the darkness he reached for her and dully she lifted her nightgown to accommodate him. His efforts were strenuous and brief and soon afterwards he slept. Elisabeth did not move. She lay on her back, her skirts around her waist and her legs still parted, staring upward into the ghostly folds of the linen she had hung from the roof as protection against the mosquitoes. The pale stuff clung to the darkness like smoke.

They had cut his throat while he slept. She closed her eyes tight, her fingers pressing down on the lids, but it came all the same, rolling through her like nausea: the sultry night sky pierced with white-hot stars, the baleful suck and hiss of the drowsing bayou, the whisper of feet, the pale gleam of linen as the flap of his *baire* lifted, his sleeping face, his arm thrown back above his head, his discarded boots, worn soles upward, the shimmer of oiled skin as the dark figure raised the blade — and then silence, a stillness like a gasp that stopped the night and silenced forever the ceaseless scream of the cicadas.

She wrenched herself over onto her side, her pulse hard in her neck. Beside her Artur snored, his mouth open, and her treachery tightened her throat and clenched her fists. She had not hoped to grow fond of her new husband, only that she might serve him uncomplainingly. She had accepted him in the certainty of loneliness, in the vague, bleak hope that in the isolation of the plantation and the drudgery of the work, she might find a kind of peace.

She had not reckoned on that hot fierce part of herself that refused to believe that he was gone, that it was over, but clung instead to the conviction that, one day, if she strained for it enough, she might be able, through the force of her own will, to force upon the story a different ending.

The room, pressed in upon by shelves and shelves of ledgers, was dominated by a large desk of dark wood. Its feet were cracked and splayed, pale green with mould. Behind it stood a tall man with a broad, imperious head and the large-boned fleshiness of a man who had once been muscular. Though he had been in the colony more than a year, his skin was pale, spotted with pale sand-coloured freckles. His abhorrence of the sun was well known. Whenever he walked in Mobile, he wore always a distinctive wide-brimmed hat of fine straw. His eyes, set deep into his skull, were cold and grey.

The man gestured at Auguste to close the door. Then, still standing, he extracted from the pile in front of him several pieces of correspondence and set them to one side. He did not invite Auguste to sit. He leaned upon his steepled fingers as he studied the papers, eyeglasses perched upon the end of his nose, a slight frown puckering his brow as though he calculated figures in his head.

'You sent for me, Commissary?' Auguste asked. His shoulder ached as it always did on damp days. In its sleeve his arm hung awkwardly, the palm twisted away.

'You had a profitable expedition?' the commissary asked.

'Not entirely, sir. The English have been busy.'

'But surely the Choctaw are our allies?'

'It has been our habit to trade one deerskin for two-thirds of a pound of gunpowder. The English offer one pound.'

'But that is outrageous. We cannot do business on such terms.'

'Nor shall we. After long discussion, the Choctaw chief agreed to accept three-quarters of a pound. As for food, they will accept our goods and forgo trade with the English.'

'That is the best you could manage?'

'It is a fair arrangement, sir. The English goods are more plentiful than ours and of a higher quality.'

The commissary sighed. Then he nodded, gesturing at Auguste to sit.

Auguste hesitated.

'If that is all, sir, I am needed at the storehouse. The manifest — '

'The manifest can wait.'

He fixed Auguste with a look at once indifferent and intense. Auguste bowed his head, but something in him stiffened.

'Sit,' the commissary ordered him.

Auguste sat. The commissary did not.

'You find yourself in an awkward position, I think,' the commissary said at last.

'I am afraid I do not know what you mean.'

The commissary's mouth tightened.

'I would advise against disrespect. It will not favour you.'

'I intend no disrespect, sir.'

The commissary frowned. Then he sat. He said nothing but lowered his gaze to the stack of papers on his desk, squaring the pile with the flats of his hands. Then, taking a folded handkerchief from his pocket, he removed the eyeglasses from his nose and set about polishing them. He worked meticulously to the perimeter of each lens, holding them up to the light to check that they were spotless before hooking them once more around his large ears.

'Louisiana is the property of the Mississippi Company, M. Guichard. It does not and never has belonged to Sieur de Bienville, whatever he may think to the contrary.'

Auguste said nothing. It was no secret that the commissary had been a close confidant and ally of de l'Epinay who, during his short-lived tenure as governor of the colony, had quarrelled with all of his subordinates and Bienville in particular. Now de l'Epinay was returned to France and Bienville governor in his place.

'Sir?'

'I would counsel strongly against wasting my time. I am not a patient man.'

'I do not know what it is that you want from me, sir.'

'I want your cooperation. It is almost certainly too late for the governor. It is not too late for you.' The commissary cleared his throat and took a paper from a pile upon his desk. 'Perhaps you would begin by telling me why it was that you left Mobile. It coincided, I think, with the removal of Sieur de Bienville from the position of commandant?'

'Not precisely, sir. In 1712, when the King granted the banker Crozat the lease on

328

Louisiana, Crozat sent Sieur de Cadillac from France as governor, though Sieur de Bienville continued to serve as his lieutenant. It was some weeks after his arrival that the new governor sent me north to the Illinois as translator to one of his expeditions.'

'And the purpose of that expedition?'

'The governor believed we should find mines there.'

'Did he indeed?'

'Yes, sir.'

'But you did not?'

'No, sir. Though we returned several times we found nothing.'

'Unfortunate for Crozat.'

'Unfortunate for Louisiana, sir.'

In the months after Cadillac's arrival, there had been a brief flowering of optimism among the inhabitants of Mobile. After years of protest, they had finally succeeded in persuading Bienville to move the settlement south to the mouth of the river. While the sandy soil there was unfavourable for cultivation, it was less prone to flooding, and the settlers rebuilt their houses quickly, determined to put the years of hardship behind them.

Their hopefulness was short-lived. Embittered by his failure to find precious metals, inflamed by the abominable conditions in which he was required to exist, Cadillac had exacted his revenge upon the colonists. He prohibited all trade with the natives, including the lucrative trade in liquor, and instead established a single company store in Mobile where credit was refused and a pair of stockings cost forty *livres*. Any man unable to provide documentation in proof of his noble blood was forbidden to wear a sword under the penalty of imprisonment.

In penury and desperation, the settlers had staggered forward away from the past. Subsistence became an accomplishment. Elisabeth Savaret had married an indentured Rhinelander with nothing in his pocket but a contract promising a grant of land when his time was served. The women of the town had ground acorns for coffee and told each other that pride came before a fall. Months later, when the news of Elizabeth's marriage reached the Illinois, Auguste toasted the bride with savage moonshine and wept into the hair of a girl who stroked his pale shoulder with her copper hand.

Cadillac was fired and de l'Epinay despatched to Louisiana in his place, but he lasted barely one year. In 1717, Crozat, faced with a massive tax bill from the Chamber of Justice, had remitted his privileges to the King. When Auguste's expedition returned to Mobile, Le Caën's daughter was grown up and married to a cannoneer, the white opossum Ponola was dead, and Louisiana was the possession of the newly minted Mississippi Company.

For a time it had seemed that the colony's fortunes were finally to change. With the support of the Regent and the newly minted Banque Royale in Paris, John Law's Mississippi Company would hoist Louisiana onto its broad shoulders and make it rich. The Company had been granted not only exclusive rights of trading

330

but also the free possession of the coasts, ports and harbours of the colony, ownership of the forts, stores, houses, guns and ships in the colony belonging to the French Crown, the right to make war or truce with the native tribes, and the right to appoint all colony officials. In exchange, Law, the colony's new merchant prince, had promised seeds, supplies and three thousand Negro slaves, as well as six thousand new colonists. Sieur de Bienville, restored to his position as the colony's governor, was triumphant. A new era was begun.

In those months perhaps one hundred men sailed to Louisiana from France, agents of the noble *concessionaires* with orders to cultivate the land and return the profits, and a few wives too, widows with small children or bad debts, daughters too old or troublesome or impoverished to secure a husband. Respectable people, half stunned by the heat and the privations of the voyage, they made their way unsteadily to their grants while the settlers at Mobile squabbled over the contents of the newly stocked warehouses and waited for more ships to come.

And so they came. They brought flour and wine and inferior brandy and before long a different kind of colonist. For all his grand plans it seemed that Law could not persuade sufficient Frenchmen to travel of their own volition to the New World. So instead he scoured the orphanages. He emptied the prisons. He put bandoliers on the streets of Paris to round up throw-outs and cast-offs, any kind of human excrement that might be scraped together so that he might meet his commitment of human freight. It was said that Law's Company paid a bounty for every vagabond arrested and put to sea. They paid nothing to those expected to receive them.

There is no man bitterer than he whose ambitions are exposed as a folly of his own invention. He must suffer his humiliation in the certainty that it has been from the very first an inevitability, with nothing to relieve the shame of his disgrace but the polishing of new curses and old grudges. The long-time habitants of Louisiana, who had suffered so much, responded with resentful garrulousness to the enquiries of the increasingly distrustful commissary. Of course the governor had always feathered his own nest. There was no smoke without fire. Personal commerce with the savages in goods granted for diplomatic purposes; the clandestine sale of stores intended for the garrison; use of the King's boats for the transport of furs for his own profit; trade in savage slaves; favours to favourites. Like suspect coins, the old rumours were once more bitten on and rubbed up shiny.

The commissary cleared his throat.

'I understand that the governor has granted you a concession. Why would he do that, do you think?'

Auguste thought of Bienville, his finger on a map, his shirt open to expose the time-softened tongues of serpents, his sleeves rolled up as though he meant to dig the triumphs of his future from the earth himself.

'Yours,' he had said, pointing at a square of

land. 'Make something of it.'

The years had aged the governor, stripping the flesh from his boyish face and pouching his eyes, but he had made no mention of the past. It was not in his nature.

Auguste regarded the commissary evenly.

'So that there might be as much land as possible under cultivation,' he replied. 'It is important that the colony lessens its dependence upon the savages.'

'I say he seeks to reward his friends. You are one of his friends, are you not?'

'He was a just and tireless commandant. He will make a good governor.'

'Don't play the innocent with me, Guichard. We know full well that Bienville continues to deal with the Spanish at Pensacola on his own account in direct contravention of Company law. Just as we know that he and his cohorts trade in French goods intended as gifts for the savages. Damn it, man, the lot of you have been at it for years. Do you think me stupid?'

The commissary slammed his hands down hard against the desk. Auguste observed the flush in his neck, the reddening of his large ears, and something loosened a little in his spine.

'With respect, sir, the governor's enemies here have sought repeatedly to slander the commandant with accusations of this kind. None has ever been proven.'

'Not yet.'

'There is no man in Louisiana who is more dedicated to the colony's prosperity.'

'There is no man in Louisiana who has done

more to promote his own.'

Auguste was silent as the commissary picked up the sheaf of papers in front of him. He shuffled through them, extracting a sheet of onion-skin scrawled on in faded ink.

'But I think you may be able to help me with that,' the commissary said, and he struck the sheet of onion-skin with the back of his hand. 'What, for example, do you know about an ensign by the name of Babelon?'

Auguste did not blink but set all his attention upon expressionlessness.

'Babelon, sir?'

'Yes.'

'Jean-Claude Babelon was a Canadian from Quebec, one of the first settlers here, I think. But he has been dead some years.'

'I hear that he traded on the governor's account. That you assisted him.'

Auguste shook his head.

'No, sir. We traded with the savages in exchange for food. Without such trade, the people of Mobile would have starved.'

'And what of the goods you took from the storehouses, the goods intended for the colonists?'

'We have always been required to secure the friendship of the savages with presents, sir. Without those alliances we would not have contrived to hold the colony for one month, far less nearly twenty years.'

The commissary regarded Auguste. Then he looked back at the papers he held up in front of him.

'This Babelon. He came to an unfortunate end, did he not?'

The commissary peered over the papers, his eyes narrowed. Auguste kept his gaze steady, but his neck prickled and the breath in his chest was as heavy as water. From where he stood, it was not possible to see the page that the commissary held in front of him, but in his mind Auguste saw it precisely: the crushed onion-skin browned with age, the ragged edge where it had been torn from the notebook, the words scrawled in his own clumsy hand.

'Yes, sir,' he said quietly. 'He was killed by savages.'

'And what cause did they have to kill him?'

'It was rumoured that they were perhaps encouraged by the English, though there was no proof of that. They robbed him. That may have been enough.'

'You yourself were satisfied with that explanation, were you?'

'During my time here, the savages of Louisiana have killed many white men. They have seldom troubled to explain themselves.'

The commissary pursed his lips. Then he looked down again at the papers in front of him. Auguste breathed carefully, inhaling the reek of rotting sweet potatoes.

'When the death of Ensign Babelon was reported to the garrison, what was the response of Sieur de Bienville?' the commissary asked.

'He sent a raiding party to the Chickasaw to avenge him.'

'Did he? And was any attempt made to

335

discover which of the savages was in fact responsible for the ensign's untimely demise?'

'It seemed that one of them had boasted about Babelon to his fellows. When our soldiers reached the village, they killed him and several other warriors with him and brought several more savages to Mobile as prisoners.'

'A bloody reprisal.'

'The nation of the Chickasaw has ten times our strength. The commandant desired them to know the severity of their offence.'

The commissary pursed his lips, tapping at his papers with his fingers. Auguste thought of the savage warrior, set upon by three French soldiers, his head and all the recollection in it bludgeoned to pulp with a rock. With his death no proof remained, no trace of what had been, but for a letter on onion-skin paper torn from a notebook written in a man's awkward hand.

Several minutes later, Auguste was dismissed. He walked slowly from the room, closing the door behind him. Whatever it was that the commissary had held in his stack of papers, it was surely not his letter to Elisabeth. Which meant that he had nothing. He could prove nothing. Or not yet.

That night he soothed himself with brandy, but still Auguste slept poorly, plagued by restless dreams whose images eluded him. Before dawn he rose. Uneasiness greased his stomach. Outside in the dying night, the air was almost cool, the black trees huddled together like cattle. Auguste drank more brandy and watched as the new day stretched and spread, insinuating itself among the trees, but still he could not blur them, the words on the onion-skin paper in his own unpractised hand.

It is decided. The trap is set. His death shall be an act of savagery to put fear in every white man's breast.

Dear Elisabeth, if you love him, do not let him go.

The child inched away, her eyes upon a lizard of poisonous green. Elisabeth looked up. For a moment the lizard was no more than an inked outline on the page of a notebook hatched with shading and labelled in Auguste's careful letters. She squeezed her eyes shut. There were days when, without warning, a part of her would sheer away, dropping like a stone into the past, and she had to stretch out over the chasm of herself to haul it back. Clasping tight to her elbows, she cleared her throat. The child's slate lay abandoned on the dusty ground.

'Petchi,' she bid the girl, resorting to the child's native language. 'Sit down.'

The child hesitated and, reaching out her hand, tried to snatch up the lizard. With a flash of its green tail, it was gone. The girl stuck out her tongue.

'Le lézard vert vif,' Elisabeth said crisply, laying the stress on the article. 'La fille très désobéissante.'

'No disobedient,' protested the girl in French. 'The lizard — ' She hesitated, frowning. 'The bright green lizard. He wished in the lesson.'

'He wished to be in the lesson.'

'There! You saw it also.'

The child was sharp as an arrow. Elisabeth's head hummed. She tightened the grip upon her elbows.

338

'Enough! *Caheuch*. Come here now.'

The child regarded Elisabeth with her dark eyes. There was neither insolence in her expression nor the slightest deference. Elisabeth held her gaze as the heat massed beneath her skin. The eyes were the girl's own, but the mouth, the narrow fullness of it, the way the lip curved upward at the top so that it appeared to be outlined with a circle of paler flesh, the mouth was an anguish. The child puffed out her lips consideringly. Elisabeth did not blink. Then, without rising from her haunches, the child shuffled back to sit at Elisabeth's feet and took up the abandoned slate.

She had been baptised at the same time as her mother, and given the name of Marguerite. Once, during a lesson, the child had asked Elisabeth what the meaning of her name was.

'Pearl,' Elisabeth had said. 'It means pearl.'

'What is pearl?'

'It is a white jewel. In France rich ladies make necklaces of them and sew them to their dresses.'

'Like a bead?'

'Like a very precious bead.'

Elisabeth had thought she would be pleased. But the child had only frowned and pursed her unbearable mouth.

'A bead is not a very interesting thing,' she had said.

The clay pencil dangled on its leather thong as Marguerite licked her finger, drawing shiny black circles on the tablet's dusty face. Elisabeth straightened a little. Her hands were clamped so tightly about her elbows that her knuckles ached.

Slowly she brought them into her lap, cradling one inside the other. When they had first come to this place, the men had been obliged to travel abroad for days at a time, hunting meat and gathering wild indigo for cultivation. When the rains came, Jeanne had brought the child into the main cabin so that they could watch her while they worked. The child had stared up into the spidery roof and smiled her father's secret smile. She had hardly ever cried.

'A spelling test.'

Immediately Marguerite grew attentive, the tip of her tongue caught between her teeth.

'*L'homme*,' said Elisabeth. '*La femme. Le garçon.*'

She waited, watching Marguerite's bent head as she carefully formed the words.

'*La fille.* Not so hard. You will break the pencil. Next. *Le fils.*'

Marguerite wrote, frowning with concentration. Then with her head on one side, she studied what she had written.

'Please, Madame, excuse for asking but how can there be son without saying father?'

Elisabeth hesitated.

'In my language, there is no such word,' the child added.

'And in French there is. Spell it.'

Obediently the child wrote. Elisabeth watched her, her stiff fingers laced tightly in her lap. *Le fils.* F-I-L-S. But it came all the same, the memory of Rochon on the porch of the house at rue d'Iberville on the day he left for the Chickasaw. He had told her then that in various

340

of the Indian tongues there was no word for son but only for son-of-someone. The curiosity was that since the Indians traced their descent through the maternal line, someone was never the child's natural father but rather his uncle, the eldest brother of his mother. While he might show indulgence towards his children, and his people would always be welcomed by the child's tribe, a father wielded no authority. He had looked at her then, in that grave way he had that always seemed on the verge of laughter, and it had taken all her strength to bid him goodbye. He had walked away without turning. The seat of his worn-out coat had been rubbed to a darker sheen.

The child curved the *S* with a flourish and held out the slate, admiring her work.

'So please, what is the word for the daughter-without-father?'

'*La fille.*'

'Just the same?' The child looked disappointed. 'But why?'

When she pouted, her brows twisted and her bottom lip protruded in a bow. The sight of it made Elisabeth light-headed. She frowned, looking away.

'No more questions. Next. *L'infant.* Write it. *L'infant.*'

★ ★ ★

It was no good allowing oneself to remember things, Elisabeth knew that. Memories were like slaves. They had an instinct for weakness. You

341

showed one a little latitude, permitted it some small privilege or attention, and before you knew it they were all there, hands outstretched and noses pressed against the palisades, half wild with the need for it.

Nothing fixes a thing so intensely in the memory as the wish to forget it.

At the plantation, Fuerst insisted upon locking the Negroes in their enclosure at night. He considered it vital for their safety. The Negroes of Guinea, raised from infancy to believe that the white man purchased them for no other purpose but to drink their blood, distrusted their master as a frog distrusts a snake, in the meat of its bones. He was a fair master, all the same. He believed that, like horses, slaves would only be ruined by violent and continual labours and should instead be set to work moderately and with adequate rest and nourishment. He gave them clothes and blankets and something on which to sleep, for he knew that it was a simple matter for men who want for every necessity to turn to thievery. He praised them when they worked well and whipped them only when they deserved it, and when the beating was done, he had the sore parts washed with a salve of vinegar mixed with salt and a pinch of gunpowder.

Fuerst treated his Negroes well, and they worked hard for him and did not make trouble. Yet he was careful to mistrust them as they mistrusted him and more careful still to conceal from them his dread of them, for he knew there was nothing so dangerous as an enemy who smelled your fear. He tried to conceal it from

342

Elisabeth too. He wished to protect her. He did not see that she had learned the lesson long ago.

Meanwhile their neighbours the Chetimachas had grown bolder. The savage war parties no longer troubled to wait until nightfall. They carried English guns. Elisabeth knew she should be afraid. On plantations upriver cattle had been killed and taken, their bodies dragged away into the forest. On one occasion two of Fuerst's men had spotted a band of savages in a canebrake only a few hundred feet from where they stood, and several blasts had been fired before the red men had been forced to retreat.

Fuerst was thankful that the Rhinelanders had proved poor shots, for savages were pitiless in revenge, but he knew also that matters could not continue as they were. If he could ill afford to lose his precious cows, he was in no position to lose any of his men.

'I have no choice but to appeal to the commandant,' he told Elisabeth that night. 'He must make peace with those damned Chetimachas or we shall never be free of danger.'

She said nothing but placed her hand over the scorch mark on the table.

'Do not be alarmed,' he said, and he sucked on his pipe till the bowl gleamed red. 'You are safe here. The savages are ferocious but they are cowardly. They would not come so close.'

She pressed down hard on her hand, spreading her fingers wide.

'No one is ever safe,' she said.

Fuerst hesitated. Then he leaned back against the wall and studied his pipe. The clay was stained dark around the rim of the bowl, and the stem bore the ghost prints of his lips.

'I cannot go,' he said at last. 'Not now. Even if he is at New Orleans, there is too much to be done. And I shall not leave you here alone. A letter, that's the thing. The river is busy this time of year, a trader will take it. Quick now, fetch me paper and ink.'

What little ink there was had all but dried in the bottle, and Elisabeth was required to add a few drops of water to get it to flow. In its damp box the paper had grown brown around the edges and, together with the ghostly pallor of the diluted ink, it gave the letter the air of something written long ago.

Elisabeth put her face close to the page, inhaling its smell. Her handwriting was small and cramped, long accustomed to the scarcity of paper. She thought of Auguste's spiky hand, of the paper fine as onion-skin, so that the ink showed through. It had been torn from a book so that while one side of the paper was jagged, the other was smooth, with a trace of gold along its edge.

Dear Elisabeth, do not let him go.

'Are you listening, Elisabeth?' Fuerst asked, frowning, gesturing at her with his pipe.

Elisabeth turned away from him.

'Why must you smoke that thing in here? It makes my eyes sting.'

'Then pay attention and we shall be done the sooner. *If my men go out ever so little, they are daily in danger of seizure or death — '*

Elisabeth forced her attention back to the words on the page, taking care to form each letter with the precision her brother's tutor had required of her and which she in her turn demanded from the child. When she scratched the paper with the nib, she thought of the girl and the squeal of pencil on slate. The hairs on her arm pricked.

'*Your faithful servant &c &c.* Very well, we are done.'

The paper was coarse and the pale ink already dry. His pipe clamped between his teeth, Fuerst read the letter through slowly, his eyes narrowed against the smoke. Then he set it down on the table and, taking the pen from Elisabeth, signed his name at the bottom.

'Do we have sealing wax?' he asked. 'Or must we make do with tallow?'

She reached into the wooden box and brought out a flat-sided pebble and a lump of wax the size of an acorn. Careful not to burn her fingers, she held it to the light, letting the molten wax fall upon the folded paper. She waited a moment for it to cool and pressed down upon it with the pebble. His seal had been an elaborate *J-C* entwined with vines. He had had the matrix carved for him by a savage from a piece of moss oak.

The pebble was smooth and warm in the palm of her hand.

'Husband?' she said quietly.

'Let me see.'

He picked up the letter and examined the seal.

'I am expecting.'

Fuerst blinked at her. His pipe ducked in his mouth and he snatched it out, crushing a corner of the letter.

'A child? You are certain?'

'Yes.'

Jeanne knows, she wanted to add. We have never spoken of it but I see how Jeanne takes the heavier of the burdens, thickens the stew with squash fried in bear grease so that the infant might grow fat. I see the squash she leaves on a dish among the trees at the boundary of the plantation so that the bad spirits might fatten too and forget their spite.

'It may not hold,' she said instead. 'I am old and I have not been lucky.'

'No. But a child? A child! Come, this is excellent news.'

There was no concealing his pleasure. It creased his farmer's face and flexed his blunt farmer's fingers, setting them to twitching against the stem of his pipe.

'So when? When do you think?'

Elisabeth shook her head. She did not expect to feel things any more, not in the ordinary way, but still it surprised her a little, the numbness of it.

'December, perhaps sooner. I cannot be sure.'

'A child.' Fuerst shook his head, his smile widening. 'Perhaps it is a boy.'

It came upon her suddenly, the pendulum creak of the rocking chair at the rue d'Iberville, the stiff clay-skinned creature with the cap of dark hair and the pelt of curdled blood, and she had to close her eyes to hold herself steady.

'Perhaps.'

'Or a girl. No matter.' He grinned at his wife. 'Karl-zu-klein's wife and now you. It shall give faith to the others.'

'Shall it?'

They had never told her where they buried her child. She had lain in Perrine Roussel's cabin, her eyes fixed upon the brown stain shaped like France that spread beneath the window and her arms around her shins, curled tight against the ebb of poison from her body that abandoned her to life. Waking was a torment, the stretch and lift of her chest, the breath in her mouth and the flicker of her fingers on the sheet. The sun had moved through the room and then the moonlight, marking out in slices of shadow days that were not hers. The baby had not lived long enough to be baptised and Elisabeth had never named her, not even in her dreams. A name was a hand held out to a stranger, permission to touch. Elisabeth would not let anyone touch.

Fuerst frowned.

'You should not do the heavy work. If we were to sell the girl — '

'No!'

'Elisabeth, consider your duty. This infant — '

Elisabeth's eyes snapped open.

'Consider my duty? I am here, am I not?'

Fuerst blinked.

'You are my wife,' he said evenly.

'And she is my slave. Mine. You know the law.'

'You would threaten me with the law?'

'She is only a child! She would fetch nothing.'

'Enough to — '

'I will not sell her, do you hear me?'

Fuerst's mouth tightened. He turned away.

'Why do you oppose me? You are my wife.'

'Yes,' Elisabeth said more gently. 'And I shall not let you act recklessly. Wait until she is older, until she is worth something. We can manage as we are.'

He did not turn round. But very slowly his back softened.

'A child,' he murmured. 'It is fine news.'

'If it holds.'

'If it holds.'

He turned round. Taking the chair from its place on the other side of the table, he set it next to hers and slung his leg across it.

'It is fine news,' he said again, and he nodded to himself, reaching over to pat her awkwardly on the arm. 'Think of it. A son. Uberto for my father.'

She shifted in her seat, moving her arm out of reach.

'No German names,' she said.

'The child shall have a German name. A child of mine will always be German, wherever he is born.'

'No. He shall be of this place. The Islands of the New World.'

'And the blood of generations of Rhinelanders will flow in his veins. He shall have a name to honour his forefathers. He shall not deny his history.'

'Then he shall be as much of a fool as you are.

348

Our histories are nothing but ropes around our necks.'

There was a silence. Then Fuerst rose, slamming the back of his chair hard against the table. Elisabeth did not look up. She hunched over in her chair, staring at the wall. Near the floor a moth clung to the rough plaster, its dust-brown wings shut tight. Perhaps it was dead. The door wrenched open, banged shut. The moth trembled in the echoed silence but it did not fall.

* * *

It was much later when he came in. Elisabeth lay on her side, her face turned away from him, deepening her breathing so that he might think her asleep. At nightfall Jeanne had come to tell her that the child was sick. There had been no sign of it. She had done her chores as usual and a little before dusk had swum as she always did in the river, beating the water with her habitual excited ferocity to frighten away the alligators.

But with the darkness had come a violent fever. When Elisabeth went out to the hut with Jeanne, the child on her sleeping mat was hot as a sun-baked stone. Jeanne sat down cross-legged, sliding her arms under her daughter, taking her into her lap. Marguerite whimpered and shivered and arched her back into a bow, pressing her burning face against her mother's belly. The rough violence of her coughs shook her small body until it rattled.

Elisabeth had brought a tisane of red willow.

349

Jeanne lifted the child a little and Elisabeth knelt before her, spooning the medicine between her lips. When it was drunk, she sat back on her heels. She wanted to reach out, to touch Jeanne upon the shoulder, but she did not. The slave did not look at her, and she said nothing. They waited together in silence as the child sank back into a fitful sleep. They watched as the fever coursed through her, causing her limbs to jump, her eyes to flutter. Elisabeth gazed at the floor so that she might not see the stricken look upon the slave's face, who endured her own trials with a distant and ancient composure, the way her fingers clenched in a knot so tight it had seemed to Elisabeth that the bones must poke through the skin.

Once, when Marguerite was a baby and would not settle, Jeanne had whispered to her of the terrible sickness that had come to her village when she herself was a girl. The sickness had filled the mouths of the sick with sores and covered their skin with scarlet lumps fat with slime. Though the medicine man pleaded with the spirits to yield up a remedy for their afflictions, his appeals were not answered. A great number of her people died. When at last the sickness was exhausted, the village was too big for those who were left. Several of Jeanne's sisters had been taken to another village a long way away where they might find husbands. In their own village there were no longer enough men to go around. From her corner of the cabin, Elisabeth had listened, rocking herself for comfort, and she had known that this was the nature of lullabies among her people too, that they should stand not as a kind of solace but as a warning.

When the child at last was still and the heat in her a little diminished, Elisabeth bid the slave goodnight and returned quietly to her own cabin. Alone in her bed her fears were stronger. She told herself that the child was strong, that she would soon be well, but when she closed her eyes she saw only Jeanne's clenched hands, her wide, frightened eyes. It frightened Elisabeth that Jeanne too could be frightened. She had grown accustomed to the strength of her, the quiet succour that she carried in the air around her.

It was Auguste who had chosen her name, Auguste who arranged for her and the child to be baptised. By then they were his, to do with as he pleased. He had told Okatomih that in the Grand Village of the white men, Jeanne meant 'mother to the first of the Great Suns'. He had not told her it was also the name of Jean-Claude's mother, who was dead. Perhaps he had not known.

Rochon had pleaded with her not to do it. He would find her another slave, he promised her, an obedient girl unhampered by the demands of an infant, but she would not hear him. She could no longer bear the confines of Perrine's house, was recovered enough to return to the cabin on rue d'Iberville. The clemency of numbness, so long a refuge, had grown to be a gaol.

She had them sleep not in the kitchen hut but in the house, where every cup and fork recalled the touch of his lips and the back of the door was stained with the greasy shadow of his hat. The cabin had been shut up for many weeks. She and Jeanne took down the mouldy platille from the windows for washing. They swept the cobwebs from the ceiling and scrubbed the floor with sand. As they worked they breathed life into the dead air, setting the ceaseless shadow of him dancing in its dark corners. The pain of it had stunned her. Elisabeth burned Okatomih's old white dress and in a tunic of deerskin the slave was no more than a dull and constant ache.

To look upon the child was an agony.

The bed shifted as Fuerst sat heavily and pulled off his boots. Elisabeth waited, one hand gripping the edge of the moss-filled mattress, the other upon her belly. The boots fell, two dull thuds, before he rolled over to lie beside her. He smelled of pipe tobacco and, faintly, of cypress. He placed his hand upon her hip and she stiffened, waiting for him to raise her nightshift. Instead he rubbed at her hip bone in little circles as though it were a blade requiring cleaning.

'A child,' he said.

Suddenly Elisabeth was filled with fear. She curled herself into a tight ball, squeezing her eyes tight shut.

'If it holds,' she whispered.

'It will hold. You'll see.'

Auguste was late. The braid of his new wig rustled between his shoulder blades as he hurried along the dusty lane, the silk ribbon whispering to the brocade of his heavy coat. Auguste insinuated a finger beneath the unfamiliar weight of horsehair and scratched at his freshly shaved scalp. His skin prickled with the heat and the awkward vanity of the unaccustomed dandy.

As he mounted the steps and went in through the open door, he could hear the clink of glasses, the gurgle and creak of voices taking up the night-time chorus of the frogs. The commandant's house had been rebuilt and was entered now through a vestibule. It was a fine residence. Though there was still no glass in the colony for windows, the governor had hung a small gilt-framed looking glass on the plastered wall, and set wax candles in an eight-armed candelabrum. Auguste held his hand up, spreading his fingers so that the flames seemed to leap from the ends of them. He had not seen candles for many years. He had forgotten that lights could smell so sweet.

He had ceded his grant. After his interview with the commissary, he had gone to Bienville and told him that he would not be taking it. He said that he did not wish to be a farmer. The governor had tried to persuade him to reconsider.

'The commissary can do nothing,' he had said. 'The past is past.'

Auguste had only shaken his head. He had never comprehended why the white man resolved to think of time as a straight line and life a course set always ahead. Like the Ouma, he knew that time was a series of loops like knitting, so that the then knotted itself about the now until each was as much one as the other.

'It shall serve neither of us,' he had said firmly and, placing the papers on the governor's desk, he had turned to leave.

'Wait,' Bienville had said. 'There is perhaps another way.'

Auguste breathed in the sweet syrup smell of the melting wax. In the glass his face gazed back at him unsmilingly. His skin was dark against the powdered grey of his wig, burned brown by the sun. He tried to imagine a white woman's pale fingers against his cheek, the rise of her pale neck and slope of her pale bosom, but instead he thought of the slave girl Okatomih. The moon had been full that night. It had lit the white dress that she wore like the shade of a lamp, imprinting on it the dark curves of her body. She had pulled at the ties that fastened it and it had fallen away, a pale puddle at her feet. Beneath her bowed head, the smooth, swollen curves of her had shone like polished wood, a dark grain running from the stub of her protruding belly button to the shadowed tangle between her thighs, dividing her in two. She had said nothing.

354

She had only knelt by the bed and reached under the rugs, her fingers cool against the flush of his skin. He had smelled the musky oil in her hair, felt himself harden. When he had asked of her what it was she thought she was doing, she had replied simply, 'You are master now.'

In the parlour beyond the door, a woman laughed, a shrill screech like a crow's cawing. Auguste pressed his knuckles to his lips, and in the glass the man in the wig did the same. He knew nothing of her, only that she had come from Paris and that, when Bienville proposed it, there was immediately a certainty in him, as though he had known she was coming. That afternoon he had dressed with great care. He had donned a clean shirt and sponged his breeches until they were spotless. Then, very carefully, he had slid his arms into the sleeves of his new coat.

The coat was the finest thing he had ever owned, and the most expensive. In the guttering candlelight, the silk brocade shimmered like water, causing the double row of close-set crystal buttons that ran the length of its front to glitter and dance upon its surface. Delicate and easily broken, the buttons served only as embellishment and could not be fastened. The buttonholes that would never receive them were trimmed with sleek bindings of scarlet kid, like ranks of little red mouths. The pockets were trimmed with silver braid. Auguste slid his fingers into the slit of one, feeling the smooth silk of the lining and, deeper, the sharp corners of a folded-up piece of paper. A bill in brown ink acknowledging the receipt of payment in full. But he had not paid for it. The coat had been a gift from the governor.

'Consider it a wedding present,' Bienville had said with a grin. 'From Louisiana's own Mr John Law. It is the very least he can do, in the circumstances.'

Auguste had not taken the slave into his bed. The smell of the dead man had been too strong on her, the shape of her the shape of treachery, of madness. He had dreamed of her though, and when in the dark hours he reached down to comfort himself, it was her mouth that encircled him, her high breasts that he spattered with his seed. In the mornings when she brought his breakfast, he could not meet her eye. He was ashamed but he was grateful too. He could not have borne to have dreamed of Elisabeth.

Later, when the child was born, Auguste had insisted that both mother and baby be baptised with French names. The beginning of a new life in the sight of God, the Jesuit had called it. The slave had held the child in her arms, her head bowed, and as the Jesuit made the sign of the cross over their heads and spoke her new name, and of the name of her child, she closed her eyes and the savage song she sang over the child's sleeping head flowed from her like a stream of water.

It was in the first days of the governorship of Sieur de Cadillac that he had received word from the Jesuit that Elisabeth wished to buy back the slave. The priest, who was a good man, had begged him to deny her. Her body was still weak from the ravages of the poison, he said, and the Devil worked in her, disturbing the order of her mind. After all that had happened, the presence of the slave, and of her child, in Elisabeth's house would only undo her further. The weight of her mortal sin bore down upon her. He had said very quietly that penance was a matter for God.

Auguste had listened courteously to the priest. The next day he had made arrangements for the sale as Elisabeth had asked. They met only to set their signatures upon the papers. She had been gaunt and pitifully frail, her skin wax-grey, her eyes dark holes punched in her white face. By then it had been agreed that she would not be called to trial. The governor spoke of clemency but it was plain that pragmatism, not mercy, had prevailed. Among the frantic problems of the colony a failed self-murder was hardly of pressing concern. Her exoneration had not prevented the other wives from branding her a criminal, a lunatic, but he had seen then that there was no madness in her, only the indifference of someone with nothing left to lose. She asked him to promise that they would never meet again. He had given her his word.

And he had kept it. Some time later she had left Mobile. Recently there had been rumours that the husband held her captive, that he meant to take her to the Rhineland. The Company had forbidden all departures, but the ships were frequent these days and the chaos at Dauphin Island beyond imagining. There were plenty of sea captains hungry for specie and for France. Perhaps she was already gone.

Auguste straightened up, staring at himself in the glass. He looked, he thought with a sudden rush of shame, like a peasant dressed up in his master's clothes. The sudden impulse to flee overcame him. He did not know what it was he thought he was doing here. The past was not the past. A man could not shed his skin like a snake. He was not ready.

From the house there came the clatter of approaching heels and, distinct from the frog chorus, a man's voice, prickly with impatience. Hastily Auguste turned, smoothing the creases from the skirts of his coat.

'Governor,' he said, and bowed.

Bienville stopped in the doorway, squinting as his eyes adjusted to the gloom of the vestibule. Behind him stood le Pinteux, junior clerk to the governor's office since Auguste was a boy. The clerk's wig was crooked and his sparse eyebrows twitched restlessly upon the sun-reddened dome of his forehead.

'Guichard? What the devil are you doing lurking out here?'

'I am just arrived, sir.'

'Then you are late. Look at you, though. Sieur de Guichard makes quite the popinjay, wouldn't you agree, le Pinteux?'

The clerk scowled, a droplet of water quivering on the end of his peeling nose.

'Of course you cannot expect easily to impress a man of mode like M. le Pinteux,' Bienville sighed. 'If only we could all boast his natural

Parisian style and ease of manner. Look here, I have business with the commissary but I shall be back directly. Go on in. You are reasonably safe, I think. Barrot accompanies her, and that shrivelled old prune of a schoolteacher. Between them they should keep you from harm.'

'I am comforted.'

Bienville grinned.

'I shall need to see you tomorrow. There is trouble again between the Choctaw and their Chickasaw neighbours. Have you word of it?'

Auguste shook his head.

'With the ship come it will not be long before the chiefs start sniffing around,' Bienville said. 'Both nations are sure to send deputations. We must be prepared.'

'Yes, sir.'

'Till tomorrow then. And do not think you can slip away the moment my back is turned. I shall return.'

'Do not hurry on my account.'

'Trust me, I would take a party any day over an hour pettifogging over specks of flour with the commissary. Hell, I should take a wife.'

'Come now.'

'Truly. Any one of them. Even the old schoolteacher, I swear it.'

'But not Mlle le Vannes?'

Again Bienville grinned.

'Guichard, you have a disturbingly distrustful nature. You shall find the Mademoiselle as charming an almost-widow as you could hope for. Blue-eyed, plump as a peach and legal owner of a fine indigo plantation. Truly, my friend, I am green with envy. Now, if you will excuse me — '

Auguste bowed again as the commandant hastened from the house, the pink-nosed clerk scurrying behind him. The candles dipped, gold-tipped brushes painting flourishes of gold on the darkness. Then, clamping his hat more tightly beneath his arm, he walked towards the light.

'Mlle le Vannes, I would like to introduce you to M. Guichard. M. Guichard is one of the longest-serving of our colonists, is that not right, old boy?'

'Perhaps.'

There was a silence. Guichard held her fingertips awkwardly, away from his body, and looked about him as though seeking a place to put them down. His tentativeness dismayed her. She wanted him to seize her hand and crush it in his own, to address her vigorously, without hesitation or ambiguity. She wanted him to demand that she raise her head so that he might get a proper look at her. She wanted to disappoint him. Instead she waited, her hand wilting on its wrist, and stared at the crystal buttons that edged his coat. They were fine and bright, like chips of ice. She imagined taking one in her mouth.

'So. Please.' The physician, whose name she had already forgotten, cleared his throat purposefully. 'Mlle le Vannes, sit down.'

'Thank you.'

Awkwardly she pulled her hand away and sat down, busying herself with her skirts. When Guichard turned away to set his hat upon the table, Vincente observed that the bow securing his queue was lopsided, foolish, one loop of ribbon much larger than the other. He did not turn back. He doesn't like me, Vincente thought suddenly, and she swallowed. His neck was narrow, burned brown, and his shoulders were sharp beneath the expensive coat, his damaged arm pulling awkwardly at the seam. It was an ugly coat, she thought, absurd in its courtly pretension. It did not even fit him. The cuffs fell over his hands like a child playing at dressing up.

'M. Guichard knows everything there is to know about Louisiana,' the physician announced. 'A proper authority on plants and animals and so forth, if you have an interest in such matters. Used to have an extraordinary garden, full of herbs and whatnot, though that was years ago, of course, in Old Mobile. Do not listen to him, however, when he tries to tell you that the savages know more about medicine than French physicians. I have no desire to be called to your bedside to undo the damage.'

Though Vincente forced something of a smile, Guichard gave no impression of having heard the physician at all. He stood quite still, his hands cupping his hat and his head tilted, as though he listened to something very far away. It was hard to see beneath the coat the extent of his affliction. His fingers looked quite ordinary.

He turned to look at her before she could look away. Flustered, she dropped her head. The tips of her slippers protruded from beneath her skirts. They were the old ones that her mother had threatened to throw away in Paris, but Vincente had wrapped them in paper and hidden them in the bottom of her trunk. She had worn them so often that she could see the shape of her toes in them even when they were empty. The floor of the commandant's house was of wooden planks, not splintery like the schoolteacher's, but rubbed to a smooth sheen. The physician's shoes were shiny too, with bright silver buckles. Guichard's shoes, by contrast, were almost as worn as hers.

The physician tried again.

'Of course he's been here an eternity, haven't you, old boy? Almost raised by the nation of savages known as the Natchez, though luckily for you, Mam'selle, he lived to tell the tale. People like to claim that the Natchez are the most civilised of the lot because they dress respectably but, my dear, do not be deceived. Last year, when the wife of their chief died of a fever, every one of her retinue was strangled, hung from scaffolds and strangled, so that they might accompany her to the next world. Infants too, a score of 'em, strangled by their own fathers and then trampled underfoot by the coffin-bearers until they were in pieces. Pieces, I tell you.'

'But that's horrible.'

'That's savages,' the physician said firmly.

'The Ouma.'

'What's that, old chap?'

'It was the Ouma with whom I lodged as a boy. Not the Natchez.'

His French had a guttural rasp, as though the words formed not upon his tongue but bubbled up from the back of his throat.

The physician blinked.

'Is that so? Ah, well, it is all the same to Mlle le Vannes, I imagine. One red man much like

363

another and all that. Ah, excellent, excellent. Drinks. We haven't seen a vintage this fine in the garrison in months. Mlle le Vannes, will you raise a glass? A toast to new arrivals, then. And Godspeed the ships that bring to us parched colonists the sweet, sweet blessings of French women and French wine.'

The physician laughed and drained his glass, seizing another from the tray before the boy had time to move away. Vincente murmured and set the glass to her lips. Over the rim she saw that, though he stood quite still, against his sides his fingertips tapped restlessly, each one lightly touching the pad of his thumb in sequence as though he counted them.

'It falls to M. Guichard to make sure that we live in peace with our red neighbours, as far as such a thing is possible,' the physician declared. 'Which means he does his damnedest to keep them fighting with one another so that they have neither the men nor the appetite to fight with us! Isn't that so, M. Guichard?'

'Something of that kind.'

'As you can see, Mlle le Vannes, M. Guichard is a man of few words. It is fortunate for him, perhaps, that he has at his disposal so great a host of outlandish languages in which to speak them. Now where has Mme de Boisrenaud got to? She assured me she would be gone only for a moment.'

The physician raised himself up on his tiptoes and strained his fat neck. Vincente was reminded of a dachshund which she had often seen in the Tuileries as a little girl, whose extravagant ambitions with dogs several times its own size caused her nursemaid to snigger and press her red hand over Vincente's eyes.

'Can you see the boy? Ah, here he is. I'll take that, I think. More for you, Guichard? No? You should drink it while you can, old boy. Anything of a decent vintage is gone in the blink of an eye. I'm only glad your savages prefer the hard stuff.'

'Yours too, of course.'

'I beg your pardon?'

Guichard said nothing but only looked stonily at the physician, who began to splutter.

'If you accuse my slave of drunkenness, it is a baseless slander. I'd beat her from here to Pensacola for so much as sniffing a cork.'

'A prudent master.'

'So which savages *do* you refer to then?' the physician demanded, gesturing at him with the wine bottle. 'Come on, man. Spit it out.'

'It is of no consequence.'

'On the contrary, if you troubled to say it, I should say it was. Well?'

Guichard was silent. Then he shrugged.

'I referred to the savages at the garrison,' he said quietly.

'The garrison? But there are no red men at the garrison.'

The physician frowned, baffled. Then he tossed back the last traces in his glass and emptied the rest of the bottle into it.

'*Mon Dieu*, Guichard, enough of this nonsense. You are not yet so much of a native you cannot address us in ordinary French. Now, it is time I went in search of sustenance and the elusive Mme de Boisrenaud. You will excuse us, I'm sure. Mlle le Vannes, would you accompany me to supper?'

Vincente hesitated. When Guichard said nothing, she took the physician's proffered arm and allowed the little man to help her to her feet.

'No,' Guichard said abruptly. Startled, Vincente turned, and their eyes met. His were the grey-green of the Mobile River. She looked away. 'You go on, Barrot. I shall escort Mlle le Vannes to the tables presently.'

'Well, if the fair lady is content to wait a little. I must say, the spread looks very fine.' Barrot licked his lips. His round eyes greedily followed the dishes of food as they were carried through the room, the aroma of roasted meat fattening the air. 'Mam'selle?'

Vincente blinked.

'Yes. Yes, of course.'

'Excellent. Good. Well, very good then.'

The physician sprang away from them as if released by a catch. Vincente shifted awkwardly. She could feel his gaze upon her. She did not know where to set her own.

'So.'

'So.'

There was laughter from the far end of the room and the clatter of forks. Vincente examined her wine glass.

'You are hungry?' Guichard asked.

The emptiness in her stomach curled tight as a walnut.

'No. Thank you.'

There was a long pause.

'You are not long arrived,' he said.

'I — I have been here twenty-three days.'

'How do you find it?'

Vincente stared at him. She wanted to laugh, to scream, to beat him with her fists. She wanted to thrust the engraving under the nose of this impassive man and demand to know what lies there were that that devil Mr Law had not told. She wanted him to tell her how to endure such a place, the fear and the squalor and the grind of it, the heat and the swamps and the grim austerity, the snide disparagements and petty thefts of the schoolteacher, the spiders and the alligators and the snakes and the tormenting mosquitoes, the coarse, oily slabs that passed for bread and milk that cost fifty *sols* a jug, the whispers and the slid-away stares of the Salpétrière girls, the rough men and the whores and the half-naked savages and the soldiers so drunk that they fell against you in the street, the boils and the sores that would not heal, the cabin with its straw mattress that would hardly have sufficed for a shepherd, the sun that beat down so powerfully at midday that it could strike a man dead, the savages with their tattoos and their devilish magic and their taste for human flesh.

What kind of a deal had her mother done with the Devil, could he tell her that? To send her to a place where the church was no better than a byre for cattle and the chaplain, God's agent on earth, a lascivious drunkard who had fled France to avoid punishment for his disorderly life and who, since arriving in Louisiana, had seduced a

367

woman while hearing her confession and fathered a child? What was the enormity of her offence that she, who had endeavoured always to live an upright and pious life, must be discarded in such a place, from which even God averted His face?

And where was it, she wanted to plead with him, where had they hidden the magical land they talked of in Paris, where the savages read Latin and crowded the elegant churches, where the meat cast itself onto a man's plate and the savage so venerated the Frenchman that he made of himself a willing slave? Where were the noble colonists, carving a paradise from the virgin soil? She had found only a midden, a foul dustheap where villains and rogues might be thrown to rot. Every day she had thought that she must die of it. They were dying everywhere, the coffins piled up like flour crates, except that there was no flour, only the vile pap of the savages, and no more coffins either, so that in the shallow, uncovered trenches, hands and feet poked mud-stained from the ill-wrapped winding sheets.

She swallowed.

'It is not like Paris,' she said.

'I have never been to Paris.'

Vincente waited for him to say something more, but he only stood there. He made no attempt to set her at her ease. She wanted to seize him by the arm, to demand his attention. She wanted to run from the room.

Instead she stared at her feet. It defeated her, how it was possible to converse in the ordinary way with a man who had lived among savages, a man who had taken a savage woman in shameless concubinage and fathered a half-red bastard whom he had sold for profit. To Vincente's disgust, the schoolteacher had reported his history as though it was hardly a scandal. Worse, she had rebuked Vincente for her repugnance. Auguste Guichard was a sober man, she had said sharply, able to support a wife in reasonable circumstances, and well regarded by the commandant. Vincente would be fortunate to make such a marriage and, without the schoolteacher's considerable influence, would doubtless have fared much worse. Louisiana, if she had not noticed, was not Paris. In Louisiana an almost-widow was in no position to be particular.

The next day, and in the days that followed, the schoolteacher had been cold with her, speaking to her only when necessary, and declaring her spoiled and perverse. Vincente wept as she crouched in the kitchen hut at night. She would rather die than marry an unvirtuous man, she told herself, and her tears mingled with the handfuls of unknown, uncooked food that she crammed blindly into her mouth. It was to be another three days before she had finally relented. By then she had been in Louisiana long enough to learn that French goods, however badly broken or soiled, still exceeded the means of most settlers.

'So,' she said at last. 'You seek a wife.'

'Yes.'

'Because of the plantation?'

If he was perturbed by her candour, he did not show it.

'The plantation is a good one. But there is no want of good land in Louisiana.'

'Merely a want of marriageable women.'

'Indeed.'

There was another long silence. He studied her thoughtfully, without embarrassment. Vincente flushed and looked away, but the knot in her chest loosed a little. There was something about the gravity of him that settled her. He was not a man who would be made a fool of.

'And you?' he asked quietly. 'You seek a husband?'

'I seek to do God's will.'

The words came out bunched up, like too-tight stitches. The flush in her neck deepened. He regarded her steadily and said nothing. She swallowed.

'I — yes,' she said. 'I seek a husband.'

There was a long pause. Vincente watched as a boy carried a large milk jelly to the supper tables, its pale flesh quivering. She had always abhorred milk jelly.

'I was born in La Rochelle to Auguste Guichard, docker,' he said. 'I am employed as a trader and emissary for the Mississippi Company, which pays me an annual subsidy of eighty *livres*. I am the owner of a single-storey house on the rue Dugué and an Indian slave of the Colapissas tribe. I am in good health. Might I call on you?'

Across the room a woman in a dark red dress raised a spoon and plunged it into the milk jelly. Cut low at the front to expose the woman's ample breasts, the dress was trimmed with golden ribbon that had begun to unravel a little. Her mouth was wide with dark red paint, and she wore a yellow feather in her piled-up hair. The physician stood very close to her, paddling her plump arm with his fingers.

Vincente pressed her lips together.

'In Paris I wanted to enter the convent.'

'But you did not.'

'My mother would not permit it.'

'She wished to see you married?'

'She wished to profit from the sale of a daughter into marriage. My mother was very fond of money.'

'Your mother is dead?'

'No.'

'M. de Chesse is dead. Your mother's arrangement is no longer binding.'

'But I am here. The law says I am not permitted to leave.'

'There shall be a convent here too. The commandant must have a hospital for his New Orleans, a school.'

'How soon?'

'Five years perhaps.'

'Five years is too long.'

'Then you must make the best of it.'

Vincente looked at him. He held her gaze. Then she looked away. The supper tables were strewn with half-eaten dishes, the hollowed-out carcasses of roasted birds. The craving was sudden and violent.

'Very well,' she said quickly. 'You may call for me. Now please, I should like you to find me the schoolteacher. I have to go home.'

Seventeen days later the priest du Mesnil married Vincente le Vannes and Auguste Guichard in a brief ceremony in the tiny unadorned church of the garrison. Vincente wore the mantua of dove-grey silk trimmed with silver lace chosen by her mother, and her old slippers. The dress was uncomfortably tight beneath her arms and the sole of her left slipper had come loose, so that the sharp point of a tack nudged her big toe. The governor, who had promised to attend, had been called away to Pensacola on urgent business and sent his apologies. In his place the schoolteacher and old Jean Alexandre, the master joiner, stood as witnesses. The priest was a wan old man, with brown wrinkles and a wisp of a beard on his tapered chin. He put Vincente in mind of a turnip. When he required her to speak her pledge, she felt the jab of her sister's furtive elbow in her ribs and the fear of what was to come dried the spit in her mouth, so that the words came out gluey and stuck together.

Afterwards there was a brief celebration at the house of the school-mistress, attended by a handful of guests. Vincente, who for the previous days had been kept under the close surveillance of the schoolmistress, recognised only one or two of them. They shook her hand, regarding her with ill-disguised curiosity. When they left she went with her new husband to her new home.

Auguste's house was a low wooden building thatched with cypress that opened directly onto the rue Dugué, a narrow lane towards the rear of the settlement. Like all of the houses in the colony, it was dominated by a single simply furnished room with a fireplace but, unlike the schoolteacher's cabin, this room was long and reasonably broad. It was adjoined by two smaller rooms, one leading into the next so that one was required to pass through one to reach the other. Though it was simple, it was not so ill-built as many of its neighbours. Its walls were white-washed with an approximation of lime and the floor was laid with wooden planks. At the rear it boasted a wide porch that ran the length of the cabin and a sandy yard with a small vegetable patch staked around with canes.

Someone had brought her boxes from the schoolteacher's house. The trunk containing her trousseau had been placed in the alcove of the smaller of the two bedchambers, its leather top soiled and greasy against the clean white wall. She did not open it. Instead she walked restlessly from room to room. There was nowhere of comfort to sit. In her head she placed her mother's settle, with its needlepoint pattern of unicorns in a forest of emerald leaves, in front of the fireplace. As a child Vincente had crouched beside it, the silk of the stitches soft against her cheek, and pretended herself into its green depths, her legs astride a unicorn and her hair streaming out behind her like a flag. She had begged her father not to sell it when they were

374

obliged to move the first time. Her mother had said it displayed a peasant's taste to prefer the settle over the Gobelins cabriole chair, but the chair had only pink roses and ribbons on it. Pink roses and ribbons would not carry you anywhere.

That night Vincente went to bed alone. Some time later he came to her. She had known he would come. Still, when he slid into the bed beside her and lifted her skirt and she felt the graze of him against her flesh, she had to bite her lip to stop herself from screaming. She lay stiffly on her back, her arms at her sides and her eyes squeezed shut, as he rubbed and pressed her flesh with his hands. Its compliance disgusted her, the thick dough of it coating her bones. His mouth was wet and hot, and the flickering slime of his tongue unspeakable. He groaned and she turned her face from him, her mouth in a tight knot, waiting for it to end. When he entered her, it was the shock as much as the pain of it that caused her to cry out.

When she woke the next morning, there was dried blood on her thighs and upon her petticoats. She bent her head over her breakfast and could not look at him. When he asked if all was to her liking, the sound of his voice caused her skin to burn with mortification. She answered him in monosyllables. When at last he bid her goodbye, passing his hand lightly over her shoulder as he passed, she flinched at the touch of him, sickened with distaste and with shame.

That night, he came to her again. She wanted

to weep, to scream, to take up the musket that stood propped and ready behind the door and thrust the barrel hard into his chest. Instead she closed her eyes, digging her nails hard into her clenched palms, and in the darkness all her disgust and disappointment, all of her wretchedness, hardened inside her until she could hardly breathe. At that moment she hated him so utterly, with such certainty and strength, that there was a kind of triumph in it.

Knees locked and head wrenched to one side, she stiffened herself against him, the soft, hidden parts all stone. She did not move as he pressed himself against the pliancy of her breasts, her belly. If he dared trespass upon her again, she would grind him like corn between her bones.

He covered her mouth with his. She clenched her jaw, locking her teeth against him. His mouth slid over the hard curve of her chin and found her neck. His breath was hot, his tongue urgent. His fingers closed around her breast. She ground herself down, down into the centre of herself, where the hatred was fiercest. She wanted him to die.

And then he thrust himself inside her. This time the pain was sharper. The force of it sprung a lock deep in her belly. Despite herself, she arched against him, her head thrown back, the cry caught in her throat. For that moment, adrift in the thick, hot darkness, she was free of him. The man who lay upon her was not M. Guichard, husband and employee of the Mississippi Company. He was not even a man. He was the darkness, the night made flesh, turning her own flesh inside out. In the astonishing pleasure of it, she forgot him. She strained only towards herself, towards the point of light that was release. When it came, she cried out and dug her fingers hard into his back.

In the morning she was no more than herself and he was a man again, an ordinary stranger with a twisted arm and an unfamiliar face. The distaste was the same and the shame greater. The ordinary exchanges of the morning caused her to redden. As they had the previous day, they ate their breakfast in silence.

* * *

That night and the next night, he came to her again but it was not the same. Whatever enchantment he had placed on her had lifted, leaving only a faint impression of intoxication, like the memory of a dream. Two days later he left Mobile, despatched on a Company matter to a savage village several days' journey from the town. Vincente listened to him as he explained the expedition and longed for him to be gone. And yet, when he had rounded the corner, she stood for a long time in the lane, looking after him, her hand sheltering her eyes from the slanting morning sun. It was only when Mme Driard threw her slops into the lane that she slowly let her hand fall to her side. She watched the water run through the dust, the stream narrowing to rivulets that spread across the lane like roots. Then, smoothing her hair from her brow, she went inside.

She was quite alone. The slave was in the kitchen hut and in the garden the boy worked, his back bent over. Outside the birds shrieked, their calls shrill and contemptuous, but in the cabin all was still. She thought of Blandine and Marie-Hélène whispering and giggling with their mother, the way they stopped when she entered a room, their lips pressed together and their eyes round, and the explosion of laughter when she blinked at them and turned away, and she felt a pang of something that was almost grief.

Hurriedly Vincente picked up her Bible, turning the fragile pages in search of a favourite passage, but the words blurred before her eyes. During the weeks at the schoolteacher's cabin, she had gone half mad with the need for solitude. All day long the cabin clattered with a mismatch of ill-clad youngsters, both red and white, and several of them visibly a mixture of the two, to whom Mme de Boisrenaud gave elementary instruction. Vincente had been obliged to assist her. Afterwards, when the yearning for silence rose up in her like a scream, she was assigned her share of the household duties, during which the school-teacher kept up an unceasing stream of complaints about her innumerable infirmities, to which she was devoted. At night they slept in the cabin's only bedchamber in a pair of curtainless cots no more than an outstretched arm from one another. The rasp of the old woman's snores rattled up and down Vincente's spine and set her teeth to throbbing in her gums. It required considerable will not to throttle her but to lie quietly until she was certain she was quite asleep. Only her night-time forays to the kitchen hut had kept her steady. Sometimes, as she knelt upon the dirt floor, her mouth and her fists frantic with food, she had thought she might weep with gratitude and relief.

In the cabin on the rue Dugué, there was nothing but silence, broken only by the ominous shrieks of the forest that pressed up against the town as though it meant to snatch back the land. Silences were all different, Vincente knew that well enough. In the Place Royale the silence had been all muffled rage and clamped-down expectation, while in the convent the cloistered stillness had gleamed like an undisturbed lake. In the convent the veils and loose grey habits obscured the awkward angularities of form and disposition and made everyone right. No one in the convent had ever raised their voice to her. They had not declared her tiresome or ugly or dull. Though she had visited almost daily, no one had ever ordered her away. When the abbess had taken Vincente's bony hands in hers and counselled against the too-bright flame that burns itself out, she had done so gently and with a tender pity in her soft face, so that Vincente had thrown her arms around the old woman's neck and clung to her, her face pressed against the old nun's shoulder, inhaling her comforting dusty smell. The abbess had patted her back and blessed her, calling her *my child*.

'I am your child,' Vincente had whispered. 'I am.'

'Do you love me?' she had asked later. 'Do you think me good?'

'The Lord loves all His children,' the abbess had replied, and she had detached the girl's arms from around her neck. 'And you shall be a good girl if you say your confession and live according to His holy commandments.'

Vincente had announced her determination to take orders during a fierce quarrel with her mother. Mme le Vannes had struck the table with her fist and declaimed her as the most insufferable of daughters, and Vincente had been flooded with a fierce and bitter-tasting exultation. Her Father in Heaven had chosen her, Vincente le Vannes, for His handmaid and she would give herself to Him entirely, surrendering all that she was and all that she would ever be to a life of silent prayer and contemplation.

Two months later they had sold her into marriage. Distraught, Vincente had gone to the abbess to beg her intercession, but the old nun had only shaken her head and advised her to accept the will of God. Vincente had not given up. Aboard the *Baleine* she had tried again, declaring her vocation to Sister Marie and pleading with her to accept her as a postulant. Sister Marie's refusal had been quick and contemptuous. If Vincente cared to demonstrate her piety, she had said sharply, she could begin by teaching the godless Salpétrière girls their catechism. Vincente had managed just two awkward hours of lessons before the seasickness came, rolling through her in a terrible, unstoppable wave. When at last the sea calmed and the ship reached Havana, her dress hung loose from the knobs of her shoulders.

'I was not sick,' Sister Marie declared with satisfaction as Vincente stumbled onto dry land. 'And the girls have their catechism despite you. The Lord is merciful.'

Past Havana there was no wind and the sea glared flat and smooth. During those long drifting weeks, Vincente spoke to no one. She had consoled herself with her Bible, which proved poor comfort, and with a great deal of milk and cheese and butter, which did not. Once or twice, half-heartedly, she put her fingers down her throat but, weary of its old convulsions, her body refused her.

Now she was plump. Her face was full, her breasts also. Her thighs nudged each other beneath her skirts, and she grew breathless when she walked. She hardly cared. She wore the supplementary flesh like an undergarment, without thinking it a part of her. She had never imagined it might hide pleasure in its yielding plush, such pure intensity of sensation that the sight of the tumbled bed was enough to sharpen her skin to gooseflesh.

The thought shamed her, and she shook herself briskly and went to her trunk, thinking to cheer the house a little with the linens she had brought from Paris. In the alcove, above the trunk, her husband's clothes hung from crude wooden pegs, his expensive silk coat beside the brown tangle of garments sewn from deerskin and nettle-bark linen. The smell of the old clothes made her shudder. Carefully she lifted the silk coat off its peg, smoothing out its gleaming folds, and threads of remembered pleasure glittered like silver between her thighs.

'And put a knife to thy throat, if thou be a man given to appetite,' she whispered, but there was no heat in it. Perhaps the abbess had been right. Perhaps the flame had indeed burned itself out, all the psalms and proverbs in her descending, with the last scraps of nourishment in her belly, to the bottom of the great wide ocean.

The day stretched ahead of her, empty and endless. For the sake of something to do, she turned and walked out into the yard. Smoke came from the chimney of the kitchen hut. Above the chattering of the birds, she could hear the slave pounding maize for bread. The slave's name was Thérèse. Vincente leaned in the frame of the open door, watching her. The slave did not look up but continued to pound in slow thuds, the sinews straining in roped stripes along the bones of her forearms. Vincente knew that she should return to the house and the pile of mending that awaited her, but she remained where she was, watching the sliding movement as the tight, round fist of muscle at the top of the slave's arm moved slick beneath her skin. Rough yellow cakes of cornbread cooled on the bench and something bubbled in the large iron pot on the fire. The bread of Louisiana tasted to Vincente like it was baked from greasy sawdust, but the soup smelled good, thick and meaty.

382

Vincente felt the pull of saliva drawing up into her mouth.

'It smells good,' she said.

The slave glanced up and did not cease in her pounding. She did not smile. Vincente was not certain if she understood her. Auguste had told her that the slave was from the nation of the Colapissas and that though she had a French name, she knew only a few words of the French tongue.

'The soup,' Vincente persisted, pointing at the pot and rubbing her stomach with the flat of her hand. 'Delicious.'

The slave Thérèse stopped pounding and wiped her hands on the broad apron she wore around her waist. Her brow was oily with perspiration. Reaching up to a shelf above her head, she took down a cloth and laid it over the pounded grain. Her head hung forward, too heavy for her thin stalk of a neck. Then slowly she turned towards the fire and squatted before it on her haunches, her apron falling between her thighs. Her upturned knees were as sharp as teeth. Taking up a ladle, she dipped it into the iron pot and brought it to her face, her nostrils wide as she inhaled. The smoke curled upward, spangling her eyebrows. Something about her stillness made Vincente think of Auguste. She wanted to ask if she might taste the soup.

Instead she watched as the slave returned the ladle to its place and took up a long spoon. Her plait fell over her shoulder as she stirred, and the ridged jut of her spine pushed pale against the curve of her brown neck. Beside her on its hook, the iron ladle glistened, its bowl speckled with flecks of meat. A bead of gravy slid unhurriedly from its rim and fell silently to the floor. Round and round, the slave stirred with her long spoon, pushing the fragrant smoke up into the air. She did not look up as Vincente jerked herself away from the door jamb, snatched up a cake of the still-hot cornbread and, tearing it into wads that burned her crammed mouth, walked back across the yard to the empty cabin.

It was late afternoon. The shadows were lengthening and the bats swooped, scattering snipped-out scraps of black across the pink-gold sky. The men and the Negroes would soon return from their work. The women in the lower compound were cooking. Smoke drifted over the sun-baked ground, and the air was greasy with the smell of roasting meat.

Elisabeth sat upon her bench, her hands desolate in her lap, and let her head fall back against the rough plank wall. Fuerst had been adamant. He had seen it before, he said, in the Rhineland and knew how it would be. The venomous quality of the child's sick body was volatile as liquor and would quickly putrefy her breath and infect the outward air. Like a garment that retains the smell of sweat or of fire smoke, the air would bear the pestilence to the rest of them, insinuating itself through the tiny holes in the skin to corrupt the spirits and the humours within. The venom threatened them all, but Elisabeth, being with child and unnaturally inflamed with heat, would be most susceptible. When she had protested, he had simply shaken his head. The child must go.

It was very quiet. Jeanne's corn paddle idled against the wall of the cooking hut, and the mortar was closed, covered with a piece of wood weighted down with a rock. Her fire circle was cold, muffled with ash. Since the slave's departure, the wife of the man they called Karl-zu-klein, who was near to her time and little use for outdoor work, had ground their corn and brought supper to the cabin. Her flour was coarse, her sagamity lumpy and indigestible. Fuerst made no remark of it, but only ate more fastidiously than usual, swallowing his mouthfuls with water.

For years they had worked alongside one another, slave and mistress, bound by exile and by silence and by the child who had known no life but her own and could not mourn what was lost, their days as distinct and as appended as the oak and the cow byre. With Jeanne gone, the wind blew through Elisabeth and made her shiver. It seemed to her that the shadowed forest played a child's game with her, creeping a little closer every time she turned away from it.

She worked ferociously, making candles from tallow and scrubbing the cabin with sand till her hands were raw, but steadiness eluded her. Without Jeanne the silence was different. Elisabeth did not know who watched here when the slave did not. Quietly, when she had thought her mistress not looking, Jeanne had pulled the stray hairs from Elisabeth's comb and buried them, and her nail clippings too. It was the savage belief that the bad spirits made powerful magic with such plunder. The previous morning, as she had combed her hair, Elisabeth had wrenched a knot from it. When she returned to the cabin in the evening it was still there. She had stared it at a long time. Then, pulling the tangle of hairs from the comb, she had walked down to the lower compound where the Rhinelander woman prepared the fire for dinner, and thrown it into the flames. The women had watched her warily, clumped together around their pots and kettles. The smell of burning hair had been powerful and unpleasant.

In their pen beside the live oak, the cows shifted, swinging their bone-boxed flanks. In the hurricane months, when the wind whipped up from the river and tore across the bluff, the beasts pressed up against the tree as though the oak was a cow also, and the lichened bark striped their hides with green. They wanted milking. Marguerite liked to watch her while she worked, swinging from the rough bars of the pen. Often she got splinters in the palms of her hand and Elisabeth was obliged to work them out with a needle so that they might not become corrupted. In Burnt-canes, even scratches were slow to heal.

Once an alligator had ventured from the bayou all the way into the yard and, when the child cried out, Elisabeth had turned on her stool to see it staring at the fire as though transfixed. It was a young creature, perhaps six feet in length, but its appearance was as ancient and appalling as the monsters of antiquity. Hissing at the child to stay quite still, Elisabeth stood very slowly and backed away towards the rear of the pen before slipping between the bars. The creature did not move as she ran to the cabin to fetch the musket, but it seemed to her that it watched not the fire but the child. She seized the gun, cocking it and raising it to her shoulder as Fuerst had taught her, but before she could shoot, she saw that Jeanne had taken up her corn paddle and was striking the alligator with great force upon the head. She lowered the gun, her arms shaking, but Jeanne only issued a final blow to the alligator, who sprawled senseless in the dust, and, smiling at her round-eyed daughter, carried the paddle to the bayou so that she could rinse it clean.

The child turned in her belly. Elisabeth sighed and placed a restraining hand upon it. She wanted to be angry but the anger was not in her, only weariness and a tipping kind of unease. It was not only the savage spirits that were capricious.

★ ★ ★

The arrival of the pirogue stirred the smoke-smudged air and set the birds to clattering in the trees. Elisabeth was halfway across the open ground before the Jesuit emerged from the canebrake, his small retinue at his heels. When she saw him, she stopped short, her face slackening.

'Father?'

'Elisabeth Savaret.' He hastened towards her, his hands outstretched. 'Look at you. It has been a long time.'

'Yes. A long time.'

There was a silence. Then, very slowly, Elisabeth reached out her hands. Rochon seized them, pressing them between his own.

'We are headed for the mission at the Illinois,'

he said. 'Might we beg your indulgence and lodge with you a while? We bring letters for your husband from New Orleans and supplies too.'

'Why — yes. Yes, of course. I — forgive me, Father. It is so unexpected. I thought you returned to France.'

'Oh, I went. Then I came back.' He shrugged. 'I missed the mosquitoes.'

She did not smile. He studied her, his head on one side.

'Are you well?' he asked.

'We manage.'

'I had hoped to find you in Mobile. The place is full of strangers.'

'I am here now.'

'So I hear. They tell me that you have not once been back. I would not have expected you so devoted an advocate of the rural life.' He smiled at her wryly. 'Your husband, the Rhinelander, he flourishes?'

'It would appear so. Like the indigo, he seems strangely well suited to this place.'

'He is not alone. There is something about Louisiana that draws a man back.'

When she did not reply, Rochon sighed.

'How long since you have seen a priest, Elisabeth?' he asked gently. 'Since you have seen anyone at all?'

'A while.'

'Then I am glad I am here. You shall make your confession and in exchange I shall say Mass and fill you in on the latest news from town. You are a long way from life here, Elisabeth.'

Elisabeth was silent.

'I was startled to find Mobile moved,' he continued in a lighter tone. 'I had assumed its name an irony.'

She looked up at him then. His smile was wry and very tender.

'There was a flood,' she murmured. 'Not long after you left.'

'So they tell me.' Rochon shook his head. 'You know the soil in the new town is all sand? Yet again they manage to settle in a place where nothing grows.'

'Naturally. If the soil was fruitful, the good people of Mobile would have to till it. It is less wearisome to complain of injustice and to wait for white flour from France.'

The Jesuit laughed.

'My dear Elisabeth, I am so glad to see you. I have missed our friendship.'

Elisabeth swallowed the cramp in her throat.

'Will you stay long?' she asked.

'Three or four days. If we may beg your indulgence.'

'I would be glad of it.'

'And I.'

They walked together towards the main cabin.

'You know it is not only you that lures me here,' Rochon admitted. 'I have taken comfort in the thought of Jeanne's cooking since I set sail from France.'

'Then you shall be disappointed. She is not here.'

'No?'

'My husband has sent her away.'

'Perhaps it is for the best.'

'You misunderstand me. The girl is sick. My husband feared that — I am myself with child. Several months. He sent her away.'

'A child? Praise God.'

'I begged him to allow her to stay, begged him, but he would not listen. She should not have been required to travel, she was too weak, and the Bayagoulas are not her people. How may she grow stronger among strangers?'

Her voice tore. Rochon laid his hand gently upon her shoulder.

'Her mother is with her. She will be well cared for. And your husband is right to be prudent, though my stomach curses him for it. You have the child to think of.'

'But it has been weeks. Still she ails. Oh, Father, what if she dies? What if she dies?'

'She is baptised, Elisabeth. Guichard saw to that. When her time comes, she will take her place in Heaven.'

Elisabeth's shoulders crumpled.

'She cannot die,' she whispered. 'She is all that I have left of him.'

'Then it is time to let her go, whether she lives or nay.'

★ ★ ★

When evening came they ate roasted roebuck with the Rhinelander woman's rough cornbread. Rochon drank a good deal of Jeanne's maize beer and described his failed attempts to settle back to life as a priest in provincial France. Elisabeth had forgotten the distinctive infectiousness of his laughter. Even Fuerst, weary and irked by the unwelcome encumbrance of company, unbent a little, nudged to grudging tolerance by the Jesuit's generous wit and irrepressible good humour.

When he came to relate the situation at the coast, however, Rochon's tone grew uncharacteristically sombre. As a result of Mr Law's pledge to enlarge the colony, he had plundered the streets and jails not only of Paris but of Lyon, Rochefort, Orléans and Bayonne, and heaped his finds into ill-provisioned and overcrowded ships. The confusion at Dauphin Island was indescribable. What lodging there was available was pitifully inadequate, hardly more than hovels of a few stones roofed with cane. The demands from hundreds upon hundreds of empty bellies were ceaseless and overwhelming, and the already insufficient provisions were frequently seized by organised gangs of felons or by bands of disaffected soldiers from the garrison. No food could be raised on the blinding white sand. The men who waded out to gather oysters a gunshot from the shore returned scarlet and half crazy from the burning sun. Most sickened; many died. Rats swarmed, reduced to gnawing on the stocks of guns. And yet still they languished there, the indentured and the pressed and the merely desperate, half starved and ailing, for there were no boats to spare to convey them onward.

It was impossible to imagine how they might manage when winter came.

'Mr Law is a charlatan,' Fuerst said. 'That or a

damned fool. Can he not see that if we are to make something of this place, it is slaves we have need of, not felons?'

'A felon has hands,' Rochon observed. 'He might be put to work.'

'Except that it costs more to feed that manner of man than his work is worth. You cannot make gold from stones.'

'That is true. But with enough picks you can hew it from the bare rock.'

'If Law would treat Louisiana like a mine, then he should send miners. We are not a dunghill onto which he can throw all the dregs of France.'

'These men have been spared the gibbet. A thankful man is a hard worker.'

'And a thief is always a thief.' Fuerst pushed his plate away and reached for his pipe. He nodded at Elisabeth as she rose and began to gather together the dirty dishes. 'That wasn't half bad.'

Rochon watched her, sipping at his beer.

'So, what other news do I have for you?' he said at last. 'The war with Spain goes on and the fort at Pensacola is French once more. Your old friend Renée Gilbert is married again. To Trégon, the merchant.'

Elisabeth thought of little Renée Gilbert and the tilt of her chin as she had gazed up at her tall cannoneer. The cannoneer was long dead and her second husband too. Years of drudgery and famine had threaded white into Renée's thick brown hair and set her jaw hard as metal. She would be glad of Zacharie Trégon. The merchant was prosperous, unflinching in

393

matters of business.

'Burelle sends his regards,' Rochon continued. 'His tavern licence has finally been restored and he has a fistful of new grandchildren, all nourished to unnatural good health by his strongest ale. More astonishing still, at the ripe old age of whatever she is, it appears that the schoolteacher has finally abandoned all hope of marrying the commandant. She claims infirmity and a large pension and petitions to return to France.'

'Good heavens,' Elisabeth replied drily, lifting the beer jug. 'How shall the children of the colony get by without her?'

'They shall not quickly find another to answer to her description, that is certain.'

They smiled. Elisabeth refilled Rochon's mug and offered the jug to her husband.

'I must check on the Negroes,' Fuerst muttered, frowning as he scraped back his chair. 'I had thought priests not permitted to drink ale.'

'Some prefer to avoid it,' Rochon conceded. 'But the Lord is merciful. He has my pledge of celibacy. He does not insist upon sobriety too. Or not every day.'

Fuerst scowled.

'I shall not be long. When I return I must sleep.'

Without speaking, Elisabeth took the piled dishes and set them on the porch. The dusk was thickened with clouds of biting insects and the outline of her husband as he walked away past Jeanne's empty hut was powdery and indistinct.

Quickly she closed the door.

'Forgive my husband's discourtesy,' she said, turning back to Rochon. 'He is unaccustomed to company.'

'It is I who should apologise. My tongue is too sharp.'

'Not for me.'

'No. Not for you.'

It had grown dark in the cabin. Elisabeth reached up to take a tallow candle from the high shelf.

'I shall be back directly,' she said.

'In a moment. I wanted to speak with you of Guichard. He is come?'

Elisabeth fumbled with the candle, almost dropping it.

'Come here? No, of course not. Why would he come here?'

'You have not heard?'

'Heard what?'

'That Guichard is finally married.'

Elisabeth set the candle down. The saucer rattled on the table.

'Married?'

'Yes.'

'Not to the black-haired urchin, Le Caën's daughter?'

'No. Not her.'

'Then whom?'

Rochon hesitated.

'Well?'

The Jesuit sighed, spreading his fingers upon the table.

'Before his death, Sieur de Chesse made plans

to marry. Perhaps you know this. He arranged for a wife to be sent to him here, from Paris. As part of their contract of betrothal, he named her his sole heir in the event of his death.'

'I don't understand. What has this to do with Auguste?'

'The wife is now in Louisiana. And married to Guichard.'

Elisabeth stared at him.

'Elisabeth, Auguste Guichard is your new master.'

'No.'

'Yes.'

'But he will never come here. Not here.'

'On the contrary, he has resigned from the Company. He is to come here, to reside here. Permanently.'

'No.' Elisabeth looked wildly at Rochon. 'It is not possible. He gave his word.'

'He comes all the same.'

'Who comes?'

Fuerst stood in the doorway, a lit torch in one hand. The flame painted his face like a savage's, orange and black. Elisabeth covered her face with her hands.

'Herr Fuerst,' the Jesuit said gently. 'All is quiet, I trust?'

Fuerst gestured at him with the torch.

'This will light your way. Goodnight, Father.'

'Yes, yes, of course. Goodnight to you both. And thank you for a fine supper. I am most grateful for your kindnesses.'

The priest stood. Coming around the table, he stood for a moment behind Elisabeth's chair.

She did not look up as, very lightly, he set his hand upon her head.

'May the Lord bless you this night and always. May I?'

Taking the torch from the Rhinelander, the priest touched the flame to the wick of the tallow candle, filling the room with its smoky yellow light. When he made to leave, Fuerst stood in the doorway, his legs wide, blocking his path. Then he stepped to one side. Holding the flame before him, the Jesuit went out into the frog-shrill night.

'Slippery bastard,' Fuerst muttered, pulling off his boots.

Elisabeth did not reply.

'Who comes? The religious said someone comes.'

'Yes.'

'Who comes?'

'We have a new master.'

'When?'

'I — I don't know. I was not really listening.'

Fuerst looked at her. Then he nodded.

'To bed now,' he said. 'I tell you, I am weary to the bone.'

Elisabeth stared into the tallow candle as her husband crossed the room behind her. The wick had been too hurriedly dipped and it burned fast and fierce, spitting sharp sparks of buffalo grease that stung her hands. She heard the crackle of the bed, the drawn-out sigh as her husband broke wind.

'Elisabeth,' he called to her, his words stretched into a yawn. 'Come.'

Slowly Elisabeth stood. Her back ached with

weariness, and her shoulders too. Fuerst said nothing as she set down the candle and struggled with the fastenings of her bodice. Before she was free of it, he was asleep. Snores caught in his throat and whistled out between his parted lips. Cupping her hand around the flame, she blew out the light.

The bed was damp and smelled of sweat and mouldy moss. Fuerst's grunts scraped at the underside of her skull. She lay first on one side and then the other, but sleep did not come.

She thought of Marguerite, grey and glazed with fever, without whom she was hardly alive. And she thought of Auguste Guichard, who had loved her once and was now her master. The one man in the world she had trusted never to see again, the one man whose presence was unendurable. It was a mistake, she told herself. Rochon had misunderstood Auguste's intentions. He would not come to Burnt-canes, he would never come, for she was here and was she not at least as intolerable to him as he was to her? He would not forgive her. She did not hope for that nor did she desire it. She wanted only the absence of him, so that she might set her gaze on her feet and go on, she might continue to go on.

He would not come. If he came, how might either of them pretend to forget? Elisabeth sat up in the darkness and the fear rose up in her like vomit. Was that why he came — because he wished to make her remember?

'And how is the life of a married man?'

'I hardly know.'

'Never fear. With luck you shall have plenty of time to tire of it.'

'I shall hold my thumbs.'

'Luck seems to have favoured you this far.' Bienville shook his head. 'I only wish the Company would see fit to send us a few more Mme le Vannes. My Canadians can no more make wives of the whores they discard here than the garrison can make soldiers of murderers and thieves.'

Auguste said nothing. The governor himself had never married, though naturally there had been offers. Rumours persisted, many of them contradictory. Some years before there had been a scandal when the priest at Mobile had refused to allow the commandant to serve as godparent at a christening because of alleged improprieties with a French serving maid. She had been a pretty enough thing, Auguste remembered, with a swagger to her walk that presaged ruin. Although it had been the priest who had emerged from the incident the more damaged, it had done nothing to enhance Bienville's already dubious reputation with the court at Versailles. Five years of deference under Cadillac's ill-fated governorship had been a harsh punishment. Since he had finally been restored to authority,

Bienville had either ceased in his adventuring or he had become more careful.

'Of course I write to Paris, but I might as well talk to myself,' Bienville went on. 'The redoubtable Mr Law appears unable to grasp that I cannot turn roving *coureurs-de-bois* into sturdy colonists while they are running around after Indian girls in the woods.'

'A wife cannot always prevent that.'

Bienville rubbed his palms on the thighs of his breeches. Then he stood.

'So what do you think of our New Orleans?' he asked. 'Salt smugglers are cockroaches, but so far at least they have proved themselves capable of industry.'

Auguste looked about him. On the bluff that rose above the wide yellow crescent of the river, there were perhaps sixty men engaged in all manner of work, filling the air with shouts and the ringing of axes and hammers. Already a wide area of ground had been cleared and perhaps one hundred rectangular plots had been laid out around a central *place*, many of which already boasted cabins or the beginnings of them. At the rear were two large warehouses of wood and a long, low building thatched with palmetto that served as a barracks. Everywhere the signs of building were in evidence. Newly dug ditches were stubbled with a faint green beard of regrowth, the dirt matted with broken branches and fans of cut palmetto, and the splintered bones of trees jutted from the underbrush.

And still the forest pressed back against the attack, the ancient trees splay-footed and

400

resolute, slung about with shadows and Spanish wig. Beyond the ravaged bluff, where the land sloped back to the river, swamps of cypress and tangled reeds choked the riverbanks and snagged in the low, heavy skies, drawing them downward. The air was thick and cumbersome, sticky with the reek of river water.

'Shall it not flood?' he asked.

'*Vierge*, man, you are as blinkered as the dolts in Paris. Are embankments beyond the wit of man? You know there can be no ruling Louisiana without control of the Mississippi, and here there is a natural harbour, deep enough for the largest of vessels. When the wharf is properly completed, New Orleans shall challenge the finest ports in the world. It maddens me that they cannot see it. Instead they would have me travelling up and down from Mobile. We should have moved the capital here months ago.'

'I am sure, sir, that you shall have plenty of time to tire of her.'

Bienville grinned.

'If it is the possession of a wife that sharpens your wit so, perhaps I should be grateful that we suffer such a scarcity of them.'

The two men strolled together along the edge of the bluff. Below them the wide river slid unobserved, its yellow wavelets turned upward like pricked ears.

'The King's plantation shall be directly over there,' Bienville said, gesturing towards the opposite bank.

'A fine position.'

'Fine indeed. And how goes yours?'

'My wife's.'

'Then yours. How do you find it?'

'I have yet to go there.'

'But it is only a few days' travel from here. Surely you — '

'I will, sir.'

The two men stopped, looking out over the river.

'You have my word,' Auguste said.

Bienville sighed.

'It is not over, you know,' he said. 'The commissary is to send another report.'

'The commissary knows nothing.'

'Perhaps not, but like any man unequal to his post, he abhors his superiors. He would stick a blade between my shoulders for the pure sport of it. Besides, the people of Mobile have long memories and short tempers.'

'There is only rumour and insinuation.'

'Since when was that not enough?'

Auguste did not reply. Bienville sighed.

'The grant you were to have,' he said. 'It is to go to a cousin of the commissary.'

'I heard.'

'You have always served Louisiana faithfully, Guichard. It is not forgotten.'

'Then perhaps it should be, for all of our sakes.'

The commandant rested his hand briefly on the younger man's shoulder.

'It is some solace, I hope, that the de Chesse plantation is worth the trouble of a wife,' he said. 'You are fortunate in the Rhinelander Fuerst. There are not many foremen who would work the land as he has without a master and his whip. Indigo was a prudent decision. And is he not married to — ?'

'Yes. Yes, he is.'

'An irony, in the circumstances. Still, it will be a comfort to your wife, I imagine. An experienced woman to show her the ropes.' Bienville jammed his hands in the pockets of his coat. 'A new edict had been passed that prohibits royal governors from the possession of plantations, did you know that? Now that they have finally conceded me the title, it transpires that I must sell the concession that came with it. I am permitted to hold only sufficient land for a vegetable garden.'

'That seems a little unjust, sir.'

'A little? It is fortunate that I consider vegetables essential to a healthy constitution. Fifty-four acres should suffice, don't you think?'

'Shall that not provoke the commissary?'

'Of course. Everything that I do provokes him. Do not give me that look, Guichard. I have come to regard the commissary much as I regard the mosquito. One must succumb to the harassment of neither if one is to make something of oneself here. This is my country, damn it. I have given my life to this place and at last it offers up something in return. I shall not let some bean-counting bureaucrat confound me.'

★ ★ ★

The next morning, Auguste sought passage on a Company boat preparing to depart for the coast.

403

In his coat he carried in paper certificates the money pressed upon him by the governor and a number of letters to be delivered to the fort at Mobile.

Summer was ending. Alongside the sloop at the makeshift dock, several pirogues were being loaded with provisions. The roughly hewn canoes sat low in the water, squat and bundled about with rope-bound sailcloth, putting Auguste in mind of the cradle the Oumas had called *ullosi afohka*, or infant receptacle, a bent bark pod lined with Spanish wig from which the child peeped like a not-yet butterfly wrapped in the rolled brown leaf of its cocoon. For the whole first year of his life, a child resided in this cradle, either on his mother's back or propped against the trunk of a tree so that he might see more clearly the world into which he had been brought.

Jeanne had not made a cradle for her child. Instead she had bound the infant to her body with a length of linen. Often too she had carried the child in her arms, the tiny skull cupped in her palm like a nut in its shell. He had understood then that, as a mother was a suckling's whole world, so might a child be land and sky and village to its mother.

At last the sloop was loaded and ready for departure. There were shouted orders, the squeal of ropes through their wooden blocks, the crack and gasp of the sails straining to catch the faint breeze as the vessel pulled into the fast-flowing channel at the centre of the river, the yellow water tumbling in spirals around its prow. A Negro in a torn shirt pushed past Auguste, hauling at a rope coiled at his feet. Auguste did not move. He knew from long experience that wherever on the deck he chose to stand, he would find himself in the way of someone.

Instead he crossed his arms across his chest, watching as the chopped-out settlement disappeared from view and the forest reclaimed the land. On both sides of the river, the dense mass of trees hunched black against the sickly sky. The swamp waded waist-high into the water, reaching out towards the sloop while, trailing in its wake, whole tree trunks turned in the yellow churn, their shattered branches held aloft in silent appeal.

He had meant to go. He had sent a message with the Jesuit instructing Fuerst to expect him. He wrote that he wished to inspect the concession, to identify those supplies necessary for the further development of the land, including the construction of a house for himself and his bride. He had assured Fuerst that he had heard nothing but praise for his efforts at the plantation and that he looked forward to meeting him. In the meantime he asked that the Rhinelander pass on his sincere regards to his wife, Elisabeth, whom he hoped was in good health. He would be pleased to remake her acquaintance.

She had asked that they never meet again, and he had bowed his head and given her his word. It had been, agonisingly, a reprieve. She had not mentioned the letter. Perhaps he might have asked for its return or that she destroy it, but he did not. He wanted her to have it. The letter was hers, a sheathed blade that might be drawn when time had passed and the howling churn of anguish no longer drowned out anger or rendered it absurd. He knew it as a kind of justice, that she should hold in perpetuity the possibility of vengeance, and that he should continue forever in the shadow of it. She had lost her husband and her child. There was nothing else he had to set against the terrible vastness of her grief.

Now he would break his word. There was no help for it. He could not continue as he was, without knowing. And yet, when the day had come, he could not. Instead he had informed the men that they would travel directly to New Orleans and from there back to Mobile. The men had mocked his urgency and made crude observations about the appetites of newly-weds, but they were glad to be going south. In New Orleans, where the church remained no more than a square of earth marked out with timbers, the whores had already set up business and makeshift taverns pushed up from the newly turned earth like mushrooms.

'So go on then, Guichard, tell us. What's she like?'

Auguste stared at the soldier. See her there, he wanted to say, her head slightly averted and her dark hair looped beneath her cap? She is honest and bold and tender and fierce and quite without vanity. She is educated, worked

406

fine with book-learning, and yet she is always curious. Intent upon a task, she presses the tip of her pink tongue between her teeth and a V forms between the twin arches of her eyebrows. She cries silently, her hands in fists. But when she looks up at you and her mouth curves upward and her cinnamon eyes soften, the world slips sideways and you have to hold tight to keep from falling.

Except that she cannot look at me. Her eyes are dead and all the soft, bold, curious parts of her are dead also. Because of me. Because I murdered her husband.

'Will you look at him? The man's gone all misty-eyed. And there was me thinking it was only those fancy plants of his that got him stiff.'

'Spill it, Guichard. She must be something special to make you moon like that.'

'In Louisiana? A smile and a pulse makes a girl special in Louisiana.'

'There's more to Guichard's wife than a smile, I can tell you.'

'Tits to make a Jesuit beg for mercy.'

'So what's the story, Guichard? Feel as good as they look?'

'Ah, the man's barely been married a minute. Give the bugger a break.'

'Your bugger's getting it for free, which is more than can be said for the rest of us. Since when did he deserve a break?'

The nearest man nudged Auguste hard in the ribs. Auguste stood and walked away from them.

'You should not speak this way of my wife,' he muttered.

'If you ever spoke of her yourself perhaps we wouldn't have to!'

The men laughed. Auguste stared out over the river. His wife. He strained to summon her likeness, to recall the shape of her face, the colour of her eyes, the feel of her flesh beneath his hands, but his head was dazed and disobliging.

Sharply he ordered the men to strike camp and load the boats. They would start south immediately. As the men worked, he forced himself to attend to the proper loading of provisions. Improperly stacked they would dampen and spoil.

'In the first pirogue,' he ordered the thickset man they called Le Fût. 'Right up front, in the bow.'

Le Fût did as he was bid and straightened up, wiping his brow with his sleeve.

'A married man, eh? Sweet Jesus. You're a lucky bastard and no mistake.'

'Is that so?'

'Ungrateful bugger. You'd better watch out, you know. They need more than that, women, to keep 'em sweet.'

'Do they?'

'Mark my words. They all love you at the start but you wait. You just wait.'

'For the love of God!' Auguste cried, and he struck Le Fût in the soft part of his face with his fist. Around the camp the other men turned to stare as Le Fût staggered backwards, falling hard against the pirogue. Blood streamed from his nose.

For a moment Auguste stood there, his breath coming in jagged rips, his fists still raised. Then, dropping his hands, he turned and strode away into the forest.

It was not possible to be a married woman in Mobile and to avoid company. Mr Law might have convinced the Paris newspapers that the port of Louisiana was a small city with more than two thousand residents, but the truth was that for more than a dozen years, it had numbered fewer than two hundred souls, even when the garrison was included in its count, and though it was grown five times as large, it could not shake the habits of familiarity. The people of Mobile were city folk, tradesmen and clerks and taverners. Inquisitiveness, which they called neighbourliness, was in their blood.

Once married and the mistress of her own house, Vincente le Vannes found herself taken up by what passed in Louisiana for the respectable women of the town. Just as Louisiana was nothing like Paris, nor were these coarse women with their rough hands and rougher humour like anyone Vincente had ever known. They were ignorant, shabby and shockingly godless. None knew so much as ten words from the Bible. But though she recoiled from them, she recoiled more from the prospect of isolation.

Vincente had never liked to be alone. The company of others was a looking glass she held up to her face, less for vanity than for reassurance. If they could see her, then she must be there. She was startled always by the solidity

410

of others, their loud voices, their heavy footfalls, their strong smells. Even the nuns in their silent robes exhibited a containment and a certainty she could not imitate, for all her pains. Denied the proof of her reflection, she was filled with a dread that she had already begun to disappear.

The women of Mobile made poor looking glasses, but they were better than no glass at all. They spoke French and knew her troubles. She was consoled by their undisguised interest in her and by their blunt acknowledgement of her despondency. They had all of them despaired at the place, they told her, when first they came. She would grow accustomed to it as she would grow accustomed to marriage. It was a matter of arranging things to one's advantage.

The wives were as eager to teach as Vincente was to learn. Under their tutelage, Vincente learned which of the families of the town were decent and upright, where she might find the least disreputable of the savage traders, and how to treat her linens so that they would not immediately mould. She learned that the taverner Burelle might always be depended upon to find a little white flour when the Company stores were empty and that while she might exchange nods with the Taensa woman who was the mother of the children of the merchant Charly, the Alabama wife of the carpenter should never be acknowledged. She learned that since the transportation of whores and felons from France, the town was no longer what it had been, obliging the rigorous observation of propriety.

'You must attend Mass at least one Sunday in the month,' Gabrielle Borret instructed her. 'It sets an example to those *debauchées* who do not know a church from a lump of cheese.'

In Paris, Vincente thought, she would have assailed a speech of such impiety with every psalm and proverb in the Bible. Now she only nodded, her eyes sliding sideways to confirm that Perrine Roussel and the others did not mock her. It caused her ears to burn still, the recollection of the morning when, horror-struck by the depravities of a *curé* insensible to vice, she had begged the assistance of the wives in defeating the vast and terrible empire of the Devil in the New World. The women had not sighed gravely and clasped her hands, as she had hoped they would, nor had they been roused to righteous anger. Instead they had looked at each other, sucking in their cheeks as though the screws in their jaws had been tightened a half-turn. Then they had burst out laughing. The shame of it had caused her to flee.

Later that day Renée Gilbert had come to see her.

'You are possessed of a dry wit, Madame,' the older woman said quietly. 'But we would prefer if you would desist from such humour. Life in Mobile is hard enough without the bony fingers of saints poking us in the ribs, even in jest.'

For two days Vincente had remained at home. She read her Bible. She knelt on the floor, her hands folded, and said her prayers. The splintery floor caught in the stuff of her skirt, tearing holes. She thought of the coarse rag rug she had insisted upon for her attic bedroom at the Place Royale and of the silk carpet with its delicate patterns that was too big for her mother's parlour. On the third day, she rose and washed her face and went to join the women at the market.

She did not know how she would have managed without the instruction of the women. They showed her how to make candlewicks from twisted milkweed silk, brushes and brooms from corn husks and tough-stemmed weeds, soft soap from a mixture of lye and buffalo grease. They taught her that a paste made from the pith of the sassafras wood worked wonders for redness and swelling of the eyes, and that inhaling the smoke from the burning leaves of jimson weed eased congestion in the chest. They instructed her in the best ways to prevent meat and slaves from spoiling. From them she learned that goods that were scarce or wanting might always be acquired for a price, and that the women of Mobile might endure upon a diet of cracked corn, but they would do whatever was necessary to acquire new sleeves or a collar from France when the ships came into port.

Her own trousseau was stroked and sighed over, the lace-trimmed silk streaming like foamy water through the women's fingers. Vincente, who in Paris had clamped her jaw and jutted her hips and refused to utter a word even as the dressmaker stuck her with pins, no longer despised the dresses so ardently. Sometimes, alone at night, she unfolded the mantuas and the chemises and the petticoats and the cloaks from

413

the chest and laid them out upon the bed, their skirts spread and their sleeves outstretched. The heavy silks were lustrous and cool to the touch, and the approving murmurs of the women drifted from their folds, easing the knot in her belly.

She had been married almost a month before she ventured with Germaine Vessaille to see the widow Freval, who let out the seams to their limits. Germaine, whose husband Jacques le Brun was a gunsmith, had a sweet smile and the harried abstraction of a mother overburdened with infants. Some days later, Vincente visited her at her own cabin and, amid the sticky-handed clamour, asked hesitantly if she would accept a lace *fichu* for which Vincente could find no use. Germaine said nothing but only gasped and pressed her hands over her mouth while a chap-mouthed child tugged unheeded at her threadbare skirts. The pleasure of it pinked Vincente's cheeks.

It was Anne Negrette, wife of the Canadian they called Le Grand, who was first to quiz Vincente about her husband. The hour was early and the women gathered before the baker's ramshackle shop, waiting for him to raise his shutter.

'So, tell us,' Anne said, nudging Vincente with her basket. 'What is he like?'

Vincente flushed, startled at the impropriety of the question.

'Why,' she stumbled, 'he is a decent enough man, I am sure.'

'Decent? Come, Madame, you shall not satisfy

414

us that way, shall she, ladies?'

'I — I am sure you know him better than I,' she said, unsettled by the women's laughter. 'We have spent hardly seven days together.'

'And seven nights also!' Yvonne Lereg interjected.

The laughter grew louder.

'I should grant you the advantage, all the same,' Vincente muttered.

'We hardly merit it,' said Gabrielle Borret. 'He is never here. His affairs are all with the savages.'

'Peculiar, isn't it? You'd think he'd want nothing to do with those brutes after what they did to him.'

'If I were him, I would not have been able to look them in the eye.'

'He did a great deal more than look,' Yvonne Lereg said with a giggle. 'Remember that slave of his?'

There was an awkward silence.

'What?' Yvonne protested. 'It is hardly a secret. The child's parentage is there in the parish register for anyone to see!'

Perrine Roussel cleared her throat.

'Still, your husband was lucky,' she said. 'If the missioner had not arrived, those devils would surely have killed him.'

'And he still has his arm.'

'Thank the Lord. You remember it was Le Grand they asked to cut it off, when they thought it could not be saved?' Anne Negrette smiled at Vincente. 'If your husband was lucky, so was mine. He always said that he would have needed more *eau-de-vie* than Guichard, just to

415

go through with it.'

Gratefully, Vincente smiled back.

'Those were terrible times,' Gabrielle Borret agreed with a shudder.

'Nothing to eat. The savages running wild. Everyone afraid they would be murdered in their beds.'

'So many bad memories,' Perrine Roussel agreed. 'The sight of Elisabeth holding up that dead infant still haunts me, even now.'

'No one could accuse Elisabeth Savaret of a want of grief,' Anne Negrette added, and the two women exchanged a look. 'She was a fool for that man, a perfect fool.'

'She was a fine midwife,' Anne Conaud protested.

'She was a lunatic,' Yvonne burst out, unable to support her sulk a second longer. 'And not just because of you-know-what. Imagine marrying a virtual labourer without a *sou* to his name.'

'Perhaps it was another of her great unions of love,' Anne Negrette said drily.

'It is Vincente who shall tell us, now that she is as good as her mistress.'

'Well, so she is! Now, Vincente, I would counsel you to manage her most sternly. Pride and vanity make miserable helpmeets.'

'Oh, yes, beat her often, do!' Yvonne laughed, butting Vincente playfully with her basket.

'Poor Vincente hasn't the first notion what it is we are talking about!'

'Elisabeth Savaret came over with Perrine on the *Pélican*,' Gabrielle Borret explained.

'And was trouble from the very first. It was

Elisabeth whose first husband was murdered in mysterious circumstances.'

'Anne Negrette, you are a scurrilous gossip-monger!'

'She tried to murder herself in a surfeit of grief.'

'She failed, of course. The child in her womb was not so fortunate.'

'In France she would have been tried, imprisoned. Here she goes free!'

'And now she is married to the foreman of your plantation. I wonder what you shall make of her?'

'I fear no one in town was ever much fond of her.'

'The Jesuit Rochon was kind to her,' Anne Conaud protested. 'And Perrine here could not have done more.'

'She certainly had her admirers,' Yvonne giggled. 'Guichard used to trail after her like a lovestruck puppy dog!'

The silence that followed was broken only by the bang of a fist against a jammed shutter.

'At long last,' Perrine Roussel announced brightly. 'Ladies, form an orderly queue, if you will. The bakery is open.'

After the Jesuit had gone, heat clogged the slow days, thickening the air to mud. Fuerst was gone at dawn and did not return until the first stars pierced holes in the indigo sky. When branches snapped or the shadows shifted in the trees, Elisabeth's heart leaped. But still no one came. In their enclosure the cows hung their heads in the scanty solace of the shade, their sides moving in and out like bellows. She kept a full pitcher of water in the cabin, for messengers.

It was not until after the full moon that a savage came from the village on the other side of the forest. His face was expressionless as he crossed the yard. Elisabeth watched as he gained upon her, and she pressed herself back against the rough wall of the cabin.

'I bring word,' he said unsmilingly in halting Mobilian.

'The child,' she said, and her mouth hurt with the shape of it.

'Yes.'

Elisabeth bowed her head. She wanted to cover her ears, to reach up into the sluggish sky and rip out the burning sun by its roots, hurling it back towards morning.

'Bad spirits gone.'

Elisabeth exhaled so suddenly it was almost a laugh. Awkwardly, the savage mimed his message. The child was still weak, her improvement slow. She could not yet leave the village. But the fever had broken. The spirits of death had been thwarted.

Elisabeth tipped back her head and the thankfulness in her was hot as the sun.

'Praise God,' she whispered. When she fetched the savage messenger water and something to eat, her hand shook, splashing water on the beaten earth floor.

Inside her belly the child kicked.

'Hush now,' she murmured, pressing her hand flat upon the curve of her belly. 'I have not forgotten you.'

In the yard the savage squatted patiently in the shade. Elisabeth picked up the cup and then set it down again, looking about her. Aside from the table with its two benches and the chest set behind the door, the cabin was almost bare. There was no ornament, no rug on the floor nor plaited basket upon the table, not even a pretty curtain at the window. Nothing that might catch or snag on a splinter of memory. Nothing to hold fast to, when things were unsteady.

On the wall behind the door, there was a single plank shelf. Elisabeth reached behind the old black-bellied kettle and a battered corn-husk brush and took down Marguerite's slate. The pencil dangled on its leather thong, its tip worn blunt. Upon it in the child's laborious rounded hand was written

le beau fils
la belle fille
les beaux enfants

The words were pale against the powdery ground. Elisabeth clasped the slate with both hands and thought of the tip of Marguerite's tongue pink between her teeth as she shaped the unfamiliar letters, the knobs of her spine pushing up against the nape of her bent neck.

The fever had broken. Marguerite would live.

'Prepare yourself, Elisabeth. Do you truly believe his wife will permit them to stay?'

Elisabeth shook herself like a dog, but the Jesuit's words clung to her, insistent as burrs. It had been evening, Rochon's last. The men had not yet returned from the fields, and in the yard the shadows stretched their long fingers across the dusty ground. The Jesuit had spoken gently, without emphasis, as though he only reminded her of something she already knew. The shock in her face had made his eyes soften with pity, and she had had to turn away.

'It has been years,' she had protested shakily. 'Six years. How shall she even know?'

'In Mobile?'

She had been glad of the shadows then, glad of the men clattering up from the fields, the empty commotion that filled the yard. The next morning, as the guides readied the pirogues, Rochon and Elisabeth had walked out to the boundary of the indigo fields. They spoke little, neither wishing to acknowledge the necessity of parting.

'It looks a fine crop,' Rochon said, gazing over the sea of green.

'You say that as though you know what a fine

crop would look like.'

Rochon smiled.

'I shall be very sad to leave you,' he murmured.

'I am not worthy of your affection,' she said, and she thought of the letter and the barrel behind the wood store and the poison in her blood and the urge to tell it rose suddenly up in her, like tears.

'Nor I yours. But I am very glad of it.'

'If you knew — oh, Father, I have done such wrongs.'

The words were in her mouth. With her eyes on the ground and her feet moving, she might have allowed them to fall. But he stopped. He stopped and he extended his hands to her and he bid her look at him.

'Is there something you wish to confess, child?'

And she had looked at his wise, kind face and seen the lines that sketched the shape of a frown around his mouth and the space between his eyebrows, which in the soft, milky light of early morning were no more than faint pencil marks, and she had shaken her head.

Later that morning Rochon had left.

'Be strong, Elisabeth,' he had said as he bid her farewell. 'Think of your husband, of the child in your belly. Think of Marguerite.'

Elisabeth stared at the slate. Then, snatching up the pencil, she drew a firm line through the first and the third line. At the bottom of the slate, in hasty capitals, she printed

She set a slice of cold roasted pumpkin and
some cornbread on a plate and took it with the
water to the savage. The youth ate and drank
slowly, squatting in the shade. When she gave
him the slate, his fingers made dark circles on its
dusty face.

'Take this to the girl,' Elisabeth said in her
clumsy Mobilian and he nodded, eager to be off,
the sinews in his thighs twitching like the
haunches of a deer. He was halfway across the
yard when Elisabeth called him back. She held a
hairpin in her fingers. Taking the slate from him,
she tied the pin to the leather thong that secured
the pencil, testing the knot to make sure it held.

'Go well,' she murmured in French, and a curl
of hair unspooled itself slowly from the smooth
cap of her scalp.

★ ★ ★

It was Rochon who had urged her to sell the
slave. Her husband was buried, his remains
committed to the earth and his soul to the mercy
of God, and what was done was done. She had
her unborn child to think of. The presence of
Okatomih and the sin in her, swelling beneath
her shift, would not ease her widow's burden; it
did no good to keep her. Besides, there was a
buyer in the town who had made a good offer, to
be paid in Spanish *piastres*.

Elisabeth did not object. She signed her name

clumsily, one arm held tight about the curve of her belly. Huddled inside her, the child had become a quiet thing. He seldom moved. They endured together, fists clenched, heads bowed, arms clutched tight around shins. Sometimes, in the dark hours of the night, something stirred inside her and she knew it was not a child that grew in her belly to rip between her thighs in a rush of blood and slime, but desolation.

It was some weeks later that the women of Mobile observed to one another that the slave they called Okatomih was unquestionably with child.

'They say her time is close,' Perrine Roussel said to Elisabeth, her eyes round with rapt outrage. 'Which means it happened under your roof, Elisabeth. Under your very nose. And after all you'd done for that boy. Still, I suppose we must give credit to the degenerate Guichard. In buying the slave he has honoured his obligations and has not tried to deny his part. I hear he wishes the infant properly baptised.'

That afternoon, for the first time since she had buried her husband, Elisabeth went for a walk. The child sat heavily upon the base of her spine as she walked, so that the ache divided her in two. At Auguste's house on the rue Condé she hesitated. Then she knocked.

There was shock in his face when he came to the door, shock and sorrow and a kind of dread. Then his expression flattened and blanked, and she was looking at nothing.

'Elisabeth,' he said.

'Don't,' she said.

He waited.

'I cannot — I must ask you something. I ask only that you answer truthfully.'

Auguste looked at her and, though his ruined arm hung twisted at his side, his shoulders were square.

'The child. The slave's child — '

She broke off, struggling to compose herself. Auguste took a step towards her.

'No!' She stepped away from him, her hands trembling. She clasped them together. 'The child. It is his, isn't it?'

Auguste regarded her, his grave grey eyes holding hers.

'Well?'

'No,' he said very quietly. 'The child is mine.'

Elisabeth stared at him, disbelief unhooking her ribs. When she shook her head, the ground lurched beneath her feet.

'No,' she whispered, her mouth dry. 'No. You are lying.'

'The slave's child is mine,' he said again and there was no evasion in his eyes, nothing but sorrow and defeat.

She closed her eyes. She was hardly able to breathe.

'Jean-Claude — '

' — is innocent in this, whatever else he has done. I am sorry.'

'No.' Her eyes snapped open and she shook her head. She shook it again and again, the weight of her head jerking at her neck. 'No.'

'Yes.'

'Why do you lie to me? It is his child. I know it

424

is his.' She was pleading with him now, the desperation wild in her voice.

Auguste pressed his lips together and bowed his head.

'Do what you must,' he murmured. 'There is no punishment in the world too harsh for my offences.'

Taking up her skirts, Elisabeth stumbled blindly from the cabin, wrenching at the clumsy door and lurching up the street. At the corner the wife of the carpenter called out to her in sympathetic greeting, but Elisabeth barely heard it. Her breath came in jagged rasps that screeched like screams in her ears. What terrible thing had she done?

She did not stop running until she reached the wood store.

By the time she saw the slave's child, saw in the infant face the unmistakable curve of his brow, his smile pressed into the corner of its mouth, by the time she knew for certain, there was no righting it.

After a brief exchange of pleasantries, the meal passed in near silence. She had spread a cloth he had not seen before upon the table, a fine damask with a trim of lace. He ate carefully so that he might not splash it. A storm was coming. Auguste could feel the prickling of it in the soles of his feet. As the light faded, Vincente rose and lit the tallow lamps, setting the dusk to dancing in the darkening corners of the room. The storm was in her too, he could see it in the twitch of her shoulders, the restless fluttering of her hands. She had hardly touched her supper.

He watched as she smoothed the wrinkled cloth, straightened a plate upon the dresser.

'Come,' he said gently. 'Sit with me.'

She sat. Auguste swallowed his last mouthful and, pushing his plate away, smiled up at her. She blinked at him and looked away. Her neck was very white. In the blind dream-warped burrow of the night, she pressed her soft heat against him, her nightdress already raised above her waist, her hands and mouth eager for his. Now those hands lay locked together in her lap and the points of her teeth pressed into the plump spill of her bottom lip. Her back was straight as a cypress. She wore a lace cap, also very white. Only a tendril of hair, escaping its pins to cling to the damp nape of her neck, whispered faintly of abandon.

'There will be a storm,' he said.

'Yes. They said that, at the market.'

The ocean roar of the cicadas swelled in the silence. They were always shrillest before a storm. Auguste listened, straining to pick out the calls of the nightbirds above the clamour of them. At the rue d'Iberville, he had never heard the cicadas. The evenings there had been filled to the brim with words, so many that they tumbled over one another in the effort to be spoken. Auguste had thought that the measure of happiness, the number of words you could share out between you and still not come to the end.

He thought now that he had been mistaken. Several times he had observed Vincente in the marketplace, surrounded by the women of the town, and he had thought of the chief of the Ouma who had asked him once how it was that the French understood one another when, like angry bustards, they squawked all at the same time. It had grieved the chief that the white man wasted words just as he wasted the carefully husbanded resources of the land, neither planting nor tending but only eating and drinking and smoking tobacco as though the earth was not his mother but his slave, his property to do with as he desired. His ships crushed the rivers, his stinks stifled the skies. And yet when the floods came, and the famines, he was angry.

'A bishop,' Auguste said suddenly. 'Do you hear it?'

Vincente looked up, her face creased into the fierce frown of a child. The vehemence of it surprised and stirred him. He smiled again, this time almost tenderly, and immediately her frown deepened, as though their faces tugged at each other with invisible threads. So this is marriage, he thought, and, though the thought startled him, the sensation of it was not entirely unpleasant.

'A bird,' he said. 'Not a cleric. Listen.'

The bird's song spilled like mercury into the smoky room. He watched her frown falter a little, easing the twin notches between her eyebrows. There was the faintest of hesitations. Then she leaned forward and the notches returned, more deeply etched than before.

'I want to come with you,' she said. 'To the plantation.'

Of course the women would have told her. He thought of them crowding about her at the market, hissing and chattering and choking the earth with their dung.

'To the plantation,' he said.

'Yes.'

'I do not advise it.'

'Really? And why is that exactly?'

'The situation is perilous.'

'The Lord is with us whithersoever we goest.'

'The bishops I am familiar with have feathers.'

Vincente flushed.

'Do not laugh at me. I am not afraid.'

'Perhaps you should be,' Auguste said gently. 'The Chetimachas attack our expeditions and ambush the plantations. You would be safer here.'

'What about you?'

'I would be safer here also.'

Vincente hesitated.

'So you shall stay?'

'No.'

'Then you must let me come with you.'

'I shall not be gone long.'

'Then I shall be quickly returned to safety.'

Auguste considered his wife, the tips of his forefingers against his lips. There were smudged thumbprints of pink in her habitually pale cheeks.

'You are determined,' he said at last. 'Why is it that you are determined, when there is no sense in it?'

Vincente looked away.

'There is every sense in it,' she said. 'It is my plantation, is it not?'

'It is.'

'It belongs to me by law.'

'That is true.'

'And we are to live there, are we not?'

Auguste's mouth twisted a little and his fingers pressed together.

'Yes.'

'Then I must come with you. Arrangements must be made. Now, forgive me but it grows late. I am to bed. Goodnight, husband.'

Tipping her chin into the air, Vincente seized the candle in one hand and her skirts in the other and swept away from him towards their chamber. Though it was clear that she intended a display of victory, there was something about the slip of her shoulders that lent her the air of a child dressing up in her mother's clothes. Again somewhere in the soft parts of him, Auguste felt the bruised press of tenderness.

'Goodnight, wife.'

He was not sure if he had spoken the words aloud. The curtain to the bedchamber swung loose, obscuring the doorway and setting the lamp on the dresser to shivering. Auguste unfolded his hands. Never before had they spoken to each other so freely and at such length. The flame bent and straightened, exhaling a kinked smear of black smoke as the silence sighed, settling itself once more over the room.

From behind the curtain he could hear the small noises as she readied herself for bed, but he did not go to her. He thought of the darkened bedchamber, the unspoken world beneath the rugs where there were no words, and he knew that for tonight at least that place was lost to him. The words had torn it open, letting in the light. The light was impossible.

A long, low growl of thunder set the heavy air to trembling. Auguste pressed his fingers into the sockets of his eyes. Then, pushing back his chair, he walked slowly across the room to the dresser. Low in its dish, the tallow candle hissed and spat, smearing soot over the rough saucer and painting a second shadow on the wall. Auguste blew it out, then pinched his dampened fingers over the red eye of the wick.

Out in the yard he paused beneath the shelter of the porch, his back against the lintel as the thunder snarled again. Though a faint and twisting draught stirred the very tops of the

430

trees, there was no freshness to the night. It clung to his face, greasy with slime and rot. There was a sudden slash of white light that slit the darkness and then thunder again, no longer a warning but a war cry as the rain hurled itself in great gobbets to the ground.

Auguste extended his hand, feeling the slap-sting of water against his palm. He wondered if Vincente slept, her face pressed against the pillow, the sticky click of her breathing catching in her throat. The rain hammered on the earth, and when the lightning came, it froze the night into shattered sheets of glass. Did it rain one hundred leagues north, on a bluff above the Mississippi River? Did she lie in the arms of her Rhinelander as the yellow waters rose, washed clean of anger and of grief? Or did she run the tips of her fingers over the stumps and loops of his clumsy script and think — today?

The rain was easing, the storm rolling out to sea. Above the trees a few stars shivered dew-like in the clearing sky. She was his wife, this stranger whom he reached out to in the other-world of the night. He would take her with him. It would alter things, it would surely alter things, but it would keep him steady. If the worst was to come, she would have to know it also. They would know it together.

He turned and went back into the cabin. In the darkness the hulk of the table was heavy and unfamiliar. He had grown almost accustomed to it, the small changes to the place that presented themselves when he opened the door. A shawl of

431

soft green wool across the back of the hewn-pine bench. A linen towel by the washstand. A woven spread across the bed, trimmed with silk ribbon. Her chest was a kind of magic box, ever-yielding up new treasures of a kind he had never seen before. The day before he had found beside the bed a small stool with curved mahogany legs. On its seat, picked out in needlepoint, was a posy of spring flowers, tied with a silk ribbon.

In the bedchamber he peeled off his wet clothes and stood shivering beside the bed. She lay curled like a crayfish, the rugs thrown off and one pale foot thrust out, suspended in the darkness. Gently he eased it back. She murmured in her sleep, throwing out an arm towards him. He sat, absently brushing away the scattered crumbs that clung to the soles of his bare feet, and slid into bed beside her, cupping her warm hand between his cool ones.

In the darkness it was simple.

The port at Mobile was clamorous, a jostle of noise and activity. A sloop had just docked and men shouted to one another as the sails were brought down and ropes properly secured. Men crowded together on the narrow deck, sun-blistered and unkempt, their heads low. There were women too and children, thin faces half hidden by the confusion of crates and ropes and ragged clothing heaped up around them.

Standing alongside the Company vessel that would take them as far as New Orleans, Vincente watched as her husband made the final arrangements for the safe embarkation of their boxes. They were not the only passengers bound for New Orleans. A gentleman come from Picardy by the name of M. de la Houssaye was to join them, along with several men he had brought from France, and, under the close supervision of a red-faced foreman, several rough-looking labourers. She had heard that they were to be taken to the de Catillon concession, situated only a day's travel beyond their own. Even she had heard of the de Catillon brothers, probably the wealthiest financiers in Paris.

'My daughter's neighbours,' she heard her mother say with satisfaction, and she shook herself hard, like a wet dog.

There appeared to be some confusion about the manner in which the luggage might be stowed aboard. Auguste was irked, she could see it in the twist of his bad shoulder. But he did not raise his voice to the savage as the other men did, hardening the consonants until the words bristled and the spittle flew from their mouths. He did not gesticulate with his fists, rolling his eyes heavenward. He spoke slowly, his mouth rolling easily over the awkward syllables of their strange tongue. When they spoke, he was silent, attentive, as though he conversed with equals.

It was a mortification to her, the differences in him.

'All of our husbands,' the wives of Mobile often said. 'Except for yours.'

'I know!' she declared then, rolling her eyes in mock despair, but still the breach opened up between them, cutting her adrift. Their husbands did not speak the savage languages. They were carpenters and gunsmiths and taverners. Even as she recoiled against their coarseness, Vincente frowned at her own husband, wishing him more like them. Meanwhile, the women called him the white savage and made jokes about warpaint and about the bones of his deceased ancestors, which Yvonne Lereg liked to imagine he kept in a pot in the kitchen hut.

'Make sure it is truly deer bones that slave of yours puts in the soup,' she giggled, and Vincente laughed with the others and wrapped her arms around her belly and did not know which she wished more, that Yvonne Lereg loved her or that Yvonne Lereg was dead.

'A fine specimen.'

Vincente turned. The physician Barrot stood

beside her, gesturing at the sloop where a boy was trying to coax a large bay horse down the narrow gangplank. The animal's flanks were scummed with foam, its eyes wild as it thrashed and danced, twisting away from the rope.

'You would think it glad of dry land,' Vincente said.

'Dry land? In Louisiana?' The physician chuckled, his jowls shuddering above his neckcloth. 'I admire your optimism.'

On the gangplank the horse stretched its throat and neighed, trumpeting its distress. There was a clattering and shouts of warning as, its front legs pawing at the air, it pulled free of the boy and skittered wildly onto the dock. Men ran to grab it, clustering about the creature and reaching up to restrain it. It neighed again, its eyes rolling in its head. On the deck the men and women waited, huddled in uncertain clumps as the boat hands pushed among them, hoisting boxes and barrels onto shore.

'So I hear you are to go and live among the savages,' Barrot said. 'Husband taking you back to meet the family, is he?'

'We are to go to our plantation.'

'Oh, come now, do not glare at me so fiercely. It was just an old man's little joke. We all know how Guichard loves those damned savages.'

'There is hardly a need for curses,' Vincente said stiffly. 'The savages are as much a part of God's creation as we are ourselves.'

'Indeed. Just like the snakes and the venomous spiders and the alligators who would snap off your leg as soon as look at you.' Barrot stared

435

balefully across the dock towards the pettyaugre. Beneath his wig his brow was shiny with sweat. 'Louisiana is certainly the sewer for the Almighty's least successful experiments. Madame, I shall see you on board.'

Pulling a handkerchief from his pocket to mop his brow, the doctor bowed and bustled away. Across the dock Auguste turned his head and nodded at her and she nodded back, her arms tight across her chest. She did not know why she had defended the savages to Barrot when her abhorrence for them was like sickness in her throat.

When she had told the wives of her plan to travel to the plantation, their voices had shrilled with pleasurable disgust.

'Among the savages?'

'How could you?'

'They scalp their prisoners alive!'

'They throw babies, live babies, onto the fire to appease their gods!'

'They feast on human flesh!'

Unnoticed, the slave Thérèse spread wet linens across the nearby shrubs to dry. Vincente's stomach turned over.

'But I promised I would go with him,' she had confessed unhappily. If the wives judged her decision imprudent, she comforted herself, she would heed their counsel. It would not be so awkward a matter to change her mind.

'Are you sure you should?' Anne Negrette said. 'I mean, it is hardly safe for the men.'

'It is hardly safe here,' Renée Gilbert said. 'Now that we are at war. Trégon says that if the

Spanish are prepared to besiege Dauphin Island, there is no telling what else they will try.'

'Unlike the savages, the Spanish stop short of murdering you in your bed.'

'*I* should not go,' said Germaine Vessaille. 'I should be too afraid.'

Anne Conaud shook her head and patted Vincente reassuringly on the arm.

'Do not listen to her,' she said. 'M. de Bonne, the attorney general, has taken his wife and children to his plantation. And M. Dubuisson took his sisters to the de Catillon place. It cannot be so very dangerous.'

'I only know that I should not wish to be a farmer's wife,' Anne Negrette said. 'Life is hard enough in the town.'

'The food will surely be more plentiful,' Anne Conaud countered.

'And the poisoned arrows too.'

'I think Vincente does not trust her husband to go alone,' said Yvonne Lereg slyly. 'Oh, come, do not give me that look. I can hardly blame you. I would not trust my husband either.'

'Auguste asked me to go with him,' Vincente said in a choked voice.

'I should want to go,' Anne Conaud. 'After all, the effects of the estate are hers.'

'If there are any.'

'But of course there will be,' said Gabrielle Borret. 'De Chesse brought crates with him when he came, do you remember? The place is likely full of treasures.'

The women's eyes opened wide.

'De Bonne brought a carriage,' said Germaine

Vessaille. 'Did de Chesse bring a carriage?'

'Don't be ridiculous.'

'But there will be furniture. Proper French furniture and French linens. Perhaps even carpets. Imagine carpets!'

'How unjust it is, that it is to those that have that more is given,' Yvonne Lereg pouted.

'Fortune favours the brave,' Anne Conaud said with a smile.

'And those betrothed to dead noblemen.'

'Yvonne Lereg, you are sour as a lemon,' Anne Negrette said. 'Pay her no heed, Vincente. You shall be returned before you know it.'

'Of course you must promise to bring something back for us,' said Renée Gilbert. 'A token of your affection.'

'A handkerchief perhaps.'

'A piece of lace.'

'A carriage!'

'Yes, promise!'

The women laughed and nudged her, and Vincente laughed too because there was nothing else to do. After that it appeared that the matter was decided. The wives helped her collect provisions for the voyage, advised her upon suitable clothing, the proper oil to rub upon her skin to repel the mosquitoes, and the tide of the arrangements bore Vincente onward despite herself.

Alone in the cabin, she watched the slave Thérèse as she worked and wondered with a shiver at the nature of the devilish imaginings that filled the slave's shuttered skull, the wild superstitions that fermented in her fleshless chest. She told herself that God was in His heaven, even in Louisiana, that however barbarous the savages' habits, their spirits were nothing but false idols, the imaginings of the ignorant and the credulous, signifying nothing. And yet, at night, when the pull in her belly was too much for her and she crouched in her bare feet in the porch, cramming her mouth with the cold sagamity left over from supper, when the bats beat the darkness with their leathery wings and the owls howled like souls in purgatory, she knew that it was not God who presided over the night but the malignant animal spirits of the savages, snaking between the cabins like vines to claim back the tiny scratched-out patch of civilisation that clung precariously to the hem of a lost and lawless land.

At night she drew the body of her husband on top of her and the weight of it kept her from scattering in the darkness.

Vincente watched as Auguste pushed his way through the jostle. Not for the first time, she felt a tug in her belly, a stretching sense that, the closer he came, the less clearly she could see him. When he reached her, she gave him a polite smile and looked away.

'Is everything arranged?' she asked.

'Yes. We are to take pirogues from New Orleans. I am afraid you shall find it uncomfortable.'

'Yes.'

There was a pause. Though Vincente had grown accustomed to them, the still and silent spaces when it seemed that her husband slipped

439

out of his skin, they still disquieted her. Her mother's disparaging voice echoed in her head, deriding his poor breeding and the unnaturalness of his conduct. Anyone, she sneered, would think he was not French at all. Vincente sighed, smiling up at him.

'Shall we board?' she suggested.

Clasping her arm with his good hand, he steadied her as she stepped aboard. His grip was firm and, when he released her, the impression of it lingered on the fine stuff of her sleeve. She followed him towards the stern of the pettyaugre, noticing the way that his coat puckered over the warp of his maimed shoulder. She could not look at it, not in the light, but her fingers knew the jutting lumps where the bones had healed awkwardly, the waxy smoothness of his scars.

'Are you truly not afraid?' Gabrielle Borret had whispered the day before, when the wives came together to bid Vincente farewell. 'So far from the town and the safety of the garrison, shall you not be terrified out of your wits?'

The other women had hushed her then and talked of the ordinary business of the town, the rebuilding of the church and the seventh confinement of Germaine Vessaille. It was only as they came to leave that Vincente confessed to them that she was indeed afraid. They were kind to her then. They held her hands and patted her arm and told her that she was fortunate. Her husband spoke the savage tongues, knew the strangeness of their ways. He was a friend to them, as much one of them as it was possible for a white man to be. She would surely be safe with him.

Vincente was grateful. She wept a little and clung to them and allowed herself to be comforted. It was only after they had gone that she remembered their reassurances and wept again. In the town her husband passed for a Frenchman. He ate like a Frenchman and dressed like a Frenchman and kept company with Frenchmen with as good a grace as he could muster. In the town she was a wife and he a husband, a white-skinned man who, for all his peculiarities, was not so very different from all the others. But among the savages? Who knew what kind of a savage he himself might become among the savages?

The pettyaugre began slowly to pull away from the dock, the water rolling out from beneath its stern, the pilings of the dock easing away. The sails slapped. The clamour of the quayside grew fainter. In the marketplace the women would be greeting each other, exchanging the news of the day. Vincente held tightly to the bench with both hands. The prospect of the voyage appalled her and yet, now, as she stood watching the water stretch between her and all that was familiar, she knew why she had come. She thought of Auguste Guichard, who was hers in law, speaking in another language, walking over another land, smiling at a woman who was not his wife. Elisabeth Savaret. He had loved her. He had been no more than a boy, the wives had declared, but not one had said it was not true. Auguste was to go to the plantation where

441

Elisabeth Savaret, whom he had loved, lived with her slave, who had been Auguste's concubine, and with his bastard child, whose name was written in the parish records. What place would there be for her in such a ménage, who was only his wife?

In the town, with the wives about her, she knew her fears groundless. She told herself that the threads of the past were gossamer-fine against the solid chains of matrimony, and she believed it to be true, in the town. Mobile was not Paris, but like Paris it was arranged in the French manner, a grid of lanes and hours and customs that might be depended upon to remain unaltered.

Not in the wilderness. In the wilderness savages lurked in the shadows and the prodigious forest nosed and slid and crept and coiled upward without ceasing. The licentious suck of it rotted the roots of the trees and pushed blindly up through the decaying luxuriance of its half-digested self, an eruption of snaking coils and crude excrescences bursting from the thick black slime. Its fecundity was as grotesque as it was shameless. It throbbed in the ceaseless thrum of the cicadas, in the suck and gasp of the reed-choked bayou. It draped itself from the trees, smearing their trunks with velvet, hanging in gluttonous hanks from their branches and exploding into pale, fleshy mushrooms at their roots. There was no shape to the forest, no order. There was only ungovernable profusion, blotting out the light, gorging on the lush compost of the dead.

★ ★ ★

'I wish to learn the savage language.'

Auguste stood at the bow of the pettyaugre, his elbows on the rail.

'Sickness passed?' he asked.

'Yes. Thank you.'

'Good.'

They stood together in silence as the boat slid through the yellow water. Vincente fixed her gaze upon the dense brakes of cane that sprawled half submerged along the banks of the river. There was no way of telling where the water ended and land began.

'I should like you to teach me,' she said. 'We could begin directly.'

'There is no need of haste. You shall pick up the rudiments soon enough.'

Vincente shook her head.

'I shall require more than the rudiments,' she said, and the certainty was bright and shiny in her.

'In German perhaps. The men are mostly Rhinelanders.'

'You misunderstand me. How else may I school the savages, if I cannot speak with them?'

'School them?'

'The children,' she said tightly. 'There are children on the plantation, are there not?'

He nodded.

'What?' she cried. 'Why do you look at me that way? Do you think me unable to do it?'

'Of course not.'

'The old crone schooled all the children of

443

Mobile, red as well as white. They learned their catechisms, to write their alphabet, to count. Even the ones that were not half-French.'

Auguste said nothing.

'The savages are God's creatures too, for all their ignorance,' she said. 'For as long as I am among them, it is my duty to bring them into His light. There are women at the plantation, are there not? Wives of the men. They shall help me. We shall make a school of it, you wait and see.'

'I do not doubt it.'

'Then why do you frown like that?'

'I do not. I — it is unexpected, that is all.'

'Unexpected?'

'Yes.'

'But not folly.'

'No. Not folly.'

They were silent, side by side. A sail cracked.

'I thought you might help me,' Vincente said, and without looking at her husband, she extended her arm and touched his sleeve.

There was a long pause. Auguste sighed, stretching out his arms. Awkwardly Vincente took her hand away.

'We run ahead of ourselves,' he said, gripping the rail with both hands, and though his lips smiled, his eyes did not. 'There is a great deal to be done before then.'

They reached the plantation in late afternoon. The sun was low and, in the rush-choked shallows, the bullfrogs sang a chorus harsh enough to split trees in two.

'This is it?' Vincente said faintly as the guides secured the pirogue.

'This is it,' said Auguste.

He clambered from the canoe and stared up at the bluff, where a few ramshackle huts clustered together. There was a lightness in his head, a dizzy blend of apprehension and disbelief and a kind of exultation at his own recklessness.

'But there is nothing here,' Vincente said, and it was not the desolation in her voice but the calmness that caused him to stop and turn around. She sat in the pirogue, her arms about her, her head put back, taking in the forest, the rotting cabins, the crumbling bluff. The pirogue rocked slightly from side to side.

'I am sorry,' he said.

'The other plantations. They are like this one?'

'One or two have mills, I think.'

She bit her lip.

'It is not like Paris,' she said.

He looked at her. His wife. Her hair was unkempt, her face blotchy with insect bites. Since New Orleans the journey had been arduous and uncomfortable, and yet she had not once complained. She had said little, crouched in

445

the prow of the pirogue with her skirts gathered tight around her, her hands clamped between her knees, her face shut tight against the secret terrors of the swamp.

'I have never been to Paris,' he replied softly.

She blinked at him and looked away. At night she smuggled food into her *baire* and ate it alone, frantically, as though she might never eat again. He did not ask her why. She thought he did not know.

They had lodged in the dilapidated old cabin in New Orleans that had belonged to de Chesse while they waited for the pirogue that was to take them north. It had been six months since Auguste's last visit and already Bienville's little town on the curve of the river was losing its struggle against the wilderness. Fearing inundation by flood, Bienville had had a ditch dug about the entire settlement and further ditches on all four sides of each and every lot. When spring came and the waters rose, the town had become an archipelago of tiny isles, each one with its own frail hut of cypress board, fenced all about with wild copses of weeds and stranded in a black and stagnant sea. The slimy ditches slithered with snakes and alligators, and at dusk swarms of mosquitoes rose from their slumbers to cast shadows against the violet sky. The aspect of the whole place was wretched.

In New Orleans Auguste had dreamed he waited for Elisabeth in a canebrake. There was a river close by; he could hear the tumble and churn of it as it raced away. The cane shifted and snapped, bright with hidden eyes, but though he

446

strained to see, he could see nothing. Beneath his feet the ground was swampy and treacherous. He wore no boots. The cold mud squelched between his toes. He stepped backwards, away from the sound of the river, but the mud grew deeper. It swallowed his feet, pulling him down. Auguste thrashed frantically but the mud was stronger. It closed over his knees, his thighs, his waist, his chest, crushing and squeezing, as muscular as a snake. It closed over his shoulders. There was mud in his mouth, his ears, his nostrils, the sockets of his eyes. He could see nothing but mud. Mud and the white gleam of the distant moon. And then the moon grew closer and it was not the moon but skulls, hundreds of them, thousands, constellations of skulls in an endless mud sky.

'Monsieur?' the savage guide murmured. 'We unload?'

The bayou whispered and sighed, its surface dappled gold by the tree-sieved sun. Auguste thought of a day many years ago when he stood upon the banks of another bayou and watched as the yellow water bore away the only world he knew. Somewhere on the bluff, Elisabeth was waiting for him. Slowly, the savage guide beside him, he walked back towards the pirogue. When he held out his hand to his wife, the ground was firm beneath his feet. Their land, for better or worse.

'We are arrived,' he said quietly. 'Welcome home.'

★   ★   ★

447

The sloping path led up the bluff into a dusty square of cleared ground. Auguste walked towards the largest of the cabins, whose wide roof offered some shade from the relentless sun. In a dilapidated pen at the far corner of the yard, a heat-stunned cow swayed, its mouth slack. There was no one about. Silence hung in the air, turning slowly in the sunlight. Auguste imagined her crossing the yard, her hair escaping its pins, her arms heavy with water or wood. So many times, backwards and forwards, the curve of her path worn into the earth. There was a bench against the wall of the largest hut, a plank bench like the one at the cabin on rue d'Iberville where she had liked to sit in the evenings, a knife in her hand, peeling vegetables as the evening shadows lengthened.

She liked to see them before they saw her, she told him once, and after that he could never turn the corner without hoping for a glimpse of her as she was without him, without either of them, alone and unawares. For a time Babelon had taken to whistling to her, as if he summoned a dog. It amused him, perhaps her too. One evening when he whistled, she had leaped so eagerly from the bench to greet them that she had upset the basket and the vegetables had spilled onto the ground. She had laughed. She had kissed her husband and leaned into him, her shoulder against his arm, and as Auguste bent down to retrieve the scattered vegetables, he had been pierced by a loneliness that stripped the years from his bones and made a boy of him again.

A lifetime ago.

The Rhinelander was a good man, they said. A hard worker. He rapped with his knuckles upon the door of the largest cabin.

'Hello?' he called. 'Hello?'

No one came.

'It is nearly harvest time,' he called to Vincente. 'They must all be in the fields. Wait here in the shade. I shall be back directly.'

He walked across the yard that sloped away towards the forest. They had been a long time in the pirogue and his legs were unsteady. On the lower ground, he could see an enclosure of cypress, its door open, and, across the way, a second hustle of makeshift cabins. There was the burned circle of a fireplace, a broken palmetto broom, a blackened kettle hung from the forked branch of a twisted locust tree. Spread on bushes, a few scraps of linen dried in the sun. Close by, beneath the shade of a machonchi, which the settlers called the vinegar-tree, a woman snored, her head tumbled back, her legs and her mouth sprawled open.

Not Elisabeth.

He walked slowly down towards the sleeping woman. She was big with child, so big that her distended belly was like a great stone pinning her down. Her skirts were crumpled about her knees and her swollen ankles spilled from her shoes like rising dough. The shoes were worn-out moccasins, savage-made shoes, soft as butter and decorated with a pattern of tiny shells. He had wanted to procure some for Vincente, to replace the old and battered

449

slippers she wore every day, but he did not know the size she wore and he had not known how to ask.

He cleared his throat.

'Madame?'

The woman sucked on her teeth, twitching her face as though bothered by flies, but she did not wake. He stepped closer.

'Madame?'

The woman started. Clutching her huge belly, she cracked open one reluctant eye, her face pulled tight against the afternoon sun, and muttered something in an unfamiliar tongue. Auguste shook his head.

'*Parlez-vous français?*' he asked. 'Or Mobilian, perhaps?'

The woman yawned widely. Her teeth were large and uneven. Then she pointed, jabbing the air with her finger as though to pop the bubble of each spat-out word. Auguste heard the name of Fuerst.

'Mme Savaret?' he asked.

'Frau Savaret?'

The woman puffed out her lips, grumbling to herself as she dragged herself to her feet. Auguste thought of the Ouma chief who had told him once that there was no purpose in learning the white man's tongue when every white man he had ever met wore his meaning clear upon his brow. As the woman shuffled splay-legged towards the woodpile, he turned and walked slowly back up the slope to Vincente.

★ ★ ★

Fuerst was a small man, thickset, with tufted sandy hair and a frown burned into his brow. Alerted by one of Auguste's savage guides of his new master's arrival, he had hurried back from the fields to greet him. His face was red and smeared with dust.

'Welcome, sir, madame, to your plantation,' he had said in careful French. 'I am only sorry there was no one here to greet you. You come at a busy time.'

Soon afterwards, awkwardly but without apology, Fuerst had returned to the fields. The sun had already slipped down behind the trees when at last he brought the men in. Auguste waited, listening, still as a hunter. The men's voices lent a bass note to the insect shrill of the forest. It reverberated in the soles of his feet and in the churn of his stomach. Below, in the lower camp, a fire smeared the gold hem of the sky with smoke. There was the sound of shouts, the bang of kettles. In their pen the cows lowed, impatient for evening milking.

And still Auguste waited. It was some time before Fuerst appeared. Behind him limped the pregnant woman, a pot of food against her swollen belly.

'You and your wife,' Auguste said, keeping his voice steady. 'I hope you will eat with us?'

'I shall, sir. But this is not my wife.'

Clattering three wooden plates onto the bench, the woman served them in silence, banging her spoon hard against each plate in turn. Three plates of thin stew and beans, three cups of Indian beer. Fuerst bent his head over

451

his supper. He did not eat like a man but fastidiously, his mouth moving in neat circles. When he had eaten, he set the bowl of his spoon precisely at the centre of the plate and pushed the plate away.

'That wasn't half bad,' he said quietly.

Vincente did not eat. Her face was pale, her eyes ringed with purple. When Auguste set down his spoon, she excused herself. He watched as she crossed the room, her head dropping forward with fatigue. Their cabin, Fuerst's cabin, was small and bare but tolerably clean, the curtainless bed softened with a mattress of Spanish wig. It was not Paris, but then he was not exactly sure what it was about Paris that she might miss.

Auguste took out his pipe and motioned to the foreman to do the same. Fuerst took a twist of grass from his pocket and set it in the flame of the tallow light until it caught. He lit his master's pipe first and then his own. Neither spoke.

'I hope you shall be satisfied,' Fuerst said at last, exhaling, and though there was deference in his voice, there was pride also. 'We have done what we can.'

Auguste regarded the Rhinelander. He held his head low, bent forward from his muscular shoulders as though he meant to ram through life with the crown of his skull.

'It will be a good crop?' Auguste asked.

'God willing.'

'The men work hard?'

'They know they must. It is indigo that will pay their wages.'

'And the Chetimachas?'

'A perpetual hazard. We fear attack daily.'

There was a silence. Both men smoked, their exhalations sketching idle curlicues in the thick air.

'Where is your wife?' Auguste asked, more abruptly than he had intended.

Fuerst was silent, contemplating the red glow in the bowl of his pipe.

'I understood you had a wife,' Auguste persisted.

'I understood that also.'

'And a slave. Is there not a slave?'

When still the Rhinelander did not reply, Auguste struck the table with his fist. The spoons jumped on their plates.

'Answer me, damn it!'

Fuerst flinched. Then, leaning forward, he reached out to the plate in front of him and carefully straightened the crooked spoon.

'The slave's child was sick. I was obliged to send them away to the village of the Bayagoulas they called Puchiyoshuba, six leagues from here.'

'And your wife? She is sick too?'

'No.'

'So where is she?'

'I am told she is gone there also. To the village.'

'You do not know?'

Fuerst's mouth twisted.

'I returned from the fields two days since to find her gone. She went with a savage to fetch back the slave, that was all that *dummkopf* of a woman could tell me. That a savage had come

453

and she had gone with him.'

'And you did not go after her? What if she were tricked, taken against her will?'

'Go after her? It is harvest time, sir. Who shall gather the indigo if I am not here? Who shall manage the Negroes?'

'It is six leagues, not six hundred!'

'With respect, sir, I have put my sweat into this earth, my blood. I shall not be disgraced. As for my wife's will — '

He broke off, staring at the table. For a while the two men sat in silence, sucking on their pipes. Between them, in a dish of pressed clay, the tallow lamp spat and sighed.

'Anyone may be betrayed,' Auguste said at last.

Fuerst said nothing, but only exhaled with a mirthless laugh, two plumes of smoke rushing from his nostrils. His mouth twisted as he laid his hands flat on the table, one on either side of the tallow lamp, and stretched out his thumb and forefinger like callipers, as though he measured it. He looked at the lamp for a long time, his eyes squinting against the smoke from the pipe clenched in his teeth. Then, impatiently he pushed it away. Where the lamp had been, there was a mark on the table, a half-moon scorch where once, long ago, someone had carelessly set a hot kettle.

'She took my musket,' Fuerst said, and he hunched his shoulders, the fibres in his neck tightening like ropes. 'She shall defend herself.'

454

A messenger had brought back the slate. He was not the same one who had come before. The slate had been wiped clean. The clay pencil dangled from its strip of leather, but the hairpin was gone. He stood before her, his head bowed, his chest rising and falling, and her heart closed, and she held tight to the slate, to the last breathless moments of not knowing. In the late-morning drowse, the birds sang, and the frogs. A pale blue butterfly blinked its wings. In their pen the cows dozed and flicked their tails against the flies. The savage's copper skin shone with grease and perspiration. When he had recovered his breath, he raised his head. His brow was creased, his eyes grave.

'I bring bad news,' he said.

Elisabeth shook her head, her hands tightening on the slate.

'The fever spirits. They take her.'

'No.' She shook her head frantically. 'She was better. They said she was better.'

'We bury her according to her customs, but the elders are not satisfied. Others among us are now sick.'

'No.' Elisabeth wheeled around, her hands clenched, fighting the breathlessness that threatened to overwhelm her. 'No.'

'Still we hope. The child is young, but she is steadfast. She wails over the turned earth and

455

does not cease in her vigil. She brings honour to her ancestors.'

Elisabeth froze. Her lips moved but no words came.

'The dead woman is not of our nation. We mark her passing and provision her for her journey. Some of the women, they cry also, from respect and from fear of the spirits. But only the child mourns.'

There was a long silence.

'Jeanne,' Elisabeth whispered. 'Jeanne is dead.'

'Yes.'

Elisabeth closed her eyes, and the sadness rose from her belly in a violent gush and streamed down her cheeks. The savage waited quietly, his leathery feet set apart in the dust, and said nothing. When the tears ceased, Elisabeth set down the slate and wiped her face upon her apron. She smoothed back her hair.

'She should have been buried here,' she said quietly.

The savage shook his head.

'She may find peace only among her own people.'

Elisabeth was silent. Then she walked slowly to the cabin and took down a cup from the shelf. She filled it with water from the pitcher and brought it to the savage.

'Forgive me,' she said, holding out the cup. 'You must be thirsty.'

The savage took the cup and drank. Elisabeth went back into the cabin. Kneeling before her trunk, she lifted the lid and rummaged beneath the small pile of folded aprons and woollen

456

stockings. Her fingers brushed a yellowing fold of lawn and lace, and for a moment she paused, searching with her fingertip for the hard scab of a darn beneath one tiny sleeve. Then she pulled from the trunk a moth-holed shawl and closed the lid. On the table, in a covered dish, there was cold porridge cut into slices and one half of a roasted wood pigeon. She put a little on a plate. The rest she wrapped in the shawl.

'How far to your village?' she asked the savage as he squatted to eat.

'From dawn to the third part of the day.'

'You return directly?'

'Yes.'

'Take me with you.'

The savage sat back on his heels, his eyes averted.

'My village is a good village and friend to your nation,' he said slowly. 'We desire your allegiance. We do not take from you what is yours.'

'Take me with you, I beg you. If we hurry we could be there by nightfall.'

'I cannot.'

'The child is mine. My kin. I must mourn with her.'

The savage was silent.

'You cannot stop me,' Elisabeth persisted. 'If you refuse I shall only follow you.'

'The unskilled hunter does not see the deer.'

Elisabeth hesitated. Then she went back into the cabin and, on her hands and knees, reached under the bed. The musket was loaded, the cock twisted, ready for the Chetimachas if they dared venture so close. Months ago, when the troubles had started, Fuerst had taken her out into the yard and shown her how to use it. She could feel the shock of it still in the curve of her shoulder.

The savage stood as she came out. He eyed the musket, his fingers reflexively seeking out the knife that hung from the band that he wore about his waist.

'Take me with you,' she said, and she held out the gun to him. He stepped forward, sliding a hand over the barrel as though it were a frightened animal. Elisabeth pulled it away.

'When we get there,' she said. 'You may have it when we get there.'

★   ★   ★

The savage walked silently and with a swift grace, careless of the uneven ground, the tangling undergrowth. He carried her bundle slung easily over his shoulder. Elisabeth stumbled behind him, the musket bumping against her back, unable to match his long stride. Her eyes smarted, raw with heat and perspiration, and the strap of the heavy firearm bit into her neck. Her back ached.

They did not stop. They walked through forest dank with cypress and through thick brakes of cane. Several times they crossed narrow creeks, the savage holding his knife aloft as he waded through the slow water. Elisabeth knotted her skirts about her thighs and lurched after him, one hand beneath the swell of her belly and the other on the gun in case of alligators. Jeanne was dead. She was sick with grief and fatigue.

And yet she derived a kind of solace from the setting of each spent foot before the other. All her life she had waited as a woman must and left the living to others. In the confines of the settlement and then of the concession, she had succumbed without objection to incarceration in a few square *arpents* of cleared land, the limits of her world set into the earth like palisades, the ceaseless course of her footprints around its perimeter like the circles worn into the hard dirt of a gaoler's yard. In that way Louisiana had proved no different to Paris.

The sun flattened to a bronze disc and slid into the earth. The dusk thickened and still the savage walked on. The forest thinned. Elisabeth trudged behind him as they skirted tall fields of corn, the tasselled heads nudging the darkening horizon. Her hair, escaped from its pins, clung to her face and fell in damp tendrils about her neck. It bewildered her now, the simple ease with which she had swallowed the certainties of her gender. A woman could not work her own land, but she could choose to let it lie fallow. She could not propose marriage, but she could decline it. She had thought it a rule, that a woman's power to act lay only in refusal, in the craven treachery of omission.

By now Fuerst would be returned from the fields. By now he would know of her unauthorised departure. He would know that she spoke halting but quite comprehensible German. When she returned, and she would have to return, there would be consequences. Things would be different because she had made them

459

so. The thought of it tightened around her heart and spurred on her weary legs.

The moon was high by the time they reached the village of Puchiyoshuba, and it spilled its white light on the hive-shaped huts of the savages. Between the huts a great fire licked at the fringe of the sky, bleaching it to ochre. There was the sound of music, the beat of drums and gourds and calling voices and, above them, like a faint breeze, the ghostly keen of a cane flute. Dogs barked in quarrelsome cacophony and the faithful frogs and cicadas continued their ceaseless chants. But though Elisabeth strained her ears, she could not hear the cries of a child.

When they were almost at the village, the savage stopped and held out his hand.

'Gun,' he said.

'Take me to the girl. Then you may have it.'

'Gun first.'

'No.'

The savage regarded her, his eyes gleaming in the darkness.

'Please. She is the place I seek. Take me to her.'

Very slowly he let his hand drop. Then, without speaking, he led her past the village and down the shallow slope of a meadow, rough with tangled grass and flowering weeds. Their shadows splashed across the pasture like ink and the grasses whispered into her skirts, pressing their faces against the ragged stuff.

Above them the sky was huge with stars. Mostly their patterns were pricked out with perfect precision, but across the centre of the sky there were so many that they smudged together in a swirl of greyish powder like the face of a much-used writing slate.

And then she heard it. The wailing came like the muffled shriek of a distant owl borne upon the night breeze, discordant and eerie, tracing the arc of the night sky. Elisabeth had never heard a cry like it. It pierced her with a sadness that was as old as the stars and as uncontainable. As the sadness in her own breast rose to receive it, she began to run, the barrel of the musket hard against her back and the sorrow streaming out behind her like a banner.

★ ★ ★

There were several of them, kneeling in a close circle around the heaped-up grave. One was very small. They held blankets over their heads as they wailed in solemn disharmony, the cries undulating in waves that rose up to meet the vaulting sky before falling away to mingle with the freshly turned earth. Close by, a group of young children played together and their gleeful shouts caught in the dirge and made a kind of music of it.

Quietly Elisabeth turned to the savage and gave him the musket. He bent his head and handed her her bundle.

'Thank you,' she murmured.

Taking the bundle in her arms, she walked round the circle until she stood behind the smallest mourner. As the raw cry began to rise once more, she set her bundle on the ground and tipped its contents out onto the ground. Then she draped the shawl over her head. Behind her, intent upon a game of chase, the savage children squealed with delight.

When Elisabeth knelt silently beside her, Marguerite did not turn. She only put back her head and wailed to the sky as though she meant to draw every last star down from the heavens and into the cold earth. Elisabeth closed her eyes and put her hands together against her breast and felt the cry in the clenched-up parts of her chest.

The night deepened. The savage children were at last despatched to bed, and the glow from the distant fire grew faint. And still the mourners cried out to the sky, sending forth in the tumult of their music all the wordless sorrow of the world. From time to time, two or three of the blanketed figures rose from the circle and quietly walked away and immediately their places were taken by others who came forward, knelt, drew their blankets over their heads and took up the woeful song.

When at last Elisabeth stood, it was almost dawn and the trees traced black lace against the pink-grey hem of the departing night. Her throat was raw. The savage women bowed their heads and were silent. The air was new and still, broken only by the birds who sang without restraint, delighting in the new day. Then they stood and, turning to the child, guided her with the utmost gentleness to her feet.

Marguerite looked up. Her face was smeared with dust and her dark-ringed eyes were huge.

462

'Madame,' she whispered in French.

'Marguerite,' Elisabeth whispered back, and she held out her hands to the child and the girl took them in her small ones, pressing them hard against her thin cheeks. Elisabeth knelt down, the pain in her stiff knees causing her to flinch, so that their heads were level. She longed to take the child in her arms but something stopped her, something she could not explain that was to do with separateness and with respect.

'You came.'

'Yes.'

'My mother — '

'I know.'

Marguerite blinked, biting on her lips.

'The night was clear, did you see? She would not have got lost.'

Elisabeth remembered then what Auguste had once told her, that according to the savages the great swirl of stars at the centre of the sky was the trail of souls leading to the Great Village of the hereafter, where the hunting was abundant and it was always spring.

'The brave and the loyal do not get lost.'

'Was my mother brave?'

Elisabeth closed her eyes, pressing the girl's forehead against her own. She could feel the child trembling between her hands.

'Yes. She was very brave.'

Marguerite pulled away. Her eyes were bright with tears. She scrubbed at them with her fists.

'I am not brave,' she muttered.

'Oh, but you are.'

'No. I am afraid.'

'We are all afraid,' Elisabeth said. 'The brave are afraid. That is what makes them brave.'

It was morning. The sun spilled over the trees, slanting into their eyes, and the village was busy with the noises of the day.

'Come,' she said gently. 'It is time to eat, to rest.'

Marguerite did not come. She stared instead at the piled-up heap of turned earth, at the knee prints pressed into its soft crumb.

'The crying is almost done,' she said. 'Then my mother's spirit will be safe and she can come to me. In my dreams. Like the spirits of my ancestors.'

'Yes.'

'When do you take me?'

Elisabeth hesitated. Pulling her shawl from her shoulders, she folded it carefully, smoothing out the creases until it made a neat square.

'I — I am not here to take you with me,' she said. 'You belong with your own people. You should go back to your village, to the place of your ancestors. I came to grieve your mother and to wish you *bon voyage*. I have no more claim on you.'

'I am to go free?'

'Yes.'

She watched as the child knelt at the graveside, her head bowed, her hands burrowing into the loose earth.

'You do not want me any more?'

'Oh, child,' Elisabeth said. 'I want you with all my heart. It does not make you mine.'

'Then whose am I?'

'You are a child of the proud nation of the Yasoux, the tribe of your mother. You belong to your kinsfolk, who share your blood, and they to you.'

'You would send me to live among strangers, because I share their blood?'

'They are your people.'

'No,' Marguerite said, shaking her head. 'You and the master are my people. You and the cows and the Negroes and the cross-faced men with the funny voices.' Her thin shoulders shook. 'Please, Madame. I belong with you.'

Elisabeth looked into the small tilted-up face and her throat closed in a knot.

'I will study hard,' Marguerite said pleadingly. 'I promise.'

Elisabeth could not swallow. Instead she reached out and very slowly smoothed the child's hair away from her forehead. Marguerite closed her eyes, leaning into her touch.

'I will try to be good,' the child whispered.

The tips of Elisabeth's fingers brushed the curve of the girl's ear, the sharp jut of her jaw.

'I miss my mother.'

The child's neck was smooth and warm. Elisabeth could feel the jump of her pulse against her fingers, and she remembered a night long ago when her fingers had tightened around another neck and she had thought anguish unendurable.

'I know,' she murmured, and she stroked the child as she stroked the cows when she milked them, to steady them both.

465

The savages came at night. They came all the way into the yard and slaughtered one of the cows and her half-grown calf with her. Dark puddles stained the dirt of the pen and there were splashes of blood on the rails and on the trail behind the kitchen hut that led into the forest. No one knew how they had contrived to kill the beasts without waking the settlement. The gate to the pen stood open, and looped over the post were the two collars with their metal bells. The cow that remained had not escaped. It huddled against the fence, its flanks pressed against the splintery bars and waited, as it always waited, for milking.

'Those bastards,' Fuerst muttered. 'They would destroy everything we have worked for.'

Auguste said nothing but only blew on his sagamity to cool it.

'I suppose we must after them, harvest or no?'

Auguste shook his head.

'Not directly. Let them think themselves safe.'

The men went to the fields, muskets slung across their backs. Auguste went with them. In the silent yard Vincente pressed her brow against the cow's flank, her hands tugging at the udders in the way that the German woman had shown her. The milk did not come. The cow twisted against its rope, jarring her neck. Vincente straightened up a little, pulling the stool closer,

466

and began again. The udders slipped in her hands. The cow stamped its protest, barking her shin with its hoof, and almost kicking over the bucket.

Hot tears sprang into her eyes.

'Stop it, you stupid animal,' she hissed at the cow, and she jabbed her shoulder hard against its belly, crushing the teats in her clenched fists. Fuerst's wife always did the milking, that's what the Rhinelander woman had told her as she balanced her bulk precariously on the milking stool. The woman was big with child and the effort of reaching for the teats had turned her face brick red. Her name was Nellie. Fuerst's wife had had a knack with the cows, Nellie had said. No one else could get milk from them like she could.

It was at that moment that Vincente had determined to master the knack of it. It was not so simple as it looked. Vincente tugged again, her brow creased with vexation.

'The child mistakes ferocity for feeling, and as for melody!' she heard her mother murmur, with her tinkling laugh. 'She wields that harpsichord as though it were an axe.'

Vincente's stomach was empty. It moaned a little, stretching up beneath her ribs, and her head swam. When she closed her eyes, tiny silverfishes darted through the darkness. She thought of her mother then and of the shrinking disgust that would compress her mouth if she were to see her daughter, a le Vannes who could trace her lineage through marriage to the noble families of France, in a place like this, milking a cow like a peasant girl. The cow had the warm, frowsy smell of a slept-in bed. She rested her forehead against its flank, and the gurgle of its stomach made echoes in her skull.

The food she had brought with her from Mobile was almost all gone. The previous night, while Auguste slept, she had crept to the kitchen hut, but the door was locked, and though she set all her weight against it, she could not open it. Instead she had slid to the ground, the need in her belly straining the fibres of her, stretching her fingers from her palms, splaying her toes, every nerve strung shrill. To steady herself she had pressed down with her hands into the dirt, closing her fists around handfuls of dust and pebbles and tendrils of dried grass and, for a moment, she had been seized by a violent impulse to cram her mouth with earth.

Instead she had opened her hands and the dirt had run out between her fingers. She had put her head back against the door, the splintery wood snagging her scalp, and she had stretched up her neck as though she would fill her mouth with darkness. The sky was vast above her, so crowded with stars that in places they swirled in a milky soup, blotting out the night.

The kitchen hut was a few strides from the gate to the cow pen. If the savages had come then, if they had found her there, crouched like a criminal by the kitchen hut, they might have taken her instead. They might have cut her throat with their flat knives and carried her away, wrists and ankles bound tight together over their hunting pole so that as they walked, she swung a

468

little from side to side like the deer when they brought them out of the forest. Her blood in a spreading pool in the dirt, her life leaking from her to fall in dark petals into the dust of a savage land.

They would have hardly noticed she was gone. Auguste and the Rhinelander left always before dawn, leading their trail of almost-men behind them and the women too. It was nearly harvest, Fuerst said. No one could be spared. Vincente was left alone all day with Nellie, who wheezed through her mouth like a mule and spoke only to protest at her discomfort. The list of her complaints was inexhaustible. Vincente tried to ask her about Elisabeth Savaret, about the slave, but the Rhinelander woman only shrugged and muttered about the ache in her back. Alone in the heat of the afternoon, Vincente swallowed mouthful after mouthful of rough yellow bread, but though she could seize her flesh in both hands she felt as though she were disappearing. She knew that in Mobile the wives would have already begun to forget her.

Dumbly, Vincente pressed her brow into the cow's warm flank. The heaviness in her chest caused her back to bow. Carelessly, like a child playing at pretend, she moved her hands on the udders. The cow shifted a little and made quiet chuntering noises in its throat. Slowly at first, and then faster, the milk hissed into the bucket.

★   ★   ★

469

That evening a hunting party came to the plantation. When the Rhinelanders saw the savages, they ceased in the eating of their dinner and made to stand up, several of them bunching their fists and calling out to one another excitably. The clamour raised Auguste, who had gone with Fuerst to the upper settlement. Quickly he snatched up his gun, cocking it ready.

'Stay here,' he said to Vincente, who hesitated and then followed him, clutching her apron about her. It would be worse to be left alone.

When he saw the savages, Auguste let the gun fall.

'These men are not of the Chetimacha tribe,' he said impatiently. 'They are Bayagoulas. Our allies.'

He listened gravely. When they were finished he turned to Vincente.

'Tell Fuerst that they bring word from the village they call Strayed Pigeon,' he said. 'His wife is safe there and the slave girl too.'

Vincente did as he bid. When she followed Fuerst from the cabin, she saw Auguste point towards the fire in the men's camp. Later, when food had been brought for the savages and a camp struck, she saw the men talking again with Auguste. He carried a bundle in his arms, which he gave to them.

'What did you give them?' she asked when at last he came in to supper.

'Not much.'

'What manner of not much?'

Auguste paused in the pulling off of his boots and looked up at her. Her ears pinked a little. It

470

disturbed her, the way he had of finding the meaning of things under the words, but, like a blush, the sensation was not entirely disagreeable. She smoothed her skirts, jutting out her chin.

'Gabrielle Borret says that the French have always given too much to the savages. She says it is the reason they grow greedy.'

Auguste regarded her.

'It is their custom to give and receive gifts.'

'So what did you give them?'

'Not much,' he answered, and dropped his boots on the floor. 'A few trinkets, beads and the like. A little gunpowder and shot. Some brandy.'

'They say the savage will do anything for brandy.'

'And so we bring God's light to the Devil's empire.'

He intended to provoke her. Angrily Vincente clattered his plate before him.

'So Fuerst's wife condescends to come back, does she? How much longer must we wait?'

'A few days, perhaps. Until her business is complete.'

Vincente pushed her own food around her plate. She could not eat, not while he watched her.

'Who in the Devil's name does she think she is, this woman?' she demanded. 'Conducting business with the savages?'

Auguste was silent. Then he shook his head.

'I do not think I know,' he said.

'I have heard no good of her, I cannot deny it. Anne Negrette, Perrine Roussel, they . . . '

She trailed off, the words shrivelling under the light of his unblinking stare. In the silence that followed, he lowered his gaze, straightened the spoon beside his bowl. Then he picked it up and began to eat. He chewed and swallowed, then raised his spoon again. Neither of them spoke. He finished eating and pushed his bowl away. The grease on the bowls hardened and turned white. Somewhere a dog howled, dragging its cry down the slate-dark sky.

At last Auguste leaned forward and cleared his throat.

'I have spoken to Fuerst. I go tomorrow to the Ouma. Harvest or no, we cannot permit the Chetimachas to trespass onto our lands, to kill our livestock.'

Vincente nodded.

'What shall you do?' she asked.

'There are always Chetimacha at the Ouma village. I shall seek their help in brokering a peace.'

'Alone?'

'Yes.'

'Is that not dangerous?'

'Perhaps a little.'

Vincente was silent.

'I am sorry,' he said quietly. 'I should not have permitted you to come.'

'You did not. And yet I am here.'

'Yes.'

The silence stretched out between them. As he looked down at his hands, Vincente scraped back her chair and gathered up the dishes. At the door she paused. He sat perfectly still, his head bent.

472

'Be careful,' she whispered, and she set down the dishes with a bang loud enough to scare off the Devil.

★   ★   ★

He left before dawn the next morning. It was still night when he rose from bed, and he fumbled for his clothing, stumbling a little as his foot caught in his breeches. Vincente lay in the darkness, listening, as he gathered his pack and took up his musket and tiptoed quietly from the room. She strained for the sound of his feet as he crossed the cabin, but they made no noise on the hard dirt floor. The door to the yard creaked open, its leather hinges protesting against the hour. In the dark hours of the night, he had held her and her skin had clung to his. On impulse, she threw back the covers and hurried across the bedchamber. He did not turn. She wanted to call out to him, but she did not. The door closed, its swollen hem drawing a fan in the dust.

She watched him go from the window. He walked briskly and did not turn round. The men walked behind him like dead men, their eyes half shut. They carried scythes in great baskets over their shoulders. The womenfolk followed them, dinners bundled in shawls. Then the whip cracked, sending up squalls of startled birds as the Negroes were hustled from their enclosure.

They were not the first Negroes Vincente had seen. In the days when they were rich, a cousin of her mother's had owned a Negro boy. A round-faced cherub with skin the smooth brown

473

of milky chocolate, he had been a favourite with the children. They had petted him, dressing him up in a suit of silk and, around his neck, an ornamental collar with a padlock picked out in gold. It had amused them to take him walking in the gardens on a leash of scarlet leather. Then he had grown and his round face had hardened into angles and he had gone, sold to a merchant in Rouen.

'Like a bear,' the cousin had observed sagely when asked her opinion of the matter. 'Perfectly sweet when a cub and then frankly unsafe.'

The Negroes were not roped together. Led by one of their own and followed by two of the Rhinelanders, whips aloft, they padded in a ragged line across the yard, showing the pale soles of their feet. The palms of their hands were pale too, and the shiny scars that striped their unclothed backs. Otherwise they were quite black. The intensity of their blackness was a shock to which Vincente could not accustom herself.

Then they were gone, and in the sudden hush the forest edged a little closer and the fear rose up in her like heat from the strengthening sun. Fear of the savages, of the Negroes, of the bovine Rhinelander women who looked at her as though they might trample her if she came too close. Fear of the feverish heat and the alligators and the venomous snakes, fear of fever and exhaustion and loneliness and a clutching kind of terror at the prospect of the Rhinelander's imminent labour. And all the time the persistent dread that Auguste would not come back and

474

there would be nothing left to cling to, nothing at all between her and all the fear in the world.

★　★　★

She was mistress still. She had Fuerst give her the key to the kitchen hut, and when the men were gone she crammed food into the pockets of her apron and took it to the cabin, hiding it behind a big book on the shelf by the door. At night she took it down and ate, hurriedly, blindly, without lighting a lamp. She did not want to see her hands. Sometimes she closed her eyes, squeezing them tight as though even the backs of her eyeballs might push down hard against the emptiness and force it out of her.

There was no key to the windowless cabin where de Chesse had stored his effects. Fuerst was required to break the lock.

'Most of it he took,' he said, and he struck the door hard with an axe until it splintered.

Inside, the hut was dim and damp as a church. Apart from the cobwebs, it was mostly empty. But propped in the corner she found a silk carpet only a little eaten about its edges, and a few small items of furniture: a walnut table and a looking glass and a chaise upholstered in stained blue velvet. There were boxes too of linens, grown rather brown.

Vincente carried them into the cabin, setting the table and chair together in one corner, the flyblown looking glass against the wall. Light spilled from it like silver. Then, on her knees, she smoothed the carpet carefully across the hard

475

dirt floor. The silk was cool and soft against the palm of her hand, the blown roses creamy and exquisite against the pale green ground. She lay down and set her cheek against it, and she imagined what the women of Mobile would say when they saw it and whether they would lie on it too, all of them in a row like beans in a pod, and the thought of it was a comfort to her and a torment.

★　★　★

She had not known that ordinary work could be so punishing. Auguste had assured her she would be required to do only as much as was necessary for the subsistence of the settlement, but the drudgery of it was unending. In her head she heard her mother's appalled protestations at the impropriety of such low work, the disgrace that it brought upon the family, and she hunched her shoulders and wrapped her blistered hands and brought the paddle down upon the unground corn so hard that the kernels spilled from the shallow mortar and made yellow patterns in the dust. Then she cursed Elisabeth Savaret with all her heart, who had lured her here and abandoned her here and would have her die here, crushed by the gruelling toil that was rightfully hers.

At night, though, a ceaseless prickling twitched in her limbs and stung her into an exhausted wakefulness. She lay on the floor then and drew the wives about her for comfort, their faces soft with sympathy and admiration, but the creaks in the cabin walls startled her and she could not hold them steady. Fuerst too seemed possessed of a wariness that was almost agitation. At night he had the men take it in turns to sleep on a deerskin laid out beside the cattle pen. As for the foreman, he slept in the wood store that, set just behind the kitchen hut, was the cabin closest to the forest. He kept the door lashed open so that the pale moonlight fell on his face and drew a line of shadow beneath the musket he laid at his shoulder.

Vincente did not open her Bible. She lay upon the carpet, her eyes closed, flat against the carpet as though the stuffing of her was all leaked out, and she waited for the blind, black hours of night when her hands were no longer hers and could comfort her.

On the fifth day, in the sun-drugged hours of the early afternoon, Elisabeth Savaret came back. The men's dogs slept in the shade of the live oak tree, their tongues hanging from their open mouths, and the cow drowsed in its pen, only occasionally bothering to twitch away the flies that clustered round its eyes. Somewhere Nellie slept too, for her baby had come down, its head hard and heavy between her thighs, and her time was near. The dazed hum of the heat was broken only by the dull clunk of metal against wood.

In the shade of the main cabin, a rag wound around her head, Vincente split watermelons with a field knife. The red juice stained her fingers and her apron was flecked with flat black seeds. Beside her on a great wooden platter, she piled the broken hunks of fruit. Inside the curls of green rind, the white flesh melted into scarlet like blood-stained snow.

She did not see Elisabeth at first, only a chit of a savage girl swinging from the bars of the cow's pen, her hands reaching out towards the animal. Barely more than an infant, she was calling out to someone in her own tongue.

Vincente's heart stopped.

'Get away from those animals, do you hear me?' she shouted in French, and she brandished her knife above her head. 'Get away!'

The child turned round, her hand shielding

her eyes. Then she climbed off the fence and ran back towards the forest. Vincente blinked dizzily, the knife loose in her hand. All was silent. A fat fly settled on the cut fruit.

Slowly, squinting against the glare, Vincente walked out into the stunned afternoon. She held the knife thrust out before her, the handle clasped in both hands. The heat pressed down on the crown of her head. Beneath the trees and between the mean cabins, the shadows swarmed with the bright heads of spears, the slick black points of poisoned arrows. Her skin was sticky with melon juice. Somewhere in the shade, swollen and stranded, Nellie waited for her baby to come.

The cow jerked up her head and skittered sideways, bumping against the bars. Vincente wheeled around. A savage stood before her, his glossy skin patterned with black marks. The savage child loitered beside him, her tongue caught between her teeth, and a little behind them both there was a white woman, her skin burned brown by the sun, dressed in a much-patched gown of sprigged cotton. Vincente let the knife drop. The woman was old. Her face was lined and her hair, which she wore pulled into a loose knot at the nape of her neck, was streaked with grey. She wore no cap, no stays. When she stepped forward, Vincente saw that she was pregnant.

'Mme le Vannes,' she said, and Vincente blinked and hid the field knife in the folds of her apron.

'I — yes. You startled me.'

'I am Elisabeth Savaret.'

Vincente said nothing but only stared at Elisabeth, unable to match the woman who stood before her with the Elisabeth Savaret of her imaginings. When she had asked Perrine and Anne and the others, they had sighed and agreed that Elisabeth was proud, that she was vain, that she was selfish. That she had always thought herself too good for the rest of them, that stuffed full with book learning, she knew everything and cared for nothing, nothing, that was, but herself and her ambitious husband. They said that, if it had pleased him, she would willingly have watched them starve. After that, whenever Vincente dreamed of Elisabeth Savaret, she always had a heart-shaped face, wax-smooth like a doll and with a doll's round eyes and fixed expression. The face of her sister Blondine.

'My husband is in the fields?' Elisabeth asked.

'It is harvest time,' Vincente replied, a bewildered elation rising in her chest. This woman, who was worn and old, her body misshapen with child, this woman was Elisabeth Savaret.

'And yours? He is there also?'

Vincente stiffened and in the folds of her apron, her hand tightened around the handle of her knife.

'Your master is away,' she said sharply. 'You chose a poor time to run out on us.'

'Yes. Forgive me.'

'You must ask the master for forgiveness. In the meantime there is work to be done. The

480

harvest comes in and no one can be spared.'

★ ★ ★

That night Fuerst slept as usual in the wood store, the musket beneath his shoulder. Some time after midnight, Nellie's waters broke. By dawn, when her husband came for Vincente, the contractions were coming regularly.

'Come, please,' he said in German. 'It is her first. She is afraid.'

Vincente frowned at the Rhinelander in dismay.

'Me? But I — surely one of the other women — '

'They are ignorant. She asks for you.'

In the yard the whip cracked and the dogs set up a frenzy of barking. Vincente swallowed.

'They will know what to do,' she said. 'I — I do not.'

When she turned away, the Rhinelander caught her by the sleeve. She looked at his fingers, at the broken nails. The creases in his skin were black with dirt.

'Please,' he stammered and his grip tightened, pinching her skin. 'Please. I do not know what else to do.'

Nellie lay on a deerskin in the corner of her dark cabin, her eyes round with fright. The pains were coming regularly and she moaned, her head back and her swollen legs straining against the dirt floor. Her knees were parted. Vincente squeezed her eyes shut. She felt sick.

'Help me,' Nellie pleaded, gasping for breath.

481

'Oh, God in Heaven, help me!'

'I — ' Vincente pressed her fingers against her temples.

'Oh, God — '

'Mme Savaret,' Vincente said desperately. 'Mme Savaret shall know what to do.'

She backed away towards the door.

'Don't — don't leave me. The baby — oh, God — '

'It's all right. Don't be afraid,' Vincente said shrilly, and she ran to the door and flung it open. 'Everything is going to be all right. Elisabeth!'

She ran to the yard. The savage child stood in the doorway of the kitchen hut, a pile of dirty bowls in her arms.

'Elisabeth!'

'She is gone for water, Madame,' the child said in French.

'Then fetch her. Now!'

The girl clattered the bowls to the floor and set off across the yard.

'Tell her Nellie's baby comes,' Vincente called after her. 'Tell her to come quickly.'

Elisabeth did know what to do. She brought brandy and bear fat and bid Vincente have the child boil water and find clean rags. When she slid her hand between the Rhinelander's thighs, Vincente had to turn away, but Elisabeth did not flinch. She gave Nellie instructions in a low, clear voice that seemed to calm her. Shaky with relief, Vincente clasped the labouring woman's hand and wiped her brow with a cloth soaked in cool water and tried not to see the streaks of blood that striped the woman's mottled legs.

It was a long labour but not a difficult one. That night, a little after the men had finished their supper, the child was born. Nellie had long since ceased her hollering and the cabin was hushed, the air hung about with tallow smoke and shadows. Vincente watched as Elisabeth deftly knotted and cut the cord and slapped the infant on the back. The scream was tiny and furious, raw with newness.

'A boy,' she said, and she placed him onto his mother's belly. He lay there, curled tight into the familiar shape of it, slick with blood and rheum and a whitish scum like the curds of cheese, the stump of his birth string like a twist of purplish meat, and Nellie took him in her arms and Vincente looked up at Elisabeth and they smiled, both of them, at the wonder of it.

'It's sore, I know,' Elisabeth said when Nellie wept. 'But you'll heal.'

Later, Elisabeth and Vincente walked together up to the yard. The night was soft, the stars strewn like fine white flour across the sky. Glory to God, who has created Heaven and earth, Vincente thought, and though she could not remember the verse exactly, she was filled with a quiet awe.

'A child of the New World,' Elisabeth said, and there was wonder in her voice also. 'It will not be strange to them, I suppose.'

'I don't know. I think every place is strange to a child.'

'Alone, perhaps. But held in the arms of their mother?'

Vincente shrugged.

'Then it is stranger still.'

Elisabeth said nothing. Vincente watched the tips of her worn slippers as they nudged at her skirts. At the top of the slope, she turned towards her cabin.

'Goodnight then,' she said. 'I am glad you were here. For Nellie's sake.'

Elisabeth did not answer.

'Praise God,' Vincente said. 'A fine strong boy.'

'Let us hope he makes a better place of these lands than we have managed.'

Elisabeth's sprigged gown was an ashy smudge on the darkness, her face obscured by shadow.

'The slave girl,' Vincente said suddenly. 'The child. She is my husband's, isn't she?'

The words clung to the fleshy air.

'Marguerite belongs to me,' Elisabeth said finally.

'That is not what I meant.'

'No.'

'Well?'

'Her mother was Yasoux. Her father was French. Both are dead.'

'I have friends, you know, in Mobile. They have told me everything.'

'Naturally they have. They cannot help themselves. But in this they are mistaken.'

'And the parish records, they are mistaken also?'

'Yes.'

'My husband is the child's father. He signed his name.'

'That it is written does not make it so.'

'Then if my husband is not the father, who is?'

484

'Mine.'

Vincente gaped.

'Yours?'

'The child's mother was our slave. She was very beautiful. My husband bought her. Or stole her. I don't know. Then — when my husband died, Auguste — your husband — he thought that if he could only — he took her away. I think he thought I did not know, that no one knew. When the child came, he claimed she was his.'

'And why would he do that?'

'To spare me. To spare my husband. He was always kind to us both.'

Vincente shook her head disbelievingly.

'Then why does he still not have her?'

'Because I begged him to sell.'

'But why?'

'So that I might not forget.'

'Your husband's sin?'

'My own.'

Vincente stared at the dark lace of the trees and at the star that rose beyond them that seemed suddenly to shine brighter than the rest. Above her the bats swooped, spatters of black against the mercury sky.

'It is a pretty story,' Vincente said, and she pinched her mouth shut.

'Not so very pretty. My husband did not know how to love. I think perhaps neither did I. We did not deserve so faithful a friend as Auguste Guichard.'

It was the tenderness that Vincente could not endure, the softening of her voice. Her belly squeezed in the old familiar way, flooding her

485

with the furious misery of righteousness.

'May the Lord forgive your lies,' she hissed. 'I know the girl is his!'

Elisabeth was silent. Then she turned and walked away.

'*Marriage is honourable in all, and the bed undefiled: but whoremongers and adulterers God will judge*,' Vincente called after her. 'And liars too!'

There was a long silence, and then Elisabeth's quiet voice reaching back to her through the night. There was no anger in it, only a piercing sorrow.

'If you think I lie, look at the child. Jean-Claude, my — ' She broke off. When she spoke again it was so softly that Vincente could hardly hear her. 'She is his in every particular.'

Vincente thought of Anne Negrette, who had called Elisabeth's marriage a great union of love, and of Germaine Vessaille, who was big with her seventh child.

'A wise friend once told me that if there is such a thing as a good marriage, it is because it resembles friendship rather than love. And I pitied him.' Elisabeth gasped, a strangled splutter. 'I pitied him.'

For a while Vincente said nothing. 'What friend?' she asked at last. 'Was it my husband?'

'Your husband?' Elisabeth sounded startled. 'No, no, it was not him.'

Vincente wrapped her arms around herself. For the first time she thought: a child of our own.

'I thought I understood,' Elisabeth said softly.

'I thought I grew wise too.'

'Perhaps you did.'

'No. I thought — I have done such terrible things.'

'We are all sinners. At the Day of Judgement, the Lord shall be merciful.'

'No,' Elisabeth murmured. 'No. Not to me.'

Vincente held up her hands.

'What could you have done,' she asked, 'that is too bad to be forgiven?'

But Elisabeth was gone.

He saw her first. The yard was silent, and she was quite alone but for a yellow dog that slept in the shade of the live oak. He saw her but he did not call out to her. He did not know why exactly, except that there was a breathlessness to the moment, the quiet expectancy of the not-yet, that he was not ready to relinquish. The dog stirred, lifting its head as he crossed the yard, his feet muffled by the dust, his breath barely stirring the air. The nape of her neck was pale above her collar, and her mouth puckered as she fixed upon the dip and pull of the stitches. He could see the rise and fall of her chest, the glint of perspiration on her forehead.

He was but a few steps away from her when she looked up. He saw immediately that he had misjudged things, that he should have called out to her, given her time to compose herself. There was something almost prurient about his proximity, her unguarded self as pale and private as unclothed flesh. She fumbled the sewing as she scrambled to her feet, ducking her head so that he could not see the confusion in her eyes.

'You are back,' she mumbled.

'I am back.'

There was a silence. Under the live oak, the yellow dog hauled itself to its feet and, its tongue lolling from its mouth, limped across the yard to settle at Auguste's feet. Slowly Auguste reached out and took her hand. She did not pull it away. She set her other palm against his shirt, so that he felt the press of the rough knots against his chest. They stood there like that for a long moment and the silence between them grew thick, bound over and over with the filaments of unspoken words.

'Thanks be to God,' she said.

It was disquieting, the way her face was at the same time strange and quite familiar. She had a freckle on the lobe of her left ear. He could not recall if he had known that before. She was nearly as tall as he was.

'You look tired,' he said.

'The harvest, it is nearly all brought in. And Nellie's baby is come. A son, Karl, for his father.'

'That is fine news.'

'The Negro who sickened is improved.'

'Good.'

'And Elisabeth Savaret is returned.'

He had expected it. His face did not change.

'Fuerst will be glad,' he said evenly.

Vincente turned away, bending down to retrieve her mending. The needle glinted, dangling from its thread.

'You will find her at the lower settlement. The child too.'

'Perhaps later.'

She hesitated. Then she reached for the needle, sliding it into the collar of the shirt.

'You must be hungry,' she said.

'Not too much. The Ouma gave me victuals for the journey.'

She nodded, folding the shirt and setting it in

the basket on the bench. This time the silence between them was empty.

'I must find Fuerst,' he said.

'Yes.'

He hesitated.

'I shall see you later,' she said, and without looking at him, she picked up the mending basket and walked away into the cabin.

'Wait,' he cried as she pushed at the door with her shoulder, and it startled him, to speak without thinking. 'Wait.'

She paused, the basket jutted on her hip, as the words jostled inside him, forming and reforming themselves into ever more impossible patterns. He opened his mouth and closed it again. His bad shoulder ached. He took a deep breath.

'I — ' he tried. 'That is to say — '

'Yes?'

'Perhaps I am a little hungry after all.'

They walked together to the kitchen hut. Vincente pulled a key from the pocket of her apron and unlocked it.

'So you see I am become the mistress of the house,' she said lightly.

'It becomes you.'

'On the contrary. Look, my hands are the soles of two worn-out slippers.'

She gestured at Auguste with her palms, but when he reached out to take them she laughed awkwardly and snatched them back. Auguste watched her as she took down a plate and set upon it some cold corn-bread and roasted pumpkin. She moved about the small space with an easy familiarity, reaching down salt and a heel of cheese from the higher shelf without fumbling. It was not difficult to imagine her here in the dark.

'Eat with me,' he said, and he held out a piece of pumpkin.

'I'm not hungry.'

'Please. I should like it. Eat with me.'

She hesitated. Then she took the pumpkin from him and put it in her mouth. She chewed it, her jaw working as though it were a gristly piece of meat, and swallowed.

'There,' she said, and she dragged the back of her hand over her lips.

'Thank you.'

She blinked, looking away from him. There was a long pause.

'The Chetimachas desire peace, I am sure of it,' he said at last. 'They are tired of fighting always with their neighbours who are our allies.'

Vincente nodded, her face still turned away.

'Do you know,' he went on in the same conversational tone, so that she would not know that he saw her tears, 'one of the Ouma warriors asked me why the white man is never content. When I asked him why he supposed such a thing, he said that the white man is always frowning and his eyes bulge from his head as though he seeks something he can never find.'

Vincente pressed her fingers to her eyes.

'And what did you tell him?'

'I said that while the savage steals his property and makes war against him, the white man has no choice but to be vigilant. As for the frowning, he must squint all day against the relentless Louisiana sun.'

Vincente smiled a little then, and he was glad of it. They stood side by side without speaking in the cramped kitchen hut and there was peace in it. It did not matter that it was not true, that he had said nothing at all but only listened in silence as Tohto declared it the fate of the white man to go mad, because he thought with his head, while the savage thought with the heart and might therefore walk the true path, untroubled by the dodges and deceits of the intellect. He had listened and watched the fire as it burned itself out, and he had reflected how curious it was that any man may sometimes speak the truth, whether he be a scholar or a perfect fool. Tohto was a braggart and usually drunk, for he traded skins for *eau-de-vie* and he was a fine hunter. He had seldom been right about anything but hunting.

In the yard the cow set up a plaintive lowing.

'She wants milking,' Vincente said, covering the dish of pumpkin and setting it back on the shelf. 'I must go.'

'You have learned to milk?'

'I have learned many things. You have been gone a while.'

She hesitated, her hands lifted. There were dark patches beneath her arms. His stomach tightened but he did not move.

'I have to milk the cow,' she said.

★ ★ ★

492

He meant to go to the fields. He walked out beyond the Negro enclosure and along the edge of the forest before his steps circled around and took him along the lower path into the men's settlement. The yellow dog followed him a little way. Then it was gone.

The ramshackle cabins drowsed in the heat. Behind the fire circle, the calico bushes were shrouded with drying laundry, and the low-hanging branches of the moss-oak blossomed with battered pans and kettles. In the shade the child looked up from the half-made basket in her lap, her fingers twisted among the sharp filaments of palmetto. He walked slowly towards her.

'Hello,' he said.

The girl blinked up at him. She was thin and none too clean, her dark hair tangled about her face. Still, the resemblance was striking.

'You are the new master,' she said.

'Yes.'

'I don't remember you.'

'No. But I remember you.'

Tucked into the child's lap was a doll of blackened Spanish wig. It had a dress of woven grass and startled shell eyes that stared at Auguste from between the palmetto bars of the unfinished basket.

'Your mistress,' he asked. 'Is she here?'

The girl shook her head.

'She is at the bayou. Today is laundry day.'

'Which way?'

At the edge of the yard, he turned. The child held her doll close against her face, whispering something into its black ear. When she saw him watching her, she stopped speaking and sat up a little straighter. The two of them, girl and doll, stared at him with their round eyes. He raised his hand. Then he turned and made his way down through the canebrake to the creek.

She was not alone. Another woman, one of the Rhinelanders, bent over the washboard, her hair a rough rope against the damp of her bodice and her sleeves rolled up above the elbow to reveal strong red arms. Beside her Elisabeth was thin as a child. Both women wore burlap aprons over their knotted-up skirts and straggly palmetto bonnets that shaded their faces from the sun. In the brown water their bare legs were pale as fish.

'Elisabeth Savaret,' he said quietly.

She looked up and her arms fell slack and the shirt that she held reached out its white arms and wrapped itself like a shy child about her legs. The harsh light inked the lines on her face in black. He felt the pull of her on his heart like a memory of childhood, sharp and wistful. Then, briskly, she plunged the shirt into the water, rinsed it, wrung it and threw it on top of the other wet linens in the large basket.

'What is it that you want?' she asked, and there was no softness in it. The Rhinelander woman glanced at Elisabeth. Then, setting the washboard more firmly against her legs, she resumed her vigorous rubbing.

The urge to walk away was overpowering. But he thought of Vincente and of the commissary and of the years stretching away into the forever, each one scrawled on and smudged with the spidery marks of his own hand, and he sucked saliva into his dry mouth and set upon his tongue the words he had so many times rehearsed.

'I cannot do it, Elisabeth.'

'You gave your word.'

'I have tried to stay away, I swear it, but I cannot.'

'I have nothing to offer you.'

'I have no right to ask this, I know, but — ' He faltered, swallowed. 'Elisabeth. I must know my future.'

'Your future?' She gave a choked little laugh. 'I should have thought it plain.'

'Then tell me. I do not want your forgiveness. I could not endure it. But I have to know.'

'Your future.' Elisabeth bent over, working the shirt roughly in the water. 'You shall grow indigo. Unless the crop fails. In which case, you shall grow poor.'

'You would grant me that?'

'You are the master here. You may grow poor without my authority.'

Auguste was silent. The Rhinelander woman sang tunelessly to herself as she ground the linen in her hands against the washboard.

'Please,' he said. 'Walk with me a while.'

'I cannot. We shall never be done.'

'Please.'

Elisabeth hesitated. Then she sighed. Wiping her hands on her apron, she waded out of the water, unbundling her skirt so that it fell once more around her ankles.

'Quickly, then,' she said without smiling, and

495

she untied her apron and slipped her feet into a pair of worn-out moccasins.

They walked a little way along the bank to the place where the canes grew so thickly that a man could not pass.

'You are pregnant,' Auguste said. 'I did not know.'

Elisabeth did not reply. She held herself tightly across the chest, her sharp elbows aloft, staring out over the bayou. Auguste looked at the swell of her belly beneath her arms, and he felt again the echo of the old, familiar twist in his heart and he told himself that he was glad.

'I cannot forgive you,' she said at last.

'I cannot forgive myself.'

'Nor could I endure your forgiveness.'

'Mine? What need have you of mine? If I had only — '

'Don't. I — don't.'

There was a tightness in his chest, as though she wrung water from his lungs. The frogs screamed. Above the forest the sky was white, the morning's blueness quite bleached out. Elisabeth reached out, placing one hand on a stalk of cane, and he saw how the cane and her finger resembled one another, tough and fleshless with prominent knuckles, lined in brown.

'I shall not stay,' he said at last.

Elisabeth's face was shuttered, her eyes blank.

'It is your plantation,' she said.

'I should not have come.'

'You gave your word.'

'I know.'

'But then I suppose you are the master now,' she said bitterly. 'And the master does as he pleases, is that not so?'

'No. You know that is not true.'

'No?'

'He does as you please.'

'Don't.'

He heard the danger in her voice and the pain, but he did not heed them. He had nothing left to lose.

'Don't what? I cannot change what is, Elisabeth. You have the letter.'

He watched her. She stood quite still, though there was a quiver beneath her skin like a deer.

'The letter?'

'I do not ask your clemency. I — I have no right to ask anything of you at all. I have no right to be here, standing here, before you. But I — I have a wife now who depends on me. For her sake, for mine, I must know. Shall you use it?'

'Use it?'

'I should not blame you. It is what I should do, I think. If I were you.'

Elisabeth raised her head, her face crooked with shock and grief.

'Did you, oh, God, Auguste,' she cried. 'Did you think that I would keep it?'

Auguste stared at her.

'I — '

'When the paper caught it — it rose into the air. As if it were alive. The flame was green.'

She closed her arms around herself. So that the pointed teeth of her spine rose beneath her dress. She was silent a long time. Then she raised her head.

'It does not matter what happens next, don't you see? He is dead because of me.'

'You know that is not so. By the time — it was too late.'

'No.'

'There was nothing you could have done. My letter — you weren't there. How could you have stopped him if you weren't there?'

Elisabeth's fingers pressed into the dents between her ribs.

'You promised you would not come,' she whispered. 'You gave me your word.'

'Oh, Elisabeth, I am so very sorry.'

His fingers reached out to her before he could stop them, and she recoiled as though he burned her, turning her back to him.

'Goodbye, Elisabeth,' he said. 'We shall not meet again, I swear it.'

She did not turn. He plaited his fingers together, pressing down hard upon his knuckles.

'Forgive me. I should not have come.'

'You may do as you wish,' she said dully. 'The plantation is yours.'

'It is my wife's. And she prefers the town.'

He waited. Still Elisabeth did not turn.

'We shall leave tomorrow. The situation with the Chetimacha shall hold. I have a little money and fair credit. I shall send more slaves. And when your husband's indenture is complete, I shall help him secure his own grant. He is a good man and a hard worker.'

The evenness of the words, the expediency of them, steadied him.

'It shall be a good crop,' he said. 'I am indebted to you both.'

He had lived many years among the savages. Silence was a habit with him. And still the words flooded his mouth like spit.

'Your own farm. There shall be profit in it,' he said. 'A future. For you. For your child. Perhaps at last we shall learn to belong here.'

He looked out over the bayou into the tangled thickets of reeds where the snakes coiled and the black earth sucked at a man's legs to pull him under, and he thought of Vincente, who had eaten from his fingers and had learned to milk a cow.

'It is not Paris,' he murmured.

Elisabeth closed her eyes, her hands upon her belly.

'It is endurable if you are quiet,' she said. 'If you stay still.'

Auguste was filled with pity and a powerful desire to be gone from her.

'The girl,' he said. 'The look of her.'

'I know.'

'I don't know how you endure it.'

'Do you imagine that without her I would forget?'

'Perhaps if we purchased her, took her with us? So that you — '

'No. She wants to stay.'

'And you? What do you want?'

Elisabeth shook her head, her lips pressed into

a tight twist of a smile.

'I thought she was my punishment.'

Auguste was silent.

'It was done,' he said at last. 'Before I wrote the letter, it was done. I should never have — you could not have stopped it.'

'I could have made him stay.'

'How, when the letter came too late?'

'But it didn't.' Her face tightened, her jaw white as an alligator bone. 'I went home that day. I got your letter. I knew. And I let him go.'

Auguste stared at her. She stared back.

'I thought — ' he said.

'Yes.'

'You knew?'

'Yes.'

Neither spoke for a long time. Beyond the canebrake the river sighed.

'I never should have sent it,' he said finally. 'There was nothing you could have done. He betrayed the colony. They would not have let him live.'

She stared at him with pity and a kind of weary contempt.

'Does that comfort you?'

'He betrayed you. He betrayed us all.'

'And we him.'

'We had to.'

'Did we?'

Auguste did not answer. The frogs clamoured, filling his head with noise. Elisabeth turned away from him, smoothing her apron over her swollen belly, and suddenly the breath caught in his throat like a bone. He thought of another white day, when Elisabeth had stood before him on his threshold. She had moved her hands like that then, tracing the curve of an infant.

'The child,' he stammered, and he shook his head, his lips clumsy. 'The slave's child. That day, the day you came to me, the day you asked me, asked me straight out — '

'Don't.'

'You knew the child was his and I lied. Oh, my God, Elisabeth, if I had not lied — '

'No!'

Her knuckles were white, her face tight. He stared at the water, the shock opening slowly inside him.

'I must get back,' she said finally. 'The laundry.'

She walked ahead of him. His legs were unsteady and several times he stumbled on the rough ground. The strings of her apron were frayed, the skirt patched. Strands of hair escaped from the loose knot pinned at the back of her head and clung damply to the nape of her neck. Above her collar the skin was burned brown from the sun.

When they were almost at the laundry place, he reached out, catching her arm.

'Elisabeth. Please.'

She twisted away from him, her back arched with reluctance.

'I — when I — if I had known — ' The words burned his throat.

'Let me go,' she said softly.

He hesitated. Then he released her and she walked away. Above the frayed strings of her apron, an oval of sweat darkened the stuff between her shoulder blades. She did not turn back.

The next day, when the sun was up, he took Vincente away. He did not explain why they were leaving so suddenly. He said only that he had done what he had come for, and that while the Rhinelanders were there to manage the concession, there was no requirement for them to stay. At Vincente's request, they rolled up the carpet with the pink flowers and wrapped the looking glass and the walnut table in skins so that they might not be damaged and packed up the boxes of linens and stored them all in the bottom of the pirogue.

When it was almost time to go, Vincente walked down to the lower settlement. Nellie held the infant up for her to kiss and Vincente took the heavy child into her arms and held him close, feeling the sticky dampness of his cheek against her neck. By the smoking ash pit, Elisabeth rinsed beans. Vincente handed back the child to Nellie and walked across the yard. The water in the crock was grey, leprous with bubbles.

'I came to say goodbye,' she said.

Elisabeth nodded and wiped her forehead on her sleeve.

'Shall you manage here all right?' Vincente asked. 'With the child coming?'

'I have Nellie.'

'All the same — ?'

'We shall manage. There is peace with the Chetimacha, at least.'

'If it holds.'

Elisabeth gave her a look Vincente did not understand.

'My husband thinks that the English shall not cease in their trouble-making, not now so many people come,' Vincente said. 'He thinks they shall do all they can to stir up the savages against us.'

Taking up a stick, Elisabeth poked the ash pit, her eyes narrowed against the stinging smoke.

'Should you have come here,' she asked quietly, 'if you had known?'

Vincente watched as Elisabeth set a lid upon the crock and, squatting, lowered it into the smouldering pit. White flecks of ash clung to her skirts like tiny butterflies.

'I don't know,' she said.

'*I know well from what it is I flee but not what it is that I seek,*' Elisabeth said softly.

'I'm sorry?'

'They say that in Paris fathers tell their incorrigible children, 'One word more and I shall send you to the Mississippi!' '

'When I left Paris everyone was to be a millionaire. Shopkeepers took seats at the opera and coachmen bought chateaux and their own equipages.' Vincente shrugged. 'It is only another kind of madness.'

The two women were silent, gazing at the submerged pot.

'I should go,' Vincente said at last.

'Yes.'

'Perhaps — if you are ever in the town?'

Elisabeth nodded. Briskly she wiped her hands on her apron.

'Marguerite?' she called, and her voice cracked a little. 'Marguerite, come here! It is time to bid the mistress farewell.'

The child did not answer.

'Goodbye then,' Vincente said, and she held out her hand.

Elisabeth hesitated. Then she took it.

'Godspeed. May the Lord keep you safe.'

'And you also.'

Gathering up her skirts, Vincente hastened away up the bluff. Behind her Elisabeth stood amid the broken-down shacks, her hands upon her belly, and called out again and again for the savage girl and, in the shade, roused by her cries, a yellow dog put back its head and howled into the thickening day.

The year drew to a close and still the baby held. Elisabeth grew large. Without Jeanne there was much work and little time for lessons. The slate grew dusty on the shelf and her own books beside it. When they were established at the new place, Elisabeth thought, they would begin again. There might be money then, a little. They would be working on their own account at last. In the spring the period of Fuerst's indenture would come to an end, and in accordance with the terms of his contract, the Mississippi Company had granted him a five-*arpent* concession on the Bayou Saint-Jean on cleared land that had until recently been a savage village. The soil was rich and Fuerst would be permitted to purchase slaves from the Company on two years' credit, though the scarcity of Negroes had pushed the price of them sky-high. The sun had burned a furrow between Fuerst's eyebrows, but sometimes as he walked to the fields he hummed, very softly, under his breath, a song from the old country. This would be their last winter at Burnt-canes.

Meantime she kept Marguerite close. She showed her how to fashion cloth from the bark of the mulberry tree and buttons from the plates of armour beneath the alligator's thick skin just as Jeanne had once showed her, how the sharp-toothed jawbone of a garfish made for the

506

finest comb and the bones of choupic and patassa the best needles. And when the weight of memory pressed down too strongly upon her, she taught the child the colonist's skills, the dipping of tallow lamps and the manufacture of soap and butter and soft cheese. It was Marguerite's duty to milk the cow, and the girl had grown quickly and fiercely fond of the animal, giving her a name of her own in the custom and language of her own people. It had startled Elisabeth at first to hear the child calling out to the beast in the unfamiliar tongue. The child was so young and no one at the plantation spoke to her in Yasoux. She had thought the girl would have forgotten it.

She refused to think upon her own confinement. Fuerst did not speak of it, and on the few occasions that Marguerite pressed her on the subject, her answers were brief and discouraging. It was only when her time was very close that she summoned Nellie and explained to her the rudiments of midwifery. Nellie listened closely, her brow furrowed with the effort of it, repeating Elisabeth's precepts after her as though she swore an oath.

'But what if I forget?' the Rhinelander asked several times, tugging anxiously on her fingers. 'What if when it happens I forget?'

'You shan't,' Elisabeth assured her. 'And if you do, I shall be there to remind you. I do not intend to leave you there alone.'

Nellie laughed then, a frightened scrape of a giggle, and her red hands twisted into knots. She wore her own son in a hammock of cloth tied over one shoulder so that she might carry him with her while she worked. He stirred and Nellie placed a hand upon him, soothing him with a low, wordless chirrup. Elisabeth thought of the infant Marguerite then and of the other infants, the nameless wraiths like midnight shadows that darkened the darkest parts of her, and she put her hands upon her own belly and closed her eyes, so that she might collect herself.

Sometimes as she worked, Elisabeth heard the steady thump of Jeanne pounding corn, but when she looked up there was no one there. She looked at the covered mortar, the paddle propped idle against the wall, and she bent her head and counted the thumps of her own heart quiet in her chest. When evening came and the mosquitoes gathered in the darkening sky, the long shadows over the yard had the shape of her. Elisabeth watched Marguerite as she crooned to the cow, and she wondered what the child thought of and what she saw when she was all alone, but she did not speak of it. Sometimes she would look up from what she was doing to find the child looking at her from beneath the tangle of her hair and she would smile and hold her gaze until the child blinked and bit her lip, her own smile pressed tight into the corner of her mouth. It was enough. They had lived with scarcity as long as they could remember. The habit of hoarding was strong in all of them.

It startled Elisabeth, then, when the child spoke to her of the baby. They were gathering wood for tinder and, near her time, Elisabeth was required to pause frequently to catch her breath.

'You shall not care for me so much,' Marguerite said, her face averted as she dragged a recalcitrant branch from the tangle of the undergrowth. 'When the baby comes.'

'But of course I shall care for you.'

Marguerite shook her head.

'I shall not be the one you like best.'

'A heart is not like a melon,' Elisabeth said softly. 'You shall not have a smaller slice because there are more to feed.'

'You will like the baby better,' Marguerite insisted. 'Because it grew in you.'

'As you do. Every single day.'

Marguerite frowned.

'You will not remember the new master's garden in Mobile. You were only an infant then. But it was a fine sight, especially in spring. He loved plants. Everywhere he went, he gathered new ones to plant in his garden. Some he grew from seeds that hold the tiny plant all curled up inside their shell and have only to be planted in the earth like maize. But others he grew from cuttings, which were the limbs of plants already half grown. It made no difference. They flourished just the same.'

'It does not hurt the plant, to take its limbs?'

'Not at all. They grow another.'

'The master cannot grow another arm.'

'That is true.'

Marguerite glared at Elisabeth.

'So plants are not like people. Not like at all.'

Something sharp rose up in Elisabeth then,

burning the back of her throat. Marguerite's shoulders squared, her frown deepening. Elisabeth thought of Jeanne, of her quiet endurance and her low voice and her strong hands like a cap around the child's head as she suckled. Bending down, she looped the hemp rope around the stack of wood and hoisted it onto her shoulder.

'No,' she agreed softly. 'Plants are not like people. Unless they dally so long that they put down roots. Come now, my little chickweed, quickly, shake the earth from your feet. The sun is low and it is almost supper time.'

★   ★   ★

The first pains came as she stood knee-deep in the river, the wash-board between her knees. Elisabeth gasped and staggered backwards, slipping on the weed-slick stones so that the washboard fell with a splash into the water. The pain crept backwards as, whimpering, she gathered the half-rinsed laundry into her arms, then reached down to retrieve it. Beneath the slab of sodden linen, the skin of her stomach was hot and taut as a drum. She stumbled to the bank, hauling the washboard behind her. She knew enough of labour to know that she was not necessarily begun. Many times she and Guillemette had been called to a lying-in to find the child not yet descended and, though she was not certain, she did not think herself ready. A mother on the verge of giving birth complained of the weight of the child upon her bladder, while the readied head obliged her to walk with an awkward splay-legged gait. Elisabeth had not yet suffered such discomforts. And still she could not contain the fear that rose in her and the clamour, the voices and the shadows that she had swallowed for so long that she had grown accustomed to the ache of them always in her throat. They crowded in on her, the noise of them raucous in her ears, and she held onto the bank with both hands, winding the grass around her hands in hanks and pressing the roots of her fingers hard into the dirt.

She did not know afterwards how long she had sat on the bank of the river, only that when the pains had passed and she dragged herself shakily back to the settlement, the mud had spread like a brown bruise across her bundle of wet clothes. Though she banged the pots together to drive it off, still the fear soured her breath, drying her mouth as she built up the fire and prepared supper, and the past was wild in her.

Later that night, when Fuerst went out to check on the Negroes, she reached up to the shelf above the table and took down Montaigne. Like them, he too had aged. His covers were nibbled and frayed, marked with a waxy grease, and mould bubbled beneath the damp leather bindings, but the weight of the book was solid in her hands. She pressed the softened corners of the book against her belly, holding it close, her fingers moving over the familiar swirls and dimples pressed into its tooled cover. Then, tugging the bench closer to the fire, she opened the book and began to read.

She could not reach him. His words were there, unchanged, dry and sharp and clear, but though she knew he stood before her as he always had, without dissemblage or disguise, she could not reach him. The print danced and blurred before her eyes, but even as she strained for it, it bore her away, a relentless crush of fear and recollection like a mudslide that stole the ground from beneath her feet and pulled her under. When she closed her eyes, pressing her fingers into their unyielding jelly, the book slipped from her lap and fell to the floor.

When Fuerst returned to the cabin he found her hunched upon the bench, her arms around her shins, her thighs pressed into the swell of her belly. On the floor beside her sprawled a heavy volume, open and face down. He picked it up, smoothing out its crumpled pages, and set it on the table. He waited, observing his wife. She did not move. Gently he touched her shoulder.

'Come to bed,' he said.

She lifted her head, staring dazedly at her husband.

'The baby,' he asked. 'Is it coming?'

She shook her head, then let it fall onto her knees. The fire was almost out.

'Then come to bed.'

He patted her awkwardly and turned away. Elisabeth closed her eyes and the darkness was splashed red, livid with the coals of the dying fire. Behind her, her husband dropped his boots to the ground, one thud and then another.

'Forgive me,' she whispered, and the words hung in the silence like smoke.

'You are afraid,' Fuerst said quietly. 'It is to be expected. But we have worked hard and you are strong. God shall be merciful.'

Elisabeth pressed her hands against her face.

'Forgive me,' she said again into the cup of her fingers, and in the stretched-out scream in her chest the words closed round her heart like a noose.

★   ★   ★

The tallow lamp spat and guttered, coughing scrawls of black. Elisabeth pinched it out, the red eye of the wick sharp against her thumb. It was a dark night, the moon no more than a slit in the sky. As the fire paled to ash, Fuerst's breathing slowed and deepened, the rasp of it scoring the darkness. He was a wary man and cautious, but there was no fear in him. Already he was of this place, his feet growing down into the earth. She might try to pull him out just to see the torn-out hole he left, but she could not uproot him.

She breathed in, filling herself with his exhalations, but still the child moved in her, and the fear, and she did not know which was the stronger. When the dreams came, she hardly knew herself asleep. A part of her watched them from the other side of wakefulness so that she thought always that she might wake, that she could make herself wake, but she did not. She could not stop them. They came like contractions, iron hoops around the barrel of her to drive the memories from her, each one stark and sudden as though lit by lightning, outlined in black, the colour all bleached out, and there was no pity in them.

When the news of his death had reached Mobile, the commandant had come himself to break it to her. She had opened the door and seen the solemnity in his thin, boyish face, and she had held on to the jamb of the door with both hands and told him she could not see him. She had thought that if he did not say it —

He was dead. She had watched him go and she had said nothing. The loss of him stole her balance from her, filling and filling her with a bitter black brine that rose up to choke her, roaring in her ears. Day after day, in the room with the stain the shape of France beneath the window, she had crouched over the swell of her belly, holding in her arms the child, oyster-pale, that stirred inside her, the child whose faithless father was dead and whose sibling at that moment curled like a reflection in another woman's womb.

And then, one heat-clogged afternoon, the click of Perrine Roussel's tongue against the roof of her mouth. Elisabeth tried to twist her mind away from the pursed lips, the pale peel of potato from her rough red hands, but the words came clearly, nails banged into wood. *After all you have done for that boy. At least he has honoured his obligations and has not tried to deny his part.*

Auguste standing in his doorway, his grave eyes, the defeated sag of his shoulders. The weight of the child like a bruise on her spine.

Jean-Claude is innocent. The slave's child is mine.

514

The impossibility of it, stuck like a scream in her throat. He had gone north and she had said nothing. *The trap is set.* She had watched him go and she had known, and she had said nothing.

The pain in her side as she ran, the slash of breath in her throat. Okatomih's child was not his. Guillemette's words in her head all the comfort she could summon. *Belladonna is a poison, of course. An excess of it will kill a man.*

Elisabeth twisted away, turning her face from the press of memory, but it was upon her now and the force of it too strong for her. The yard, wide as a windless sea. The squint of the sun. The heat-swollen latch of the wood store that stuck. The frenzy in her, stronger than fear, stronger even than grief. The rush of saliva into her mouth, the hunger and the smell of cypress. The tilt of stacked wood beneath her feet, the frantic clatter of the logs that covered the wide-open mouth of the barrel. There had been so many. The weight of them and her clumsiness, the splinters beneath her fingernails, her groping fingers closing on air. The clawing off of the rags, the prising out of the stopper. And then the clatter of the earthenware jar against her teeth. Its thick rough lip, like scouring sand. The blessed sticky rush of the liquid down her chin. The rough texture of linen against her greedy tongue.

The images slowed, fragments now, stretched and misshapen. The cold of the cabin floor. The convulsions. Blood spreading in a black pool. The cold spreading through her, and the pain emptying her, scouring her. The light fading, leaching out colour. The table, the chest, the basket vague and flat, like smudged charcoal sketches. Then darkness. Such darkness, filling eyes, ears, mouth, closing over her like a frozen sea. Down, down, into the abyss. Terror like the table in the darkness, there but not there, but for now a desperate, blessed numbness that was almost peace.

Ashes to ashes, dust to dust. Sinners to everlasting damnation. The end.

Thanks be to God.

Then at the end of darkness a wash of grey light behind her eyelids like dirty water, and birdsong. A dog barking. The ordinariness of it, as though death were no different from what had gone before. Except for the fear. The fear spreading through her, and the cold. So cold. The convulsion of shivering that set the pain to screaming in her. The sickening flutter of her heart in her chest. The draught of sour breath in her mouth, the gluey stick of her throat as she swallowed. Through the fringed slit of her eyelids the familiar shapes of the table, the chest and the basket.

She lived. Oh, God, she still lived.

After that, only the fainting agony of movement and the meaty grey-blue string between her legs and at the end of it, of her, the tiny grey shape. Blood-blacked, empty, fingers stiffened into bird feet and bones hollow light, wrapped around with skin.

A girl.

Perhaps she screamed. The echo of it seemed

to hang in the darkness as, wrenching herself from sleep, Elisabeth pulled her legs from the bed and sat up. She hunched over, stiff and very cold, waiting for the sobs to slow. Then, stumbling a little, she rose to her feet and crossed the cabin to the door. It was not yet dawn. The starless night pressed black against the porch, matted with shapes and shadows. She closed the door and leaned against it, rubbing her arms with her hands. On the other side of the cabin, swaddled in a twist of rugs, Fuerst sighed and turned over.

Afterwards, from pity or perhaps as punishment, Perrine had told her that they had found her in the street. She was half naked and covered in blood and in her arms she held the dead child, its birth string still uncut. She would not let it go. When they took it from her, she screamed as though the Devil himself was in her.

The delirium had persisted for days. Some of the women took it in turns to sit with her, but they could not quieten her. She tore at her sheets, clawed her body, bit her lips and fingers till they bled. She raved and screamed, pleading with Death not to abandon her. Childbed fever, they said, and they had sucked their teeth and waited for her to die.

She had not died. On the seventh day the fever broke. Anne Conaud called it a miracle from God. Most of the other wives shared the opinion of Renée Gilbert that there was strength in madness. But they could not abandon her. There were too few of them for that.

Around the edges of the night, the darkness

was beginning to fade. In the grainy light of early morning, the ordinary outlines of the cabin gathered themselves together. The bench, the chest, the scrubbed wood table. There was something on the table, a dark, square shape. Slowly Elisabeth crossed the room. She did not pick the book up but she set her hands upon it. Then she placed them on her belly and closed her eyes.

Whether offering or blind error, the thrum of life had persisted in her. It was no longer hers alone. She carried in her womb a child whose father was a good man. Though it was six years since she had read them, the words returned to her then and the face of the man who spoke them, who was a good man also. *What a wonderful thing it is that drop of seed, from which we are produced, bears in itself the impressions, not only of the bodily shape, but of the thoughts and inclinations of our fathers!*

Picking up the book as gently as if it were a child, Elisabeth closed her eyes, touching her lips gently to the greasy leather. Then, setting it carefully on the table, she knelt before the fire, readying herself for the new day.

From the plantation they took the pirogue south as far as New Orleans, where they would find a pettyaugre to take them the rest of the way. When they reached the settlement, there were several small craft tied up at the muddy dock and, beyond the bluff heaped with the carcasses of cypress trees, the mud-slick hulk of a new embankment.

They walked up to the place together. At the rear of the square, a makeshift market had been set up where savages laid out deerskins to display their wares. Above them a faint breeze toyed with the flag of the House of Bourbon, three golden lilies on a white ground.

'Business is good?' Auguste asked one of the traders.

The savage shrugged. She had a dark streak pricked across her nose and another down the middle of her chin, and she wore several necklaces of kernel stones, so highly polished that they resembled porcelain.

'White men come,' she said. 'Our village is moved to the shores of the lake so that they may have land to cultivate.'

When they had bought bread, they picked their way to the de Chesse cabin. The storms had come late this year, bringing down cabins and flooding all of the lower part of town. The ditches that surrounded the cabins, dug for

519

drainage, were dark with stagnant water that gave off a powerful and noxious stink. Even the lanes were criss-crossed with planks to prevent the unwary walker from sinking to their knees in the mire. Where the cleared area ended, on rue de Conti, the marshy cypress groves pressed forward, shrubs and saplings like foot soldiers advancing across the narrow trenches. It was too wet, too densely wooded, for grazing. Instead, the settlement's animals roamed the town, as aimless and excitable as the men who, late at night, staggered from the illegal drink shops that pushed up like weeds across the settlement, insinuating themselves into the cracks of sheds and stables.

Close to the de Chesse cabin, they were obliged to wait their turn while a large pig idled between the ramshackle dwellings, his chin bearded with mud.

'And yet the town seems a little less wretched than I remember it,' Vincente said, looking about her at the sloping cabins propped in their plots of slimy weeds.

Auguste smiled.

'The savages say it is impossible to return to a place, even after a short absence, and find it quite unchanged,' he said. 'They say that time alters the shape of a man's eyes.'

Later that day he went in search of news. The taverner, a red-faced man with unsteady hands and eyes like sucked bonbons, poured Auguste a pot of beer, and slopping it a little as he set it on the splintery counter, assured him that despite the season sloops continued to run between New

Orleans and Mobile.

'Bringing up the commandant's favourites, aren't they?' he said sagely. 'Not to mention materials. You should see the house he's building himself here. Never saw nothing like it.'

'The commandant is here often?'

'Most always. Happened by him just yesterday, in fact. Though naturally I keeps my head down. Not what you might call a martinet, is he, the commandant, but all the same, best not to stick your neck out, if you knows what I mean.'

The next day Auguste arranged their passage on to Mobile. He was not fool enough to hope that his brief presence in New Orleans would pass unremarked but, like the taverner, he had no wish to summon attention to it. Besides, his wife was eager to return home. He watched her as she stood at the bow of the pettyaugre, straining forward over the yellow river like a horse in a harness, and it pleased him to oblige her.

★   ★   ★

A week later they were settled once more in the house on rue Dugué, their arrival so swiftly effected that no word of it preceded them. At the marketplace on the first day, Vincente saw them near the baker's shop, their heads bent together as they awaited its opening, and the anticipation in her swelled like a bubble as she hastened towards them. She waited until she was almost upon them before calling out to them, and it was only when they turned, their mouths pulled wide with pleasure and astonishment, that she saw the stranger among them and the smile on her face and the swell of anticipation in her shrivelled, as though they had been sprinkled with salt.

The wives gathered round her, bombarding her with questions, and though Vincente did her best to answer, she could think only of the stranger in their midst. She was young, younger perhaps than Vincente, and her grey dress was faded and worn. As the women talked, her eyes flickered from one face to another, as though she would pull them to her with the force of her concentration. But when she looked at Vincente, her eyes were narrow, her mouth pinched.

It was Anne Negrette who pushed the girl forward.

'You have not yet met Mlle de Larme, have you?' Anne Negrette said. 'She came on the *Charente*. Her mother also.'

The young woman ducked her head, glancing at Yvonne as though seeking reassurance that Vincente would not bite her. Vincente tightened her hands around her basket and wished her dead.

'She is to marry the widower Martin,' said Perrine Roussel.

'Mlle de Larme, that is, not the mother,' Yvonne Lereg added, slipping her arm through the young woman's. 'Martin was quite clear about that.'

The women laughed, and the plummet of it was a stone in Vincente's belly. She smiled and the smile stiffened on her face.

'It is a pleasure to make your acquaintance, Mlle de Larme.'

'Yours too, Mme le Vannes.'

Vincente watched as Yvonne Lereg leaned over to murmur in the young woman's ear, and the hunger that had lain quietly in her turned over, opening its jaws.

'You heard, I suppose, the sad news of Germaine Vessaille?' Anne Conaud said, laying a quiet hand upon her sleeve. Vincente shook her head. 'Her confinement . . . there were difficulties. She did not have the strength for it.'

'Her eighth child,' Anne Negrette sighed. 'And all the others no trouble.'

'The infant lives, thank the Lord.'

'And thrives. A savage wet nurse has her.'

'But a Tensaw? I would not leave my child with one of those.'

'Beggars cannot be choosers.'

'Nor drunks neither. The gunsmith is become a perfect souse.'

'He will shoot his foot off one of these days.'

'He will be lucky if it is only his foot.'

As the women rattled on, Vincente let her spine soften. Her shoulders unhooked from her neck and her hands opened. She looked around the vigorous faces of the women as they talked, and she thought of Germaine Vessaille and her brood of children and the pleasure that had pinked her cheeks when Vincente had given her some trifle from her trousseau, and the fear tasted thin and foolish in her mouth. They were so few and so far away. The loss of any one of them was a hole in the fabric they made.

She was kinder to Mlle de Larme after that, though she could not help but dislike the intimacy of the younger woman's friendship with Yvonne Lereg, the way they whispered and smiled together as though they shared secrets that none of the others were permitted to share. All the same it was not until she stood with the other wives at the celebration of her marriage to old Martin that she understood that there was nothing to fear. The younger woman's arrival had not pushed her out. It had pushed her in. To Mlle de Larme, Vincente was not the latest of the wives or the least. She was one of them, a stalk of palmetto woven into a basket of many stalks. It startled her to realise that her arrival had done precisely the same for Yvonne Lereg.

★ ★ ★

They had been in Mobile some weeks when the summons came from the governor. Auguste had been expecting it. When the boy had gone, he went out onto the stoop, gazing out over the blank winter yard. He had never attempted to grow anything here and the neglected garden was overgrown, choked with half-dead grasses. There was no purpose in cutting them back. When spring came and Fuerst took up ownership of his own concession, they would return to Burnt-canes and Auguste would begin again. He had already drawn up plans for a garden of medicinals, the savage remedies of smutwheat, goldenrod, elderberry, catnip and jimson weed, as well as the imported simples such as ammoniac, antimony and rhubarb: remedies to ease pain, to reduce swelling, to deter corruption.

'It is a fine idea,' Vincente said when he told her. 'What better place to trade medicines than New Orleans? There is more pestilence in the air than there are mosquitoes.'

Auguste shook his head.

'I do not mean to trade them. They are for us, for the plantation.'

'But why, when there will be more than we can use? Why not profit from it?'

'Because we shall have enough without it.'

'And with it we shall have more.'

Auguste squatted down close to the porch, his fingers feeling in the cold earth. The soil was sandy and loose, and he scooped it up, letting it fall in crumbs from his hand. Then he rose and went as he was bid to the commissary.

Afterwards he returned to the house. Vincente knelt before the fire, struggling to light the mess of tinder. The curve of her back was soft, her arms plump. He did not know if she ate still secretly, at night. He thought perhaps she did, but less often than before. The swell of her belly in the darkness was round. Soon, perhaps, it would grow rounder. In the meantime, he waited and he hoped.

She sighed, rolling back on her heels.

'The wood is wet.'

'Be glad you are not in New Orleans.'

'Anne Negrette said that when the burial ground flooded in New Orleans, the soil gave up its dead.' Vincente shuddered. 'Spat them out, as though it could not wait to be rid of them. Imagine it. Scores of them, she said, just floating there.'

'Those women say many things.'

'She said that the pigs ate the bones.'

They were silent, staring at the fire.

'What did the governor want?' Vincente asked at last.

'Consolation.'

Vincente gave him a curious look.

'And you were able to oblige him?'

'I don't think so.'

'Because there is none?'

'Because there is no fixing past mistakes. There is only the making of new ones.'

★ ★ ★

Auguste closed the door behind him, watching the governor as he paced the room. There was no trace of his habitual dry humour. When he seized the back of the chair, slamming it against the floor, his knuckles were white and the features on his face jerked as though they meant to escape him.

'It is over,' he said to Auguste, and his voice was high and thin. 'Law's bank is collapsed and the Mississippi Company with it. It is all over.'

Auguste frowned at him.

'You are quite certain?'

'Mandeville arrived this morning on the *Portefaix*. He came here directly. All of Paris is in uproar. There are riots in the streets. Do you know what Law said to the Regent in his final audience before he fled for his life? He said that he had made mistakes but that his mistakes had proceeded always from the noblest of aims.' Bienville exhaled a mirthless laugh. 'As though that somehow set things right.'

Auguste said nothing.

'All of the paper money issued by his bank is worthless,' the commandant said. 'Law himself set bonfires of it and the stock certificates too. All of it, up in smoke.'

'It is not new for us to have nothing.'

'We can expect no more ships, not now. No more supplies or slaves. Once again the mother country will turn her back on us.'

'Perhaps we are old enough now to fend for ourselves.'

'And with what? I have for a garrison a miserable dustheap of thieves and deserters. Do you think that they will not mutiny now, when there is no pay?'

'We have many allies among the savages.'

'And how long do you think we may rely upon their friendship when the storehouse is empty?'

The two men were silent.

'The existence of this colony is no more than a prolonged agony,' the governor said quietly. 'The very principle of life is wanting in her.'

'But still she lives.'

'And for what? Mr Law has proven her not worth a straw.'

'To the financiers of France, perhaps. But we are not in France.'

'It was only months ago that those primped

527

and perfumed nobles at Versailles were proclaiming Louisiana a perfect paradise,' Bienville said. 'Now they damn her as the charnel house of the Devil himself.'

Auguste shrugged.

'Louisiana made them rich. Now she beggars them.'

'And not one of them has her soil upon their shoes.'

'Then we have something to be grateful for.'

Bienville shook his head.

'You are an optimist, Guichard. I should not have guessed it.'

'Not an optimist. But I know that no place in the world is either as fine or as rotten as we would wish it. Nor any man either.'

'Except the commissary.'

Auguste inclined his head.

'With the possible exception of the commissary.'

'I am hoping his losses distract him from my persecution,' said Bienville with a bleak smile.

'Then you too, sir, are an optimist.'

'I am governor of Louisiana. What other choice do I have?'

★ ★ ★

When it was time for Auguste to take his leave, the commissary was waiting in the outer room. He too roamed restlessly around the small space, his hat twisted between his hands.

'So I suppose you have heard the news?' the commissary said.

'I have.'

'If you have any sense you shall get out. Return to France while there are still ships to sail on.'

'Thank you, but I mean to take my chances here.'

'Do not think you can depend this time upon the friendship of the governor.' The commissary blew out his cheeks, shaking his head. 'There is not enough meat left on this miserable carcass even for him.'

Auguste regarded him steadily.

'Then I shall depend on indigo.'

'And doubtless you shall prosper. If you survive the famines. The English. The savages. Oh, and the hurricanes,' the commissary said, counting them off on his fingers.

'On indigo, then, and good fortune.'

'A perilous stratagem.'

'Are there any others?'

There was nothing more to be said. The commissary held out his hand and Auguste shook it. It swung in his as if the bolts that attached it to the wrist had worked loose. Neither man smiled.

Auguste was at the door when he paused, his hand upon the latch.

'Did you hold stocks in the Mississippi Company, sir?'

The commissary's mouth tightened but he said nothing. Auguste settled his hat upon his head. Then, pushing open the door, he walked out into the sunlight of a spring afternoon.

Elisabeth's child was born at dawn two days before the feast of Mardi Gras. It was an unseasonably cold morning, the damp air chill as wet clothes. Fuerst slaughtered the deer he had trapped and skinned it, skilfully slicing and stripping the hide from the animal's purple flesh so that he might wrap the infant in its still-warm embrace. The deer was a large one and the hide handsomely marked. It would do very well.

When it was time, he called the men together. The Rhinelanders' wives had roasted the deer meat and they ate heartily and drank beer brewed from Indian corn. Nellie, who since the birth of her own child had come to occupy a position of authority among the women, raised her cup to toast Michel Fuerst. His father sat among them and smiled awkwardly, made bashful by his own joyfulness. On a battered hide spread close to the fire, Marguerite squeaked out a tune on a flute of cane, while beside her, like an upturned beetle, Nellie's child rolled on his back, gurgling and kicking his fat legs in the air. The air was full of singing and smoke. Soon they would be separating, each man going to his own grant of land. The three-*arpent* lots were strung along the Mississippi north of New Orleans like beads on a string. It would be, they joked, a superior colony, a little piece of the Rhineland in the New World.

Alone in the cabin, Elisabeth lay quiet among the mess of rugs, the infant asleep in her arms. The birth had been long and the pain terrible, as though the child would tear her in two. The raw force of it had startled her. She had thought her nerve-strings numb, but as she laboured in the throes of birth she was nothing but pain. She pushed her son out into the world with all her strength as though she would hurl him from her, desirous of nothing but to be rid of the anguish of him. And yet, when Nellie lifted him and placed him on her breast, she was split with a new anguish, and she held his slippery body against hers and wept.

'It's sore,' Nellie said, her face split in a wide grin. 'But you'll heal.'

Elisabeth's need for the child was powerful and immediate. There were animals, it was said, who when their newborn offspring are endangered, attempt to eat them that they might be returned to the shelter of the mother's womb. When Fuerst was permitted to enter the cabin, her arms locked around the infant and she would not let him go. The birth string was cut, the stump tied off, and already it grieved her, the drift of him away from her.

Fuerst knelt beside the bed and put out a finger to touch the boy's head.

'He is Michel,' she said, and Fuerst said nothing but only nodded, and she saw the softening in his work-scoured face and something in her softened too.

'Take him,' she said, and she watched as he lifted his sleeping son into his arms, and

531

immediately the softness was gone and she pressed her fists into the mattress so that she might not snatch him back.

That night the child cried. Elisabeth walked with him back and forth on the hard dirt floor and told him of his father, who said little and worked hard and who moved among the fields like the river, certain of his course. She told him of the farm on the Bayou Saint-Jean, which one day would be his if he wanted it, and the books in her trunk, which would be his also, whether he wanted them or not. And she told him of the Jesuit Rochon, who was as slow to judgement as he was quick to laughter and who would, one day, if he was willing, stand as the boy's godfather.

'You have another godfather also,' she whispered over the child's thin wails. 'Though no one but you shall ever know it. His words shall guide and comfort you always.'

When the infant did not quieten, she lifted the latch and took him outside into the yard where the stamped-out moon raised the sky and drew shadows sharp as ink on the beaten ground. It was cold and her breath made dandelion clocks as she walked towards the byre, singing to him softly as she settled him into the curve of her shoulder.

When she pushed open the low door, the cow raised its broad head, pushing gently at her skirts. The child hiccupped, his cries no longer so certain, and his tiny fists uncurled a little. The cow had a white blaze that ran the length of her face and a tight whorl of curls upon her forehead that lent her an anxious look. Gently Elisabeth reached out and stroked her smooth neck. The cow snuffled, pressing her head against the woman's shoulder, and Elisabeth leaned against her, inhaling her warm ripe smell.

'Perhaps when you are older,' she murmured, 'Marguerite shall show you how to milk her.'

But the child was asleep. His eyelids were lavender, etched with blue, and between the startled curves of his faint eyebrows, his skin was dry and flaky. Elisabeth tightened her arms around him, pressing him against the tingling in her breasts. *Mon fils.* A word like a kiss, with a kiss's soft sibilance, lingering on the lips. His face twitched and his fists reached up to beat the air, but he did not wake.

The fatigue came suddenly with a lurch of light-headedness. Cupping the child's head with her hand, she lowered her bruised and battered body to the milking stool and closed her eyes, leaning her head against the mud-rough wall. The straw rustled as close by her the cow shifted and sighed. In the villages around Paris, the peasants brought their animals into their huts with them in winter. Elisabeth had always assumed the advantage all to the cattle. She thought now that perhaps there were a great number of things that she had not properly understood.

She was almost asleep when the scraping of the door roused her. She blinked, her arms tightening reflexively about her sleeping child.

Marguerite stood in the doorway. The moon caught silver in her hair and drew the narrow shape of her beneath the rough linen of her shift. She looked at Elisabeth and then at the floor, scraping a circle in the dirt with her toe.

'I could not sleep,' she said.

'Nor I,' Elisabeth said.

'You were sleeping just then,' the girl protested. 'I saw you.'

Elisabeth smiled, rubbing her eyes.

'Come,' she said. 'Sit with me.'

The child hesitated.

'This is Michel. I have already promised him that when he is old enough you shall teach him how to milk the cow.'

'Michel.'

'That's right.'

'Is it French?'

'Yes.'

'What does it mean?'

Elisabeth hesitated.

'Does it mean bead?' Marguerite demanded.

Elisabeth smiled.

'No,' she said. 'It has many meanings. But to me it means wise friend.'

Tentatively Marguerite reached out and touched a grubby finger to the baby's head.

'Wise friend,' she said. 'He looks like a turtle.'

Elisabeth looked down. The mottled deer hide curved over the baby's head, leaving only his fists and the crown of his head emerging.

'You are right,' she said, and she smiled. 'He does look like a turtle.'

'Perhaps you should call him turtle instead.'

'Perhaps. But I think his father would prefer Michel.'

'In my language we say Olo. I think I shall call him Olo. He should have one of our names as well as his French one. Like my mother did. Like I do.'

Elisabeth stared at her.

'You have another name?'

'Of course.'

'I did not know.'

Marguerite shrugged a little.

'He's so small,' she said, and the curve of her dirty hand fitted the infant's head like a cap.

The cramp was sudden and unexpected, and Elisabeth gasped as she folded over it, her face twisted in a knot. The child frowned.

'Are you ill?' she asked.

'Not ill. Sore.'

Elisabeth took a long breath as the cramp faded. Marguerite watched her warily.

'Shall you die?'

'Some day. But not yet.'

Marguerite was silent. In the darkness the cow's wet nose gleamed palely as she stretched out her neck to nudge the girl's stomach. Marguerite put her thin arms around the beast's neck, crooning to her in her savage tongue. The beast lowed softly, shuffling closer. When her hoof struck the milking stool, Elisabeth felt the shock of it in her belly.

'What is your other name?' she asked.

Marguerite hesitated. Then she shook her head.

'It is something between me and my mother.'

'Like a secret?'

Marguerite frowned, puffing out her mouth consideringly.

'Like when I call the cow,' she said. 'And I know she'll come.'

The baby stirred on Elisabeth's shoulder. She lowered her face to his brow, inhaling his sweet grassy smell.

'I should like to have a name for you like that,' Elisabeth said softly. 'One just for us.'

Marguerite leaned against the cow's broad brow, pulling on her ears.

'It has to mean something. Like wise friend. It can't just be a thing like a bead or it doesn't work.'

'Like girl with no comb?'

'No!'

'Like little chickweed?'

Marguerite was silent.

'Yes,' she said finally, very quietly. 'Like little chickweed.'

★　★　★

The moon rose high over the clutter of cabins that huddled on the bluff. In the shadow of the great live oak, the stillness of the cattle byre was stirred only by the sonorous breathing of a drowsing cow. Close by, beneath a tattered palmetto roof, a mother slept and a father and an infant who opened his round eyes and stared up at the roof as though the very shape of the air astonished him. The yard was still and bleached with moonlight, empty but for the girl who stood in the middle of it, her head tipped back and her arms stretched up towards the swarm of stars that filled the sky, and the shadow that marked the shape of her, as definite as day.

Author's Note

I first came across the story of the first French settlers in America when researching my previous novel, *The Nature of Monsters*, which is set in London in the same period. In 1720, London's nascent stock market had crashed when the South Sea Bubble had spectacularly burst. Paris's own stock market had collapsed just six months earlier in similar circumstances, driven by the spectacular rise and then fall in the value of shares in their great trading company, the Mississippi Company. Living at a time when shares were soaring in value, while house prices spiralled ever upward and governments claimed that such growth was indefinitely sustainable, my curiosity was piqued by the hubris of Europe's first — but hardly last — speculators.

More captivating still were the tales of the women who became known as the 'casket girls', young girls of marriageable age who were sent from France to Louisiana as wives for the colonists. Paid a stipend for a year or until they were married, whichever was the shorter, these girls embarked upon a perilous voyage of several months, sold as brides for men they had never met in a country of which they knew nothing. Already the seeds of Elisabeth's character were starting to take hold.

By 1703, when the *Pélican* set sail from La Rochelle, Louisiana had been in French hands for only two decades. The French has established New France in the north in 1608, but it was not until 1678 that a Frenchman, Cavalier de La Salle, was charged by Louis XIV with the exploration of the areas south and west of the Great Lakes, making him commander of any forts he might construct there. The following year La Salle began the descent of the Illinois River, eventually reaching the mouth of the Mississippi. There, in April 1682, he erected a cross and claimed the territory as a French colony, naming it Louisiane in honour of the King.

However, when La Salle attempted to return to the Mississippi two years later, the mist was thick and he failed to locate it. Though he built a fort at Biloxi Bay, his men were mutinous and murdered him in 1686. It was to be another twelve years before Pierre d'Iberville, a Canadian from the Lemoyne family of Normandy, sought permission from Louis XIV to occupy Louisiana. With his brother, Bienville, he left France in the autumn of 1698, at the head of a fleet of five ships, determined to establish an outpost to secure the French claim to the Mississippi River. Besides officers and soldiers, Iberville brought four families of colonists to settle the land.

Iberville constructed his fort at Mobile Bay, where the island that he named Massacre Island offered protection and adequate harbour, and moved there most of the garrison previously posted at Biloxi. When he returned to France, he left his brother, Bienville, in charge as the fort's commandant. By 1704 the town consisted of eighty wooden cabins roofed with palmetto, with a population, including soldiers, of fewer than two hundred souls.

From the outset, the colony struggled. Louisiana was a territory many times larger than France, stretching from the mouth of the Mississippi for three thousand miles north, taking in the present-day states of Louisiana, Mississippi, Arkansas, Missouri, Illinois, Iowa, Wisconsin and Minnesota, as well as parts of Canada. This vast land mass was uncultivated, largely unexplored and inhabited only by tribes of Native Americans. No one knew what treasures it contained, most of France had no notion of where the colony even was, but rumours described it as a kind of paradise, rich with gold and silver and awash with precious stones.

But the area chosen by Iberville for settlement was poor, the soil too sandy for the successful raising of crops. The wheat that the Frenchmen had brought from France came up well, but the damp climate rotted the ears before they could come to maturity. There were fertile lands farther inland but no one dared risk his life there alone. Besides, the French had not come to Louisiana with the intention of tilling the soil. The first settlers were not farmers nor hardy pioneers of the English type, but city dwellers, mostly poor and unskilled, who had crossed the ocean with dreams of instant riches, of fabulous mines and tame buffaloes. They had no intention of scraping a living from the land. Instead they dragged out an idle existence around the forts of

Mobile, and to a lesser extent, Biloxi.

Everyone, including the officers and soldiers, traded with the Indians and the Canadians who came down from New France. They raised a few cattle, pigs and chickens; in summer they hunted and fished. Otherwise they waited for the ships from France to bring them what they needed. But the mother country was distracted by war in Europe and her resources were more urgently required elsewhere. To find serviceable ships and supplies to send to Louisiana was an almost insuperable problem, to the extent that Louis XIV seriously considered abandoning the colony. To those who were there, it must have felt as though he had already done so. In winter when food was scarce, they threw themselves on the mercy of the Native Americans. One Frenchman, Picard, was said to have taught the women of the Colapissas to dance the quadrille in exchange for a dish of sagamity.

It was with great excitement, then, that the colonists greeted the arrival in 1704 of two ships from France, the *Loire* and, some months later, the *Pélican*. The ships brought supplies, soldiers and, of course, twenty-two girls who would, Iberville hoped, give solace to the dissatisfied men and form the basis for an eventually populous colony. He had originally asked Pontchartrain, then Minister of the Marine, for one hundred girls, but a lack of funds, not to mention the difficulty of convincing 'young and well-bred' girls of the advantages of life in Louisiana, made a less ambitious number more feasible. Certainly the demand for wives far outstripped supply. All but one of the girls aboard the *Pélican* were married within a month.

The *Pelican*'s passenger roll still exists today, and many of the names upon it appear in this novel. Elisabeth Savaret is herself the amalgam of two real-life passengers, Elisabeth Deshays and Gabrielle Savaret, though the situation of her marriage to Jean-Claude Babelon is entirely imagined. We have little information about the details of these women's lives, for the women of Louisiana kept no journals of this time and any letters they may have written are few and far between. Their lives are mapped only by the stark records of marriages, baptisms and deaths contained in the Mobile parish register.

These show how commonly infants did not survive beyond baby-hood, which prompted some to claim that the Louisiana climate made women sterile. The records also show that it was common for colonial men and women to marry three or four times, and that it was not unusual for a widow to remain unmarried for only weeks before finding a new husband, though, as in France at this time, a wife was always referred to by her maiden name. Interestingly, under Louisiana law, established in 1712 in line with the law of Paris, a wife enjoyed a number of economic protections; even in a first marriage, a husband did not acquire full rights to his wife's property, while, in any subsequent union, he enjoyed no marital power over her assets at all. In the novel Elisabeth's slave therefore continued to belong exclusively to her even after her marriage to Fuerst; Vincente's estates too remained entirely hers. This continued to be the case until the Spanish took control of the colony in the 1760s.

The lack of women caused significant headaches for both Bienville and the colony's priests. Not only did many Canadians live openly with women of friendly nations, they also raided villages indiscriminately in pursuit of slave concubines. Traders exploited this by establishing a black-market trade in *sauvagesses*, seized in the interior and sold to garrison members as slaves. Children of mixed white and Native American blood, known as *mestifs*, are not uncommon in the records of baptism (Pierre Charly, the merchant, whose mixed-race child is discussed by the wives in the novel, was a real person), while interracial marriages, though not sanctioned by the Church, are also in evidence, referred to as *marriages naturel*. While mutually agreeable partnerships were made, there were also incidents of rape and other brutal treatments, especially by the Canadian *coureurs-de-bois*. It seems reasonable, therefore, to assume that the situation faced by Elisabeth Savaret, in which her husband took their slave as his lover, was not unknown.

Elisabeth Savaret is not the only character in the book based loosely on a real-life character. In March 1703, after Bienville had assembled the chiefs of the Choctaw and the Chickasaw nations in Mobile to promote a tripartite alliance, the Chickasaw took a French boy, Saint-Michel, back with them to their village. The boy was charged with learning the Chickasaw language so that he might serve as interpreter to those French and Canadians who passed through, and with keeping a close eye on the Chickasaw, whose friendship with the French was far from certain. Saint-Michel was one of four boys distributed in this way around the most important nations in Louisiana and likely, at fourteen, the oldest. By the time he went to live among the Chickasaw, he had already been in Louisiana some time and had learned the Ouma language.

Two years later, Saint-Michel found himself at the centre of a major diplomatic incident. In 1705 the French learned that the English had persuaded a number of Chickasaw warriors to seize several Choctaw families who were visiting Chickasaw villages, thereby stirring up old enmities and causing a split in the carefully constructed alliances of the French. When the Chickasaw chiefs discovered this complicity, they went to the French and explained the situation, blaming the Choctaw raid on a few renegade warriors. The Choctaw were furious. They declared the Chickasaw perfidious and claimed that they had betrayed their French friends by burning Saint-Michel at the stake.

The Chickasaw chiefs flatly denied this rumour. The Choctaw therefore proposed a test: several Chickasaw runners would be sent to bring the boy back to the Choctaw village as proof that he was alive and well. The Chickasaw chiefs, meantime, would be held in the Choctaw village as hostages. The Chickasaw agreed to these terms. What they did not know was that the Choctaw had sent their own runners in pursuit of the Chickasaw, to murder them before they could reach their own village. When the Chickasaw runners did not return, the Choctaw slaughtered their Chickasaw hostages, and thus extracted their revenge for the Chickasaw attack. It was of course a trick — young Saint-Michel returned to Mobile unharmed in the winter of that year.

This quicksand of duplicity and shifting alliances that underpinned what passed for diplomacy in Louisiana is central to the novel. History has been generous to the French colonists, suggesting that in their dealings with the Native Americans they were more enlightened than their English or Spanish counterparts. There is no evidence of this. It was rather a matter of pragmatism. With woefully insignificant military muscle (in 1713 there were a mere sixty-seven soldiers in the Mobile garrison, ten of whom were too old or infirm to serve), the French had to exploit the military strength of the largest nations or see the hinterland between the Appalachians and the Mississippi fall to the English, who, richer and much more numerous, exerted relentless pressure from their colonies along the Eastern seaboard. Indeed, Bienville was quick to set the tribes against each other if it served French interest, and boasted of one conflict that 'it has not cost one drop of French blood, through the care I took of opposing those barbarians to one another'. Given the paucity of French supplies with which to purchase friendship and the better quality and prices of

English goods, his adroitness in managing these alliances to French advantage was nothing short of remarkable.

Relations between the French and a number of their Native American neighbours eventually grew so warm that some nations, including the Houma, relocated to the coast to facilitate trade, and Bienville's envoys travelled regularly up the Mobile and Mississippi rivers, as Babelon did, to purchase maize from the nations there. It was not long before Bienville was accused of profiteering from the sale of native food and, in 1708, a commissary was sent by Louis XIV from France to investigate the claims against him. The inquiry, though rigorous, failed to elicit sufficient hard evidence and the matter was quietly shelved. These days historians tend to agree that the accusations against Bienville were not entirely unjustified. The illegal trading in the novel is an invention, then, but one that might bear more than a passing resemblance to the truth.

Certainly the scandal that accompanied the trial in France not only discredited Bienville's family but also the colony in general, and went some way to explain why the Crown was content to sell the claim upon it to a wealthy private financier, Crozat, in 1712. Crozat ploughed more than 1.5 million *livres* into Louisiana, and specifically into the search for mines. But in 1717, faced with a massive tax bill and in the absence of a single significant mineral find, he was obliged to relinquish his concession and the colony returned to the Crown.

Meanwhile Louis XIV had died in 1715, leaving his country more than two billion *livres* in debt. In desperation, the Duc d'Orléans, who was to act as regent until the five-year-old Louis XV might come of age, turned to a Scotsman, John Law, to reverse the country's fortunes. Law proposed the creation of the first national bank in France, financed by shareholders and underpinned by the most powerful conglomerate the world had ever seen, the Mississippi Company, with exclusive rights to all commercial interests in Louisiana. To ensure the success of his venture, Law granted large concessions of land to influential noblemen and pledged to supply to the colony seven thousand new French settlers and three thousand African slaves.

Law's Louisiana propaganda machine was immense. France's official newspaper, the *Nouveau Mercure*, wrote rapturously of a latter-day Eden, cooing over its temperate climate, its fertile soil, its rich seams of gold and silver. In 1719 the newspaper described New Orleans as a prosperous town of 'nearly 800 very comfortable and well-appointed houses, each one of which has attached 120 acres of land for the upkeep of the families', while the quantity and purity of the mineral finds exceeded that of 'the richest mines of Potosi'. 'Nothing almost is wanting,' one journalist declared, 'but industrious people and numbers of hands to work.' Investors stampeded Paris. In a matter of months, the share price rose from 150 *livres* to more than 10,000.

Meanwhile the colony was struggling to stay

afloat. By the end of 1717, only five hundred prospective colonists had set sail for America. At least one nobleman, like Vincente's dead husband-to-be, wrote imperiously to the Ministry of the Marine to send him a wife, but enthusiasm for such emigration was already on the wane. Though Bienville banned colonists from returning to France without his express permission, rumours of the miseries in America inevitably found their way back to the motherland.

As the stream of voluntary colonists dried to a trickle, Law was obliged to fulfil his obligations to the colony through force. Prisons were emptied; gangs of *bandoliers* scoured the country for beggars and vagabonds, receiving a bounty from the Company for each one arrested. Louisiana became a dumping ground for undesirables, smugglers, criminals and prostitutes. When the Mississippi Company finally crashed in 1719, Louisiana had become in the French imagination a kind of hell on earth, a vast pestilential swamp where the midday sun struck men dead, the natives were all cannibals, and the frogs were so big they ate children whole.

In 1720 the Banque Royale folded, and Law fled France. In a bid to straighten out its affairs and to appease its impoverished shareholders, the Mississippi Company implemented drastic cuts. The remaining settlers of Louisiana suffered dreadfully. Law's paper money had penetrated the colony, and when his bank collapsed, it lost 80 per cent of its value. Supplies were in pitifully short supply. A pair of stockings in poor repair, for example, which in France would have cost six *sols*, in Louisiana cost six *livres* — one hundred times as much.

Famine and fever continued to devastate the colony. Then, in 1723, a terrible hurricane devastated the new capital of New Orleans. Crops were ravaged, farms blown away and three ships in port completely wrecked. For a period of months there were two deaths a day in the settlement. As the colonists sought to drown their sorrows, drunkenness and gambling became so excessive that Bienville was obliged to outlaw gaming altogether.

But the colonists rallied. By the end of 1724, they had rebuilt the town, this time partly in brick. Though Law's legacy was hardly the one he had hoped for, his Mississippi Company had transformed Louisiana. Between 1717 and 1720, of the thousands that undertook the perilous voyage to Louisiana, more than half died en route and hundreds more on arrival from disease or starvation, but the population had grown from four hundred to nearly five thousand. Slaves had been introduced by the hundred and the establishment of sizeable plantations had begun the vital process towards self-sufficiency.

The French Crown was to cling on to her American colony, through war with the Natchez and other Native American nations, until 1763, when the Treaty of Paris ceded the territories to the east of the Mississippi to England, those on the western side to Spain. France would not regain control of the colony until 1800, and her triumph was brief. In 1803 Napoleon sold Louisiana to President Jefferson for $15 million, or four cents an acre, doubling at a stroke the size of the United States. Upon completion of the agreement, Napoleon declared that 'this accession of territory affirms forever the power of the United States, and I have given England a maritime rival who sooner or later will humble her pride'. Though divorced from their newly acquired compatriots by their religion, customs, law, governance and language, the descendants of those first French colonists, by now known familiarly as Creoles, would surely have derived some comfort from that.

Acknowledgements

I owe a significant debt to those writers, past and present, who have sought to cast light on this little-known period in American history. There are far too many to mention here, but I should like to express my particular gratitude to Jay Higginbotham for his extraordinary history of Mobile, *Old Mobile: Fort Louis de la Louisiane 1702-1711*, without which I should never have been able to write this novel. I have leaned heavily on the definitive histories of Louisiana by Charles Gayarré and Marcel Giraud, as well as plundering George Oudard's *Four Cents an Acre* and Peter J. Hamilton's *Colonial Mobile*. The journal *Louisiana History* also proved an invaluable source of articles covering every aspect of the region's colonial history.

A range of contemporary accounts provided crucial insight into the period, in particular *Fleur de Lys and Calumnet*, the journal of a carpenter in Louisiana, ably translated and edited by Richebourg Gaillard McWilliams, and *History of Louisiana*, the observations of Le Page Du Pratz, a Frenchman who arrived in Louisiana in 1717. The journals of Sauvole, the first governor of Louisiana, and of Pierre d'Iberville, the latter translated and edited by Carl A. Brasseaux, were also enormously useful. For access to these and other rare volumes, I would like to thank the staff of the Williams Research Center in New

Orleans, where I was also able to draw upon a matchless collection of contemporary maps and prints.

For details of Native American life in the early eighteenth century, I am indebted to Jon Manchip White's *Everyday Life of the North American Indian*, to Daniel H. Usner Jr's *Indians, Settlers & Slaves in a Frontier Exchange Economy*, and to Angie Debo, not only for her terrific *A History of the Indians of the United States* but also for H. B. Cushman's *History of the Choctaw, Chickasaw, and Natchez Indians*, which she so capably edited and annotated. As for the story of John Law, it would be difficult to find a more erudite and enjoyable source than Janet Gleeson's *The Moneymaker*.

My final acknowledgement, however, must go to Michel de Montaigne, whose *Essais*, more than five hundred years after his death, continue to rouse, inspire and delight all who read them. To him, and all the other scholars whose works I have plundered, I would like to extend my heartfelt thanks. The weight of their scholarship underpins this novel, while any errors that may be contained within its pages are entirely my own.

We do hope that you have enjoyed reading this large print book.

Did you know that all of our titles are available for purchase?

We publish a wide range of high quality large print books including:
Romances, Mysteries, Classics
General Fiction
Non Fiction and Westerns

Special interest titles available in large print are:
The Little Oxford Dictionary
Music Book
Song Book
Hymn Book
Service Book

Also available from us courtesy of Oxford University Press:
Young Readers' Dictionary
(large print edition)
Young Readers' Thesaurus
(large print edition)

For further information or a free brochure, please contact us at:
Ulverscroft Large Print Books Ltd.,
The Green, Bradgate Road, Anstey,
Leicester, LE7 7FU, England.
Tel: (00 44) 0116 236 4325
Fax: (00 44) 0116 234 0205

THE NATURE OF MONSTERS

Clare Clark

It is 1718 and, in a parish near Newcastle, Eliza Tally, a girl of sixteen, embarks on a love affair that will prove her undoing. When her lover casts her off, she is forced to travel to London. There she takes up a position in the house of an apothecary, Grayson Black, whom she trusts to salvage what remains of her reputation. Black, however, has a quite different plan in mind. Shunned for years by the men of science, the apothecary is convinced that he is finally about to achieve the fame and success he thinks he deserves. And it is Eliza he is determined to exploit to realise his long-held ambitions, with consequences that are terrifying for all who inhabit the apothecary's house.

SEX AND STRAVINSKY

Barbara Trapido

The time is 1995, but everyone has a past.
Brilliant Australian Caroline can command
everyone except her own ghoulish mother —
things aren't easy for Josh and Zoe, her
husband and twelve-year-old daughter. Josh
has bizarre origins in South Africa, but now
teaches mime in Bristol. Zoe reads girls'
ballet books and longs for ballet lessons.
Meanwhile, on the east coast of Africa, Hattie
Thomas, Josh's first love, has taken to writing
girls' ballet books from the turret of her
fabulous house — that's when she can carve
out a space between her alpha male husband
Herman and her crosspatch daughter Cat.
From far and wide, they are all drawn
together; drawn to beautiful, mysterious Jack.
Or is he Jacques? Or Giacome?

TRUTH TO TELL

Mavis Cheek

Nina Porter appears to have it all: husband, home, family and security. But her life turns upside down when a marital row over truthfulness sets her thinking. Isn't she dishonest herself, always playing the good wife? Shouldn't she try to live without the little white lies that support us all? Her husband thinks it can't be done. But when he goes away on a business trip, Nina sees no reason to refuse the offer of a few days of research in Venice. Or to resist the attentions of the charming, if slightly sinister, Italian who wants to show her the city. As Nina entangles herself in a web of deceptions, it starts to look as though honesty might not always be the best policy.

THE WIVES OF HENRY OADES

Johanna Moran

In 1890, Henry Oades undertakes the arduous sea voyage from England to New Zealand to further his family's fortunes. Once there however, disaster strikes in unexpected ways . . . A local Maori tribe kidnaps Mrs Oades and her children, and vanishes into the hills. Henry searches ceaselessly for his family, but they must be dead. In despair he ships out to San Francisco, where he eventually marries a young widow. Meanwhile, Margaret Oades and her children finally make their way back to town, five years after they were presumed dead. Discovering that Henry is now half a world away, they are determined to rejoin him. So, months later, they arrive on his doorstep in America and Henry Oades discovers that he has two wives and many dilemmas . . .

TRESPASS

Rose Tremain

In a silent valley stands an isolated farmhouse, the Mas Lunel. Its owner, Aramon Lunel is an alcoholic, haunted by his violent past; his dogs starve and his land is in ruins. Meanwhile, his sister Audrun, in her bungalow within sight of the Mas Lunel, dreams of retribution for the betrayals that have blighted her life. Into this world, from London, comes disillusioned antiques dealer Anthony Verey, hoping to remake his life in France. He looks at properties in the region, but his arrival at the Mas Lunel marks the beginning of a frightening and unstoppable series of consequences. Two worlds and two cultures collide. Ancient boundaries are crossed, taboos are broken — a violent crime is committed . . . whilst the Cévennes hills remain, ever cruel and seductive.

CARTE DE LA LOUISIANE ET DU COURS DU MISSISSIPI — Dressée